A Novel

GRACE
AT BENDER
SPRINGS

A Novel

GRACE AT BENDER SPRINGS

VINITA HAMPTON WRIGHT

BROADMAN
&HOLMAN
PUBLISHERS

Nashville, Tennessee

© 1999
by Vinita Hampton Wright
Printed in the United States of America

0–8054–2127–0

Published by Broadman & Holman Publishers, Nashville, Tennessee
Acquisitions and Development Editor: Leonard G. Goss
Page Design and Typesetting: Desktop Services

Dewey Decimal Classification: 813
Subject Heading: FICTION

Library of Congress Cataloging-in-Publication Data

Wright, Vinita Hampton, 1958–
    Grace at Bender Springs / by Vinita Hampton Wright.
      p. cm.
    ISBN 0–8054–2127–0 (pbk. : alk. paper)
    1. Title.
    PS3573.R548 G73 1999
    813'.54—dc21
                                                                99–49700
                                                                CIP

1 2 3 4 5 — 03 02 01 00 99

To all the folks
and all the ghosts
of Cherokee, Kansas.
And especially to Grandmother and Grandma Virgi,
whose stories are my history,
and to Great-grandmas Sellars and Longston,
who have gone home
to live with God.

Acknowledgments

Many, many thanks to my editor, Rod Morris, who greatly improved my writing and my story through his careful reading, constructive criticism, and ongoing encouragement. Special thanks to Lil, Lynn, Beth, Joan, Ramona, and other friends who cheered me on and kept the excitement going when I felt like abandoning the whole thing.

Grateful thanks to my agent, Sara A. Fortenberry, for finding a home for this manuscript. Also to Len Goss and others and Broadman & Holman for taking a chance on it.

And a one-of-a-kind thanks to Jim, my husband. We met at an artists' retreat, and he read my stories. It's been nice to discover that he still likes my writing, even after the courtship and honeymoon are over. And it takes a true friend to live with a person while her book is going through the revision process. Thanks, babe, for all those good-luck kisses.

CONTENTS

PART ONE: JUNE   1
THE HISTORY: THE FARMERS, 1888   3

1. BENDER SPRINGS, 1997   11

2. MAMIE RUPERT: THE DREAMER   17

3. TONY GARDINO: THE DARK CHILD   23

4. DAVE SEATON: THE TOWN GUY   35

5. SARAH MORGAN: THE PASTOR'S WIFE   47

6. MAMIE RUPERT: LAYING ON OF HANDS   63

7. DAVE SEATON: PERKY'S TAP   71

8. THE MIRACLES ON MAPLE STREET   83

9. MAMIE RUPERT: HANDYMAN   91

10. SARAH MORGAN: FEARS   107

11. TONY GARDINO: THE JUNE REVIVAL   117

PART TWO: JULY   131
THE HISTORY: DISSENSION SPRINGS, 1890   133

12. SARAH MORGAN: THE SIGH   139

13. DAVE SEATON: LENA   149

14. MAMIE RUPERT: THE CONVERSION   163

15. TONY GARDINO: LENA   173

16. SARAH MORGAN: JOURNEYS   183

17. DAVE SEATON: JULY EVENING   189

18. MAMIE RUPERT: NEW LIFE   201

19. DAVE SEATON: THE EVIL IN THIS WORLD   209

20. SARAH MORGAN: SUMMER'S END   217

21. RANDY KLUVER: THE JULY REVIVAL   229

22. TONY GARDINO: RESCUE THE PERISHING   239

23. DAVE SEATON: LOVE YOUR NEIGHBOR   253

PART THREE: AUGUST   261
THE HISTORY: DISSENSION SPRINGS, 1893   263

24. TWO PASTORS   269

25. TONY GARDINO: THE PAINTING   275

26. MAMIE RUPERT: THE PAINTING   283

27. DAVE SEATON: DORIS, HIS MOTHER   303

28. SARAH MORGAN: THE AUGUST REVIVAL   315

29. TONY GARDINO: AFTERMATH   327

30. SARAH MORGAN: THE VISIT   333

31. MAMIE RUPERT: RECONCILIATIONS   345

32. DAVE SEATON: WATER   351

33. MAMIE RUPERT: MEMORIES   359

34. DAVE SEATON: SUMMER'S END   363

35. THE MIRACLES: REDEMPTIONS   369

36. SARAH MORGAN: JACOB'S WALK   377

37. TONY GARDINO: SUMMER'S END   385

38. MAMIE RUPERT: DREAMS   391

THE HISTORY: DISSENSION SPRINGS, 1895   395

FOREWORD

When you write a story that has some truth to it, people are bound to assume more is true than isn't. Bender Springs and Helmsly are fictitious towns. They are similar in only a few ways to the actual towns of Cherokee and Pittsburg, where I grew up. Bender Springs is meant to represent any number of small farming communities in southeast Kansas that were also mining towns. Some of my relatives were coal miners, who emigrated from England in the late 1800s and ended up first in McCune, Kansas, and finally in Cherokee. When my grandmother talks of her girlhood years, she describes a Cherokee that had ceased to exist by the time I was born. A town that no longer has its own grocery once possessed multiple retail businesses, a newspaper, banks, and hotels. When my grandmas mention old friends, they are often evoking the names of families that founded the town. All that is left of such towns now are a few small communities that dot the farmland, this due to trends affecting both farming and mining—and due to people, like me, who keep moving to the cities.

The characters in this story are not based on any actual people, living or dead. A few familiar names crept into Bender Springs, only because they were familiar. Mamie Rupert, for instance. The moment I conceived her, I knew what her full name would be, as though she had marched out of my subconscious wearing a name tag. Only sometime later did I realize that *Mamie* is a variation on my great-grandma's first name, and *Rupert* was the name of some family in Cherokee I never even knew; I probably heard relatives mention it. This is the way writing works. Your mind brings to the surface names, gestures, and snatches of conversation to be reinvented in an entirely new setting. Most of the time there is no actual memory to blame, and you really don't know why this person has that name or why that person possesses a particular fondness for zucchini bread.

I made no effort to follow actual weather patterns in Kansas history, although the 1873 drought referred to was quite real and wiped out the corn crop that year. There were also mineral springs in some areas of the state, and there was a time when "water witches" did a booming business.

I grew up surrounded by religion, touched by Pentecostal, Baptist, and Methodist theologies. I believe I have kept the best parts of all those. *Grace at Bender Springs* explores them with eyes that see both the dark and bright sides of believing—and a heart that can't help but keep the faith.

Part One

JUNE

The History:
The Farmers, 1888

Lewanda Thompson walked with a purpose, her dark skirt flapping against the stiff grass. The wind was hot. She bent over and watched the tip of the forked stick tremble in indecision. She followed its nod into the churchyard and then back out of it, down the small slope. She bent toward the earth so that the people in the prayer service couldn't see her. The flat lands in the distance moaned, papery grass meeting wind in the near darkness, while inside the plain church house another hymn commenced to the wheezes of Annie Bryant's pump organ.

Lewanda traveled farther from the church, its sounds following her—snatches of "There shall be showers of blessing" and "While on others Thou art calling, Do not pass me by." The voices slipped through open windows only to turn thin and disconnected in the air that whipped around corners and over the hard ground. Lewanda felt herself showered with grit and the smells of scorched grass. The small farming community had gathered to pray for rain.

She had watched from the porch of the general store as families wandered in from their dying patches of cultivation. Their children were cranky from the heat. A couple of the more stalwart women had come with their umbrellas, sure that God rewarded faith, even now, as wells turned brackish or dried up completely and as the Blue Horse Creek turned into a trickle. Elders murmured about the drought back in '73. Lewanda had watched them all march with a diligence of belief that impressed even her, an apostate.

Only a few members of the community had not come to the church that evening. They were the folks who had never believed, except for one. As the hymns began, church member Thaddeus Seaton had made his way quietly in the hot orange sunset, coming up from his place with a pick and shovel. He had come to the porch of the store and approached Lewanda without speaking. She had risen and taken the dowsing stick from where it had been concealed in the folds of her skirt. They had started in back of the store.

The forty-three-year-old spinster now followed the pull of the slender branch, her hips squared and the work boots scuffing up small clouds of dust. Thaddeus followed behind her, unhurried, glancing back at the church from time to time. His wife, Florence, was in there, her sturdy alto voice undergirding the rest. Florence had managed to bring God with them to Kansas, although God seemed to treat them differently in this place, a land of both extreme cold and heat and ground tough and matted with high grasses. Thaddeus traced the sound of his wife's voice now as it lapped toward him on the ebb and flow of warm wind.

Darkness ate away the streaks of sky in the west, and the church lights glowed brighter. Lewanda's stick brought them back around from the north, not far from the back wall of the squat church building. This time they went again down the slight hill the church stood on, but away from the other buildings and to the east.

"It's here," the woman murmured. Thaddeus could no longer see her face, but his mind's eye saw the taut, brown cheeks, heavy-lidded eyes, and thin lips stretched tight from age and maybe sorrow. It was rumored in the community that Lewanda was half Osage Indian, that she'd had a family once, on what had been the old reservation southwest of here some thirty years ago.

Whatever Lewanda's history, it was well hidden now, her entire person protected from the world by heavy work clothes and an expression that refused to be interpreted. She existed at the edge of the rest of them, just north of Pritchard's Farm, in a small shanty with chickens and a few hogs and a garden. She came to the general store rarely and briefly.

Thaddeus would not have known of Lewanda's dowsing skills had he not been forced into her place during a sudden gully washer last spring. The shanty had come into view through the sheets of water. Lewanda was at the small window and motioned him in. They waited it out, talking—naturally—of the weather.

"I knew it was coming," the woman had said, nodding at the rain. "I always feel it."

"Rheumatism in your bones?" Thaddeus asked.

"Oh no. Since I was a young girl, I just feel natural occurrences before they come—most of the time. I can find water too. With nothin' but a branch."

Thaddeus eyed her with interest. They had never spoken to one another before. "I had a great-uncle who was said to have found his wells that way," he said.

"I've found wells and springs from South Carolina to West Texas to Ohio," Lewanda answered quietly, as if listing the achievements of a son or a daughter.

The storm ended and Thaddeus went home, thinking little of it. Until July. Nine weeks and not a drop from heaven. He knew that Rev. Harkness and the more religious folks would consider what he was doing now to be on the dark side of miracles and prayers. So Thaddeus didn't speak of it to Florence or anyone else, just sauntered down to Lewanda's while running other errands. A simple appointment to make. So here they were.

"Here," Lewanda said, her voice cracking on the word. Thaddeus could barely see where the black-sleeved arm was pointing, but he could tell that the grass was higher and thicker here. The church was not a hundred yards from them. "They can't hear in this wind and with all that singing," the woman said. Thaddeus nodded and swung the pick hard. It hit the ground sharply.

"Gonna take a while," he said.

"No longer than they will," said Lewanda. He could tell from her voice that she had turned her head back toward the church. He raised the pick and brought it down again. And again. The people were praying now, a ghostly murmur that came to Thaddeus and Lewanda in snatches. Two or three voices rose above the rest—Ellie Perkins and Rhoda Sellars, older women with many children. Their sounds were hysterical and pleading, intercessions streaked through with accusations at a God who seemed to have abandoned them. Thaddeus was glad for the wind and the grating clunks of the pick; it pained him to hear prayer anymore.

Lewanda stood by soberly, her hands folded in front of her.

They hadn't brought a lantern, so Thaddeus dug by feel. Lewanda started with the shovel once the ground had begun to give. The prayers droned on. Someone was crying. Was it Florence? Thaddeus tore at the earth with all his force.

"Feel here," said Lewanda.

Thaddeus knelt and placed his hand near her voice. The earth was cool, damp. It clung to his fingers when he raised his hand to see, although seeing was impossible by this time. He swore in disbelief, and Lewanda chuckled at him. They both went to their knees then and pulled out dirt by the handful, scraping large swaths of it back with their forearms.

Near dawn, the Rev. Bernard Harkness stepped out the back door of the hot church house. The service had left his control hours ago. His parishioners drooped about the tiny sanctuary in exhaustion; some of them slept. A few continued to mutter prayers, tears somehow present in bodies that had gone bone-dry. The Reverend had a headache, and his eyes felt as though every grain of Kansas grit had lodged in them. He leaned against the back wall, sliding down into a squat. From there he looked out into nothing. A few stars still spotted the pale, near-dawn sky.

He had looked out here many times, wondering about his spiritual influence in such a place as this. He was a minister among dirt farmers, people with much of the life sucked out of them by the terrain they had chosen for their homeland. Some of them had not chosen. The Perkinses came through a year ago, on their way farther west to get some land the railroads were selling. Their axle broke two miles from town, and they didn't have the money to buy a new one. They stayed, even after there was money for an axle. This place was like that, made people feel obligated after a while to make it fertile, to redeem it from its own forsakenness.

For the most part, the folks in Bernard Harkness's community were not very spiritual. They weren't much educated either. Harkness remembered with fondness the Presbyterian church back in Boston under his father's care and the civility of people there. But God had great plans for Bernard, because he was a visionary and he held a high moral ground. Both vision and morals seemed to lapse more easily here. Perhaps because a person could look most any direction and see no end to the land, it became more and more easy to believe that other boundaries had ceased to exist also. The constant wind and the waving of the grass made a wildness grow in people. They became too independent. Their minds began to blur. And their spirits forgot important definitions of the faith. The country was more and more settled now; even the Indians had been cleared out pretty much. But the miles of fields could feel vast and empty, and such feelings set people to wandering like sheep sometimes. That's why Rev. Harkness had come. In his mind the horizons were still quite clear. And his memory latched onto spiritual principles like a blacksmith's vice.

The reverend folded his hands behind him and walked down the little slope from the church. He enjoyed communing with God at this time of the day. Jesus had prayed in the early morning, surely an example worth following. And although the minister had been up all night and hard at prayer, he wanted his moments alone with God now, out of hearing of the people he worked so hard to lead.

When Harkness reached the bottom of the slope, a small, dark pool came into his vision. He stopped, frightened for an instant by the sensation of seeing what no other sense or memory told him should be here. Was it a vision? But no, upon a closer look, upon bending to dip his hand into the liquid, the reverend knew it was no vision. It was a miracle. An answer to prayer. He fell to his knees and wept, then prayed for a few awe-filled moments, there alone as the sky lightened, giving pale blue color to the circle of water before him. Then he strode back to his sleeping church. A few people were on their way out, intent on doing their morning chores. The pastor's announcement, loud on the morning air, turned their direction to the pool. Soon the entire congregation stood there, dipping into the silvery stuff with their hands, weeping and praising God. They worshiped and hugged one another.

Had the events stopped there, the community would have been known as Miracle Springs. In fact, leaders in the little crowd began to plan a naming ceremony then and there. But Rev. Harkness tasted a few drops of something besides water. The taste was sweet and full of blessing. He felt the land swell beneath him and the Holy Ghost trembling in his bones. He began to stride around the circle of people who clustered about the pool, and he began to speak fervently of sin and repentance and of prayers and righteousness. He began to preach, waving the large Bible above the water. As the few people who hadn't attended the prayer service gathered at the edges of the group, the Reverend preached louder and harder. His presence grew like a storm cloud, like a whirlwind. He bore down on the people, who became quieter and quieter.

"The Lord hath opened the earth and brought forth water from dry ground! The Lord hath done this! We have cried out, and the Lord hath answered us in his mercy. Where God's people are, there will be made a way through the wilderness! Where God's people repent and pray and turn from their wickedness, God will bring sustenance and water the earth and the fields thereof." The congregation murmured awed affirmations. Never had their pastor been so eloquent, so full of truth and power.

But Thaddeus Seaton stood in the crowd, alone in his growing agitation. He had long resented the way Harkness regarded all of them, as though they were ignorant heathen. As the man waved his arms and cried out over the spring, Thaddeus felt his skin grow hot as hell itself.

And when Rev. Harkness stopped to take a breath, Thaddeus spoke up:

"Pardon me, Reverend, but there's more to know about this water."

Harkness turned abruptly, his finger raised to make his next point. Everyone else followed the pastor's gaze, and they stared as one at Thaddeus Seaton. He felt their stares, and he heard a frantic whisper a few yards behind him.

"No, Thaddeus! Let it be," Lewanda was saying. Her voice was tight with real fear, but Thaddeus didn't turn to look at her. He barely heard her.

"Lewanda Thompson found this well, early this morning, while it was still dark. I helped her dig." Thaddeus raised his arms, wiggling fingers still caked with dark earth. "That's wet soil under my fingernails." He turned to the right and to the left so that all could see. "Lewanda coaxed this water out of the ground with a willow stick. And I dug out this spring. Just so you all know the whole truth."

The morning air crackled with shock, fear, and anger. Thaddeus turned and left, grabbing Lewanda's arm as he did so. He heard a woman begin to sob behind them. He heard the pastor's ragged breathing as he struggled to know what to say next. When the words cut loose, they were filled with judgment. Judgment upon Lewanda for her witching. Judgment on Thaddeus for his part in it. As Thaddeus and Lewanda got into the wagon outside the general store and headed back to her place, they could hear the beginnings of division behind them. They had feared this would happen, but there was nothing to do now.

By the end of the day, the community had split in two. Rev. Harkness's group denounced the pool and vowed not to take a drop from it. The rest brought their buckets and filled them again and again. They did it fully confused, but in the end their livestock and vegetable gardens urged them to be pragmatic rather than spiritual. After a day and a night of gathering water, the spring was still fresh and showed no signs of ceasing. The pool refilled itself as the hours, then the days, went on.

Still the rain did not come. Followers of Harkness cut a wide path around the spring and continued to pray in shifts in the little church. The matter had become a battle between good and evil.

Evil seemed to win in the days that followed. Three families whose wells had gone dry abandoned their homesteads and traveled to Missouri, willing to start over again rather than survive on wicked water. Some families who partook of the spring began to imagine that they were cursed for doing so. Every accident or illness became a result of the spring and their part in it. They argued among themselves but kept filling their buckets. They approached the pool as though it were a wild god, ready to devour them even as it filled them.

Two people died after the spring was found and before the rains returned—one a child young and weak enough to have died in normal circumstances, the other a strong farmer who came down with a strange malady that took him home in a matter of days. People were afraid to speculate in either case. The two dead had not taken of the spring's water.

In late August the heavens rained gently and continuously for three days. But by then an awful cloud of a different sort hung over the community. The people helped one another through the mercifully short winter, their supplies sparse. The following spring things were better; folks put in crops and did their best to put the last summer behind them. They decorated the graves of their departed, just as they normally would, and in March they held a town meeting to elect the first mayor, John Saxton. John spoke of hope and a future for their little town. But when they searched for a name, the memories of dust and death worked a power over their little group. Afterward they shared lemonade and Louise Smith's honey cake. They talked of building a school. They laughed together as neighbors do. But no one felt inclined to comment on the name they had chosen for their young town: Dissension Springs.

1

BENDER SPRINGS, 1997

Saturday, June 7

Bender Springs had entered a brutal season. It was early June, and already farmers were murmuring among themselves, speculating about weather systems. It hadn't snowed enough last winter or rained enough in the spring. It had been years since a serious drought, but the older men had sharp memories of just how bad it could get.

They stood now, on a hazy, hot Saturday morning, lining the short Main Street. It was a special occasion, but they wore their work boots and overalls with T-shirts underneath just as they always did, having a smoke or a beer, looking down toward Washington Street, where three marching bands from area school districts were getting into position. Tiny baton twirlers sparkled with sequins and schoolgirl, toothy smiles. Instruments tuned up, honking and tapping in the heavy morning air.

Joe Greer had his grill going in the Lions booth, and IGA, the town's single grocery store, had established a candy/pop stand just across from the Lions. Maxie's Ice Cream Stop made its appearance nearer the senior citizen center, in the middle of the parade strip, and the nearby, bigger town of Helmsly had sent over troops with helium balloons, popcorn, cotton candy, and an assortment of patriotic stickers and hats. The small park just off the Main Street on Elm was littered with colors, balloons and streamers fluttering among the trees and park benches. At its entrance, a small booth decorated in bunting advertised a small book of eighty pages, a history of the town written by Louise Filcher. Louise herself was seated primly on the back of the blue convertible positioned behind the second marching band. The convertible belonged to Darrel, her insurance salesman husband, who sat ready at the wheel. Louise wore a white suit bought for the occasion, waiting to wave her way down the six-block parade route. Louise had been town historian for fifteen years, as well as teacher of the senior adult Sunday school class at First Baptist since Johnnie Delores had died, Johnnie having been senior adult teacher as far back as anyone with a functioning memory could recall.

This was Louise's day—her day to sell her little book and wave at fellow citizens. It was the town's centennial celebration, a day to recite a history many knew little about and to march for a few blocks and feel that their community had roots.

It was almost too late in the town's life for anyone to be excited about history. Only the most elderly citizens remembered much about Bender Springs's younger and more vibrant stages. It was now a town but two miles square, settled into a landscape of fields that alternated in soft shades of green and gold between corn, wheat, soybeans, and milo. The fields covered the land for at least fifteen miles in any direction before running into another community.

In Bender Springs, the smells of crops and sweet earth still wafted through backyards, and the town's four traffic lights regulated more pickup trucks than cute purple jeeps or sports cars. Except for a small rise here and there, every family's house was level with every other family's. And, even with phone lines and electric wires crisscrossing the town and flowing down the state highway that connected it to other towns, the skies offered their own drama from one day to the next. For once the town ended and the farmland took up as though it hadn't been interrupted, the atmosphere above became wide as the world and layered with colors that invented themselves moment by moment.

Twenty miles away, the county seat, Helmsly, remained a constant, small industry town, kept alive by the addition during the sixties of a junior college that continued to bring in residents. A lot of folks from Bender Springs worked in Helmsly's businesses and two small industries, a meatpacking plant and a tool company. But Bender Springs had actually preceded Helmsly in existence by nearly thirty years.

A hundred years before, Bender Springs had been a settlement of farmers and coal miners held together by a couple of stores, a smithy, a school, and two churches. During the coal years the place had boomed into a real town, full of life and supporting more businesses than did most present-day towns in the area. Just a few old store buildings retained those memories now. After the coal industry had come and gone, Bender Springs had shrunk back to a handful of businesses and a couple thousand people, most of whom worked in other towns. Farmers and their acreages still filled in the surrounding countryside.

Today, there weren't many parade floats, but each was earnest in its own way. Connor Ward was the great-great-great-grandson and only living relative that anyone knew about of the town's first mayor. He floated by in something that looked similar to a covered wagon, had covered wagons been jacked-up four-wheel drives. He wore a cowboy hat, although farmers and not cowboys had settled the area. Connor waved to the crowd, making faces at the present and real mayor, Jim Caruso, who played along.

The senior center was overflowing with gingham skirts and bonnets right out of *Little House on the Prairie*. The center had its own outdoor shelter; the seniors sat at the picnic tables and watched as the first band blasted into a march and headed toward them. They listened a few moments, then went back to their own conversations. Their contribution to the day was an offering of cakes and pies—everything two dollars a slice—that covered three of the picnic tables closest to the sidewalk.

Mamie Rupert had brought spice cake with cream cheese frosting. The recipe was her mother's. Mamie's mother had passed in '72. Mamie herself, still moving around pretty well for her seventy-one years, pursed her lips as Louise Filchers's convertible glided by.

"You'd think she would have appreciated some help from me," she said to Liz, Alma, and Ruthie, her pinochle buddies, who sat there in the shade with her. "After all, I was city clerk for forty years. Anybody wanted to know some piece of information, I'd know just how to find it. I organized that mess of files myself, when Louise was still a brat."

"Oh, let her have her day. Nobody gives two cents anyway." Liz was trying, for once, to blow her cigarette smoke away from them and from the desserts just a few feet away.

"It just would have made sense, is all," said Mamie, rising to peer at how her spice cake was selling. She'd already had Marie Bailey's cherry chiffon pie, and she was trying to hold herself to two desserts for the entire day. Still, it was a crime to let so much confection just sit there and get gooey in the heat. Mamie could hear Sally Bradley's chocolate sheet cake calling her name.

"It's a nice enough little history," commented Alma, on her second dessert at least and apparently suffering no guilt whatsoever. "I read it. The highlights are there. Nice little keepsake."

"But Mamie's right, you know. Louise didn't include a lot of things; she left out whole families, and I think got a couple of dates wrong." Ruthie's face was laced with moisture, and she patted herself periodically with a handkerchief that matched her frontier dress. "When was it that the Sears store opened over at Helmsly? She's got it somewhere in the early seventies, and I could swear that's where I bought my Frigidaire in '66."

"Doesn't matter to me when the Sears store opened," said Mamie. "Matters to me that everybody be included who should be. Louise's book is mainly a history of families her family's been friends with."

Liz snorted. "No wonder it's just a pamphlet."

Dave Seaton stood outside Perky's Tap and watched the bands go by with little comment. A couple of other Perky's regulars provided running commentary on virtually every person, animal, or vehicle that passed before them. Dave got a kick out of all the dogs (and a couple of goats) with bandannas around their collars and the little kids with crepe paper flapping from their training wheels, but he didn't feel much attachment to any of it.

Partly, this was because he was worn out. His regular job kept him busy enough through the week, but the yard business he ran on the side was now in season, and he'd had to replace more mower parts than he'd anticipated and had spent a couple of late nights getting the equipment in shape.

Dave had lived in Bender Springs his entire life and had found that one day basically followed another. He'd buried a young wife two years ago and his father three years before that. He'd watched his father push brooms and mops at the high school for twenty-five years and then die slowly of a heart disorder. His mother, Doris, had left before things got too difficult, making her husband's passing even more humiliating. Dave worked on a road crew out of Helmsly. He thought about roads a lot lately, mainly roads that led to someplace different.

Sarah Morgan held up her four-month-old, Peter, to see his daddy and big sister go by on the Baptist church's float. In front of last Easter's papier-mâché tomb with its matching stone rolled to one side, four-year-old Miranda waved to the crowd as though this were the

Parade of Roses and she had been crowned queen. Her father, the pastor, stood a yard or two in front of her, grasping a six-foot cross made from an actual tree. The cross kept coming loose from its base, and there were moments when it seemed to Sarah that her husband was wrestling with the symbol of his faith. He had tried to get her to stand up with him, but she'd reminded him that she might have to nurse Peter at any point. She was glad for the excuse, because there were still a lot of people in the crowd she didn't know at all, even though she and Jacob had lived here nearly two years.

The last vehicle of the parade was not an official entry. The emerald-green van had been done over in graffiti, and the teenagers hanging out its windows weren't acting patriotic or even respectful of what the day stood for. Their hyped-up stereo system sent shock waves through the air, the vulgar lyrics eliciting gasps and scoldings from people who lined the street. Since the van had managed to get in front of the twenty or so horses that brought up the rear of the parade, Sheriff Gideon Holt was having a hard time getting to it in his squad car. He could only look helplessly at the final insult, which declared itself in violent colors across the back of the van: Demoniacs. The word itself made the bright colors and the crowd noises and the full sunlight gaudy all of a sudden. Most people shook their heads at it and turned to leave the street; the parade was all but over anyway. Others approached the kids in the van and gave them what for, which seemed only to please the teenagers more.

Tony Gardino regarded the van sullenly from the shade of Shawnee Park. He knew most of the kids inside it; he'd hung out with a couple of them. Their attempts now to be evil and rebellious looked stupid to him. He'd come to the parade only because it was a way to get out of the house, which had become a prison lately since Dad had turned it into a police state. Or maybe it always had been a police state, and Tony had only figured it out lately. He wasn't sure.

"The Tony! Hey!" A wave from inside the van brought a bored gesture from him. People he couldn't see were laughing—at him, maybe? He watched the Demoniacs turn off at the next block and hit the gas before Gideon could catch up to them. Tony sat down with a catalpa tree at his back. He watched people go by and heard sounds around him. Somebody was grilling hot dogs nearby, and he asked himself if he wanted one and decided that he didn't. His sister, Annie, two years younger, walked in front of him suddenly.

"Tony, give me five dollars."

He gave her a dead look. "As if."

"C'mon. I've got it at home, but it's too hot to walk. I'll get you something if you want—some cotton candy?"

"If I want sugar I'll go lick out the bowl at home."

"You're such a snot. Just give me a couple dollars."

"Only if you stay out of my life for the rest of the decade."

"Sure."

He handed her four dollars. "It's all I have. All."

She saw a girlfriend and was half a block away from him in the next five seconds. He watched her for that long, wondering how it was they'd ended up in the same family.

The parade was over by eleven-thirty. Events had been planned through most of the afternoon, and there would be a country-and-western band in the park later in the evening. But by two o'clock, most of the people out on the street were under the age of twenty. The seniors, visiting and fanning themselves under their picnic shelters, stayed until the heat stopped the breeze that had made the morning bearable.

Early June was already hot, and sun washed over the pavements and houses, emptying the small strips of downtown on Main, Euclid, and Washington streets. Louise Filcher's history booth continued to wave its colors from the canopy of redbud trees at Shawnee Park's east entrance. It stood like a guard over the town's memories.

2

Mamie Rupert: The Dreamer

Wednesday, June 11

Mamie's sister, Cassie, was picking orchids to put on their parents' graves. This seemed strange to Mamie, because it had always been peonies. In fact, she couldn't remember that they'd ever been able to grow orchids. Cassie was wearing her work clothes—the light blue dress with the rip under one arm and a soiled apron tied over it and her late daddy's straw hat crammed on her head. Her large behind, upturned toward the sun, obliterated her bent upper half, sort of like those cardboard cutouts some people stick in their front yards of matching Ma and Pa bent over to work, her frilly knickers peeking out from under her skirt. But Cassie was never one to wear frilly underwear, so all that showed under her skirt were dark veins in the backs of her legs.

As Mamie approached, she saw the damp spots of sweat on Cassie's dress. Coming closer, Mamie could see her sister's mousy strings of hair stuck to her neck, cheeks, and forehead. She was gasping and grunting, making her outdoor work sounds.

The broom handle felt gritty in Mamie's palms. She came up to Cassie from behind, put a foot to the large, bent-over bottom, and gave a fierce shove. Cassie cried out and looked up in horror from where she lay next to the peonies. Before Cassie could speak or get up on her knees, Mamie climbed onto her, sitting on Cassie's chest. She took the broom and placed it across her sister's throat, grasping the wood on either side, and pushed as hard as she could.

Cassie gurgled, her hands flailing and her eyes popping in disbelief. Mamie couldn't seem to cut off the wind well enough sitting, so she planted both feet on either side of the purple throat, stood up, and jumped. Then she turned around and, still standing on the broom handle, grasped Cassie's kicking legs and pulled. That's the ticket. Just like Mama used to take the heads off of chickens.

The gurgles stopped, and Cassie's legs went limp. Mamie turned around to see that her sister's face had turned a horrible purple, the eyes nearly out of their sockets and her tongue lolling to one side. As Mamie watched, Cassie's skin grew darker still, then finally turned to mush, like old plum jam.

Mamie was suddenly sorry she had killed her sister. She threw the broom aside and tried to mold the plum jam back into the likeness of Cassie's face. But it spread over the ground and got grass in it. Mamie used a butter knife to try to spread the jam just right and push it back, but Cassie's face wouldn't return. Mamie realized then that she couldn't have fresh chicken tonight because she had forgotten to make noodles, and the store-bought kind of noodles just don't work with plum jam.

Mamie awoke and the room was very quiet, like Riley's Mortuary with its thick carpets. The dream was still with her, and she drew the covers up to her neck and hugged herself. Then she laughed out loud in an attempt to lighten the intensity of the shadowy room. Her dress was on a hanger, on the hook at the top of her closet door. It looked sort of like a dead person up there. The sweater draped over the chair nearby looked like another dead person, slumped forward—after having been strangled maybe.

Mamie thought of her plums down in the basement, canned months ago. If she hadn't been rummaging through the shelves for a spare jar lid she would never have known that half the jars hadn't sealed. At first she couldn't figure out what in the world she had canned, to be such an awful color as that. One whiff gave her the answer. Rotten plums. All that work. Oh, well, it wasn't the first batch of something that had gone bad in her lifetime.

Did she really hate Cassie enough to kill her? Mamie shivered, the image of Cassie's face turning to rotten plums still vivid against the water spots on the bedroom ceiling. To kill her own sister as though she were a chicken? Cassie had been dead now for nearly eight years. She and Mamie had gotten along all right. Well, they'd had disagreements over the years, as sisters naturally do, but nothing a person would want to kill over, for heaven's sake.

Mamie got out of bed and felt her way through the dark house to the kitchen. There was a dab of apple juice left. She drank it straight from the container and stood at her sink, gazing at the starlit yard outside the window. The quiet of the motionless trees and the plastic bucket hanging over the spigot gave her comfort. She stepped out the back door and walked in her bare feet through the yard—except where Bill Simpson's dog had relieved itself, just north of the sidewalk—and breathed in the heavy scents of sleeping flowers and mildewed soil near the basement windows. That side of the house was always in the shade, the windows crusted over with dirt and weeds.

She sat on the metal chair near the clothesline and looked through the black tree branches to the street in one direction and the Jeffries' yard in the other. Mamie's yard was soft and dark at night or brightly speckled with moonbeams. It was airy, and bad dreams dissipated.

For years Mamie had dreamed of her late husband, Charles. She'd dreamed both good and bad about him. Now he didn't show up too often. She felt that she'd settled all her memories of him and of them as husband and wife. She was no longer haunted by bad things she'd done or said to him. Or of things she'd planned to do with him but wasn't able to, because he died before his time. Time had weakened the grip of guilt in the case of Charles, who was so generous and forgiving to begin with. A person like Charles forgave people practically before they'd wronged him. Mamie knew that he'd gone to death free and clear. She hoped to go that way too.

But now these dreams of Cassie, of all people. Cassie had been gone a year longer than Charles had. Mamie hadn't ever dreamed of her until just lately. She had a feeling the memories associated with her sister wouldn't settle quite so well. Cassie had never been a settled person. Always in an uproar. Always suspecting bad of people. Maybe she was still after Mamie for quitting her job at the dogfood factory and getting married, leaving Cassie there by herself in that awful job with those awful people. Maybe people did haunt a person after death. Maybe the reason Mamie didn't dream of Charles was that he was simply too considerate to haunt anybody, even if he had the right. Cassie, on the other hand, would look for any excuse.

Mamie sat there in her yard for maybe an hour until she became sleepy again. She noticed how free her arthritic joints felt as she rose from the chair and climbed the steps into her enclosed porch. Night air seemed to help a lot of things.

A few hours later, after she'd caught a few more winks, Mamie sat at the kitchen table and peeled an apple. She watched her crooked forefinger guide the short blade. She couldn't remember exactly when her fingers had started turning in strange directions. Her hands looked a lot like Mama's hands had looked, once she'd gotten old. They didn't appear deformed necessarily; they just bent more than was normal, especially at the ends.

She looked at the knife and thought of Charles, who'd bought it for her years ago. The man had never been able to tolerate a dull blade. Once a month he'd be out on the porch sharpening all the knives, and Mamie would spend the week after doctoring the collection of cuts she'd gathered. She liked to be able to feel a blade in her hand without it cutting her—it sort of helped her keep her place. She liked to cut things while holding them in her hands, while Charles said that's what a cutting board was for. He'd make faces and reach to rescue her from herself whenever she held a potato in her hand, cutting inward toward her thumb. It had been one of a number of things they'd seen differently. Now all of Mamie's knives were reasonably sharp but not dangerous. She would have welcomed that danger, though, and put up with little cuts to have her Charles back, correcting her one minute and kissing behind her ear the next. Mamie hadn't been too organized when Charles married her, and he'd had strong opinions and had made her cry two or three times a week way back in the beginning. But he'd loved her as if she were the most precious thing God had ever created. After seven years of Charles being gone, Mamie hadn't quite got over the feeling that he should be coming in the back door soon.

Mamie scooted her chair around to face the south window so that she could watch the morning walk across her backyard. The honeysuckle on the garage was first to catch the light, then her tomato plants. By the time she finished her apple and oatmeal and read today's paper, the grass would be showing off its dew, lit up in the stillness. And when she had finished her few dishes and hung the tea towel across the rack by the refrigerator, the sun would be warming the lilac bush by the back step. Mamie thought it a shame that the lilac's blooming season was so short. A month or more ago the branches had glowed in lavender, perfuming the back porch and kitchen. She had picked a few sprigs every day to place in a tall glass of water and set on the dining-room table to freshen up the house. But spring was well over now, even though it was barely June. The heat had come early this summer. And the rains had ended too quickly. Mamie stared through the lilac's dusty, bloomless leaves. The only good thing about drier weather was that her joints didn't complain to her as much.

Mamie sat just a foot or two from the window and opened the *Helmsly Herald*. But after every few lines of newsprint, she raised her eyes to peer over the top of the page and out the window toward the alley. It was about that time. As the moment came closer, she edged the chair even nearer the window. The storm window was raised, letting morning coolness into the frame house. Mamie had her BB gun propped against the sill. At page A-7 she couldn't take the suspense any longer. She put down the news and, hitching her cotton dress up over her knees, leaned into the window.

At about 7:10, a ratty looking dog slouched through the hedge row that separated Mamie's yard from the alley. Mamie clapped both hands on her bare knees and half stood, half sat, her nose touching the window screen. She watched the dog sniff around her peony bed and lift its leg. It circled the plum tree, looked as if it might skip that, but then gave a halfhearted squirt to the trunk. It nosed through the grass and licked at the coffee grounds Mamie had deposited on the flower bed last evening. Then he made wider circles, sniffing more earnestly and twirling around a specific spot with a look of determination.

Mamie was up and had the gun in hand. She rose and stepped carefully out the kitchen door and onto her screened-in back porch. She grabbed her cane, which leaned against the wall just beside the door, and walked as quietly as she could to the back door. The dog was in a squat between the garden spot and the narrow sidewalk Charles had put in for her to walk on in bad weather.

Mamie softly cursed the mutt to perdition. She had made her way out the door and onto the stoop. The dog saw her, hung out his tongue, gazed toward the neighbors' yard, and continued his business. Mamie raised the gun with conviction then. But her dress pocket caught on the door handle, jerking the screen into the side of her head. The blow surprised her, and she kicked the cane, which was resting between her hip and the step railing. It clattered onto the walk. The door dislodged Mamie's glasses, and she had to put down the gun to readjust. By the time she had taken aim again, the deed was done. The dog kicked imaginary leaves and dirt over his deposit, sniffed the garage, and disappeared through the hedge.

Mamie let language fly she had all but forgotten. She shook all over and felt sudden heat come to her face and scalp. She had a vision then, of Charles standing behind her, still in his undershirt, coffee cup in hand, and hiding a grin as his little wife painted the sky a brighter blue than God had made it.

She saw that her cane was way out of her reach, and she muttered some more as she stepped down to get it. She pulled herself back into the kitchen and set the BB gun back in its corner. This seemed like a good time to do her dishes. Cleaning something always made her feel better after something bad had befallen her. So she filled the sink with sudsy water, plenty hot, and considered what to do next about That Dog. She didn't know the mutt's actual name, only that it belonged to Bill Simpson, a neighbor she'd never known well or liked much."

At half past ten she picked up the phone and dialed Bill Simpson's number. She let it ring fifteen times, but no one answered. She hitched up her slip and marched through the back gate to the alley. She walked down to Myrtle Street, crossed it, and continued until she reached Simpson's property. She walked up to his front door.

She could hear some game show blaring from a television in the living room. He was home all right. Mamie pounded on his front door and then on his back door as contestants won money by the hundreds and some trapped audience applauded them. After a few minutes of that, she left the yard in a huff. Screaming on Bill Simpson's doorstep was beneath her. She would just have to find another way to talk with him for the umpteenth time about his dog that had selected her property as its morning toilet.

When Mamie reentered her backyard from the alley, she began to sneeze. Several big ones ripped up through her chest and throat, causing her eyes to water and her nose to run. She walked around the fresh pile of dung, eyeing it fiercely. It seemed to her that since the dog had been depositing waste in her backyard her health had suffered more than its normal number of setbacks. If she could prove she was allergic to this dog's poop, then Bill Simpson would have to tie up his dog or go to court. Maybe she could get Dr. Meiers to write down that this dog was the source of her medical problems. She would talk with Alma when they played cards this Thursday. Alma read a lot of magazines— a wide variety—and she might just know something about allergies. She knew a lot about legal matters too.

3

TONY GARDINO: THE DARK CHILD

Wednesday, June 11

Granddad stooped over a row of what would eventually be yellow squash, poking around until his face got red, then rising for the blood to get back to his heart again. From where he sat on the back steps, Tony could hear the old guy breathing hard. The air was heavy with the smell of dark earth. Tony could see Earl Sykes messing around with his plants, too, just across the road. That seemed to be the sum of life in Bender Springs: stubborn old people and backyards tilled up and stabbed with tomato stakes.

Tony allowed himself a moment of self-congratulation. He'd made it to June (his seventeenth) still alive. January had nearly finished him off, but he was holding steady so far this evening. He thought maybe it helped that the breeze was cool. These days he never knew what would make the next hour or minute more bearable.

He stared westward, where the sun slid toward the fringe of tree-tops. The anxiety that came naturally with evening began to worm around in his gut. After evening came night, and night was when people were supposed to sleep. Tony had skipped an afternoon dose of sleep aids, the over-the-counter pills that were easy enough to hide and wouldn't get him into trouble. The bit of reefer he had left was buried under Mr. Timms's pear tree, three blocks away. He'd gone without anything today, hoping the exhaustion tonight would do its work. But his hopes were weak. Sleep wasn't something he did anymore. The drugstore junk helped him nod off for an hour or two, but then he was wide awake in the dark and felt worthless all the next day. Reefer didn't do much for sleep, but it made him more mellow about the whole subject. Now he watched the sun sliding and listened to Granddad and tried not to think about anything at all.

At least there hadn't been any of Dad's surprise searches this week. One lousy time Tony'd had junk in his locker. That's all it took. Explanations meant nothing. He'd had the junk, and he was guilty. It was Brian's junk, but that didn't matter. Tony's few experiences with real drugs had been no good, and he'd lost interest, but he'd held some for Brian just to be an OK guy. Now he should just wear a sign: Tony's a dopehead.

Actually, a smoke of any kind would be good right now. Instead, Tony concentrated on the sound of a bullfrog in the ditch out near the road. He'd chased down a lot of those things when he was a little kid. It occurred to him that this was the first frog he'd heard this year. Too dry maybe.

Early evening—that time in summer when the air is full of light but the day's sounds are winding down—seemed alive, moving across the town like the shadow of some prehistoric bird. Small squares of lamp-yellow rooms began to glow out of houses, although the light wouldn't spill onto lawns for another two hours. This time of year darkness didn't begin until nine or so, which was fine with Tony. He cared for the dark less now than when he was little. Not that anybody knew this. It was one of many facts that comprised his secret life.

"Annie, I'm not going to ask you again." Mom's voice was sounding tight. In the kitchen behind Tony, supper dishes clattered angrily, plates being set hard on the table.

Along the narrow, unpaved side street, a few people had placed outcast kitchen chairs on front stoops and porches, situating themselves on the ripped vinyl seats to enjoy this time of day when the light began to get softer. Tony had noticed the shift in light, maybe because he dreaded the dark so much. He wanted to sit here and absorb as much of the day as he could.

Before long, the daytime heat would make evening a luxury. It was beginning to stay warm enough that just cooking supper heated up most houses. That meant the Gardino family was in for more Jell-O salads and cold vegetables with salad dressing thrown over them. Of course, the meat and potatoes would keep coming, because Dad wanted it that way. Tony hadn't liked Dad for quite a while now, mainly because the guy couldn't rest until he'd uncovered everything wrong Tony had ever done or been. The dope in his locker had been some big climax, as if Dad had been waiting all along for something to prove what he'd always thought anyway. But lately Tony was noticing what being married to Dad had done to Mom. She would sweat buckets out in the kitchen every evening, making sure there were pork chops or steak or baked chicken, and the old man would lounge in the living room with his iced tea and still gripe if something wasn't salty enough.

Tony saw Granddad stretch up for a last time, look over the garden, and dust the dirt off his pants. He headed up the path of barely visible bricks that had been a decent sidewalk when he built this place a long time ago, before Tony's dad was born. He put a palm on Tony's shoulder as he walked up the two steps past him. Tony decided to wait a few more minutes before going in. Mom had said, "Supper's about ready," through the screen window nearly ten minutes ago. But Tony knew he had some time. Annie was still throwing silverware around.

Dinnertime was even harder to face since Tony's appetite had disappeared. He'd keep saying that he was full or wasn't very hungry, but this didn't register with Mom. If he didn't guard his plate, she'd plop food on it and say, like a stuck recording, "You need to eat more. Here."

Worse than dealing with food was having to engage with other family members. In spite of all society's change and progress, the Gardino family had supper together every night. It was a control thing for Dad and a Christian family thing for Mom. She always had something to say—instructions or reminders—that Tony had better pay attention to. And Dad always had something to gripe about that Tony had better hear the first time. Sometimes he felt like a dumb stuffed target sitting there with arrows flying all around him. More than anything, he just wanted his parents to ignore him. Neglect him. Anything but keep talking at him.

But Tony made a point now to do what he was supposed to do and try not to be bothered by things, even though the person inside him was ready to jump up and run. Since Howard Sheffley had slid under the semitrailer and survived. That had changed everything.

"Is there ice in the glasses?" Mom wasn't even trying to hide her irritation. There was a scuffle on the linoleum and the sound of the freezer door slamming.

Howard Sheffley. Tony contemplated the name for about the hundredth time. Howie the Shoo-fly. Horrible Howard. Most of Tony's life Howard had meant nothing to him. He was a nerdy kid who naturally irritated everybody. It wasn't anything Howard did; it was just that life had decided to be good to Howard for no apparent reason. His aunt happened to be their fifth-grade teacher, so he had passed, while Tony missed the mark by just a few points. Howard's mom's cousin happened to own Mulligans, one of the leading furniture outlets in the county, so by seventh grade Howard was working part-time in the warehouse, making five bucks an hour, while everybody else his age sacked groceries or mowed lawns. Howard's widowed grandma married a rich guy from Dayton. She had always felt sorry for Howard, since she never saw him much when he was little, and he was a slow reader and his dad never cared for him, so she asked Howard what he wanted for eighth-grade graduation and he told her he wanted a TransAm, and she went out and bought him one that week. Even though he was pathetic and totally undeserving of special treatment, good things happened to Howard. That circumstances continually fell his way was long-standing proof in Tony's mind that God had taken an early retirement.

It should have made no difference to Tony whether Howard had lived or died when his TransAm hit the 18-wheeler. But it happened on the same night Tony had carried his dad's .22 out to the shed. He must have put the barrel in his mouth four or five times. If someone had asked him why, he would have answered that if life up to now was any indication of the life ahead he'd just as soon check out early. He would have said that he'd finally found a way to use *proactive* in a sentence. He finally understood that this English class vocabulary word meant taking a thing out of someone else's hands and into your own. So he'd taken gun in hand on January 18, freezing in the middle of the night on a bale of straw next to Granddad's garden tiller.

He'd tried to pull the trigger, tried to clear his head and make everything work—until five in the morning. He still couldn't remember what he'd actually done all that time. But he had seemed to come into consciousness suddenly, and there was Granddad, silhouetted in the kitchen window, taking his blood pressure pills with a coffee cup of tap water. Tony could see him through the shed window. He knew Granddad would step onto the porch and finish the water, look into the winter morning darkness toward the backyard and the spot that would be his garden after the thaw, walk through the frosty dead grass around to the front of the house and pick up his newspaper before entering the front door that was never locked. Then he'd fall asleep in his chair, the paper spread over his pajama bottoms, his white, veined feet propped on the footstool.

It wouldn't be safe to go back into the house for another twenty minutes. Tony laid the gun across the bale, exhausted, and flipped on the small radio Granddad kept on the worktable. He huddled against the hay, the morning news crackling softly against the cold air. That's when he heard about Howard hitting a patch of ice on the bypass and broadsiding the semi. Demolished the TransAm. The trucker swerved to miss and hit a telephone pole, crashed through the cab window, and was in critical condition at St. Bartholomew's.

But Howard, who wasn't wearing a seat belt, was thrown out the door, which conveniently flew open for him, and by some feat of physics rolled underneath the semi to rest safely in the ditch, which had no water in it. He got out of it with a few bruises.

A miracle, said Ray Harris, the local news announcer, and Tony had to agree, clenching his chattering teeth between angry jaws. Howard should by all rights be roadkill, but he walked away from it.

It was all Tony could take—in such an unfair world, people like Howard walking away unhurt. Tony had looked at the rifle and thought about going over to Howard's, poking the barrel through the bedroom window, and blowing the guy's brains out while he slept. Now that would be justice.

Instead he decided he should live a while longer, long enough to make life give him something at least, to force the odds into his favor. So he waited half an hour, turned off the radio, quietly entered the house, and put the gun away.

That was why Tony tried to sit on his back porch now and just be calm. In a weird way, pathetic Howard had given him a reason to live.

There in the evening, with Granddad's garden plot growing dimmer, with Mom and Annie doing battle in the kitchen behind him, Tony felt his life shrink down to a cold little knot. He knew that there were powerful waves of something stirring up inside him and that he would drown in whatever they were before many weeks had gone by. For some stupid reason, he'd thought school ending and summer coming would make a difference. But the shift had come and gone, and Tony sank deeper and watched sun and clouds as if he were looking up from the bottom of a well. He hunkered on the back stoop, one evening at a time, and tried to conserve a little energy for getting through the night. Night was the worst.

Eventually the argument in the house subsided, and Mom's voice filtered out to him: "Supper's ready, Tony."

As Tony stood up, a '79 Impala rounded the corner and stopped at the end of their drive, dust rising like a white mist from its back wheels. Jason Worthy shifted the car into park, and it shuddered in rhythm with the engine, which sounded ready to die on the spot. Tony walked up to the driver's side and rested his hands on the hood, elbows straight, as he looked into the face of the buddy he'd known since grade school.

"Hey, what's up?" asked Tony.

"Not much. Thompson's got some stuff, if you're interested. Come over about nine."

Tony had never bothered to tell anyone his dope days were over. Too hard to explain. He was afraid he'd sound righteous or something. It was easier to show up, maybe do a joint, and leave it at that. Once things got going, nobody noticed what he did or didn't do. Tony kicked at the gravel driveway. "Hey, you know I'm under surveillance."

"You can't get away at all? Sneak out later?"

"I don't want to deal with it tonight."

"Brian's bringing." Jason said this as though it would actually raise the value of the experience.

Tony sniffed. "Too many brain cells gone."

"He's not that bad." Jason shrugged. "You're really not coming?"

"I'm beat. Catch you next time."

Jason made a ticked-off sound. "You're always beat. Like some old man, tired all the time, just hanging around the back porch, looking off at—I don't know. What are you lookin' at?"

Tony straightened, letting his hands slide off the car. "Forget it. I'll see you later." He started toward the house.

"Hey, it's fine if you change your mind."

Tony didn't look back. He could hear Jason muttering something as the car wuffled down the street.

It was getting harder to talk with Jason. Tony knew something fundamental had changed. Not that he cared about junk more or less than before. But he spent most of his energy keeping the Feeling at bay—the Feeling that had taken him over in January and kept moving in on him now, the sensation that life had ended and he was just waiting for all the information to come in. They were all on a huge airplane, eating and drinking and reading magazines, and they didn't know that the engines had cut off and they were calmly gliding to a crash.

This summer he would have to look for signals, that's all, signals that maybe life could be better, that things would in fact turn in his direction. It was just hard now, with sleep not coming and family around to make him relate to them. Hard to hang on and not think about checking out. He'd give it the summer. School would be impossible, feeling like this. And when he wasn't at school, he'd be home. Something had to turn around. Life would get better, or he'd off himself before school started.

Tony's eyes shifted up cautiously to study his mother's face. She had become interesting to him lately, maybe because he had begun to see her—almost—as someone not even connected to him. Now, as she set fried potatoes and onions on the dinner table, her lips were pressed together in their usual firmness, and a small vertical crease divided her face between the eyebrows. All the energy in her small body seemed compacted into that face. When a moment's peace caught her off guard, the mouth relaxed and the crease disappeared. Her eyebrows were brown and soft-looking, and her pale skin gave the appearance of being easily bruised or broken. Tony decided that his mother's ever serious expression was her main weapon against injury. Her hands were always taut bunches of knuckles and busy fingers, red from work.

Tony had finally figured out that everything Mom did or said or told him to do or say came directly out of her sense of duty—to family, to decent civilization, and especially to God. In the dictionary next to Baptist was Mom's picture. When Tony figured this out, he didn't give her so much grief. He knew that if it came down to pleasing her son or pleasing her God, Mom would choose God every time. Even Dad seemed to know that she was a living saint, and he took out his frustrations on other people, namely, Tony and Annie.

Mom paused and fixed a stare on Tony's hands. He looked down and saw the smudges of dirt, went to the sink and washed up. Mom didn't rule by screaming; she ruled by being patient and pious. When she fell into a certain still waiting, most people knew that they'd lost the battle. Mom's silence and steadfastness could dig at Tony until he had to change his ways, if not his mind. He had learned, for the sake of his own conscience, not to fight holiness.

Tonight Mom made an announcement while they were having their vanilla pudding and wafers for dessert. An earnestness entered her face and her mouth seemed to tremble a bit.

"Brother Jacob's asked us to pray about the upcoming revival meetings. He and the other pastors have put a lot of work into them." She tightened her face a final notch and poured more iced tea into Dad's tumbler.

Dad cleared his throat and studied a chip in his plate. Annie sighed and raised some split ends for closer inspection. "They gonna bring in another music group?" she asked. "The Praising Petersons or the Joyous Joneses or somethin'—what were their names?"

"There may be some music, but the emphasis of the meetings will be preaching. Each church will host a week of revival. First week will be at the Presbyterian church the last week of this month, then at the Methodist church the middle week of July, and then our church the second week of August." Mom stopped then and took a large bite of dessert.

Granddad leaned toward Dad and said, "We need to pick up another length of soaker hose." Dad nodded, and Mom regarded them with steadfast concern, but her mouth seemed to clasp over further words about the revival. Mom didn't press spiritual matters much in the presence of the men. Sometimes she seemed to be mentioning such things so that at the Judgment she could say, "Don't say I didn't tell you. I did, you know—at supper."

"Terry said I could ride along with him and Jose up to the Bensons'. They'll be leaving next week, and they're still hiring." Tony heard the words leave his mouth and a silence flatten them on the table.

Dad gave a little snort. "I already told you you're not combining this summer. Not with the grades you brought this year."

"What trouble could I get into harvesting wheat day and night?"

"That's not the point. I want you close to home, where I can see what you're doing."

For a moment, nobody said a word.

"What trouble could he get into with farm boys?" Annie's voice carried its sarcasm with ease. "He might drown in tobacco spit."

"He's not going anywhere this summer. Trust was broken, and he has to earn it back."

Annie sighed loudly. Tony watched the red rise along the side of Dad's neck. He turned to Tony.

"You'll find work around town, and you'll get there by foot or your bicycle. I already told you that." Dad was fairly attacking his pudding dish, although his voice was under complete control.

Tony swished his spoon around, watching wafer crumbs mix into the too-yellow pudding. There was no surprise in this edict, but he had to try. Combining was the best-paying summer job to be had, and the hard work, long hours, and trancelike monotony of the machinery and the golden wheat shifting and flailing would have given Tony something to attach himself to for several weeks. The other guys were usually OK to be around. And the situation was one of the few in which Tony could sleep when the long work was done.

Tony shrugged and said, "You have any ideas about what *jobs* there are in our charming city?"

"There's all kinds of yard work. The city usually hires an extra kid or two to help repair streets and things like that." Dad actually seemed pleased to be asked this question. But he had trouble swallowing his next bite when Tony responded without missing a beat.

"City won't hire me because Don Tate thinks I'm a dopehead. He'll hire people with IQs of 20, but he's real against dopeheads. And Mrs. Rupert told me everybody's lawn is spoken for."

"That's impossible."

"Dave Seaton and the Shackleford guy've got it all covered."

"Well, you better go talk to Dave Seaton then. I know he doesn't do all the work by himself. Look, I'm not going to argue with you." Dad aimed his finger of authority at Tony. "You'll get a summer job if it's washing dishes and mopping floors for free at the senior center. And the car is off limits, and you'll let me know where you are at all times. End of discussion."

Tony picked up his dishes and took them into the kitchen. Not that long ago, he would have left the table with a comment calculated to heat up the battle. But he was tired of the trouble that caused. As he came back through the dining room, Mom was wiping up a spot where Dad had dropped a spoonful of pudding. He raised his arms from the table for her. As she leaned over him she said, "I told Brother Jacob that we could feed the team one night during the July revival."

"Do whatever you want," said Dad, placing his elbows back on the damp table.

Annie gave her pudding spoon a last lick and let it clang into its dish. Dad shot a look at her. She glared back, got up slowly, and took her dishes to the kitchen. "Hey—it's Tony's turn to do the dishes."

Tony, at the foot of the stairs, turned and headed for the kitchen. He disappointed Annie by not arguing with her. They merely exchanged gestures in the middle of the kitchen. She bounced back into the dining room as Tony faced the sink.

"I'm going to Jody's," Annie announced to Mom.

"How long?"

"I don't know. Ten or eleven. We're just hanging out."

"Make it ten. Who will be there?" Mom had that look of alertness.

"Me and Jody, her mom probably. I don't know." Annie had one hand on her hip. Mom was looking into Annie's face as if she'd find Annie's plans written there.

"Is it all right with Jody's mother?" Mom asked.

"If it wasn't, Jody wouldn't have invited me over." Annie walked through the kitchen, past Tony at the sink, and toward the door, leaving Mom in the dining room. Mom moved to the doorway between the rooms and braced herself in it with both arms. It was her stance toward life. If either of her children ended up in someone else's home, doing something she wasn't sure would be right or making someone else's parents think that she wasn't a good mother—well, it would be her fault.

While Tony did the dishes, he heard the piano in the far room of the house. "Leaning on the Everlasting Arms" then "Sweet Hour of Prayer." Then "Leaning" again, until the bass and tenor parts were just right. Mom tried several different "Amens" at the end of each. Tony heard her emerge from the creaking hallway and sigh when she sat down near her lamp in the living room, across from Dad, who was watching some pseudonews program about what the government was doing to us now.

When Tony finished, he leaned over the back of Mom's chair. She was paging through the hymnal and writing numbers in two different columns in a notebook.

"What are you doing?" Tony asked quietly, so as not to disturb Dad.

"Making a list of the songs I need to practice."

"I thought you knew all of them by now."

"We sing different ones at revival time. I don't play them as often." Mom rubbed her eyes.

"If no one else is used to them either, who'll know if you mess up?" This revival thing would add knots to his mother's colon.

"You've got a point." Something like a smile haunted Mom's face for a moment as she twisted in her chair to look at Tony.

Dad broke in. "Did you finish in the kitchen?"

"Yeah."

"Everything? Wiped off the counter? Put leftovers away?"

"Yeah." Tony headed for the stairs at last. Nowadays, instead of swearing and slamming doors, he stayed quiet and out of the way. All words seemed to have lost their effect on anything or anyone in his house. Communication didn't exist. He didn't mind. They all seemed to live in another space anyway, one separate from him.

At some level, he still enjoyed the frustration he was causing Dad by being so agreeable. The old man was looking for more argument, or sassiness, or something he might punish. But Tony had discovered that immediate obedience took the wind out of Dad's huff. But the satisfaction faded when Dad started in on Mom, complaining about how "those kids never do a job all the way." Mom was saying something meant to soothe, but by then Tony was at the top of the stairs and couldn't hear her.

As Tony walked by Granddad's room, the soft sound of sleep came out past the half-open door to meet him; the old guy went to bed while it was still light. Of course, he got up two hours before any other human did. Tony put his head in the room. He could see the end of the bed and the old man's covered feet and skinny legs. A small fan was going. Granddad had a fan on year-round, claimed that his sinuses didn't block up so badly. The room felt as if it belonged to another house. It was the only one with the original wallpaper; even in the near darkness, Tony could picture the faint vertical stripes, faded into non-descript colors, that were printed on the back of his mind from earlier days. He could barely remember Grandma, who had died when he was four. He had slept with Granddad when he was small, had lain there and watched the breaths go in and out. Now hardly a word passed between them. Few words passed from Granddad to anybody at all.

Down the hall, Tony's room seemed to wait for him. All the stuff that was important was in there (except for what lay buried under the pear tree), and everything in there was his and no one else's. But the dreams had started again lately. Even with lights on while he slept—when he was lucky enough to sleep—the suffocating and panic came in black and white mostly, but some nights in full, violent colors. To sleep was to suffer, kind of like it had been back in the winter. At the doorway he nearly decided to sleep on the couch downstairs, pretending to stay up for a late movie. But Dad was still planted in front of the set, and he would think of some way to start something unpleasant. Besides, the dreams would come regardless. They had nothing to do with location.

Tony reached into the dimness and turned on the light. He stood completely still and took inventory. Sometimes objects seemed to change places without his knowing it. He stared hard to make note of the angles of furniture and which tapes were lying on top of the deck.

He began removing items from strategic places: the glass from the bedside table to a place where his flailing wouldn't knock it off—the floor lamp away from the window so it wouldn't look like a creature against the pale night sky, the radio to a closer position so that he could turn it on low when he lay awake by himself. He liked the talk-radio station; it was almost like having other people with him. He hardly ever remembered the topics they talked about, but the voices were real and alive. Tony had taped the phone number of the talk show to his flashlight, in case he ever wanted to call. They could talk about nightmares. About not sleeping.

He went to the hall bathroom and washed quickly, brushing his teeth without looking at his own reflection. At Jason's he had watched an old film where the ghost of someone kept showing up in the mirror. The poor woman would be combing her hair, and there it would come.

It wasn't something he could talk about with other people, even guys he'd known a long time—the thing that spooky movies did to him. He could remember a time when he liked getting scared with the rest of them. They still went for the goriest, creepiest videos they could find. He found something else to do or somewhere else to be. Getting thrilled by that stuff was part of another life, the Before period. Before Near Death. Time kept screwing him up. He would think he was remembering himself as a little kid, only it was something that happened just a year or so ago. That's how far away the older, normal days felt.

He put on some music and stared at the ceiling until the room grew dark. He could stare for a long time and not know how much time had passed. Sometimes it was like he suddenly became conscious again, and it would be an hour or two later, and he couldn't remember what he'd done during that time.

Finally, while he could still hear the sounds of other people wandering around the house, the snatches of conversation, the whisper of the television downstairs, he clicked off the lamp near his bed. He had learned not to try to go to sleep in absolute quiet. Silence was worse than sound; it tore up his nerves. He lay flat on his back and stared at the ceiling, at a blank spot where nothing could look like something else. He waited for his own breathing to calm down.

After twenty minutes, when he was nearing sleep and the rest of the family had settled in for the night, it came to him. Something pressed close from one corner of his room. It was standing by his desk. There was no form to it, only a feeling.

It's nothing. Your lame imagination. There's nothing here. Tony made his breath stay slow. He shut his eyes, and the thing came closer. He must aim his hand just right, so he would have the light on before he could see what was there beside him. If he saw it in the dark, he would have no power to get to the light. His muscles would freeze, and he wouldn't be able to talk or even close his eyes.

In a single movement the light was on and Tony was propped up in bed. Familiar furniture and possessions stood innocently in the quiet glare.

Tony turned on the radio and snuggled close to the light. He would listen to Jerry Rambler on *Talk Tonight*. And try to get too exhausted to dream.

4

DAVE SEATON:
THE TOWN GUY

Friday, June 13

Dave Seaton was on his front step having a smoke when the black Cavalier skidded on the shoulder of the street and stopped. He heard the kids cursing at each other and recognized the slurred speech of a teenager who had started his evening early.

The girl who got out of the passenger's side was someone he recognized, although he couldn't remember a name. She was in a silky blue prom dress, worn tight against her small form and slung low at the top. She slammed the car door and wobbled on her high heels.

"Whatsa matter?" Dave called softly as she pulled off the heels and headed in his general direction.

"Ahh! Nothin'. Everything's better now." She hiked up the skirt and jumped the narrow ditch between the street and Dave's yard. The blue of the gown gleamed in the early evening. The girl stopped in front of his walk and let her skirt down. "He's a loser," she said, looking up the street where the car had just disappeared around a corner.

"Sounded pretty belligerent to me," said Dave.

"I figured he'd get drunk later—you know, *after* the dance."

"Bad manners."

"You got it." She peered at Dave then and came up the walk toward him.

Dave sat still on the step but let his eyes wander the length of the dress and up to the girl's face. He noticed right off that her eyes seemed deep and too old, but they were set into a face that looked fresh and smooth as a little child's. Thin bangs scattered over her forehead. One corner of her mouth nudged upward, hinting at a smile.

"What's your name?" he asked. "I see you around sometimes."

"Randy Kluver," she said. "I live three blocks over."

"Your dad's Charlie . . . who does the wood carving and all?"

"Yeah, he and Mom are at a craft show in Little Rock right now." She had stopped just a few feet in front of him. The silver high heels dangled from one hand. Dave noticed dark polish on her toenails.

"Prom night, I take it," he said.

She laughed. "School's been out for three weeks. But there's a dance at the Den tonight."

Dave tapped his forehead. "I've been out of school so long, I don't keep track of when it's going or isn't." He'd heard of the Den, a place that somehow brought higher-class bands and parties here to farm country. About once a month the dance would be formal. It was one of the few places in the county that gave people an excuse to get out their good clothes.

"Randy." He reflected on the name, studying her small face. "Did your parents want a boy?"

"No. The night I was born, my dad's brother Randy was shot in the stomach in East St. Louis. Died the same hour my mom had me."

"Wow."

"I like it for a name," she said.

"Have you been to St. Louis?"

"Once, when I was too little to know anything."

"I've heard the east side's pretty rough."

"He was at a truck stop. That's all I know. I don't think anybody went to jail for it. Your name's Dave, isn't it?"

"Dave Seaton. You ever been to Kansas City?"

"Sure. A few times."

"I worked there about a year once." Dave spread a newspaper on the step next to him. "Have a seat. That's a hot dress; you're not going to the dance at all?"

She sat down and shook her head. Her fine hair was light brown, almost blond, and looked shiny in the evening light. "I guess not."

"What are we going to do with you, all dressed up and no place to go?"

Randy shrugged. Then she turned to him and grinned briefly. "It's really not a big deal."

Dave ground the butt of his cigarette into the step. "You want a cigarette?"

"I don't smoke."

"Good for you. Want a cup of coffee or a Coke or something?"

"That'd be okay."

Dave helped her up and they stepped into his living room. He walked into the kitchen and turned on a light, then glanced back at her as she walked slowly around the room. It wasn't much to look at—old sofa, a recliner with a sheet thrown over the bad upholstery, great-granddad's walnut desk, a television, and a coffee table with an empty beer bottle on it.

"A Coke with ice?" he asked.

"Sure." Randy stepped to the corner where some photos hung above the old desk. She was looking at the large picture in the center when Dave came up and handed her the drink. The photo was from several years ago.

"That's Karen," he said. The young, blond woman in the photo leaned against a railing with a reddish canyon in the background. She was wearing jeans and a T-shirt and was smiling easily, strands of hair blowing across her face and covering one eye. "My wife."

"I didn't know you were married."

"She died two years ago—some weird blood disease."

"That's awful. I'm sorry."

"We had a great marriage." Dave touched the face in the photograph. "It's something how people who spend their lives hating each other and talking about divorce seem to live until they're old. Maybe people like Karen are too good to hang around this place long."

Randy was silent.

Dave sat in the recliner, and Randy took a seat on the sofa. Then Dave got up and opened the window to Randy's left. "Hot in here."

"Thanks," she said. They sipped their drinks for a while. Randy leaned back on the sofa, stretching her neck and shoulders, and crossed her legs.

"It's nice to know your name now," Dave said, easing back himself and resting an ankle across one knee. The girl didn't seem to mind that he was looking at her. He liked how she just settled in as though she came to his house all the time.

"Where do you work?" she asked.

"Work for the county—on the roads. Before that I was a mechanic at the Truck Barn."

"Have you had a lot of different jobs?" Randy's head was cocked slightly so that the breeze from the window fluffed her hair on one side.

"I've had a few. Especially since Karen died. Had to move around. You know, get away."

"You lived in this house with her?"

Dave nodded and took a drink. "Was my dad's house, and his dad's before that."

Randy crunched on a piece of ice. Dave put his foot down and leaned toward her suddenly.

"Do you ever feel guilty for no reason?" he asked.

She studied him a moment and finished her ice. "What?"

"Do you feel guilty when you haven't done anything wrong?"

"I . . . guess. Sometimes when I do something that I don't think is wrong but somebody else thinks it is. Yeah, I do."

Dave leaned back in the chair again. "I suppose everybody goes through that."

"You—uh—feel guilty about anything in particular?"

"Hmm." He rested his mouth against the back of his hand and studied the floor. "I feel guilty when bad things happen to other people."

"What other people?"

"Oh, anybody."

Randy drained her glass.

"I felt guilty when Karen died."

Randy let out a careful sigh and put her glass on the coffee table.

"Sorry," Dave said quickly. "I'm talking like—"

"It's okay. I just don't know what to say, that's all."

"You want more Coke?"

"No thanks. Maybe I should go."

"I've got an idea." Dave stood up. "Let's drive up to Kansas City."

"Now?" She placed her hands, palms down, on the silky dress where it covered her thighs.

"Sure. You'd be out late anyway, if you'd gone to the dance. What time do you need to be home?"

"My folks won't get back from the show until Monday afternoon. My little sister's there." Randy was looking at him carefully, but Dave could see that her eyes were shining. "But she usually goes over to Granny's for the night when Mom and Dad are gone."

"Let's go then. I haven't been to the city for nearly two months. I know a great barbecue place."

Randy gave him a careful look. "I don't have much money with me."

He shrugged. "I can cover it."

She still didn't look convinced. Dave almost laughed at the suspicion on her face.

"You don't trust me, huh?"

"I just met you."

"I *live* here. Ol' Mr. Kelsey saw you sitting on my porch." He smiled. "I just want some real barbecue, see a few lights, and drive back. We could be back by one or two in the morning. This place makes me crazy sometimes."

"Yeah," she said. "I know what you mean."

"And maybe your evening won't be a total loss?" He smiled again, and she finally grinned back. Dave noticed that she had one crooked tooth in front.

"Okay." Randy got up and took her empty glass to the kitchen. Dave turned to watch her. He liked the way she walked. Easy, but not like a flirt.

"I've got to change into something I can breathe in," Randy said as she rinsed the glass and set it in the sink.

"We can stop by your house."

"No, we can't. Teri might still be there, and she'd ask all these questions. The kid's got to know everything every minute." Randy came back to the living room and stopped at Dave's chair. "I don't want to try to explain how I switched guys."

"I've got some clothes here that might fit you." Dave could hardly believe he'd just said that. But he motioned Randy to follow him into the bedroom. He went straight to the trunk under the window and unloaded the pile of magazines that covered the lid.

"Is that a cooking magazine?" Randy asked, picking up the February issue of *Eating Well*.

"Yeah. It's sort of a hobby."

"Huh. I never cook."

When Dave opened the trunk, Karen's scent flew into his face. He'd known that would happen, even after he'd washed the clothes a couple of times.

"Are you sure this is okay?" Randy asked.

"I should have given these to somebody a long time ago. You look close to her size."

"Could be freaky." Randy held up a pair of practically new Levi's.

"She's been gone over two years." Dave closed the lid and sat on the trunk. Randy was just a foot or two from him. "It won't be freaky."

"Well, let me try these on." She followed his direction to the small bathroom. He listened to her unzipping, sliding clothes off and on, and zipping again. He heard the faucet run and jumped up to find a clean towel. He knocked on the door to hand it in.

"These fit okay. How 'bout a shirt?" Her hand took the towel, and the door closed. Dave looked through the trunk and came up with a silver, silky Western shirt. He couldn't remember Karen wearing it. But they'd not gone out much, especially in the last year. She'd probably bought it, hoping the time would come when she'd feel well enough again. Dave shook out the shirt and took it to the bathroom door. "I think we'll need to iron this a little." He handed that in when the door cracked open. He heard Randy's pleased response. "Would you mind?" she asked, and he took the shirt back. He grabbed the ironing board and iron out of the hall closet. While he was pressing the shirt, the bathroom door cracked open. "I'm using your deodorant, okay?"

"Sure. Use anything you need. Sorry it's such a mess in there."

"You're pretty clean for a guy who lives by himself."

Dave smiled. When the shirt was pressed and Randy emerged from the bathroom, Dave knew he'd made a bunch of good choices this evening. The clothes fit, and the girl looked like someone he could have known for a long time. She wasn't anything like Karen, which made it easier for him. Randy had washed off the makeup, and that was an improvement too. Dave felt a surge of real anticipation.

"Does this look all right?"

"Sure. You look fine." Dave sat on the bed and nodded his approval.

"I don't want to look *too* fine."

Dave laughed. "You don't look too fine. Maybe if you had on a tight leather miniskirt—"

"Oh that *would* be too fine." She laughed too.

It's real nice of you to take me," Randy said as they left the city limits of Bender Springs.

"Sure you're not too broken up over what's-his-face?"

She sniffed. "You saved me. Jay would have given me a bad evening."

"Why do you go out with him?"

She shrugged. "Something to do."

Dave smiled slightly and glanced in her direction.

"I mean," she went on, "he's no expert."

"How old is he?"

"Eighteen."

"Nobody's an expert at eighteen."

"How old are you?" she asked.

"Thirty-two."

"Is anybody an expert at thirty-two?"

"A few of us." He smiled, then laughed. "I'm not saying who."

She fished around in his tape box and put in some Bonnie Raitt. The music gave the evening miles a comfortable feel.

An hour into the drive, Dave glanced at Randy's dark silhouette. "You feeling okay about doing this?"

"Yeah."

"I don't want to make you uncomfortable or anything."

"I'm okay. You don't set off my alarms."

"Alarms?"

"Yeah. The jerk alarms. The things that go off inside when a guy starts telling nasty jokes in the first ten minutes he knows you or he keeps trying to stand closer to you than you want him to stand, but he doesn't get it when you back away. When he's got to be the big man— make all the decisions and pay for everything. When he gets irritated if you keep him waiting or give an opinion that doesn't agree with his. He touches you when you don't give him any signals that it's okay. He won't shut up when you're trying to get in a word. Or he won't look you in the eye for more than three seconds—"

"Man, you should write a book."

"I could. Believe me. My jerk alarm is state-of-the-art."

"But you were going out with Jay."

"Jay has some good points that sometimes override my alarm system. He's an artist, and I get into painting." She sighed. "But he's still a jerk most of the time. Anyway—" She turned to Dave. "You didn't set off the alarm. And I just feel good around you."

"I feel good around you too."

"Really?"

He reached over in the twilight and found her hand. She took hold of him as though she'd been waiting. Dave felt his life up to now slip away behind them. The dark tunnel of road seemed smooth and inviting. They rolled down the windows, and sweet, grassy air whipped softly around their faces.

It was nearly ten o'clock when they entered the suburb of Shawnee Mission. Streams of cars vied for lane space all around them.

"I'm starved," Dave said.

"Me too. Haven't had barbecue for a long time."

"It's only about five minutes from here. But I need to fill up first." He slid into the far right lane and then into a large gas station, its oil-spotted pavement a sick yellow under the lights. Randy tilted the rearview mirror to look at her face while Dave pumped gas. He went in to pay and decided to use the rest room while he was at it. The attendant who sat surrounded by suspended racks of cigarette cartons looked as if she were either at the very end or the very beginning of her shift. Dave tried to be cheerful, but the woman only looked at him with dull eyes.

When he walked outside and toward the car, he saw that Randy had company. Dave stopped about ten yards from the car. He was looking at the back of a cheap suit. The person wearing it was bent over Randy's open window. Dave came around to get a better look, and the guy followed Randy's relieved look and turned straight at Dave. He was probably in his mid to late twenties. Sort of tubby. He was wearing a dress shirt but no tie.

"You need something?" Dave asked.

"I was just asking the young lady here if she knew where there might be a garage that was open at this hour." His speech was clear, but his eyes were bloodshot.

"Man—this time of night?" Dave tried not to sound too sarcastic. The guy looked exhausted.

"I know. I'm stuck, aren't I?"

"What's the problem?"

"Not sure. I think it's in the electrical system. Alternator light came on."

"Where's the car?"

The man pointed to a beat-up two-door, parked at the perimeter of the station lights, and the two of them walked over to it.

"I'm Joe Travis," the man said.

"Dave Seaton." They shook hands. "You live here?"

"Grew up in Nevada, Missouri. I'm here now at Midwestern Seminary." The guy took out a white handkerchief and wiped sweat from his forehead.

"Seminary, huh? Going to be a minister?" They had the hood of the car up and ducked under it to look things over. All the wiring looked fine.

"Yes. Another two years to go. I work as a shipping clerk, go to class nearly full-time. It'll take a while."

While they took turns starting the engine and looking at connections and moving parts, Dave was vaguely aware of Randy, who remained in his car. He looked in that direction once or twice and saw that she had put the seat back and appeared to be relaxing.

After fifteen minutes, Dave said, "Well, Joe, whatever this car's problem is, it's nothing I can fix. You're gonna have to get it to a garage."

"It was really nice of you to try." Joe walked back toward Dave's car with him. "I'll get it towed to a place near the seminary. Have to work out another way to get south, I guess."

"Where south?"

"Place called Bender Springs—hardly a speck on the map." Joe smiled. "I'm supposed to be in a meeting at ten-thirty tomorrow morning with some pastors."

"No kiddin'," said Dave. "We just drove up from Bender Springs."

"I'll be." Joe shook his head. "Small world, huh?"

They had returned to Dave's car, and Randy was looking at both of them. Dave couldn't read her expression. "Uh," he said, "Randy, this guy's on his way to Bender Springs."

"Or was," the seminarian broke in and then laughed a little.

"How's his car?" Randy asked.

"Nothing we can do. He'll have to get it to a shop."

"Gee, sorry," she said.

Joe shrugged. He put his hand out to Dave then. "Say, it was real nice of you to try to help. You folks have a nice evening."

"Sorry we couldn't do more," said Dave. He and Randy watched Joe walk toward the pay phone attached to the far wall of the station.

"Seems like a nice guy," Dave said.

"Yeah."

"Goes to seminary."

"Preacher?"

He shrugged. "I guess. Must take motivation other than money. That suit's about as old as his car."

"My granny says that preachers are called by God. It's almost like they don't have a choice."

Dave hadn't felt called to anything his whole life, and he wondered what it was like to have a vision of your own destination.

"He live in Bender Springs?" Randy asked, still watching Joe.

"Nah. Supposed to be at some church meeting in the morning."

"Oh."

Dave kicked the car's tire absently, his hand resting on the roof over Randy's head. "Not such good timing, huh? I mean, any other time I'd be happy to give him a lift."

"Why don't you, then?"

Dave shrugged and looked over the car to the passing traffic. "We have plans. I'm looking forward to getting to know you better."

"It's not like you'll never have the chance again." Randy leaned out the window and peered up at him. "Do what you think you should do, Dave. I'm just along for the ride tonight."

He regarded her for a moment, quite seriously. "If you're sure."

"I don't say what I don't mean. You may as well know that now." Her face was calm.

"Okay. I'll be right back."

Fifteen minutes later, Joe, Dave, and Randy were up to their elbows in the best barbecue sauce north of New Orleans. They all but buried their heads in the stacks of ribs and came up for air only to laugh at each other. Joe was amazed that such a delicacy existed so close to where he lived.

"Seminary students don't eat out a lot," he joked as he licked his fingers. "I've got a whole drawer of packets you add hot water to."

"Let's see, soup, hot chocolate, hot tea, what else?" Randy seemed not at all miffed that she and Dave had picked up a dinner guest. Dave watched her eat and felt happier than he'd felt for a long time. He could tell she knew how to enjoy things. And she didn't excuse herself from the table a half-dozen times to fix her face in the bathroom. He had discovered, in the course of their conversation, that she had turned eighteen but two months ago. He'd known she was young, and he wondered if she was too young, but he wouldn't let himself think about that now.

"Noodles. All kinds of noodles," Joe was saying. "And those little bean soups."

"But we already said soup," argued Randy. "And noodles count as soup. What you're saying is that you eat a lot of soup."

"Okay, you're right. I guess I eat a lot of soup. But not tonight!"

"You're not married, Joe?" Dave leaned back to give his stomach a breather.

"No. Time for other things right now. Would be kind of unfair to make a wife live on what I have."

"You plan on being a preacher?"

Joe nodded. "I'd like to be a pastor. And I hope to have a wife by then." He smiled. He won more points with Dave by insisting to pay half the tab. Dave wondered if the cash Joe pulled out of his wallet was the extent of his resources for the next week. But they split the bill, treating Randy, who grabbed an elbow of each of them as they crossed the parking lot. The downtown area twinkled in the near distance. They stood by Dave's car to look at the city lights and then turned in the opposite direction to look for stars. But suburbia spread around them for miles in every direction, and most of the lights that winked brightly at them were planes flying in and out of the international airport north of the city.

They were on the road south by midnight. Joe excused himself and slept in the backseat, his head resting on the canvas briefcase he'd brought with him.

"Thanks for not being upset about things changing." Dave placed a hand on Randy's knee as he said this.

"You're a nice person, Dave." She patted his leg in return. "Will you be able to stay awake?"

"No problem. I drove fourteen hours straight once."

"Mind if I close my eyes awhile?"

"Settle down and sleep if you want. It'll make the ride go faster," he said softly. She shifted the seat back and closed her eyes. When Dave thought she was asleep, a soft hand came up suddenly and rested on his shoulder. He bent his neck to press his face against her hand. It felt so familiar he wanted to whoop like a winning football captain or cry like a baby. Going back to Bender Springs, where he'd lived all his life, and which he had resented most of his life, didn't feel like a bad thing now.

5

SARAH MORGAN: THE PASTOR'S WIFE

Saturday, June 14

Sarah Morgan put one foot on the ground to get her balance, then stepped out of the passenger's side of the Honda Civic and hoisted four-month-old Peter onto her right hip in practically the same motion. Although she had showered this morning and dressed up, she felt her hair going limp and a trickle of sweat dampen the back of her dress. The early morning had come with a freshness that made her happy for an hour or so, but it was 10:45 now, and she was ready for another shower. And a nap. Wrestling the baby and supervising four-year-old Miranda, typing her husband's notes, and fighting two loads of laundry in and out of machines in her cramped pantry—today's dailiness had worn her down already, and the temperature was climbing.

"We're fifteen minutes late." Her husband, Jacob, pastor of First Baptist, didn't try to hide his irritation. Once again, she had slowed him down. All the planning in the world couldn't conquer two children when they had their minds on other things. Jacob's comment made

Sarah angry, and she didn't bother to apologize. She'd been apologizing way too much lately.

"Miranda, take my hand while we cross the street," she said, reaching for her daughter.

"There aren't any cars," the child muttered. True enough. One could stand on Main Street in Bender Springs sometimes for minutes at a time without any vehicles going by.

"I don't care whether there are cars or not. You always hold someone's hand when you cross the street."

"Here, Miranda." Jacob made two quick strides and grabbed their daughter's hand. Miranda didn't resist. Sarah bristled. They walked wordlessly up the walk to the new, boxlike annex that looked out of place beside the church. First Presbyterian was eighty years old, dark brick, and full of interesting angles. A giant cottonwood tree shaded most of one side.

Two girls in their midteens greeted Jacob and Sarah as soon as they entered. One of them, a skinny redhead with a long earring trailing from one ear, smiled with enthusiasm and offered a hand to Miranda right away. "What's your name?"

Miranda took the hand without a blink and pronounced her name loudly.

The teenager's face was bright. "What a cool name! We've got some games and books." And they were headed down a hallway. The other girl, slightly overweight with long dark hair, took Peter from Sarah as though this were a daily routine.

Sarah sighed with relief as the child left her arms. "He ate a while ago, so he should be okay. Right now he's into these rattly things; they're in the bag." The girl smiled and nodded, taking the bag and Peter and following her coworker.

From the opposite direction a stout, white-haired man with silver-rimmed glasses approached them. Madison Carruthers, the Presbyterian pastor, smiled and put his hand out first to Sarah. "I'm glad you came, Sarah."

"Thank you," said Sarah, genuinely warmed by the grasp of both his hands around her one.

"Sarah will help in any way she can," said Jacob, at her side. Sarah felt her own smile freeze and sudden yet familiar resentment shoot up in her throat.

"Introverts just don't fit in this church scene down here," she'd pointed out soon after they'd arrived in Bender Springs, nearly two years ago.

"Just be yourself, honey," he had answered. "You'll be fine." Yet as the months wore on, she had not been so fine, and he had begun his attempts at being helpful. Speaking for her when she was too quiet. Explaining in more detail something she'd just said. Instructing her how to respond or what to do in a given situation.

Sarah noticed that Rev. Carruthers was looking at her intently. His smile was still there, although he'd let go of her hand.

"We're meeting over here in the conference room, such as it is. We haven't quite finished this building, but that's obvious."

They entered a large room of unpainted walls and cement floors. It was sectioned into classrooms by temporary plywood partitions, with various tables, folding chairs, and teaching supplies giving some order to each space. At the far end of the room, a large table sat near a copy machine and what looked like kitchen cabinets that had been donated from someone who had remodeled since 1970. Above the copier, papers of different colors and sizes hung at angles from a bulletin board.

Chris Dancey, the Methodist pastor, was already seated at the table with a younger man Sarah didn't recognize. Dancey rose to shake Jacob's hand, then Sarah's.

"I told my wife she should come," Dancey said to Sarah. "I'll have to tell her you were here."

"Say hello for me," Sarah said. Barbara Dancey was a sweet, earth-mother type who homeschooled her three children. Like a wildflower that just sprouted up naturally in a town like this. Sarah knew that Barbara was absent not because she couldn't come but because she didn't consider pastoral meetings something she needed to be involved with. Sarah had felt that at least one woman should be here, but she sensed that this was important to no one besides her.

"Sarah," her husband said, "this is Joe Travis, the seminary student from Midwestern." The other man, in his twenties and neat looking if not particularly handsome, took Sarah's hand with a firm grasp.

"Joe, you'll be staying at our place in early August while the last week of revival is held at our church," Jacob continued. Sarah smiled at Joe and began calculating how to get a room ready for him. This was the first she'd heard anything about housing guests. It didn't surprise or dismay her, but she felt new irritation at her husband for putting her on the spot right now.

"I really appreciate that," said Joe. "Don't go to a lot of trouble now."

"No trouble, as long as you don't expect the Hilton," Sarah said, making her voice light and friendly. She turned to Madison then, who was shuffling some papers as he took a seat on one side of the table. "When exactly did you build this annex, Rev. Carruthers? I think it was here when we came to town."

"This building," Madison stated, leaning back to look at the room thoughtfully, "was the brainchild of a pastor who was here before us. Young guy with lots of vision but not a lot of staying power. Well, in the middle of it all he converted to liberation theology, and things sort of fell apart." He smiled at Sarah. "As you can probably guess, liberation theology hasn't caught on out here."

Sarah smiled. "I'm sure."

"I never met the man," said Madison. "Church was without a pastor for nearly two years after he left. Bank took back this building. The structure was in place, and I guess the plumbing and electricity were done, but that was it. A couple years ago we ironed out some agreements. This is considered a *facility* now. We finished the banquet room and kitchen first so community groups could rent the space. Fees go directly to the bank, and we keep paying on the mortgage. I'm not into building programs much myself. Figure that when we get so big we're busting out of this place, it's time to plant another congregation somewhere else."

"I agree totally," said Jacob, seated beside Sarah and leaning in toward Madison. "I don't think megachurches are the best way to go."

"Not out here, anyway. Well, I guess we're ready to get started."

While the four men began discussing logistics of the revival meetings, Sarah sat back and studied them. She wondered what composite power and wisdom they must hold, how many seminary hours they represented. How many funerals they'd preached and sermons they'd delivered. Even in her disgruntled state, Sarah held some awe toward these men sitting at the table with her, who cared for the souls of people—if such a thing were even possible. In the last couple of years, Sarah had begun to doubt that, but people who *tried to* watch over others' souls continued to impress her.

The meeting itself was uneventful. They had covered the inspirational side of things in their first meeting several months ago—about their vision for Bender Springs, about how they could truly build an ecumenical community, about how, among their three churches, they should be able to get at least 40 percent of the town in church again. Sarah hadn't been at that meeting, but Jacob had gone on about it for days.

"Whatever needs to happen here, Sare, I can't do on my own. I think this might be an answer to prayer," Jacob had said after that meeting. Sarah had looked at the new bit of hope on his face and wanted him to be right. She'd watched him trying to give faith a chance for well over a year. It wouldn't have been so hard if attendance hadn't dropped steadily since they'd come. The congregation that numbered one hundred and fifty when they'd arrived had shrunk to a little over a third that size. Jacob couldn't explain it, and Sarah couldn't either. No one seemed to be noticeably upset with them; they simply stopped attending. By the time Jacob would visit them to be sure they were all right, he would find them attending Victory Baptist in Helmsly or some other church nearby, or—in most cases—no place at all. Their reasons were always nonindicting. But Sarah and Jacob had come to feel rejected in the most fundamental way. In her heart of hearts, Sarah knew she was part of the Great Unspoken Reason. If Jacob had not quite come up to expectations, she hadn't even approached the vicinity.

Sarah half listened to the ideas volleying from one side of the table to the other. They had an evangelist for the week in June at the Presbyterian church, along with a music group from Fort Worth. For the week in July at the Methodist church there was another evangelist and a song leader from their own county's Baptist association. Week three, in early August, was still in formation, but Jacob was pretty sure an old friend from seminary would come down, and Joe Travis was scaring up some musicians at Midwestern.

The business concluded, Madison announced that they were invited to his home for refreshments. They smiled, stretched, and followed him next door to the old but classic parsonage. It was likely one of the nicest homes in town. Madison was a carpenter by trade, and the place had a cared-for, personal look about it. It was solid and freshly painted a cool blue gray with dark gray shutters. A flowerbed ruffled the base of the house. Sarah made a little sound of pleasure, reaching to touch a flower. It was a species she hadn't seen before.

"The plants are Rona's doing. She's had some inner ear trouble since February, though, and gets dizzy when she bends over sometimes. So there's not nearly as much here as usual. There's a jungle in the house too." He led them up the steps of the wraparound porch. A cushioned glider sat in the sunshine, small tables on either side. Bright begonias and petunias hung at intervals around the rim of the porch roof. A longing sprung up in Sarah. She thought of her own plain home just a few blocks away. Surely she could have worked on the place, hung a plant here and there. She dreaded seeing any more. The inside was probably a showplace too.

The inside was hardly a showplace. It held a hodgepodge of comfortable furniture and decorative items spanning several decades and undoubtedly a number of children and grandchildren. Several floor fans moved fresh air past them, and wind chimes sang from some other place in the house. It was a home that would feel like home to anyone.

Not much matched, but everything fit. And when Rona Carruthers walked into the living room to greet them, Sarah put her fears away.

She'd met Rona a couple of times, in social situations where a number of other people were in on the conversation. Sarah had been too involved with surviving the small talk actually to learn much about the older woman. Here Rona looked as though all pastors' wives must be fashioned after her. She was matronly but not frumpy. Friendly but not gushy. And capable without being intimidating. A Barbara Bush sort of woman. Rona greeted each of them with a tall glass of iced tea and directed them to a middle room full of cross breezes, where a small table, covered with a plain blue cloth, was practically hidden beneath a large platter of fruit and cookies. Dessert plates and napkins lay graciously on either side. The pastors moaned happily in approval, and Sarah gathered—since each of them, including Jacob, knew the name of the cookies—that the recipe was homemade and famous throughout the county.

A phone rang, and Rona answered it in the kitchen. "Sarah, your little boy's unhappy."

"Oh, he's probably hungry. I should have picked him up before we came over. How's Miranda?"

She heard Rona inquire. "She's fine and doesn't want to leave yet."

Sarah laughed. "Miranda never wants to leave. She could just move in with anybody anywhere." She headed toward the door they had come in. "I'll get Peter."

"Oh, Terri can bring him over. Sit down and relax a minute." Sarah followed Rona into the kitchen. Rona turned to a few dishes in the sink and motioned Sarah to a breakfast nook, surrounded on three sides by windows. "Have a seat." Newspapers and magazines, the top one with a quilt on the cover, took up most of the space on the small square table. Sarah pulled out a chair and sat down. The room, though not large, felt airy, with a fine yellow wallpaper on the upper half of the walls and light paneling on down to the floor. The cabinets were built to utilize the space perfectly; Madison's doing, Sarah guessed.

"Do you quilt?" Sarah asked, looking at the magazine cover.

"I try. My mother was an expert, and now that I have an empty nest, I've taken it up as a serious hobby."

"I've seen some patterns sell into the thousands at art shows." Sarah picked up a saltshaker, a little rooster.

"I'm not surprised. They take months. Our church has a quilting club. A bunch of us old-timers work on one every Wednesday afternoon. You should come over sometime. Do you sew?"

Sarah put down the rooster. One eye had been nicked, the unfinished white spot gazing at her. "Oh. No, not much. Most of my artistic ability goes into painting, when there's time, and usually there's not."

The long-haired girl came through the back door, just off the pantry to Sarah's right. Peter wasn't crying, but his look told Sarah that he was merely delaying his judgment of the situation. Once he saw her, his squall came out full force. She took him and bounced him on her lap.

"Do you mind if I nurse him here?" Sarah asked. Rona was at her side, cooing over Peter.

"Go right ahead. Do you need a tea towel?"

"Thanks." Sarah opened her shirt and unfastened the nursing bra. Peter took to her in seconds, and she draped the towel over her shoulder. She and Rona laughed at the gulping sounds coming from under the cloth.

"He knew exactly what he wanted, didn't he?" Rona dried her hands and pulled up a chair across the table from Sarah. "You know, my kids are grown and have kids of their own, but I feel sometimes as though they were babies just a year or two ago."

Sarah smiled.

"I saw your little girl with Jacob the other day. What a doll she is!"

"That's Miranda. Thank you. This is Peter." She grasped the baby's foot as it kicked busily in the air.

"I'm so ashamed of myself, Sarah. I was telling Madison I couldn't believe you and Jacob had been here two years. I've not even gotten to know you."

"Don't worry about it. I've not made it around like I should have."

"How are you faring over at First Baptist these days? Oh, let me get you something to eat." Rona was up and already in the next room. Sarah could hear the quiet conversation of her husband and the other three men. She wondered if they'd noticed she wasn't in the room. Rona returned with a peach and some cookies. At the cabinet she made a few quick moves with a knife, and the fruit appeared in front of Sarah, pitted and sliced. Sarah thanked her and took a bite from a piece she held in her free hand.

"So that's where you went," Madison said from the doorway. Sarah pointed to the baby. "I understand." Madison nodded. "You're on call."

"That's exactly right," said Sarah, and felt herself smile. It was becoming clear why she liked the Carrutherses so much. They introduced no pressure into her life. And they understood what her life was like. No time to visit people. A baby pulling her out of group discussions.

Sarah hadn't felt judged only to be found lacking a single time since she'd entered the house. She realized that her defenses were completely down.

"Oh, Marge Berrie's in the hospital again," Rona told her husband. "Her daughter called a while ago. Said it was no emergency, but Marge was asking where you were."

"She gets pretty disturbed when I'm not at the admissions desk to get her checked in."

"I don't know why she'd ask where you were when there's no possible way for you to know she's there. They just admitted her this afternoon. Gall bladder, I think."

"Oh, she just wants to know that I'm coming."

"She must think you have telepathic powers," said Rona, her sarcasm light but real.

Sarah laughed out loud before she could catch herself. Rona blushed a little, and Sarah felt Madison's hand clap her own shoulder lightly. "We minister types do have telepathic powers, don't we? God just plugs us into the universe when we get ordained." He waved at Sarah and his wife and turned back toward the living room.

Sarah laughed again as she watched Madison leave the room. When she turned back, Rona was looking at her. "Are your people supportive of the revivals?" Rona asked.

"They seem to be." Sarah realized she didn't have a lot of information. Most of what she knew she had heard from Jacob. "I haven't heard any real grumbling. I suppose that's a good sign." Sarah felt the intensity of Rona's eyes. "To be honest, I'm probably not connected enough to the grapevine to know what people really think. Sometimes I think I don't know anything at all."

"It can take a while to get those connections," said Rona. "For people to treat you like a real person."

"It takes longer if you're not at every meeting and informal get-together. I guess I'm not the typical personality for this position. It takes a while for me to warm up. And my pregnancy with Peter was kind of rough, and then he was colicky until, actually, just a couple weeks ago." Sarah wondered if the sugar in the peach was going to her head, making her rattle like this.

"I thought I remembered hearing about your pregnancy. I'm so sorry. Even when everything goes well, you just aren't the same human being after having a baby."

"It wasn't the way I expected my first pastor's-wife stint to go." Peter had taken a break from nursing. Sarah lifted him up and burped him before putting him at her other breast.

Rona looked at Sarah steadily. "I had two kids in diapers at the time my mother had to come live with us. And we had two or three crises in the church. All in the same spring. I still don't know how we survived. Well, the Lord's good grace."

"That's encouraging to hear."

"But even with that there were a lot of tears and sleepless nights. And times when I had to choose between giving to my mother or my babies or my husband or the church. It's an awful position to be in. I wouldn't wish those times on my worst enemy."

The women were quiet. Rona bit into a cookie, looking thoughtful. Sarah didn't feel the need to say anything. She stroked Peter's bare little leg.

"Don't overestimate the value of my advice," said Rona, "but I will say, take care of your health, whatever it takes, because it will take much longer to recover after you've made yourself sick. And don't expect God to do anything the way you've expected."

Sarah took a deep breath. "That makes sense. It's honest."

"Well, I'm just too old to waste time trying to keep up illusions."

"Sarah, ready to go?" Jacob walked in and stood over her.

"Sure, if you guys are finished."

"Where's Miranda?"

"At the church still."

"Rona, thanks so much for your hospitality. The food was just delicious." Jacob bent to shake Rona's hand, and she smiled and thanked him.

"Here, take the bag." Sarah handed Peter's things to her husband and managed to get out of the chair with Peter still attached. Good feedings had occurred so seldom with this baby that she wasn't about to interrupt him. Rona walked with them back through the sitting room. Chris Dancey and Joe Travis were in the middle of intense discussion, but they paused long enough to say good-bye. Madison opened the front door for Sarah.

"Come up and watch us quilt sometime, Sarah. I think you'd like it. Bring the kids along. We don't mind." Rona patted Sarah lightly on the back. Sarah had been patted many times in two years, but this was the first time she didn't mind.

A sadness drifted over her as they left the wide porch and walked by the flowers. She felt as though she were leaving another country—one full of things she had missed for so many months. One inhabited by someone who understood how she could have the feelings she did. She hoped she might find passage back sometime soon.

Well, that went well I think," Jacob said, after the children were both strapped in and he and Sarah were in the front seat. Sarah didn't comment, since he didn't seem to be asking her opinion.

They'd driven a few blocks when he turned to her. "So, what do you think?"

"What's to think? It's a revival strung out over three months." Sarah's reply came out sounding more sarcastic than she'd intended.

"In that case, I'm really glad you came." Jacob's tone was quite intentional.

"Oh, Jacob, please. Don't start."

"I didn't start anything."

"I think the revivals will be fine. You know I've never gotten into that sort of thing."

"Then why did you insist on coming?"

"I wanted to know firsthand what's expected of me."

"What are you talking about?"

"From this meeting, I know that I'm responsible to coordinate refreshments when the services are at our church. I also know that we'll probably have a seminary student staying with us sometime soon."

"I could have told you that."

"Yes, you would have told me." Sarah raised a finger to conduct this well-rehearsed number. "But I would have heard about the seminary guest the night before, causing me to put in long hours getting the room ready, planning meals, et cetera. And—if I were lucky—you would have informed me we needed a week's worth of refreshments two days before that week began, which would mean that I and one or two other martyrly women would have done most of the refreshment getting. Your idea of supplying information is much different from mine."

"Fine."

"Let's discuss it later," Sarah said, lowering her voice.

"Yes," Miranda's voice piped from the backseat. "When I'm out of earshot." They dared not look at each other and risk bursting out laughing. Sarah looked out her window, burying her smile in the palm of her hand. Where had this child come from? She was smarter than both of them put together.

When they arrived home, Jacob went directly to the walk-in closet he'd converted into a study. Sarah hoped he would forget her comments. Truth was, she was finding more and more in him not to like, including his inattention to detail, and she really didn't want to be asked to elaborate on her dissatisfaction. They had married for life, and she would just have to get through her irritation somehow.

Miranda went immediately to their fenced-in backyard to create dramas around the swing set. The front porch had been her stage previously, but Sarah had recently declared it off-limits. Like so many of the older houses in town, theirs had a porch across the front. This one was supported by wavering walls of cinder blocks. Jacob was not a handyman, and the church members who ordinarily did parsonage repairs were either swamped with work or sick and unable to help. The south end of their porch had sunk another inch or so during spring rains and then splintered in summer's heat and cracked completely when cold weather came. One day when Miranda had taken her dolls there for some adventure, even she sensed danger when some of her things began to roll, by ones and twos, toward the precipice and were swallowed through the black and cobwebbed fault that originated from the farthest porch post. Sarah had overheard an interesting exchange that day. Miranda commanded, "Let the earthquake come and swallow all the evil people!" Sarah had looked out to see her daughter throwing sticks toward that end of the porch, screaming in little voices, "No, Lord! We'll do what you say!" and then with a large God's voice, "You should have repented! It's too late now." The stick people disappeared into the ragged gaps, doomed to an eternity with the spiders and crickets.

Sarah sat on the sofa for a few moments, knowing that she had too much to do but not feeling like doing even the smallest task. She was about to sort through the pile of magazines at her feet when Jacob walked into the room. He sat in the chair across from her.

"Be sure to get some women to help you with the refreshments that week," he said.

"I will. Don't worry about it." Their eyes met briefly. Sarah leaned back on the couch and studied the ceiling light. It was gray with a film of dirt that had been collecting since they moved in. "What if these revivals don't accomplish what you're hoping they will?" she asked. She had expected this question to come in the middle of some heartfelt discussion, but her life felt like a continuous economy of words these days. When the energy and the presence of mind were there, she just said it. Forget atmosphere or preparation.

"I don't know. I feel as if I'm grasping at a last straw, and I hate feeling like that. I hate being desperate."

"Well, maybe things will start happening now. You never know."

"Yeah." Jacob stood up. Sarah could tell he was dissatisfied. Not that long ago she'd been full of encouragements. His cheerleader. She had so little for him now, and he knew it. She saw the unspoken anger in the way he walked out of the room. They had been experts at discussion, back in seminary, back in that other life they'd had. They could talk for hours, until their favorite coffee shop closed and then longer still, back at their apartment in Chicago's near north side. Now so much of their communication happened apart from any words at all. A set of the shoulders, a sigh, a tired look.

An hour before dinnertime, Miranda appeared right on cue, complaining of hunger. "My stomach's *yelling* for food," she said in an incredibly weak voice, pressing her hands into her tummy. "Do we have any appetizers?"

"Why, of course!" Sarah tweaked the girl's nose. Miranda giggled and beat Sarah to the kitchen. She opened the refrigerator and waited for her mother to pull out something. Sarah found the small container of carrot sticks and opened it for her daughter to see.

Miranda wrinkled her nose. "It's not an appetizer if it's plain."

"Oh, it's not?"

"No! Do we have dip?"

"No. But I've found that peanut butter is a decent substitute."

The child's eyes widened. "That would be a real appetizer."

Sarah put a bit of peanut butter in a dish and set Miranda on a stool beside the kitchen counter. The child wouldn't eat much dinner, but Sarah had decided some time ago that Miranda's system was simply on a different schedule from hers and Jacob's. Besides, she enjoyed having her daughter beside her while she worked. Sometimes they had fantastic discussions. Sometimes they just giggled a lot. Sarah felt that she'd lost a lot of joy in the last few years, but Miranda was a blessing completely undeserved. She often sensed herself turning to the child for sustenance of some kind.

For dinner Sarah pulled out a box of instant macaroni and cheese. She sliced a couple of leftover boiled wieners into it as it cooked. The vegetable of the day was frozen green beans. They looked plain in the saucepan, so Sarah chopped up a shriveled green onion and threw that in. They were practically out of instant iced tea and instant lemonade, so Sarah mixed them. She hated herself for cooking like this. She forced back memories of grilled eggplant and goat cheese and watercress salad in their one-bedroom city apartment, eons ago. She couldn't even find watercress in this Kansas wasteland. All of the art in her—for cooking or anything else—was now sucked out by daily fatigue.

"Can you go with me to visit Emmie tomorrow?" Jacob asked during the meal. He didn't notice—or at least didn't mention—that this was the second time this week they'd had some version of macaroni.

"I don't know. I'll have to see about a sitter. Wish you'd given me more notice."

"You know Sunday afternoons I visit the nursing home."

"Not always. The last two weeks your schedule's been different."

"So you don't want to go?"

"I'd like to go, but I don't know if I can get a sitter on such short notice."

"Whatever."

Sarah sighed loudly. They ate in anger for several moments. Then Sarah noticed Miranda picking at her food.

"Are you full of carrots, sweetie?"

Miranda nodded, her eyes large and serious.

"Sit there . . . five more minutes. And if you still feel full, you can go. If there's any room left, why don't you fill it with macaroni?"

"Okay. But only if there's room." Miranda folded her hands in front of her plate and looked at the clock above the sink. "Where will the big hand be?"

"On the seven." Sarah looked at Jacob then, but he was staring into his own plate. "I'll see about a sitter. I think Emmie would like the company," she said.

Jacob looked at her then and actually smiled a little. "I think you're her favorite."

Sarah didn't return the smile; it would feel too much like giving in. Peter's hunger cry whined at them from down the hall. Sarah went to the bedroom and nursed him, grateful to get away from the table and her husband. When the baby had finished, Sarah carried him into the kitchen and offered him to Jacob. The two men of the family watched television while Sarah read to Miranda in the girl's bedroom. It was their fourth time through *Charlotte's Web,* but Miranda was as involved as ever, breaking in to recite dialogue at key moments. At the end of the chapter, Sarah suggested that maybe Miranda's dolls needed to be readied for bed. Miranda got up to play mother to her three babies, and Sarah went to the living room.

"Miranda will be ready for jammies in about ten minutes."

"Okay." Jacob was playing with Peter's toes and making sounds that elicited tiny cackles. At least Jacob enjoyed being a father. He rarely complained about helping with the kids. In a few more minutes he would hand Peter to Sarah and go to Miranda's room to help her put on pajamas and brush her teeth. They had happened on to this routine naturally enough. In some ways this was Sarah's favorite time of the day, with both of them involved with the children in a quiet, satisfied mode. Now that Peter didn't cry constantly from colic, evening was often pleasant.

After Miranda was tucked in, Jacob washed the dishes while Sarah put Peter to bed. Jacob left the pan of garbage on the cabinet near the door, as usual, rather than taking it out to the compost. Sarah glanced toward the living room, where her husband dozed in front of the television. Deciding not to start anything, she pulled out the checkbook and spread their recent bills on the kitchen table. She'd feel much better if she didn't have to wake up facing this task. And maybe Jacob would walk into the kitchen for a soda and notice the garbage.

At ten-thirty, she'd written as many checks as she dared, deciding which bills were safe to delay paying. Jacob was still snoring in his chair. Sarah filed the receipts, put the checkbook in its place, and stamped the envelopes before setting them on the small table near the front door. She walked past Jacob—loudly—to do this. He didn't budge. She stood there and glared at his open mouth for a few moments and replayed the day's unpleasantries. Then she shook her head and returned to the kitchen. It just wasn't worth it, this arguing. Waiting for him to notice the garbage, when he managed to forget it every night anyway. She picked up the pan of scraps and walked out the back door.

Their one yard light had never worked. Sarah followed the narrow slash of light from their kitchen window as far as she could, then veered off into darkness and the general direction of their compost heap near the old garage.

She was still disoriented by the darkness—even after two years. There had been hardly a spot without lighting back in the city. Streets, expressways, parking lots, balconies, storefronts—any time of night or day, always a light burning or flickering somewhere. And always some indication of life—a bus or a taxi or people waiting or talking. The night sky was never black, but a luminous, pinkish orange and sprinkled at intervals with airplanes landing or leaving one of the city's three airports.

But here the night crept across backyards and streets, absorbing light and sound like a sponge. You spoke into the darkness, and your voice was snatched from you. You drove a mile out of town and found yourself groping along an empty road, your eyes begging for something to focus on, something besides snatches of unreal trees and fence posts at the very edge of the headlights.

Sarah emptied the scraps into the compost, then headed toward the small glow that was her kitchen window. From the garage it seemed to bounce in the darkness, balanced at the end of a long, unseen bridge.

Sarah groped her way to the beam of light that struck across the stiff summer grass.

When she came to the back door, she turned away from the house and closed her eyes. She took a deep breath and tried to smell the nighttime, the sweetness of cooled-off trees and moisture gathering on the ground and the green grain smell of fields just outside of town. She hated the darkness, but the aromas of earth and growing things gave her a peaceful feeling. The constant strong winds that had so irritated her in the beginning felt like old friends now, for she was sure they carried the particles of places beyond the farmland. In the dark air high above, she imagined a cloud made up of pieces of every city in the world, every lonely field, every backyard cluttered with toys. She imagined that, on an extra windy day in Chicago, a toasted sesame seed flew off a warm bagel as the baker on Adams Street pushed his cart along to make deliveries. And that seed was swooped up into the air high above the streets and then danced all the way on the weather to here. Sarah didn't have a clear idea of where that seed might have landed. But she held it on a little cloud in her mind.

When Sarah walked through the living room again, Jacob was gone. She heard water running in the bathroom and so sat in front of the television to kill time while her husband finished brushing his teeth. When his sounds moved into their bedroom, she went through her own ritual numbly. She was too tired to floss or to moisturize tonight. She got into bed and turned out the light on her side that Jacob had left on for her. He mumbled good night to her, and she answered.

At some point in their Bender Springs life, they had reached a silent agreement that lovemaking was a Friday or Sunday evening activity. Friday was Jacob's day off. Sunday was full of activities, but by evening the stress level would drop significantly. Stress and not fatigue was the main deterrent to Jacob's partaking of marital pleasure. Both seemed to short-circuit Sarah, and many times in the last year or so she had been grateful she was in her sexual-peak thirties and could actually be with Jacob without liking him much. The years of hard work and the passing of age thirty-five had begun to slow him down, so Sarah figured they were meeting in the middle these days, so far as sexual desire went. She was vaguely worried, though, that sex didn't excite her much emotionally anymore. A year or two ago she wouldn't have imagined that kind of indifference in herself. Now the main force that held her to the physical relationship was animal desire, a bodily need that had become quite pronounced and was not particular. It saddened Sarah to feel her body and emotions so divided.

She listened to her husband's breathing as he slept and tried to be in awe of him again, if for only a moment. He was a gifted man, and his spiritual intensity had drawn her to him with a force even greater than sexual attraction. And when they had put their dreams together, they had felt so powerful. Larger than life itself, with God's own Spirit giving energy to their steps. Sarah resented how small both of them seemed now, in this small place.

For the third or fourth time that week, Sarah fell asleep angry.

6

Mamie Rupert: Laying on of Hands

Tuesday, June 17

Alma slapped her cards on the table. "Ha!"

Mamie muttered that Alma's run of luck was highly unusual.

Ruthie placed her hand on the table and sighed. "Oh, mercy, I don't know what I'm doing here anyway—I've got so much work to do at home."

"Ruthie, all you've got to do at home is alphabetize your canned goods. You wanted to stop playing half an hour ago." Liz puffed on her Carlton.

They were in Mamie's living room, their knees nearly touching under the card table. It was three o'clock, and the cards were good and warm. They were on their second round of pinochle, the ice in their lemonade glasses long ago gone to clear little lozenges suspended in the yellow. Ruthie had started showing her fatigue, misreading her partner's (Mamie's) meaningful looks, giving up her best cards—and absorbing Mamie's murmurs of disgust—in an effort to push Liz and

Alma over the point mark that would end this marathon. About one more hand would do it now.

Liz jabbed fingers at the dark curls above her ears, wondering aloud if this perm would turn out to be worth the forty dollars she'd just paid for it. Alma, the trademark of serenity, grandmother of twelve, and overweight from eating her own excellent home cooking, had been out for blood all afternoon, gleeful little noises escaping from somewhere under her fake pearls and summer rayon scarf. She gathered up the cards and began shuffling them.

Mamie chose the moment to ask Alma if she knew anything about allergies.

"Well, I know there's all kinds of them."

"How can you tell if you have one?" Mamie asked.

"Generally you get congested and itchy. Some people swell up," said Liz.

"But how can you tell what it is that causes an allergy?"

"Why? What do you think you might be allergic to?" Alma looked something like a general practitioner, peering at Mamie over her glasses.

"Well, I'm just embarrassed to say."

They all looked at her, so she had to say it.

Liz exploded when Mamie uttered it. "My wonders, Mamie, where did you get an idea like that?"

Mamie explained how her condition had deteriorated since Bill Simpson's dog had begun to make regular stops in her backyard.

"It's possible, I suppose," said Ruthie. "You know, I can't eat hardly anything anymore. I think I'm allergic to nearly all foods."

"We're not talking about food, Ruthie; we're talking about dog poop!" Liz leaned back and fanned herself with a paper napkin.

"I just don't know what I'm going to do," said Mamie. "I can never catch the old man at home, or if I do, that television set's blaring so loud he can't hear the bell."

"Call him on the phone," said Alma.

"He can't hear that either."

"Hope there's never an emergency, like his furnace blowing up, if he's that hard of hearing." Ruthie looked almost as concerned for old man Simpson as she did for Mamie.

"So Mamie," said Alma, "you think this dog . . . doo . . . is what's giving you coughing spells?"

"I think it might be. I'm thinking I should go to the doctor and see what he thinks."

"I think you should," said Liz, lighting up a new smoke. "He's probably never heard that one before."

"Who's your doctor?" Ruthie wiped her perspiring face with a hanky. She perspired in all seasons.

"Meiers—over to Helmsly."

"I've heard good things about him."

"I like him because he explains everything in clear English," said Mamie, pressing a finger into the top of the card table for emphasis.

"Wish Dr. Simms did the same for me," said Ruthie. This was followed by another sigh. Liz, Mamie, and Alma ignored her. Ruthie had a way of turning everyone else's tragedy into her tragedy—and everyone else's good fortune into her tragedy too.

They seemed to notice together that someone was standing on the other side of the front door's frosted glass pane. Alma was closest to the door and got up as the knock rattled the front window. She pulled the heavy door open. A large, severe looking woman somewhat younger than they stood in a calf-length dress and polyester jacket. She smiled a wide smile, taking in all four card players.

"Hello, Rev. Miracle." Alma opened the door wide, and the woman came in. They all greeted her. Liz held her cigarette low. The cards stayed frozen in their hands.

"How can you all be inside on a day like this?" The preacher's voice sounded loud against the beige living room and its soft matching drapes. The large woman took a couple more steps into the room, and the shelf of knickknacks in the corner vibrated its collection of vases and salt and pepper shakers.

"We're old folks with creaky joints," said Ruthie.

"Well, I'll just take a minute," said Rev. Miracle. "My brother's doing handiwork around town, fixing and painting and whatnot." She handed each lady a crude-looking business card. "Since you're in our neighborhood, Mamie, I thought I'd be sure you knew."

"Why, thank you, Iris. I'll keep it in mind." Mamie glanced at the card and put it in her dress pocket.

"Are any of you ladies attending the Women's Laity Luncheon this year? I hear it's going to be quite a meeting." The large woman seemed quite settled, there in the middle of Mamie's living room. She folded her hands and leaned back on one hip, in a chat kind of stance.

"Oh, I don't attend any church," said Liz.

"You don't have to attend anywhere. It's a service for the whole community. Marie Donnington from Ecuador is the guest speaker this year. Has such testimonies to give, of casting out evil spirits."

"Sounds like too much excitement for me," said Liz.

"But it's the one thing we do each year, besides the Thanksgiving charity drive, that we all work together on. After all, the people of God are all born of the same Spirit."

The ladies murmured and scooted their chairs about. They asked one another if they were planning to go or not. Had they attended last year, and wasn't it a nice service, and, well, there's no reason they couldn't plan on it this time. Nothing was written in stone anyway. Iris smiled broadly at them and unshifted her hip. Mamie rose and headed for the door.

"Thanks for the card, Iris."

"God bless you," the preacher said, her back to them now.

"Same to you, Rev. Miracle," Alma responded.

After she left, they were quiet for a while. Ruthie sighed again, this time with an audible pitch added to the end.

"They put on a nice luncheon last year," said Alma.

"It's a good way to meet people," said Mamie.

"I know all the people in this town I care to know." Liz was leafing through a magazine that had been lying on a nearby table, one slim finger touching her lips.

"You don't mean that," said Alma.

"I most certainly do. Why get all dressed up to sit in that stuffy church and eat miniature cookies and listen to some old maid show her mission pictures?"

"Why did you say you'd go?" Alma raised her eyebrows.

Liz shrugged. "Afraid the *reverund* would start in on me or something."

"She wouldn't," said Mamie. She'd known the Pentecostal pastor since Iris was a girl growing up across town from Mamie's family. Iris Miracle was a strange one but not mean-spirited by any stretch.

"Women preachers are pushy. She would've stood there and talked at me till I let loose with something." Liz shifted in her chair and tapped one foot against a leg of the card table while she studied a hair color advertisement.

Ruthie giggled. "That would be something to hear, you telling off a pastor."

"I've done it before. When Arthur died and that idiot stood up there to give a funeral service and preached a sermon instead. Telling people they could come up the aisle right now and be saved. At a funeral of all places. I gave that man a preview of hell he'll never forget."

"That was insensitive," said Alma.

"What—insensitive! He had it coming."

"That's what I said; he was insensitive."

"Oh."

"Ruthie, I can see every card you've got." Alma sounded irritated for the first time this afternoon. Ruthie was blowing her nose, her cards in a fan, face up, in front of her.

"Well, that's my cue to call it a day," said Liz, laying her cards on the table.

"I can shuffle them, since I ruined it," Ruthie said, although they all knew her heart wasn't in it.

"Never mind. We're finished." Mamie gathered their empty lemonade glasses and took them into the kitchen.

"So anybody going to call up Iris's brother?" Liz asked.

"Oh my, I wouldn't say anything in front of Iris, but the man just drinks too much. I can't imagine him doing a decent job on anything." Alma shook her head in pity.

"I just don't like being around people who drink, period." Ruthie pursed her lips as she carefully gathered up the cards.

"I drink, Ruthie. A shot every night before bed," said Liz.

"Well, I guess I can't associate with you anymore then," Ruthie said, unsuccessfully trying to keep a straight face.

"Do hot toddies count? I put away a few of those every cold season." Alma was folding the card table.

"Everything counts."

"I add whiskey to my tea when my sinuses flare up," said Mamie, returning from the kitchen. "So, Ruthie, you've got no friends left."

"That sounds awful." Liz screwed up her face. "Whiskey in tea."

"Since I have no friends left, I'll go home now," Ruthie announced.

"I try to take pity on one stranger a week," Alma said. "Would you like a ride to your house, stranger?" She laughed a little and so did Ruthie.

"Oh, you two. It's time for my nap." Mamie waved them out of the living room. They descended her back steps. She didn't bother watching their cars back out of the drive. Alma, Ruthie, and Liz were like family. They all had keys to one anothers' houses; you couldn't get much closer to a person than that without being blood relatives. And Mamie could think of a number of blood relatives she wouldn't have lent Tupperware to.

She had just finished washing the lemonade glasses and cookie plates when a knock sounded on the front door. Once again, Iris Miracle's distinctive form loomed on the other side of the frosted glass. Mamie opened the door.

"You forget something, Iris?"

"I just want a word with you, Mamie." Iris stepped inside without invitation. "I want to say that the Lord has laid it on my heart to pray with you."

"What? What about?"

"I've seen you with your cane, and I can tell how bad you feel a lot of days. I think the Lord wants to heal you, Mamie."

Mamie stared at Iris. Then she found her voice. "Oh, but it's just a little arthritis. No need to bother the Lord with that. Not like I had cancer or something."

"God wants to heal us of all illnesses, large or small. No matter how insignificant they may seem, God wants us whole. It's why Jesus shed his blood."

Mamie looked at Iris. "Oh. Well—"

"Can we just pray together right here, Mamie?" Iris moved closer and placed a hand on Mamie's shoulder. It felt strong as a man's hand.

"Well, I suppose it can't hurt." Mamie still had a tea towel in her hand. She shoved it under one arm to free up her hands to clasp. Before she knew it, Iris's hand was clamped on Mamie's head, and a prayer had begun, the likes of which Mamie had never heard before. It sounded almost like another language. The preacher's voice got louder, and the weight on Mamie's head became so intense, Mamie thought her neck would be shorter before the prayer came to an end. She didn't know how long Iris prayed, but it felt as if ten minutes or more ticked by. Mamie felt a warmth fill her head and move down her shoulders and back. She became mesmerized by Iris's voice.

All at once, the voice shifted into a repetition of soft "hallelujahs." The hand released Mamie.

"Sister, I felt power go out from me. I believe the Lord has done a healing work here today." Sweat shone on Iris's broad forehead, and tears glistened in her eyes.

"You know, I felt something go down me," Mamie said, feeling strange and a little frightened. "Do you suppose—"

"Oh, Mamie, it was the Lord. Thank you, Jesus." Then Iris turned suddenly and gathered her large purse off the sofa. "I need to get home now." She walked to the door, leaving Mamie standing in the middle of her own living room. "I'll let myself out, Mamie. Lord bless you." The door shut, and a wave of heat from the June afternoon went through the room.

Mamie stood there, stone still, and tried to feel her body. Was anything different? She felt a little tingly. She bent her arms and legs and fingers and ankles and neck. Everything seemed to work OK. It might even feel better, but she couldn't be sure.

She went to the phone to call Alma, who heard everything first. But her hand stopped short of dialing the number. This felt like a private sort of thing. Besides, Mamie wanted to see what would come of it. If it ever rained again, she would know; the arthritis always kicked up before a rain. But it might be some time before the prayer was really tested. In a way, Mamie was relieved. Being touched directly by God Almighty was a frightening thing, and she wasn't sure it was a thing she longed for. But to be prayed over and then have nothing happen would be something of an insult. Plus, it wouldn't make the Lord look very good. It was probably best to keep this to herself for now.

7

Dave Seaton: Perky's Tap

Saturday, June 21

At about noon on a Saturday, Dave put away the mower he was repairing and headed for Perky's Tap. It felt too hot for June. The streets were deserted, most of the teenage population thirty minutes away in Helmsly, home of the closest public swimming pool. Maxie's Ice Cream Stop, at Third and Washington, was doing good business, and in backyards smaller children shrieked as they splashed one another in bright wading pools.

Dave walked by the Kluver home, which had been deserted for several days now. He wondered if his evening with Randy had been just a pleasant glitch in his otherwise below-average life. More than a week had gone by since their late-night Friday barbecue. Joe Travis had since come and gone, with a promise to stop by Dave's place when he came back to Bender Springs in a couple of weeks for the revival services. Dave was most impressed that the guy hadn't tried to get him into a church building.

Inside Perky's, Gabe had cranked up the air conditioner to full throttle, and the single unit hummed in the window, its spittle something of a relief to Dave as he walked past. He stopped to tack up a homemade ad for yard work on the square, wall-to-ceiling post at the end of the bar. Then he sat down to look at it from a distance. He ordered a beer.

Gabe supplied it, hardly breaking his rhythm of washing glasses, dealing with the cash register, and keeping up his end of a conversation with two ballplayers at the opposite end of the bar. The afternoon softball games had been canceled twenty minutes ago because many of the players were well past forty and just couldn't take heat like this; at least half of them (not counting church teams) had ended up here, in an atmosphere of smoke, sweat, and cold beer.

Dave took a gulp or two and listened without hearing. Gabe was wiping down the bar as though it were a long-loved woman, turning the cloth to a clean place every few strokes. He slowed at certain places, seeming to admire the grain in the wood. Dave couldn't be sure. He watched Gabe in an automatic way. When sitting at the bar, you looked to Gabe for everything—a drink, a refill, the weather report, an objective opinion, sometimes even an encouraging word, or free pretzels.

"Too hot to mow today—eh?" Gabe's cloth was fluttering down the wood in Dave's direction.

"I got somebody doing it for me."

"No kiddin'. Who?"

"The Azell twins. They pretty much cover everything east of the tracks."

"So you don't work no more; you just collect the money?"

"Ain't that the way it's supposed to be?"

Gabe laughed a little, glasses clinking in the sink just out of Dave's view.

"Amos Shackleford and his boy do most of the north end. Lot of big yards. He bought a second riding mower; thing's a regular tractor. I couldn't even use it most of the places I do."

"That's 'cause you take on all them widow women with their zillions of flowerbeds. Need tweezers to do 'em right."

"You hirin' help?"

Dave turned toward the voice and recognized Ax Miracle, a Perky's regular, just inches from him. He wore beat-up, mud-green trousers and a navy work shirt, dark patches of sweat in large arcs under each arm. The stubble on his face was beaded with the sweat he must have worked up walking to the bar at midday. The man reeked of a mixture of things, not all of them in the liquor group. Dave swiveled on the bar stool and leaned out of the path of the man's breath.

"I thought you were still at the brickyard," Dave said.

Miracle shrugged. "That's just Monday to Friday. I need weekend work."

John Harps, pitcher for the local savings and loan, spoke up. "Ax, he's talking about full-time work, not two hours of blowin' smoke and six sleeping behind the toilet." A couple of John's buddies laughed. Ax was a tired joke at Perky's.

Ax turned toward John Harps. Dave could see rings of grime in the folds of his neck.

"Shut up!" Ax pointed a finger. "I wasn't talkin' to you!"

"You weren't?"

Ax's tongue flew free with amazing accuracy, and the more obscene and precise he became, the louder the ball boys laughed. Dave motioned to Gabe, pushing his beer mug forward for a refill. Gabe filled it at the tap, calm as if the hubbub were three counties away.

After a minute or two, Ax returned to his booth nearest the men's room. He seemed to have forgotten his request to Dave for a job, and Dave was happy to let it pass. In his business, he couldn't afford to have a drunk running rampant over petunia patches and day lilies and plowing through rock gardens. He'd been doing lawns for elderly ladies since he was a kid, and he'd learned the hard way that they could be unforgiving if you harassed their pets, but they were downright vindictive if you messed up their landscaping.

In the sudden lull, the jingle bells on the door sounded. The thirty-something man who walked into the cool dimness looked out of place immediately. Dave heard someone down the bar murmur "Baptist preacher," whereupon someone farther back muttered something both profane and surprised. A second later the back door opened, allowing bright sunlight to flood a pool table, and a man's silhouette exited quickly.

The young preacher walked up to Dave's end of the bar. Dave swiveled quickly and gave attention to his beer as the man greeted Gabe. He introduced himself as Jacob Morgan. Gabe nodded in recognition, and Dave remembered he had seen the man before, in the grocery maybe. He was relatively new to town, evidently new enough not to know when he'd stepped somewhere his church leaders would take exception to. Perky's on a Saturday afternoon, in front of God and everybody—this guy wouldn't last. Even nonchurch people could figure that out. But the man's gumption raised a bit of interest in Dave, and he turned his ear toward the conversation.

"We have some summer revival meetings coming up, and I wondered if I might put up a flyer in here."

"Go right ahead. We got equal opportunity here." Gabe indicated the "announcement" post with a free hand. "If you can find the space, you're welcome to it. Can I get you something to cool you off?"

The pastor stepped up to the post and looked for a spot. His lime-green revival poster would compete with notices for rodeos, auctions, a newspaper clipping of some regular's granddaughter winning the district spelling bee, an '85 Ford flatbed, and a new litter of hounds for sale. A customer nearby pointed out that one of the auctions had happened two weeks ago. Jacob Morgan thanked him and carefully removed the poster and replaced it with his own.

"Actually," he said to Gabe, "if you have Dr. Pepper, that would do the trick. I can't believe this heat," he said, taking a seat two down from Dave.

Gabe put a can of cold pop in front of him. "You want a glass and ice with that?"

"Yes, please."

"Don't you pour none of that rum in it now, Gabe," Harps's voice rang out, but nobody was listening to him now.

The pastor smiled. "Not while I'm on duty, anyway," he said.

"Gonna be a bad summer, I predict," Gabe said. "These the revivals the churches are goin' in together on?"

"That's right. Rev. Carruthers and Rev. Dancey and myself. I'm surprised you've heard of it already."

"Oh, you know, through the grapevine. Charlie Peters was talking to Madison at the cafe a coupla days ago, and he mentioned that the churches were going to cooperate together."

"We're going to try."

"Sounds like a good idea to me. I'd been thinking myself how, with the way attendance has gone down everywhere—or that's what I hear, anyway—it's a reasonable idea to consolidate churches. You know—could cut down on expenses. That old Methodist fortress must soak up three hundred a month in heating through the winter."

Jacob Morgan was sipping his Dr. Pepper, not caring to hide his pleasure at the ice-cold relief. Dave turned a bit and looked at him. He seemed young. Wedding band. That's the way most preachers came. In a town like Bender Springs, it couldn't hurt to bring your own wife; most of the good women got taken right out of high school. A man who wanted to take his time was flat out of luck. Dave thought this one had some little kids too. On second thought, he didn't look any younger than Dave was himself. He just didn't seem as used up as Dave felt himself to be. But this preacher guy had only been in town a year or two. That would make the difference.

"So when did you get together on this revival thing?" Miracle bellowed from his booth. Despite his blurred state, he seemed to be awfully focused at the moment.

The pastor turned to give Ax his full attention. "Oh, we've been planning it since January sometime."

"Never in my life knew of Baptists to cooperate with anybody," Ax said.

The pastor gave a slightly nervous laugh.

"What happened?" Ax coughed, a long, heavy passage of air and phlegm.

"Well . . .," said Jacob Morgan, but he didn't seem to know how to finish.

"Cool it, Ax." John Harps spoke as though he wore a badge or something. Dave remembered Harps commandeering their high school basketball team. He hadn't liked John then, either.

"Thanks for helping me cool off," Jacob Morgan said with a smile that possibly tried too hard, but only for a second. He slid off the stool, nodded to Dave and Gabe, and was gone.

Gabe threw the money into the cash register. He started whistling "Blue Skies," one of his three tunes, but interrupted himself. "Get you anything else, Dave?"

Dave shifted on his stool, fingering the empty beer mug. "You can give me thirds." He was quiet as Gabe poured.

"How's the county treating you these days?"

Dave shrugged and tapped some ash into the ashtray. "All right. Thinking I might try for a crew closer to the city."

"Is that right? Didn't know you were looking to move."

"Not sure. Just thinking for now. Doing my homework."

"I hear Missouri don't pay worth crap. Try to stay on this side of the line."

Dave looked into the bottom of his glass, as though it were a well that went through the counter to the other side of the world. He cleared his throat. "I gave Karen's clothes away last week."

Gabe shook some packaged popcorn into a bowl and nudged it toward Dave, then grabbed a handful for himself. "It was time."

Miracle's whine rose from the far booth. "Why won't they leave me alone?" Dave looked in his direction. He was slumped over his table, clutching his greasy hair in both hands. "Why, why, why, why, why can't they leave me alone!"

"Who's after him today?" Harps asked no one in particular. No one answered him.

"Who'd you give them to?" asked Gabe, looking back at Dave.

"A girl I met. Randy Kluver."

Gabe squinted at the far wall, twisting the dish towel as he searched his memory. "Know her dad. Kind of a nut, I think. But who can say? I mostly see people when they're in here. Ha!"

Dave smiled and cupped the beer mug in both hands to take a swallow. The popcorn tasted like fake cheddar cheese.

"I bet she's a nice girl," Gabe added.

Miracle continued to moan, getting louder and more agitated.

"Time to go home, Ax," the bartender called across the counter. "You've reached your limit, buddy."

"I ain't anywhere *near* my limit!"

"Well, you've reached *my* limit. Go on."

Ax got to his feet, pulled at his underwear, and directed his body toward the back door. When he got there, he grasped the doorway in both hands and delivered a sharp kick to the bottom of the door. It swayed out into the daytime, and so did Ax.

"Good thing it's not a glass door," Dave said.

"Used to be."

Arnold Schwartz called Dave from the pool table then and asked if he was interested in a game. Dave took the beer and moved over to the table. They each placed a quarter on the mahogany rim. Arnold broke. The crack of the balls resounded in the cool alcove, nearly covering the noise of trucks rumbling past on the highway just a block away. Two or three older men wandered over to watch the game. For the moment, they huddled inward, away from the blasting sun outdoors, and concentrated on the calculated courses of the billiard balls.

I'm ready for another trip to Kansas City—how 'bout you?" Dave called across the soft early morning. It was Wednesday, hardly six-thirty, and there she was, walking down his street. Dave grinned as he watched Randy stop on the sidewalk and look in his direction. She hadn't seen him where he stood at the edge of his garden. Some plum trees formed a light screen between the plot and the street. The girl broke through the natural hedge and stood a few yards from Dave. She wore jeans and a yellow T-shirt.

"Hey, how are you?" She shaded her face from the morning sun, which was almost straight in her eyes.

"Fine. And you? Haven't seen you around."

"Out of town. Mom's aunt died, and she had to drag us all to Branson for the funeral. I hardly knew her."

"It's good to see you," he said.

"Yeah. I really had a good time the other night."

"It got interrupted though."

"Did everything go okay with Joe?"

"Oh yeah. His roommate came to get him Saturday afternoon. He'd put the car in the shop."

Randy smiled, suddenly appearing to be shy. Dave felt his own face flush, so he looked back down at his work. He'd just watered the peppers, and dirt clung to the hoe blade. He made a few chops. "I take it there wasn't any trouble, you getting in at 2 A.M."

"Nobody home. Teri was at Granny's. Mom and Dad got back Monday."

"I'd like to get together again—maybe someplace closer if you like." Dave stood up straight and hoped he didn't look too grimy. He hadn't even combed his hair yet. And he showered after his garden work and before his real job, which started at eight. He was glad Randy wasn't standing too close.

"That would be all right." Randy smiled and folded her arms. "I'm free most nights. I waitress down at the Family Cupboard Monday to Saturday until five."

"Friday's only two days away. How 'bout then?"

"Okay. I'll come over here—after I'm off work and cleaned up."

"Great!" Dave watched Randy swing her arms as she walked across his yard.

Thursday evening, Dave made his stop at Perky's. He'd put in a day's work and then done some heavy housecleaning once he got home. Now he needed a drink. He didn't mention cleaning, and he didn't mention Randy either. He'd never considered himself superstitious, but he was afraid that talking about this girl would make her disappear again.

"Hey, had another preacher in here, can you believe that?" Gabe interrupted Dave's meditation on the foam in his glass.

"Really. They trying to convert you?"

Gabe laughed. "Nah. Ax's sister, Iris—you know, the Holy Roller—charged in here wanting information about some kids around town. Asked if I'd heard about Satan worshipers."

"What?"

"Yeah, she was goin' on about kids and their devil music. I told her I never heard anything about Satan worshipers."

"I'd think you would, if anything was going on," said Dave. "I can't change my brand of motor oil without the whole town knowing it."

Gabe shook his head. "Old Iris has to have some excitement going on. She has baptized and filled with the Holy Ghost everybody who's interested. Guess she's got nothing left to do but chase the devil."

"Well, I need to go home and chase some roaches," Dave said, sliding off the stool. "I stirred up a few cleaning the kitchen."

"Try those bug bombs at the hardware store. Ask Frank which brand."

Dave waved good-bye and returned to the dry sunshine outside. The street looked washed out and barren. He walked the three blocks to the hardware store and headed home with a sack full of roach-killing chemicals.

He'd only been home ten minutes when the front door rattled under someone's knock.

A thin kid was standing there, looking fidgety. His blue jeans had holes torn in both knees. He wore a T-shirt that wasn't tucked in. Dark, shaggy hair and a faint mustache. He regarded Dave through the screen with something like dread in his eyes. Dave opened the door, and the kid stepped back.

"Hi," Dave said.

"Hi. Uh, Mrs. Rupert said you hired people to do yard work."

"Yeah, come on in." Dave stood back, and the boy stepped inside the kitchen. Dave could see now that his hair was shaggy only from his ears up; below that it was cropped close enough that skin shone through.

"What's your name?"

"Tony Gardino."

"Your grandpa's Arthur?"

The kid nodded, no particular expression on his face.

"You done yard work before?"

"Some. Mowed grass mainly."

"Not cutting many lawns right now. No rain and nothing's growing. But I work for a lot of older folks, and they've always got something they want done. They can be pretty finicky though. You up to that?"

Tony shrugged. "I guess." His eyes didn't land anywhere more than a few seconds. "When can I start?" He talked so softly Dave had trouble making out what he said.

"I go by Mrs. Rupert's on Tuesday. She's got a million flowers, so you gotta take some time. You have to clip around things. She'll probably ask you to do some watering, pull a few weeds maybe."

"Sounds all right."

"Come over here about six-thirty Tuesday morning, and I'll give you some tools." Dave watched the kid's face when he mentioned the time; willingness to be up that early in the summer said a lot. Gardino didn't flinch.

"I pay you five bucks an hour."

"Okay. Thanks." Tony turned back to the door and pulled it open. Dave followed him out and watched the kid walk down the street. Not the talkative type. Looked a little punky too. But Dave had known old man Gardino for a long time.

Dave walked around to his backyard and studied the frazzled garden spot. It continued to grow only because he pampered it mornings and evenings. It looked small this year, although it was the same spot he'd worked since he and Karen had moved in after his dad died and left the place to him in '92. He made his way through the tough grass and bent to examine his pepper and tomato plants. He'd cook dinner for Randy tomorrow night. It was easy to impress a girl over K. C.'s best barbecue, but she had to like a man's home cooking too. Dave straightened and headed for the house, the heat already soaking into his T-shirt.

It would be good to have another guy working the yards for him. With Tony and the twins, Dave would be freer to leave town on the weekends, taking Randy with him. The twins were only fourteen, too young to leave with much responsibility. But this Tony kid might be responsible enough to leave some management to, should Dave and Randy decide to spend a few days away. Dave stopped in the middle of his thoughts. Here he was planning weekends away, and he'd only spent an evening with the girl. Maybe what he really needed was to get a life, get out of this town to a place where his whole week didn't revolve around cooking up some peppers for a girl down the block.

At nine o'clock, Dave fell into his recliner, worn out. The place looked better than it had in a very long time. He was dozing off in front of the ten o'clock news when someone knocked on the door.

Randy stood on the porch, hands in her pockets.

"Hey," Dave said with surprise, opening the door wide for Randy to enter.

"Hey. Is it okay for me to be here now?"

"Sure! Come on in. Want a Coke?"

"No thanks." She sat on the sofa and looked at the television. "I just had this screaming fight with my mother, and I took a walk to cool off." She looked up at him. "It's not too cool out tonight though."

"I know. I've never seen weather like this, and I've lived here all my life." Dave sat on the sofa next to her, on the edge, so he could turn and look at her directly. "Sorry about things at home. You OK?"

"Oh yeah. We fight all the time. I just get tired of it sometimes. I won't stay long. Like I said, just out for a walk, and I saw your light on."

They sat back and watched the news. By the time the anchorman had signed off for the evening, Randy was snuggled into Dave like a kitten.

Close to midnight, a chorus of rattly car parts announced Mr. Kelsey's arrival home across the street. He'd been visiting his brother in Springfield, and from the sound of his heavy groan, he must have been driving awhile. Dave and Randy listened to the old man get out of his car and wheeze as he situated the garbage can near the back door. The sounds came through the low window and hung close to the ceiling.

"You all right?" he asked.

"Yeah, I'm fine." Randy bit a fingernail and looked into his eyes in a searching kind of way.

"Why don't you stay."

"Bad idea. Mom'll be waiting up."

"You're eighteen. Would your parents get that upset?"

"Upset doesn't really describe it. My mom can't handle me being around guys at all."

"Mothers are like that. She's gotta let go sometime."

"She's scared to death that I'll end up pregnant and she'll be stuck with a baby to feed."

"It's not like you're thirteen and not through high school yet."

"See, my parents had to get married because she was pregnant with me."

"The 'don't-make-the-same-mistakes-I-did' routine."

Randy didn't respond, and for a moment Dave worried that he'd offended her.

"She got really mad at me the second time I went out with Jay. I got in late. We'd driven through three counties to find some dance club he just had to take me to. I thought Mom was going to beat me up. She screamed at me nonstop for half an hour and ended up by saying, 'You go messing around, and you'll get yourself in the same predicament I did. Wouldn't that make you happy?'"

Dave heard Randy swallow once, close to his ear.

"And I said, 'It wouldn't make me want to die if I had a husband and some kids,' and she said, 'You've got a lot to learn about life. It's not all love and goin' dancing.' And I said, 'Well, I think life is what you make it, and I'll just worry about my own life.'"

Dave reached over and found her hand. He raised it to his lips and held it there.

"And then I said, 'I'm sorry I was such a predicament. It's not my fault you were too stupid to use birth control. I'm sorry I got born and ruined your life!' And she just looked at me with this ugly look and said that I wasn't sorry now, but I would be when it happened to me."

Dave snuggled up to her and rested his face against hers. He felt tears on her cheek and kissed them off, one by one.

8

THE MIRACLES ON MAPLE STREET

Saturday, June 21

Her name was Iris, after her late mother's favorite flower. Iris still lived on her parents' property, where seven different shades of blooms by the same name rose from the shaggy lawn every spring. The house was unremarkable, a story and a half, sided with yellow aluminum since her cousin, Ethan, had come through selling the stuff twelve years ago. Ethan was a part-time traveling evangelist. His nomadic existence gave him both need and opportunity to cultivate a number of avocations. The same gifts that helped him coax people to the altar at the end of the preaching made those same people willing also to entrust to him the well-being of their homes (siding), their health (three-book sets of home medical books), and even their memories (leather-bound, Scripture-embossed family photo albums). During a lull in business, and between preaching missions, Ethan had sided the Miracles' house. Mama had passed long before of a poisoned gall bladder; only Preacher Papa and his son and daughter remained in the old place when Ethan had come around.

The house's exterior renewal had preceded Preacher Papa's death by three months. The old man had a stroke in the bathroom and died one day when he was alone in the house. Maxwell, his only son, found him. Maxwell was himself too drunk to lift the body out of the tub; he passed out in the hallway between the bathroom and the phone. That was where Iris found him when she came home from camp meeting.

Iris had preached ten straight nights in eastern Oklahoma. When she hauled her suitcase into the quiet hallway and found her brother, she uttered a prayer, too tired to raise hands as was her custom. When she found her father, she sat beside the tub and watched the gray face for a long time. This was the only man besides Jesus who had had any lasting effect on her life, and Iris felt some pain at having the opportunity withheld from her of witnessing the old prophet's transition from one life to the next. It would have been so much more fitting for her to be there beside him, praying in tongues, singing praises, holding his hand. Perhaps the mantle of his ministry could have fallen directly and securely onto her shoulders during his final moments. But he had passed alone and without a stitch on, and Iris couldn't bear to dwell on how unglorious it felt. Her papa's lips gaped and turned blue. She called the ambulance and woke up her brother.

Maxwell was known to most people as Ax. He was burly as a lumberjack and could chop a person down to size in the space of a minute, once his tongue had cut loose. He was otherwise considered harmless.

Ax had a daughter by the woman he had shacked up with for a while. Because God wouldn't heal him of his alcoholism or give him a kind wife who might ease his pain and love him to sobriety, he chose as his mistress an unprincipled woman sure to offend both God and his preaching sister. Ax never expected Luella to take responsibility for the child that happened between them. Without so much as a legal proceeding, just a note propped up on the television, he packed the baby's things and his, too, and moved in with Iris. He knew she wouldn't turn them away. Besides, by then she had the whole house to herself and was away half the time anyway, gone bellowing through country churches as their father had done.

So they had lived, Ax, Iris, and Leah the baby. Iris cared for them, happy to be guardian of Leah's soul, since God only knew what the child would have come to otherwise. Leah's mama soon moved on, away from Bender Springs, under no pretense to keep in touch. Leah accompanied her Aunt Iris to church and grew up cradled in the hymns and phrases known intimately by those few and fervent Pentecostals and known hardly at all by anyone else. Iris considered that Leah was God's comfort to her in a demon-filled world and the only chance of redemption for her drunken brother.

The child was sturdy as an old saint, taking the crude and sacrilegious buffeting of her father in stride, caring for him when he was sick, praying with Aunt Iris every night that God would send revival to their church, town, and nation, give them boldness to witness out in the world, and deliver Daddy of drink. It was a liturgy they performed in simple rhythms, day after day, holding hands where they knelt beside Leah's bed or pausing on the back stoop or while preparing dinner, offering their praise and petition, the two pegs that held their home in its place on Maple Street.

Leah was now ten and growing serious and burdened for the whole world. Ax had maintained his sporadic work at the brickyard and his regular siestas at Perky's Tap for as long as the child could remember. She had no respect for him, having seen him reflected solely in the eyes of her aunt, who considered him damned. Leah treated her father respectfully, for the Lord required this, but the distance between them stretched without opposition from either one.

So when Ax came in Saturday evening and slouched at the dinner table and rambled about a so-and-so Baptist who had violated his realm that day, neither Iris nor Leah listened much. Iris made him hush long enough for the evening blessing, which Leah offered. Then the two women talked around and above him. It was only when Ax mentioned revivals that Iris's attention was drawn away from her leg of fried chicken.

"What are you talking about?" she asked with a seemingly severe look. Her graying hair, pulled back tightly and piled on her head, stretched the skin across her broad-boned face in a continuously tense expression.

"They're all ganging up on the rest of the town, gonna put on meetings with people coming in from outside." He turned bloodshot eyes in her direction. "How'd you miss that one? You're always up for *revivals*."

"Who're you talkin' about?"

"All of 'em. Baptists, Methodists, Pres—Pres—"

"You mean Presbyterians, Daddy?"

"That's what I said. The Baptist preacher was in the bar today."

"I thought only Methodists and Presbyterians drank," said Leah.

"You'd be surprised," said Iris, adding gravy to her potatoes.

"He didn't drink nothin' but a Dr. Pepper," said Ax.

"That's where it starts," commented his daughter. Ax gave her a look that neither she nor Iris saw, a look that came to his face often these days, as though he were watching his child slowly become mad.

"I heard something about the joint revivals," said Iris. "It can't hurt. Remind me to bring it up as a matter of prayer tomorrow night, Leah."

"Why didn't they ask us?" her niece asked.

"They're afraid of us, honey."

"Afraid of what?"

"That we'll raise our hands or shout 'hallelujah!' during one of their services."

"I wish they could learn to praise God too."

"I wish to God they'd leave well enough alone," Ax spoke miserably at his mashed potatoes.

"This town could certainly use some revival," said Iris. She hadn't yet found a way to make her brother stop throwing God's name around so profanely.

"This town needs to be left alone," said her brother, rising to sudden attention above his plate.

"Not until every soul is saved," said Leah. She was making a deep hollow in her potatoes, patting them with a spoon to make more room for gravy.

Ax shifted his glare just enough to take her in. "Don't play in your food."

"She's not playin'," said Iris.

"I don't like the gravy to leak out on the green beans."

"It all ends up in the same place," her father said with a grunt. He was chewing a fairly tough mouthful of chicken and thinking in his absent way.

"Are you about to fall asleep?" Iris asked him. It wouldn't be the first time he had nodded off at the table. "Why don't you lie down?"

"I'm not fallin' asleep," he growled. He chewed some more. "They don't understand that folks just want to be left alone."

"What?"

"Preachers. Need to leave people alone. Everything here is just fine."

Iris closed her mouth a little tighter, a practice that had replaced arguing with her brother.

"If people are left alone, they could go to hell without even knowin' it," Leah said. Iris looked proudly at her apprentice.

"If people are left alone long enough to hear themselves think," countered Ax, his voice rising, "they might just figure it all out for themselves!" He looked squarely at his offspring.

Leah folded her hands on the edge of the table in front of her and narrowed her eyes a little. "But they can't learn the truth all by themselves. That's why we have the Word of God."

Ax looked at her again, sadly, though in his state he always looked sad. By now every shade in his demeanor and mood was attributed by most folks to his addiction.

Iris had stopped paying attention to her brother's sadnesses and joys long ago. It was all the same to her. She was waiting for the time when he would be sober long enough to show something genuine. She figured it would be a long wait.

But Ax was sad now, down to his real self, seeing his little girl with her mind full of religion and her eyes growing sharp and closed like Iris's eyes. He spent the rest of his meal studying the food as he stabbed it with his fork and put it into his mouth.

After dinner, Leah gathered up the dishes and washed them while Iris scanned the newspaper and Ax watched television. The batteries in his remote control were dead, and moving across the room to the set seemed like a lot of effort to make, since he knew he would be dozing off in another fifteen minutes, so he was left to one station only, which popped with real-life stories about cops and criminals.

Iris had learned to tune out the noise; she busily took down quotes and anecdotes from the day's news, adding them to the running list in the notebook that was with her always. On another smaller pad she listed any items that might need her prayers or at least a sympathy card. Once in a blue moon her political action was required, such as the time three years ago when some big shot from Wichita tried to install a massage parlor on the town's south perimeter. Iris had had plenty of help on that one. Even non-Christian women in Bender Springs didn't appreciate such temptation around their men. Iris's luck hadn't been so good when Earl Phillips had opened another beer joint, right at the end of Main Street. A few months after it opened, Earl's wife became very ill, and they had to move west to be near their daughter, so the beer joint issue resolved itself. Nevertheless, Iris tried not to miss a single issue of the *Helmsly Herald*. She studied it like a holy detective, sharing bits and pieces with Leah, who stood at the kitchen sink across the room. The child needed to learn how to affect the world right where she lived.

That very evening the world came to them. Just as they were getting ready for bed, a blast of music rocked through the house from their church next door. It wasn't church music; in fact, the church was locked up tight. But an old sports car had pulled onto the lawn, its headlights washing over the front of the church. As Iris looked out the window another vehicle, Satan's Van, as Iris had named it after its appearance in the centennial parade, swerved into the yard and halted next to the car. The sounds coming from both vehicles emitted the essence of hell itself. Iris couldn't understand a single word, although she was pretty sure she picked out some profanity. The confusion of heavy metal tore apart the atmosphere of the entire block. Lights from a couple of the houses across the street came on.

Iris put on her robe and slippers and fairly bounded onto her own back porch. She walked around the side yard, which their property shared with the church, and was soon in the headlights herself. She heard exclamations and laughter and awful swearing, then ducked out of the bright lights so she could see the people in the vehicles.

"You!" She pointed a powerful arm at three teenagers in the first car. "Get off this property!" Her command was met by more laughter.

"This is God's house, and I won't have it profaned with this filthy noise." Iris walked right up to the car. A boy with greasy-looking hair, an earring, and stubble on his face squinted up at her. She smelled beer and tobacco and who knew what else.

"Well, if it's God's house, maybe God should come out and talk to me about it," said the boy.

Iris shook her head, hands on hips. "You don't know what you speak of, young man. If God were to come out, there'd be nothing left of you."

"Whoaaa!" Two other voices joined the driver's in mock fear.

"This is satanic music, and I won't have it here."

"We're Satan's children," a girl in the backseat said, leaning up toward the driver's window. "So it's only right we play his music."

This took Iris back for a moment. She hadn't anticipated such blatant and shameless evil. These children couldn't be out of high school yet. She breathed a prayer for Jesus' blood to protect her and bent down to speak with the girl face-to-face.

"Come out of this car. I want to know what I'm dealing with."

"No!" The girl laughed. "You're not dealing with me. Craig—," She tapped the driver's shoulder. "What's with this creepy church? You didn't tell me there were big old bats in it."

"If there's a demon in you, you won't be laughing for long. You'd better come out and let Jesus break those bonds." Even as Iris spoke, the car began backing away. Its occupants sent gestures and more language her way as she followed the car off the lawn and into the street.

"Jesus is Lord!" she shouted as the car spun out, the other vehicle right behind it. Sounds of revved-up engines filled the night air as the taillights grew smaller.

Old Dr. Lawrence and Lisa Wiggins stood on their porches, looking first at the cars in the distance and then at the preacher who stood like a state trooper in the middle of the street. Iris turned to them and lifted her arms in a motion not unlike the one with which she dismissed people at the end of a worship service. "These children need their parents sitting them down. They need a talking-to."

"We got some wild ones, all right," Doc Lawrence said. "Don't know many of them anymore." He turned and entered his house.

"Next time they bring that noise around this time of night, I'll call Sheriff Holt on them," Lisa, mother of two small children, promised.

"It'll take more than Gideon to straighten out these kids," Iris said.

"Well, I don't know about that, but he can at least make them take it somewhere else." Lisa went inside too.

Iris returned to the churchyard and looked closely at the tire marks. The ground was so hard and dry, not much damage had been done. She stood in the night breeze feeling tingly around her scalp. Her hand slipped instinctively up to her breast to still the pounding of her heart. A person never knew where or when evil would slip into a place, even a small, quiet place like Bender Springs. Iris looked with sadness across the street at her neighbors' now-dark houses. People didn't understand how high the stakes were. They didn't appreciate the spiritual realities that begged Iris's constant prayers and concern. If these children were as filled with hell as she suspected, she may well be the only person in town equipped to deal with them. The prospect was not an inviting one, but something stirred deep in her warrior's soul. Where the most evil battles were waged, glorious victory would, after all, be waiting close by.

9

MAMIE RUPERT: HANDYMAN

Saturday, June 21

Saturday morning Mamie looked out her bedroom window and uttered something between an oath and a prayer. What had she let herself in for? There was Ax Miracle striding into her yard, a moldy straw hat stuck to his head and a pair of crusty work gloves hanging from his trousers, he was about to lose.

Mamie stood back from the door and talked to Ax Miracle through the screen. She wouldn't come within two yards of that breath. He looked sober enough, though a rust spot on the screen kept Mamie's view from being too clear. He coughed when opening his mouth to speak, but he didn't spit on her walk. His hands were clean, clean enough anyway for the work he would be doing.

"What do you want me to work on first, Mamie?" Ax cleared his throat and adjusted the hat. Mamie almost said that she'd rather he address her as Mrs. Rupert, but that seemed snobbish. Still, he had no place sounding so familiar with her.

"The guttering, first of all. Scrape out the old leaves and throw them on that pile near the alley. Then the storm windows. They need to be taken down and washed, and the sills cleaned out. Lot of spiderwebs and dead bugs in them."

"You wantin' spring cleaning in the middle of summer, eh?" Miracle grinned, showing yellow teeth. He probably chewed tobacco too.

"This isn't the middle of summer; it's only June. And I don't have a lot of people around anymore to help with spring cleaning. My neighbors have their own to do, you know."

"Just kiddin', just kiddin'."

Mamie pointed toward the garage. "The ladder's in the east end of the garage, along with whatever tools you'll need. It's all near Charles's worktable."

"How long's he been gone, Mamie?"

Mamie looked at Ax in surprise. "Why, about seven years now."

"My mama's been gone seventeen years," said the man, turning toward the garage. It occurred to Mamie that Ax hadn't mentioned the old Rev. Miracle, who'd passed after his wife by a few years.

Ax disappeared into the garage. The small building leaned a bit toward the Jeffries' place. Mamie wondered if she should have it torn down and a new one built. But for what? She'd sold the car after Charles passed. The two or three problems with the engine were things Mamie could live with as long as Charles had been around to tinker with them and give her reassurance. But after Charles's death it had been simpler to sell the car than worry with it. And she'd never got around to buying another. She hated making big decisions, especially now that she was alone. She'd never driven much herself; most everything she needed was within walking distance, and she rarely went to the bigger stores in Helmsly unless it was with Alma or Liz anyway. Maybe she should have that old garage torn down and a shed built, smaller, but big enough for tools and whatnot. *Could the drunk put one together?* she wondered. She wished Dave Seaton did construction work. Such a dependable, likable type. And young enough to do the heavy work without hurting himself. Mamie wondered how long it had been since Ax Miracle had even climbed a ladder. She waited until Ax appeared with the ladder and watched him set it up and climb to the guttering. When it seemed that he wasn't going to fall or do it all wrong, Mamie turned back to her housework, such as it was. She'd cleaned up all the obvious dirt and wasn't willing to start a big project, such as sorting out the clutter in her pantry. She poured herself a second cup of coffee and looked through her little basket of cards and letters. She didn't keep up with many people anymore, but she always seemed to be behind in her correspondence. She liked to wait until she had something interesting to write about, and nothing had happened lately.

With the windows open, she could hear Ax Miracle wheezing clear across her living room, and that started her worrying again about this whole business. Why would Iris ask her, of all the widows in this end of town, if Ax could do some work for her? Well, she hadn't come out and asked directly. But she'd put the business card in Mamie's hand. And then she'd come back and prayed over Mamie's arthritis. This special service caused Mamie to feel obligated to at least give Iris's brother a try. It was probably the Christian thing to do anyway, giving work to a man down on his luck—although Mamie couldn't recall Ax's luck being anything but down for ten years or more. After a point it stopped being bad luck and just turned into a lack of gumption.

Still, it wasn't as if Mamie owed the Miracles a favor, prayer or no prayer. She probably could have hired Arthur Gardino's grandson instead. He'd already come by, asking if she had any yard work. Mamie had known Arthur since they'd grown up in the neighborhood together. She remembered him singing in a barbershop quartet years ago, when he still had hair and was courting Margaret Jean.

But Mamie hadn't been able to think of any immediate reason not to hire Ax, other than the obvious one—the man drank like a fish. And Mamie didn't know how to mention that to Iris without sounding mean. She found it difficult to talk plainly to people she didn't know so well, especially religious ones.

Ruthie called at a quarter past ten; they talked for no more than an hour, Mamie becoming agitated after thirty minutes. Ruthie took a long time to say what she meant, or to discover what it was that was really on her mind. But finally she closed with a standard end-of-conversation sigh. Mamie hung up, worn out. She realized then that she no longer heard Ax cleaning her gutters. She looked out the window where she'd noticed him last, but he had moved to the other side of the house. She stepped outside and walked around to where he was wiping down a window that leaned against the side of the house. He hitched up his pants when she came into view. She wondered why he didn't just buy a belt.

"You done with the gutters already?" Mamie asked.

"No, but it got hot on the east side of the house. Decided to work in the shade for a while." Ax pulled out a large blue handkerchief and wiped his face with it.

"All right. Just so long as it gets done. Doesn't matter in what order I guess." Mamie ambled back to the corner of the house, pausing to look over her pansies near the rosebush. Before rounding the corner she shot a glance at Ax. He was intent on the window and didn't look up.

He left the yard and went home—or to the beer joint downtown—promptly at noon. Mamie was having chicken noodle soup at the time, watching the farm report on television. She had no particular reason to watch it, but it had become something of a comfort to her. Talk of soybeans and wheat and pork and beef made her feel at home and reminded her of the farms she had grown up around. Several of her childhood neighbors had been farmers. In a world where so many children thought that hamburger was made in a factory somewhere, it was nice to hear constant news that the farmland still existed. Not a single television show had farmers in it unless they were stupid country people who didn't know how to dress. The farm report was necessary if the next generation was to have any reality attached to it.

Mamie thought these thoughts every day at noon while eating lunch. For some reason she never thought to talk about farmers and reality and the future of America when she was with Alma and Liz and Ruthie. Liz wouldn't understand, and she wouldn't care anyway. Ruthie would manage to turn the subject to herself, her life in Hutchinson, her engagement and marriage to Ralph, the war, the death of both parents, Ralph's heart attack, and finally her grandchildren, who were always getting honors at the grammar school or saying clever things. Alma would agree pleasantly. But Mamie never thought about the farm subject when they were around. It was probably just as well.

After her bowl of soup, Mamie slipped outside to inspect Ax's work. With a noble effort and not without some shaking in her knees, she climbed to the fourth rung of the ladder, which still leaned against the house next to the window Ax had cleaned and reinstalled. Grasping both sides of the ladder, Mamie leaned close to the pane, looking for splotches. She only found a couple, and they were small. Maybe this arrangement would work out.

She climbed down and examined other windows from the ground, deciding that they looked good enough. She wasn't paying much and couldn't expect perfection.

Ax returned at a little past one looking wobbly. He moved the ladder to the guttering on the east side of the house and wheezed with fresh vigor. Mamie read her latest *Grit* paper halfway through and discovered she was thirsty. She mixed up pink lemonade and took out two of her everyday plastic tumblers. She put three cubes of ice in each and poured the lemonade over them. Then she went to the door.

"Mr. Miracle," she called, leaning out from the back stoop, "I've got some cold lemonade here for you if you like." She heard him shuffle at the side of the house. He appeared at the corner, his shirt sticking to him under the arms and down the center of his chest.

"Come into the kitchen," said Mamie. She held the door until he caught it and followed her inside.

"Mmm. Thanks. This is just what I needed," said Ax. He took several long swallows. Mamie could smell the sweat on him, and she noticed his hands were gritty from the windows. She hadn't thought to direct him to the washroom.

"You seem to be coming along all right," said Mamie, sipping her drink. She didn't know what to say after that. They both looked into their glasses.

"Not hard work, just takes time." He brought the blue kerchief up to his hairline, or what was left of it.

"How old's your daughter now?" asked Mamie.

"Leah's ten. Getting long-legged." A smile hinted at his face but disappeared as quickly.

"They grow up too fast."

"Yep. She'll be out on her own before long."

"What does she want to do?"

"Be a preacher or a preacher's wife." The man's tone was flat.

"Hmm. That's nice. Not a lot of money in it, but that's not the important thing, I guess."

The phone rang from the living room. "Excuse me," said Mamie, and left the kitchen to get it. It was Alma, asking if Mamie intended to go shopping this week or next and if she wanted to go with Alma and Ruthie.

"Next Saturday's better," said Mamie. "But I can't take this all-day shopping stuff. It just wears me out."

"We'll leave right after lunch and be back by supper. Is that too long?"

"No. Not if I can sit down a few times."

"There are benches at the mall. We can always park you while we go inside the stores."

"All right. But call me the morning of, so I don't forget."

About the time Alma signed off, Mamie saw That Dog trot through the Perkins's property, across from her front yard. She put down the phone and watched from the window. The dog pranced through her neighbors' tomato plants and took a drink from a bucket someone had left near the apple tree. The dog squirted on the tree and went on its way.

"I don't understand people who let their dogs run all over town," Mamie huffed, returning to the kitchen table and Ax. He was leaning back in the chair, twirling his ice.

"Not so hard to understand." said Ax. "Dogs that travel don't cost as much to feed. They get handouts all over town."

"It's not good," said Mamie. "They run through people's yards and gardens and they—Do you want some more lemonade?"

"No thanks."

"I'll leave the pitcher out on the porch. Come and get it if you want some more."

"Thank you."

Mamie watched the saggy pants and stained shirt climb down the back steps and the frazzled hat duck beneath the sun's heat. The man stretched a bit, hitched up his pants, and headed toward the garage. He soon came out with a whisk broom. After a while Mamie heard him sweeping out the windowsills. The sound—rhythmic, short brushes against dust and dry wood—reminded her of slow summer days when Charles used to be around fixing and cleaning things. He had taken such pride in this house; nothing was left to neglect. Mamie gazed around her kitchen at the avocado paint-and-paper job. Avocado had been out for a few years now—well, a few decades if one were to be accurate. Maybe she should find another color, a nice blue maybe. Maybe Ax could handle a paintbrush.

Mamie wiped the water spots off the table, then lay on the daybed in the front bedroom. The south breeze came through constantly there, making it the coolest, most pleasant room in the house this time of year. She pulled her skirt down over her knees and arranged herself to look modest. She had no intention of having her slip show, even if it were just that old drunk happening to see her as he worked on the windows.

Ax didn't come over Sunday, but he did show up at about five in the afternoon Monday. He got off work at the brickyard at 4:30, and it seemed that he'd come straight to Mamie's to finish cleaning the crusted-over basement windows. They were in such bad shape that it became apparent Ax wouldn't finish that day either, so he came again on Tuesday. By that time Mamie had decided that the garage, rickety as it was, could stand a good sorting out. So during that week Ax and Mamie established a sort of pattern: Mamie would think of more odds and ends that needed doing, and Ax would hitch up his trousers at intervals, drink a pitcher of lemonade per day, and trot off in whatever direction Mamie pointed. The man actually did decent work, although he wasn't too quick about it. He seemed to have his own pace and manner for doing things, and Mamie could never really find anything wrong with his methods, so she left him more and more to himself, kept the lemonade pitcher full, and went about her business. She worked on her own evening meal three late afternoons in a row, listening to Ax do a funny half whistle between his teeth. He wasn't much for carrying a clear tune, but it sounded almost happy, and Mamie sort of liked hearing this accompaniment to work getting done.

By the end of the week, Mamie couldn't wrestle her mind away from the vision of a freshly painted house. Hers had gone several years without so much as a touch-up. It occurred to her Thursday morning, during her survey of the yard, that the place looked as if an old woman lived in it. Nothing kept up properly. Charles was probably doing somersaults in his grave. What had gotten into her, to allow such disrepair to go on this long? She made another round of her yard, this time with a bony arm on one hip as she did a bald-eyed measure of her walls and eaves and porches and tried to figure how many gallons it would take to set the place right again. She rubbed her left elbow, absently kneading at the arthritis for the moment, and decided that August 6 would be her deadline for getting the job done. That was Charles's birthday, and Mamie couldn't think of a more fitting way to honor his memory. It was a goal that would keep her going through this ghastly hot season. Years ago, she'd give herself five to ten goals at a time and accomplish most of them in the same calendar year. Anymore, one modest goal per year kept her occupied. Age was an irritating thing. But this house painting—well, it could give everything, including her, a fresh start.

By the time Ax was finished hauling junk out of the basement that afternoon, Mamie had her plan in order. She approached him as they sipped lemonade together.

"Have you ever painted, Mr. Miracle?"

"Huh?" The man's bald strip on the top of his head had a few strands of hair that were sticking straight up.

"Painted houses. Have you ever done that?"

"Years ago."

"Would you like to paint mine?"

Ax stretched back in his chair and twirled the ice in his lemonade glass. Mamie had noticed that he assumed this position when called upon to think or form an opinion. "Oh, I suppose. It'd take awhile."

"I want it done by August 6. That gives you lots of time."

Ax put the glass up to his mouth and tipped it, draining the last swallow of liquid. He shrugged. "Okay."

Mamie called Alma Friday morning, and the two of them went to Frank's hardware and picked out a nice gray-tinted white house paint. The dark gray Mamie wanted for the trim wasn't in, so she had Frank order some for her.

"So Mr. Miracle is working out," said Alma, sounding pleased, once they were in the car again and headed back to Mamie's. "You know, having all this work to do after his regular job just might help the man sober up."

"He never comes slap-down drunk, but there's always that faint smell of alcohol."

"People who drink a lot smell that way even when they're not drinking."

"All I know is that he shows up every afternoon and he does what I tell him to do."

"What woman wouldn't like *that* situation!" Alma said, not entirely joking.

"Now, don't get started on anything like that. The man's a complete mess. I still can't bear to get within three feet of him."

"I'm just teasing you, Mamie."

"I'd just as soon you not, thank you."

Alma pulled into the drive. It was ten-thirty. They got out of the car, and Alma helped Mamie unload the several gallons of paint from the trunk and set them on the enclosed back porch. "Remember, we're going shopping tomorrow. I'll pick you up around one."

"I'll put on some walking shoes." Mamie waved as her friend backed out of the long driveway.

Ax came promptly at five and started scraping the coolest side of the house.

"Ax, there's lemonade in the Frigidaire. The ice will melt if I leave it out. Just come in when you're thirsty."

"Yes, ma'am." The man didn't look at her; he was intent on the scraping. But his voice caught Mamie as she turned to leave. "Say, Iris asked me to ask you about your arthritis."

Mamie stopped like a person caught in a frozen blast. "My arthritis?"

"Yep. Just wanted me to ask if you were feeling better."

"Oh. Well, it's not bothering me so much these days."

"Iris's prayer workin' on you, is it?"

Mamie couldn't quite tell how Ax meant that question, and she sputtered for several seconds. Truth was, the arthritis was about the same as usual, for a dry season. She'd imagined feeling better in general over the past few days, but she wasn't really ready to make any official statement about whether the prayer had worked. In an instant of embarrassment and indecision, Mamie giggled.

"Oh, she's healed cancer, cataracts, and asthma," Ax continued, seeming not to have heard Mamie's odd spurt of laughter.

"Well, it's certainly nice of her to pray for people. I appreciate her concern." Mamie turned quickly and went back inside. She was actually trying her best not to think about the prayer's succeeding or failing. Even though the Lord was supposed to be doing this miraculous work, Mamie couldn't help but take the pressure personally. She set her mind someplace else right away.

Saturday morning, Ax showed up at ten. Mamie had hoped he'd get an earlier start—he still had a lot of scraping to do—but they hadn't really agreed on a time, so she didn't say anything. He didn't leave at noon for lunch, which made Mamie nervous. Alma and Ruthie were supposed to come by around one, and Mamie wanted to leave some instructions with Ax before then. She worried that he'd disappear for lunch at the time she needed to talk with him. At twelve-fifteen she went outdoors to look at his progress and say what she needed to say.

The day smelled like dust and heat and was too bright for a normal person's eyes. Mamie sneezed the moment her foot hit the grass, and she looked around quickly for the dog's latest deposit. It was time to call the sheriff again; obviously Gideon hadn't scared Simpson enough to do any good. But Mamie didn't see or smell dog doo anywhere. The sun nearly blinded her, even though it was directly above her. Summer insects fairly screamed in her ears. She hated summer more every year. She remembered a time, another life ago, when summer meant warm, sweet walks in her grandfather's pasture and bright, gentle blue-sky days and time—why, time to kill for days on end. But now warm had become hot, and the blue sky reflected the sun down on a person as though it were a vast sheet of aluminum foil. And time! The day was barely long enough to wake up, get dressed, clean up after herself, cook a meal or two, and start all over again. And Grandpa's meadow had gone the way of strip-mining forty years ago; somebody else owned it, and Mamie figured nobody really loved and cherished it as Grandpa had. Mamie couldn't imagine anyone looking over the white-yellow wheat field with the same romance on his face or walking the pasture to check out the pond with the same leisurely purpose. The world had gotten too hot and dirty, and the land had become something that just lay there collecting misery.

"Ax, I'm going shopping this afternoon. I'll leave lemonade in the Frigidaire and the back door unlocked. Could you be sure to pull the storm door shut when you go home?"

"No problem, Mamie." Ax glanced at Mamie, and she thought he looked the most clear-eyed she'd ever seen him. He still hadn't bought a belt. "I'll probably go home around six."

"I may not be back by then."

"That's all right. I'll be here Monday, same as usual."

"Thank you." Mamie left the man energetically scraping off old paint. The bed of pansies underneath him, still green because Mamie watered it daily, was speckled with the white chips and dust. She would be extremely glad when all this painting business was done.

Alma and Ruthie drove up at 1:05, with Ruthie in the front seat. Mamie suppressed a groan. Ruthie's voice didn't carry worth spit, and yet she would attempt a conversation with Mamie the entire thirty-minute trip, throwing her endless comments to the side for Mamie to catch from her place in the backseat. Mamie's hearing was getting as dilapidated as the rest of her, and she just nodded anymore and made a few general replies, giving Ruthie the impression that she heard everything and knew what was going on. With Ruthie's style of speaking, a person could catch every tenth word and not lose much of substance. By now Alma knew to fill in the blanks once they were out of the car, or repeat a question so that Mamie could hear, to prevent her committing herself unwittingly to some job or appointment.

Today Ruthie was more agitated than usual. Mamie had hardly got settled when she was hit with the question.

"Have you heard about those kids?"

Mamie waited a moment for some explanation beyond "those kids" and got none. "Which kids?"

"Those occult kids. Old Doc Lawrence told my neighbor Phyllis that they were carrying on something awful the other night. At the Fire Baptized church. They cussed out Rev. Miracle. You didn't hear? I'm surprised Ax didn't say something. Iris was trying to cast out demons. Do you think that stuff is real—the demons, I mean? I heard a minister say once that in the Bible demons represent other things like insanity. But I'm not well-informed on those kinds of things. They make me too nervous."

"I hadn't heard anything," Mamie said. "Mr. Miracle and I don't talk except about the work he's doing." Mamie had the feeling Alma had passed on bits of their conversation from the day before. She felt her ears get hot. Alma was a good one for priming others to do things she was above doing herself. She had stopped joking about Mamie getting too comfortable with Ax, but a well-placed word or two to Ruthie or Liz, and she could keep the subject alive and remain innocent herself.

"I've seen a couple of high school kids wearing jackets with old evil-looking symbols on them," said Alma, lifting her head to catch Mamie in the rearview mirror. "Why would anyone want to identify themselves like that?"

"I don't know. Young people are so different now." Mamie folded her hands and gazed out at Mellons' soybeans on either side of the highway. "Those beans aren't very tall, are they? And kind of pale too."

"Oh, all the crops look just awful," said Ruthie, and then she chattered on. Mamie didn't try to follow. She noticed a swing on the porch of a farmhouse they passed, and that brought to mind her latest Cassie dream, as she had come to call them. She and Cassie were young girls on the swing at the house they'd lived in when Papa ran the bakery on Main Street. Mamie and Cassie used to swing as high as they could without hitting the porch railing. They'd swing and giggle until Mama told them to settle down and reminded them that the swing was not a plaything. Mamie would obey, but Cassie wouldn't. She would keep pumping with her legs, while Mamie would put a foot on the porch floor to slow them down. The swing would swerve at an angle, and Mamie would get irritated, and Cassie would become more determined than ever to get her own way.

In the dream, they'd gone at odds over the swing, just like always. Only suddenly Mamie decided to give Cassie a taste of her own medicine, and Mamie started swinging as hard as she could. Then they were swinging off the porch, swaying out over the rosebushes by the front walk. They were headed on the backswing to the porch again, going real fast, and Cassie got scared that they would crash into the house. So she jumped off the swing, and she fell way, way down, what seemed like a mile to the ground below. She lay completely still, with her neck bent backwards severely and one leg turned the wrong way. Mamie tried to reach down and pick her up, but it was so far down there, and Mama was shouting at her to come in the house and help get ready for the funeral.

When Alma pulled into the mall parking lot, Mamie came back to the present. She'd never been an enthusiastic shopper, but she looked forward, all of a sudden, to doing nothing but wander from shop to shop and study bright merchandise that had no history. Maybe she'd find some planter or small table to put on her newly painted porch.

It wasn't until Mamie sat at the kitchen table that evening to work on her grocery list for the next week that she noticed anything wrong. She opened the drawer where she kept her coupons and grocery money. The coupons were scattered all over the drawer; Mamie had given up trying to keep them in any order. She kept the grocery money in an unmarked envelope in the back of the drawer. Every month when she got her Social Security check she would pay bills, then get enough cash to buy groceries for the month. That's what Charles had taught her to do, even before he'd helped her manage their checking account. They would never spend more than the cash that was in the envelope. If there was a special occasion coming up that required a bigger food budget, they would figure that in. But Mamie had grown accustomed to fashioning her food shopping according to the thickness of that envelope. The habit was as ingrained as brushing her teeth or stacking old newspapers near the back door.

But this night Mamie sat numbly at the table and turned her gaze on the calendar that hung down one side of the refrigerator. It was the end of June, but she hadn't shopped last week, and the week before that the envelope had been half full. Now it was flat—and completely empty.

Mamie talked to herself all the way to the Miracle home. She would not swear or act unladylike. There had to be a solution to this problem. Iris knew her brother better than anyone. Surely she would understand that he had to slip up sometimes. He'd only taken a few dollars, probably meant to give it back. Probably had run out of drinking money and knew Iris wouldn't give him any.

Mamie walked up to Iris's front door, handbag slapping against her hip. She rapped on the door, saw through the glass that there was furniture against it, and walked around to the back. She knocked on the screen door.

The girl, Leah, answered. She peered at Mamie with a seriousness that seemed highly unnatural for a child. "Yes?" said Leah.

"Is the reverend at home?"

"She's studying right now."

"I need to see her for a minute."

The child opened the door slowly. When Mamie stood inside, Leah walked into the next room. Iris appeared in the hallway.

"Why, Mamie Rupert, what brings you out in this heat?" The preacher's hairline was beaded with perspiration. She looked as if she'd been up for several days.

"I've got some unpleasant business."

"Oh?" The preacher moved toward a sunken couch, motioned for Mamie to take the chair next to it.

"Yes, I thought we should clear it up right away, just get it taken care of." Mamie covered her lap with the large purse and gripped it in both hands.

"What's the problem?"

"I don't know how to say this in a kind way. I have some money missing from my kitchen drawer. It's where I've always kept it, never had a problem. But it's missing now and I think"—Mamie noticed that Leah still stood at the edge of the room—"that your brother might have taken it."

Iris's face clouded. "Why do you think Ax took it?"

"It wasn't missing before he worked for me. I hadn't even opened the drawer until this morning. About twenty dollars—a ten, a five, some ones, and change. It's all gone."

"Might you have put it someplace else?"

"No. I always keep it there with my coupons. It's my grocery money."

Iris's lips were tight, and there were white spots at her cheekbones. Leah sat down on the other end of the couch and looked at her aunt solemnly.

"That's a serious accusation, Mamie," said the preacher.

"Like I said, I don't know how to say it kindly. But if you could just ask him about it and have him return it to me, that'll be the end of it."

"What if he didn't take it?" asked Iris.

"Well, then, I'll need to rethink it. But I want to ask him. He's the only person who's been in my house all week."

"I thought he was doing outside work," said Iris.

"I've had him in several times for a cold drink—in the kitchen."

"You've got this all figured out, don't you?" Iris mopped her face with a large handkerchief. The result was an added red tint to her already smoldering face. Her eyes snapped at Mamie. "It sounds to me like you've decided that he did it. I know Maxwell has his faults—I know better than anybody—but I've never known him to steal."

Mamie straightened in the chair. "I'd still like you to ask him. I'd just feel better about it. Maybe he saw somebody else around the house. I won't notify Sheriff Holt until I hear back from you."

"Why don't you just ask him yourself?"

Mamie's heart was crashing like there was no tomorrow. "I just think it would be easier on everybody if you talked to him in private."

"He's a grown man, and you can talk as well as I can." The angry look on Iris's face faded suddenly. "But I'll ask him—when I see him. He's out, and I'm never sure when he's coming back."

"Thank you." Mamie rose and walked to the door.

"Has his work been all right?" asked Iris.

Mamie turned back to the woman and saw more fatigue than anger on her face now. "The work's been all right. But I need to know about this money business before he can come back."

"I see. Good night, Mamie."

Mamie walked out the door that Iris held open for her and heard it shut behind her.

She called Alma the moment she entered her living room, before she'd taken the purse off her arm. Alma, as expected, tried to comfort. "Maybe he didn't take it. If you left the door unlocked, somebody could've come in while he was busy on the house."

After Alma hung up, Mamie dialed Liz's number and got a busy signal. For a person who'd met all the people in town she cared to know, Liz kept the telephone tied up pretty well. Mamie made herself some instant iced tea and took an aspirin. Then she started coughing, a tickly hack that made her feel sick to her stomach and gave her a headache. Doc Meiers had dismissed the dog dung allergy theory, but Mamie was sure it was That Dog making her cough like this. She tried Liz again and slammed down the phone at the obnoxious busy tone. She held her aching head in her hands and wondered why things had to be so hard on her. Ax taking her money and the Simpson dog dirtying her lawn. And then that Iris being mad at her, when she was only trying to get to the bottom of things. That prayer Iris had prayed over her arthritis really hadn't made any difference. So she guessed God was in on all this too. The coughing persisted, sending streams of tears down Mamie's wrinkles. She blew her nose and tried the number again. Liz answered, sounding irritated herself.

"Why did she have to have such an attitude as that?" Mamie asked her old friend, after describing her visit at Iris's. "I thought I did the reasonable thing, and that old preacher just acted like I was the one who had done something wrong."

"You know, I'm not a religious person," Liz declared, "but a woman with that kind of authority just goes against my grain."

Liz invited Mamie to have supper with her, but Mamie declined, feeling that she should stay close to the phone and see what Iris said after she'd talked to Ax.

Mamie reheated mashed potatoes and chicken from the day before and ate from her TV tray while she watched the news. She glanced periodically at the clock that sat on the television.

The phone never rang, although Mamie stayed up until nearly eleven. She thought about calling Gideon Holt right then to report her missing money, but she was just too worn out to deal with it tonight. She wanted to call Alma again, but Alma went to bed at ten, so Mamie put herself to bed, coughed and cried into the pillow, huddling on the side where Charles used to sleep.

10

SARAH MORGAN:
FEARS

Wednesday, June 25

Sarah growled at the Edsel of a computer that whirred at her tiredly. The thing was getting too old to boot up every time. On the third try the software clicked in, and she brought up the file for CHURCH.LET, the newsletter that had become her responsibility. Naomi Hunt had acted as though this was a wonderful gift the Sunday school was bestowing on the pastor's wife. It didn't matter that the newsletter had always fallen to the wife of whichever pastor was employed there at the time. This was a privilege that only pastors' wives could enjoy. *The Believer's Voice* was actually the voice of women throughout their county's Baptist association, started years ago by one of Sarah's predecessors. And only Sarah would do now as editor in chief.

"If only I could play piano, I wouldn't be in this mess," she muttered. Her lack of musical ability or the willingness to develop some had been a major disappointment to her husband's congregation—mainly because three pastors' wives before her had served as church pianist. Sarah wasn't good at potluck dinners either. At her first such occasion, she had brought a couscous salad with a light lemon juice dressing. Betty Bloom, the organizer of dishes, stirred it once or twice and took a taste, then said, "Oh, we've got salad dressings in the kitchen. I'll bring some out."

"It already has a dressing," Sarah had said stiffly, and Betty, seeing something in Sarah's face, had let it be. But Sarah had gone home with a practically full two-quart bowl of couscous salad. Sarah figured that if she hadn't been so literate on computer systems, the Bender Springs Baptists may have sent her and Jacob back to Chicago within three months.

Back in the beginning, two or three of the women had made a point of mentioning to Sarah the wonderful times they had had at the former pastor's wife's bimonthly coffee time. She would put out cookies and crackers and vegetables and dip and pots of coffee and tea—in the parsonage itself—and invite any women who wanted to come for a visit. Three or four women at least had said this deliberately within Sarah's hearing, and she had done her best to ignore it. How could she explain that her house hadn't been really clean since they'd moved in and that her pregnancy made her so miserable, some days she didn't even get dressed? Or that her stomach knotted up at the thought of a house full of women she didn't know very well—so many people whose names she would have to remember? By the time she was settled in and felt ready to handle such a get-together, Betty Bloom had stepped in as church hostess, and once Sarah had attended one of Betty's gatherings, she knew she could never compete. The woman had put out at least ten homemade food items and four drinks, all the paper products matched, and she had *made* the centerpiece.

It soon became evident that Sarah didn't cook (at least anything they liked), didn't sing or play a keyboard, and wasn't hospitable. By the time they approached her with the newsletter, she knew this was her last chance to redeem herself. They had chosen her for the job during a church business meeting, while Sarah was home cleaning up baby barf.

The very next day Naomi Hunt had appeared with a cardboard file box full of past issues of the newsletter and a floppy disk containing the template. She had handed these over with either joy or triumph, offering to walk Sarah through the first issue of the newsletter if she wanted. Sarah had declined because she liked to make unpleasant discoveries on her own, when no one was around to see or hear her reaction.

Now she stared at the screen, a nice opaque chalkboard green with yellowish type scattered down the page. There were several headings, which—Naomi had stressed more than once—stayed the same from month to month: Exciting Events, Pastor's Point, Prayers and Praises, Women's News, Member of the Month, Recipe of the Month, This Month's Feature, Community Concerns, and Corrections. Why, Sarah had all kinds of room to be creative. She could go just anywhere with This Month's Feature. Except—that's right, the feature was written by one of several "writers we have here in the association," meaning, of course, that Sarah was not one of them. Oh well.

Sarah looked through the stack of miscellaneous papers that were to become this month's fodder. Half of them were in handwriting, and some of that in pencil. She sent thanks heavenward when the phone rang.

"Oh, Sarah, I'm so glad I caught you at home." It was Heather Walker, whose voice always sounded trembly, as though she were on the verge of something life changing. Sarah braced herself; Heather was one of Bender Baptist's crisis conduits. This couldn't possibly be a short conversation.

As it turned out, the conversation was quite short. Alena Ray, who was in charge of seating at the laity luncheon, had been called out of town suddenly; her daughter's baby had been born two weeks early. And Heather, who was in charge of the greeting table and luncheon favors, suddenly had the entire floor plan to organize.

"I just can't manage the seating and the tables too. Could I come over and brainstorm with you?" Heather was always brainstorming, which amounted to sitting down with someone else and worrying them with questions and worst-case scenarios until the someone else came up with solutions. Today Sarah would be Heather's someone else.

"I'm working on *The Believer's Voice* today, and I take Miranda to her swimming lessons at eleven."

"Oh, I'm sure it won't take long with the two of us working together."

In ten minutes Heather appeared at Sarah's door, papers in hand, and soon the floor plan was scattered across the dining-room table. A mere half-hour into the process, Sarah was convinced that the hostess who worked on seating arrangements for White House dinners didn't live with such pressure. Women from the same church did not sit more than two together, and five towns participated in this luncheon, five towns and twenty-two churches, six denominations, four of them some form of Baptist. There wasn't really a head table (or so people kept stressing); nevertheless, presidents of laity committees in each church were seated together, taking up two tables nearest the speaker's podium.

The Women's Laity Luncheon had long been a focal point of spring. Sarah could tell from the conversations around church that it was next in priority only to Christmas and Easter. The planning started an entire year before, immediately after that year's program was finished. Women clamored to be on the planning committee. Sarah kept telling herself, while she and Heather drew diagrams and wrote in names, erased them, and rewrote them somewhere else, that she had suddenly risen to a place of honor.

Heather turned out to be more help than Sarah had expected, and at 10:35, she flew out the door and Sarah followed with car keys and Miranda in tow. She hit sixty-five getting to Helmsly. The farmland lay to either side of the two-lane blacktop, looking calm and sunny. Sarah vaguely noticed the occasional cows and ponds and silos, and she might not have noticed at all except that Miranda had entered a stage of needing to name, describe, and count everything they passed.

At the Helmsly public pool, Sarah tried to read a magazine as she watched Miranda splash and make friends with every person near her little wake. It was a ladies' home-and-food kind of magazine, but Sarah had bought it for the salad section and the article on making your butt smaller in time for summer. She'd bought it two months ago, when summer still lay in the future. But she couldn't concentrate now. She kept looking over at her daughter. While the sun glittered off the water, Sarah was filled with a huge and sudden sadness. This was happening a lot lately. She thought that maybe it had to do with Miranda's being named for Sarah's good friend back in Chicago. How she missed that old classmate and the city they had conquered together. Back in their poor college days, they had taken, systematically, each and every train that went out of Chicago, just gotten on at the beginning of the line downtown and ridden it all the way to its last stop. They watched unfamiliar neighborhoods come into view; they stopped and explored if they felt like it. They bought cheap food from people for whom English was a tentative, second language. Miranda Rimerez had been Jesus in the flesh, talking to perfect strangers about the things they feared and dreamed. She was one of the few people Sarah had ever known who could say "Praise the Lord" often and not sound offensive. Miranda was the personification of passion and celebration and sacrifice. Now she was in the former Croatia, working miracles among refugees. Like little Miranda in the swimming pool, the original Miranda made loud splashes wherever she went. She heard the voice of God out of thin air and churned up the world's waters carrying it out.

Miranda slapped her bare wet feet on the pavement and stood still while Sarah wrapped her in a big towel. "How was the swim?"

"Great. I can roll around and around in the water, like a seal."

"I saw you. You really learn fast."

"I *know.*" Miranda sounded awed herself. Sarah held her a little longer than usual, pretending to dry the child off. Already she felt that this baby was out in the world and speeding away from her. Miranda had no fear, and she was just nearly five. Sarah felt incapable of keeping ahead of her daughter, of making a way for her.

They stopped at Maxie's for ice cream on the way home. On swimming days they did ice cream during lunchtime and then had real lunch later in the afternoon. When they got home, Sarah sent Miranda to a quilt on the living-room floor, where it was cooler. The quilt provided Miranda's boundaries for two hours, during which Sarah gave her quiet things to do. Most of the time Miranda fell asleep with a coloring book before her afternoon surge of energy hit.

Sarah paid Nora, the teenager who had looked after Peter, and sent her on her way. The baby was sleeping peacefully in his crib, but he was due to wake up anytime for his midday feeding. The weight in Sarah's breasts told her this more than the clock did. She decided to try to get a load of laundry going before her son's cry summoned her.

On her way back to the kitchen porch/laundry room, she heard Miranda's clear little voice. She glanced into the living room. Miranda, obedient to the letter of the law most of the time, was standing on her quilt, making wide, dramatic gestures.

"Come to Jesus," she commanded an imaginary audience. "He's up on a cross, and he wants to save you *now!*" Sarah ducked out of sight and got to the pile of dirty clothes before allowing the laughter to escape. She would have to remember to repeat this week's sermon to Jacob. He had actually come up with a sermon or two based upon the unending stream of gospel emanating from his firstborn. The laughter in Sarah died down and was replaced by a niggling fear. Maybe this Miranda would hear God's voice, too, and fly away to her own adventures. Maybe Miranda and Jacob and everyone else, including all the Heather Walkers and Betty Blooms in Bender Springs, were in on God's hot line after all.

Sarah could recall a time when God spoke directly to her too—every morning at about six o'clock. This was when she sat at her desk in the dorm room, brand new to Christianity, opened her Bible, and took out pen and notebook to record her insights. Her several notebooks were still packed away in the closet. Sarah hadn't taken down anything to paper for a couple years now. God wasn't saying much these days. Or maybe she just wasn't as fervent and full of insights. She opened the Bible now and simply argued with it—or asked questions no one was going to answer anyway.

Sarah realized that she was throwing laundry into the washer without paying attention. She was *flinging* laundry. She seemed to be very angry all the time lately. She had the acute sensation that her life was on a journey backwards. She was following her husband, dragging her feet, and watching him change into a preform of who he should really be. Sarah regularly cursed the politics that had given that urban pastorate to someone else. Jacob was clearly the most qualified. The job had gone to a woman, and Sarah felt guilty for resenting that.

Peter's irritated squall erupted down the hall. Sarah slammed down a pair of jeans, frightening herself as she did so. She was angry at her baby, too, more of the time than she would ever admit to another human being. His colicky days were over, but he still cried a lot. He always acted angry with her, seemed to accuse her with his eyes of not being a good mother. From the beginning of the pregnancy, Sarah had felt like a failure, because she had felt too ill to enjoy the anticipation of her son's arrival. And once born, he appeared irritated even to be here. Sarah had read every baby and child care book she could get her hands on. She really tried to do all of it right. Her only reward was this fitful, tearful baby who seemed to never sleep and who didn't enjoy being awake either. And a husband who didn't like to be home much of the time and whom she had caught looking at her as though she had messed something up.

At this moment Sarah wished her son had never been born. She even wished she had never married Jacob. And she certainly wished they hadn't answered this awful "call" into ministry. She wished they had a nicer house to live in and that they had enough money to eat at restaurants that didn't serve food out of paper bags.

Today was only Wednesday, but already she felt the weekend rushing up to meet her. She wished that weekends were really weekends, times to go camping or travel to the city or throw backyard parties, as normal people did. But weekends were her worst drudgery, filled with church and church people. They had no respect for time of day or night, no sense of inconvenience when they had their crises or their brainstorms. Sarah cursed and cried as she walked down the hall toward her son's angry sounds.

Her own anger dissipated some when she viewed the pitiful look on the baby's face. She smelled a dirty diaper. That she could fix. She picked him up and hugged him, wiping the tears from his soft face. "I understand how you feel, sweetie," she murmured into his wisps of blond hair. "Nothing's working out for me these days, either." She pulled away to look into his eyes, raising the pitch of her voice. "Would you like to be clean?" She jostled him a bit. "Huh? Would that be better than old stinky pants?" For a moment, Peter quieted and looked at her face with interest. Then his expression crumpled into a look of utter despair and the wails started again. Sarah sighed and laid him on the changing table.

"All right. We'll do what we can, little handsome man. But you and I have got to find a new attitude. Can we work on that? Please? I'll try if you will." For the tenth time that day—and it was barely one o'clock—Sarah felt exhaustion creeping over her like a mist. She could never hate her baby. But her resentment was real, and her anger had begun to mix with an emotion she hadn't experienced in a long time: fear. She feared she would never have anything to look forward to for the rest of her life. She feared that all this anger and disappointment would choke to death her love for Jacob. She feared just getting through this afternoon.

Peter nursed in near contentment for once. He didn't fuss at Sarah's breast. She allowed herself a half-hour or so of thinking about nothing at all except her baby and the pleasant drawing within her body as he sucked. Not long ago she had been sure she wouldn't be able to breast-feed Peter. It had been so painful, and he had been fitful and uninterested. She would sit and cry, sure that her child was starving to death and that if she bumped into anything, her breasts would explode. Weeks of this. And now things were better. She had to remind herself that some things do work out.

Miranda had been an almost perfect baby. Nursed a few moments after birth. Slept well. Cooed happily within a few short weeks. Entertained herself easily but liked people too. Sarah had since decided that Miranda was God's way of setting her up. Now Miranda was nearly five and probably the main reason the members of First Baptist hadn't sent Sarah away in disgrace. Miranda charmed them all. She was proof that Sarah had done something right at some time in her life.

Miranda loved church. She loved the songs and prayer time. She loved to sit near the front and watch Daddy preach. She loved to dress up and greet everyone. "Why don't you let Miranda stand in for me for a few Sundays?" Sarah had asked her husband. He laughed. "Actually, I was thinking about having her stand in for me."

Sarah dabbed at a couple of tears while the baby nursed and Miranda continued telling the world about Jesus on the cross, who was "getting tired of all this sin." The house was quiet except for the washer bumping the wall during its spin cycle and the child's beautiful voice in the living room. More tears came down Sarah's face. She wanted to hold Miranda close, the way she now held Peter. For of all the things she now feared in life, she feared for her little girl most of all. That life would be disappointing to her too.

The laity luncheon happened on a drop-dead gorgeous morning. The heat had lessened, and the breeze felt as though it came from somewhere other than a clothes dryer. Sarah almost felt excited, dressed in a summer suit she hardly ever had the chance to wear and heading up the sidewalk to the Presbyterian annex. Other women, many women, all in summer colors and looking relaxed and happy, converged on the church steps. This would be one of Sarah's hardest moments—the time before anything officially started and she was left to make small talk and try to remember names. She did all right with women of her own church, but as a pastor's wife, she knew it her duty to break the ice with women from other towns and churches.

She looked for Rona Carruthers and found her just inside the doors to the banquet room. She was surrounded by women and appeared to be handling three conversations at once with perfect grace. She didn't notice Sarah, and Sarah decided not to bother her. Maybe later.

At least, as table-seating-arrangement person, Sarah had been able to put herself in a relatively safe place. Margaret Doublestreet, from a Baptist church on the other side of the county, was an extrovert's extrovert; Sarah remembered her from the last association meeting. Wherever the woman was, she conducted a symphony of laughter and storytelling. All Sarah would have to do was sit there. Next to Margaret, no one would expect anything from her.

But Margaret wasn't seated yet. She was four tables away, getting warmed up. A person could find Margaret by following the laugh ripples. Sarah almost walked over to join the fun, but two or three nervous-looking women were already at her table, and she knew it was her job to put them at ease. Fortunately, Anne Gaborne showed up. One of Bender Baptist's, Anne was very warm and welcoming. Sarah felt relief coming on.

They introduced themselves and sat down. Small favors—stiff, cloth crosses with tiny silk lilies of the valley in their centers—waited elegantly at each setting. They had safety pins on them and were the corsages for the day. Sarah was fumbling with hers when a pair of hands took over. She looked up into Betty Bloom's beaming face.

"You all know Mrs. Morgan, don't you?" Betty said to the rest of them. "She's our pastor's wife, and we just think the world of her." She patted the cross into place. Sarah was about to feel irritated, but she saw suddenly that Betty was genuine.

"She stepped in at the last minute and helped with the seating arrangements. And she edits *The Believer's Voice.*"

"Really?" asked the woman named Linda, dressed in a light blue suit, her short hair in perfect place. Her face, all business a moment ago, softened into a smile. "I really enjoy the quotes you include every month."

"Oh, thank you," Sarah said, satisfied. It had been her idea to include short excerpts from different books and articles every month. She knew some of them were appreciated more than others. Inspiration was a winner; comments leaning toward politics or social commentary were tolerated. Sarah smiled back at Linda. "It's my first editorial job."

"Well, you do it like a pro," broke in Betty. "We count on her every month, and we're never disappointed. You ladies enjoy your afternoon."

Betty left, and Sarah was stung with guilt. She'd hardly given Betty a chance, had decided early on that they had nothing in common. Sarah looked around the room. The women looked elegant and happy. She saw a couple in deep conversation at one of the back tables. One brought out a tissue and dabbed her eyes.

What kind of a snob am I? These women are more real than I am.

"Do you feel all right?" asked Linda.

"Oh, fine. Just trying to take it all in." Sarah felt miserable for a new reason. She started searching for excuses to leave early. Maybe tell them Miranda had a bad cold. That would be a little hard to pull off since Miranda had taken charge of the nursery the moment she entered it.

Sarah felt the room awaken around her suddenly and realized that Margaret had arrived. Almost as one person, her tablemates' faces focused and brightened as Margaret went around the table, introducing herself and asking them questions. She already knew their names. Margaret never forgot a name. Good. No need to leave early. Just be a listener. Laugh and smile.

They had a buffet lunch of salads and pie. Then Marie Donnington stood at the podium to speak. She had a manner that made Sarah think that she probably spent a good deal of time deferring to men and their opinions—too careful about the way she said everything. In spite of that, Sarah became interested. She was settling back in her chair when someone tapped her shoulder.

"Miranda fell and cut her lip," said Debbie Bailor, one of the nursery attendants. She didn't look too alarmed. "There's quite a bit of blood, but I don't think it's that bad. A butterfly bandage will probably fix it. Want me to do that?"

"No! I'll go." Sarah excused herself and followed Debbie around the tables and down the hall to the nursery. Miranda looked forlorn, holding a paper towel to her lip. The towel and Miranda's dress were spotted with fresh blood. Sarah knelt down and looked at the lip, and Miranda began to cry.

Sarah could see that the cut wasn't too deep. "It's all right, sweetie. It's not a bad cut."

"I'm all bloody!" Huge tears dribbled down the child's face.

"I know. Let's go home, and I'll clean you up." Sarah turned to Debbie and the other attendant, whom she didn't know. "How did she cut her lip?"

The girls looked at each other. Debbie finally said, "I think she was standing on that little chair. It must have tipped over."

"You *think?*" Sarah felt her blood rise. "Weren't you watching her?"

"Yes, but it happened so fast."

"What was she doing standing on a chair?"

"Pretending to be a preacher, I think. It didn't look like it would do any harm." Debbie continued to be the spokesperson. The other girl looked unwilling to volunteer any information.

"Well, I guess it did do some harm, didn't it? Come on, Miranda. I'll take you home." Sarah turned from the girls, deciding not to make a scene.

"I'm really sorry, Mrs. Morgan," Debbie said, a tear in her voice.

"Never mind. Would you get my purse? It's beside my chair at the table." Sarah walked into the foyer, holding Miranda, who was pressing a fresh paper towel to her lip, while Debbie retrieved the purse.

In two minutes, Sarah and Miranda were out on the front walk in bright sunlight. As she walked to her car, Sarah realized her legs were shaking. She buckled in Miranda, who had stopped crying and was examining the bloody paper towel. "I didn't know all this blood was in my lip."

Sarah drove home as fast as she dared. Once in the house, she sent the babysitter home, then stripped Miranda out of her dress and sat her on the bathroom sink. In ten minutes the girl was patched up, the tears gone. Sarah put her on the quilt and turned on a cartoon video. Then she sat on her own bed and cried as though the paramedics had just rescued her child from a burning car. She cried and cursed incompetent nursery workers. She cursed the summer and the laity luncheon.

She wasn't sure why the tears kept coming. She saw her own reflection in the bureau mirror across the room, and the woman there looked frightened. She could hear Miranda, apparently fully recovered, singing along with the video with great enthusiasm.

11

TONY GARDINO: THE JUNE REVIVAL

Friday, June 27

To get Mom off his back, Tony agreed to attend the first night's revival meeting at the Presbyterian church. Annie had managed to get out of this somehow. Annie still fought Mom a lot more than Tony did. For some reason, Mom had little power over her, and Annie knew it. Grand-dad and Dad didn't attend church meetings, so Mom didn't offer more than an initial invitation. At ten minutes to seven she and Tony got in the station wagon and creaked down the street toward church.

"This evangelist has had meetings all over South America," Mom said as Tony swerved around a corner, throwing dust into the sunny evening and causing her to grasp the door handle. He offered no response.

"And the music group is from Fort Worth." Tony could feel his mother's gaze on the side of his face. "They have drums and electric guitar," she added.

Tony tapped his fingers on the steering wheel as he waited for one of Bender Springs's four traffic lights to turn green. They were at the intersection of Washington and Vine, Ed's Fuel-Up being the significant landmark. Tony glanced at the fuel gauge. "Want me to fill up?"

"No, we don't have time. Service starts in five minutes."

Tony urged the car across the intersection and down four blocks. Parked cars lined the normally empty street. Mom gave a pleased gasp at the turnout.

"I've gotta be home by eight," lied Tony.

Mom's lips pursed momentarily. "I can't promise it'll be over by then. Revival meetings last longer sometimes."

"I guess I can walk home."

Evening had brought a surprisingly cool wind from the north. It licked at the dry street and seemed to perk people up. Tony lagged just behind his mother as she greeted other people who were approaching the building. They took turns looking skyward in hope of the rain clouds that usually came with June temperatures like this.

Tony was grateful his mother found a seat right away. He sat next to her and raised his eyes just enough to look over the small crowd. Heads like his mother's, with shiny beauty-shop curls that hung neatly across the white backs of necks and just above clean blouse collars. He recognized a couple of girls from school, but they weren't girls who interested him. The pews reeked of body powder and colognes that clashed. Tony noticed an air-conditioning vent close by and scooted to the end of the pew to be as close to it as possible; he had the feeling this place would run out of fresh air real soon.

The service began with the congregation standing and singing choruses, led, of course, by the legendary music group Mom had been talking about. Mom held the chorus book between herself and Tony, but Tony didn't even pretend to follow along. He regarded the musicians briefly and dismissed them. They were only about ten years out-of-date in every way. The room was already loud and feeling stuffy. It was getting hard to breathe. Tony found that it helped to examine the stained-glass windows. There was still some light outside, and the colors in the panes were at the moment faded versions of themselves. The glass was full of designs—vines and circles and other geometric shapes. No people. No depictions of God or Jesus even. Tony stared hard at the colors and dark seams and tried to get the sounds of singing out of his head. These songs meant nothing. He felt nothing, even when they all sat down and the pastor welcomed and joked and then introduced the musicians and guest speaker. All of it seemed far across the room. Tony wanted a smoke so bad he could hardly stand it. He imagined his lungs filling with sweet air and his mind relaxing. The colors of the windows helped a little, but the shade trees around the church screened out most of the western sun, and the stained glass looked dead by seven-thirty.

These ignorant people don't even know the world's ending, he thought. *They're too dense to feel what I feel.* He imagined hell bubbling under his feet, far below the carpeting and the foundation and the earth's crust. The Feeling was intense in here.

Mom nudged him suddenly, her eyes sharp, and handed him an offering plate. He passed it to the usher who stood over him from the other side. He noticed then that the still heads of the several rows of people in front of them were turned at exactly the same angle. The musicians were singing. The woman who was one of the main two singers looked like a wholesome Barbie doll. The drums and guitar droned away, and Barbie tilted her head back and closed her eyes, then crooned into the feedback of the microphone, "He thrills my soul. . . ." Tony closed his own eyes and tried to feel the air from the vent near him. He couldn't believe he had agreed to sit through this.

Things got a little better when the South American guy got up to talk. None of his witty remarks were really funny, but they were made somehow more bearable by the accent. He told some interesting stories about God's power over the evil that operated through skewed religions and the occult. He talked about his own dramatic conversion to Christianity. Midway through the talk, though, Mr. South America got louder and his face got redder, and he began to prance around. And Tony recognized the same sermon he'd heard most Sunday mornings of his life.

He looked at the clock on the wall behind them: 8:20. Everyone was so intent on the preaching, no one would notice him leave. But Tony feared this guy might call him down for trying to walk out. He'd seen that happen once, years ago. Some poor slob had tried to leave early, and the evangelist had walked over to him, put a huge arm around the guy's shoulder, and talked to him in front of everybody. Tony scrunched down into the seat as though he were warding off a heavy rain and decided to wait it out.

The invitation came at 8:35. The sweaty evangelist implored all to come to Jesus. The congregation stood and sang "I Need Thee Every Hour" as here and there a person broke from the moaning herd and slumped up the aisle toward one of the pastors who stood at the altar railing. Tony turned to his mother and mouthed, "I'm going." She did a fairly good job of hiding her disappointment.

As Tony walked to the back of the sanctuary, a moving object caught his attention. On the opposite side of the room, walking to the front of the sanctuary, was the one person who had the power to make

Tony stop and stay through the rest of the service. And Tony stood, there behind the last pew, dead still, his heart jumping to a wild rhythm. Tony watched the person who all but collapsed against Mr. South America, crying shamelessly loud. They knelt together and talked and prayed for what seemed like ten minutes. Then he took his place in the line of people who had given themselves to God that night. Each of them stood and faced the congregation, but not a single other face revealed the sheer relief and joy as that of the person on the far end. Tears had made his face shiny in the overhead lights. He looked as if he had tripped on every chemical at his teenage disposal and wouldn't come down for at least two years.

Tony heard something raspy nearby and realized it was his own breathing.

Howard Sheffley.

The guy who should have died splattered against the semitrailer. The guy who would always be too stupid to know that he didn't deserve a single thing he'd ever acquired in life. There he was, saved again, only this time from eternal hell. When the Methodist pastor asked him to testify, he cried again and blabbered at full speed about how happy he was to become part of God's family. He parroted the evangelist's words about being saved from sin and confessing Jesus as Savior, as though this were language Howard used all the time. Howard didn't seem to understand how stupid he looked, and he obviously didn't care anyway. The idiot was totally happy. He kept talking about peace. When he finished with "I just love God so much," Tony spun around and headed for the door.

Getting out of the church wasn't so simple. Blocking the rear exit were three long tables, loaded with refreshments and already staffed by several women. The only door available was the same door Tony and Mom had come in, and it was full of a small group of people who were praying intensely. Tony looked around helplessly and finally put himself in a small space between one of the tables and a bulletin board. He watched the pray-ers and prayed for them to hurry up and finish.

After the pastor dismissed the crowd with a prayer, the noise level rose immediately, and Tony headed for the prayer door. One way or the other they would have to break up now. The small crowd was already flowing into the parlor. Yet all the people seemed to be moving in a sphere just outside Tony's reach, as though he were in a bubble. He stopped hearing distinct words and sentences; the rising hum and warble of nonsense conversations made his skin crawl. Their smiles looked suddenly hideous. Tony turned around and backtracked, deciding that the refreshment tables were safer.

Somehow he managed to get around the tables and into the kitchen, where two familiar-looking old ladies chattered, large purses hung over their bare forearms. The one recognized Tony in an instant, and he remembered that she was Mrs. Petersen, from down the block. She was right beside him now, a hand on his shoulder.

"You remember my granddaughter Lena, don't you, Tony?"

"Huh?"

"She was just a year ahead of you in school." Mrs. Petersen's eyes were bright with interest. "But that was years ago—before you kids were even in high school. She's coming in July, for the rest of the summer."

"That's great," Tony murmured. The back door was a few more steps. He could hear crickets in the bushes just outside.

"You'll have to come over and visit."

"Yeah, sure. Excuse me." He felt the door give in front of him and the smell of late evening surround him. He gulped it in and put as much distance between himself and the church as he could without running like a maniac. At Ed's he bought a can of soda and a candy bar, then slowed down for the rest of the walk home.

Howard. Tony took a fizzy gulp of pop. There had to be a way to rid his life of Howard. The guy just couldn't show up uninvited wherever Tony decided to go. If it happened tonight, it would keep on happening. Howard was his personal curse. He existed solely to remind Tony that what would always come easily to Howard would never come at all to him. A new car. Money. Belief. Happiness. Peace. For the rest of his life, Tony would ride up and down the streets of Bender Springs on his old bike, and Howard would breeze by in his new TransAm. It was a decision made somewhere else in the universe. Tony finished the soda and threw the can onto a well-manicured lawn. The least he could do was mess up the environment. He wouldn't go down without making a statement.

An argument drifted through the front door of home, and Tony stopped short of entering. Something about Annie's wet towels and hair equipment all over the bathroom. Dad's whine sounded more tired than usual but insistent as ever. Tony sat on the porch step and looked at the night, breathing in some last good breaths before finding his way past people and up to his room. It felt like a long, long journey.

When he woke up Saturday morning, the sunlight that rested on his closet door sent pain through him. It was a familiar, frightening hurt. He looked at the other objects in his room—mainly CDs and a few clothes. They were contaminated too. The Feeling was all over everything.

Sitting up in bed made it hurt only more. Tony hugged his knees to his chest while his heart thudded sickly. He stared at his hands; they looked unconnected—tan rubbery things on the sheets.

He hadn't expected to feel like this again, but last night should have been a warning. Howard's presence would naturally precede something like this. Tony had thought for a while that he'd beaten this stuff; after January, he'd even felt a little invincible. But the darkness was back—the feeling that life had come to an end, that everything would close up and die and become part of black, indifferent space. Tony huddled on the bed and tried to think of a single thing that might make him happy, but nothing, absolutely nothing, came to mind.

He made himself get out of bed and stood at the window overlooking the garden. There was Granddad as usual, bent over something he wanted to grow. The sight of the old man didn't stir any feelings at all. Tony knew that the sight of anybody in his family or any of his friends would feel exactly the same, as if he were watching them on television from a place far away. He couldn't hear them, and they couldn't hear him. They couldn't touch or speak to one another. Worst of all, they couldn't understand. They didn't see the blackness, even though it was all around them. He could tell them how it felt and looked and smelled and tasted, but they would just look at him blankly.

It was the loneliest feeling anywhere or anytime, to see things no one else saw. To know that life was ending but not be able to explain that.

His gut felt like a tumor that was growing by the second. He went to the bathroom to relieve himself, and the tears started. When he looked at himself in the mirror, bottomless eyes stared back. The face scared him so much he looked away. He sat on the edge of the bathtub and sobbed as quietly as he could.

When he got over that, he went back to his room and scrunched himself into the corner by the bed. At nine, Mom called him to come eat; he lied and said he'd been up earlier and had something. He had to wait until they were all out of the house. He found a pencil and paper and tried to write something down, to explain to them, but the words all looked strange to him. He had to wait, that's all.

Tony lay on the bed for a long time then, looking out the window at pale sky and feathery bits of cloud. It was a deeply sad sky, reminding him of summer days way, way back in his life. He might even have the power to step in any direction and be some other age, like eight or eleven. Former afternoons breathed close to him. Former pains sat near him and looked on. He shut his eyes and smelled a high school football game from two years ago. He was dating Sherri Adams, and she wore a dark green turtleneck and blue windbreaker. She smelled of perfume and popcorn. The vision changed, and there was Alan Becker, the jock with red hair whom Sherri started dating a week after that game. Just like that. Tony could think of the betrayal now without emotion; it was an old movie playing in his head. The rough parts had been ground away. The general feel of his life was just that—rubbed smooth to nothing, no distinguishing marks left.

Into afternoon came sounds of people shuffling around downstairs. Annie had worn down their mother, and they were going shopping. The car sputtered to a start just under Tony's window, and he could hear it crunching over gravel as they backed out of the drive. He rose to look out the window and watch the car go down the street. He saw Granddad, mower blade in hand, headed down the same street in the opposite direction. He would be at Don Welty's little repair shop, six blocks over, for at least half an hour while Don sharpened the blade and the two of them discussed weather and current events.

Tony went downstairs barefoot and found Dad asleep in front of a baseball game on television. He snored while Tony stood and looked at him for a few moments. Tony waited for a feeling of some sort. There used to be anger. Lots of it. Nothing seemed to register now. Tony walked softly into the hallway and opened the drawer of the built-in bookcase.

Under some papers and a book of stamps the piece lay, looking hard and heavy. Tony picked up the .38 and examined it. Maybe a different gun would bring him different luck. There in the hall the memories of January rushed at him. The smell of hay and oily tools, the bite of cold invaded his senses again. It was thrilling to have a sensation at last. He found the small box of ammo and put it into his jeans pocket, then walked, holding the gun carefully in the palm of his hand, out the back door.

Outside in the afternoon light, the gun seemed larger, inviting someone passing by to notice it. Tony tucked it into the waistband of his jeans and let his T-shirt hang over it. Then he sat on the stoop while the thoughts zoomed in his head, too fast to catch hold of, and sweat popped out all over him. Where would he do it? Back up in his room, maybe? This didn't feel like it looked in the movies. In the movies there would be music that broke your heart. If he were in a movie, he would be saying good-bye to somebody, giving his prized possessions away. But the air felt dead and silent, and the yard looked unreal, as though he had stepped into it for the first time. No music at all.

He touched the gun through fabric and tried momentarily to consider the situation rationally. He remembered Mr. Arnold, the biology teacher, talking this one time about how when a person was extremely depressed some chemicals inside the brain did freaky stuff, causing irrational thoughts. Which meant that what was going on at this moment wasn't real, and even though Tony's chest was about to cave in, he wasn't actually in pain. Mr. Arnold could be pretty funny.

The black hurt welled up again, like a murky pool around his ears. Like the time he went to the swimming pool when he was eight, before he could swim, and he walked toward the center, not knowing that the water was deeper there. His feet fell farther and farther from under him, and suddenly the water was up over his chin, seeping into his mouth, and he was powerless to move back to a higher place. The weight of the water lapped him away from sure footing, and he knew he would drown. He ended up flapping around until he managed to reach the edge of the pool, but that feeling stayed with him all day, of being submerged, pushed against his will, to the slanted, deep bottom.

Tony stood up and walked toward the shed.

The small place hummed with afternoon heat and insects, white light bleaching the bench and table. He pulled a small stool from under the cabinet, set it in the shaft of sun, and sat down.

He made himself take deep breaths as he slid the gun out and held it in both hands in front of him. Dust danced around his hands as he took bullets out of the box and loaded them into the chamber. His hands shook. They had that other time too.

Just moments before, he had wanted the feel of metal against his palm, sure that the realness of it would be a comfort to him—that, and the fact that he was finally going to do something that would take the pain away. It bothered him just a little that nobody would understand that this wasn't even about dying. He was going to make the pain stop, that was all.

But now the task loomed at him, and he filled with panic. Maybe he wouldn't be able to go through with it this time either. He placed his finger on the trigger and worked the end of the barrel toward his temple, shutting his eyes against the fright of it. It was so quiet in here. Why did his ears hurt as if they'd been blasted with sound?

"Yes." He said it softly, to calm himself. He was afraid his hand would turn at the last second and he'd miss his brain. He pulled down the gun and held the opening at his mouth. How could it be so quiet in the middle of the day? His whole arm was shaking.

Hey, you really can't do this, can you? Against tons of pressure Tony opened his mouth. As the gun moved in, so close he could feel the coolness of the metal before it touched his lips, a darkness over-whelmed the shed. He heard a gasp of air and saw Granddad standing in the doorway.

The sharpened blade was in his hand, and his mouth was open in surprise, but no sound came out. Tony could barely see the man's features because the daylight was at his back, but the silhouette was in sharp focus—the tiny spikes of hair on his neck, the fold of his trousers at the knee, the point of his elbow just below the rolled-up sleeve.

Tony's arms suddenly went weak, and he could feel the scratch of the ground on his knuckles as his hands dropped. The gun, moist with sweat, slid out of his grasp.

Tony heard a shuffle and felt Granddad move in on him. He still couldn't see the old man's face clearly. But he sensed the man drop to one knee in front of him, saw the shadow of hand take the gun away, and could hear hard breaths, and bullets being emptied.

"Tony." The dark face was near his own. Had Granddad ever called him by name before?

"Tony, come to the house." It didn't sound like Granddad's voice. The pitch was different. But the man leaned back on his heel a little and light from the window came to his face. It was Granddad, all right, but strangely animated, not looking like himself.

"I don't want to go," Tony heard his own brittle voice say.

"Come to the house with me, son."

"Nothing will change."

The old man's face was still hovering close. "Yes, it will. You won't believe it in a few years, when you look back."

"I can't wait that long."

The shed filled with the sound of their breathing. Granddad shifted weight. "You'll just have to find something to get you through," he said.

Tony wondered how the old man could sound as though he really understood all this. Maybe he knew other things too. These thoughts barely connected with each other; Tony was still numb from the great interruption of his death.

"Come on," Granddad said after a moment. He was pulling Tony to his feet. Tony hadn't the energy to resist. He felt hard, old arms grasp him around the shoulders. It made him want to lean on Grand-dad.

"I don't want to go," said Tony.

"It's almost four. We've got time to walk there if we hurry."

"Where? You turning me in?" Tony tried to pull away, but Grand-dad was a lot stronger than he looked. They were walking out of the yard to the road, fast.

"Who would I turn you in to? What would the sheriff do with you now?" Granddad grunted, either from the disgust or the humor of it. They were keeping a quick pace, houses flying by on either side. Granddad's hand was fastened to Tony's upper arm, moving him forward, making his legs go.

They walked up the sidewalk to an old building. When they came to the massive doors that looked as if they were from another century, a scent of wood mixed with moldy soil tickled Tony's nose, and he remembered. Father Ricardo, those large hands and dark, strange eyes. They had frightened Tony when he came with Granddad to mass, years ago. Tony had exaggerated the situation, saying the priest glared at him and that he had smelled of beer (a lie—Tony had heard some of the kids at school teasing the Catholics by calling Father Ricardo a drunk); and Mom, who thought Catholics weren't real Christians anyway, had made her swift decision—none of her children would accompany her father-in-law to that church again. Tony wondered if Granddad had become silent in their house only after that day. Granddad was talking now.

"Just do what I do." Coolness slid across their skin as they entered the old sanctuary, and Granddad guided Tony to a pew. In the front of the room, backlit with candles and lights from the altar, was Father Ricardo, looking much older and completely harmless. He had begun to speak, his hands lifted gracefully at his sides, welcoming them to respond to what he said. Tony heard Granddad say, in yet another new voice, "And also with you." He held a book between them, moving it toward Tony, and pointed to words on the page.

Tony read without comprehension, feeling disarmed in this setting. He had a sudden curiosity about this new Granddad, or the old one who had come back to life. His face was as expressionless as usual, only washed over with some foreign emotion—belief or devotion, or something. Tony read part of the time and watched the old man the rest of the time. They stood, they knelt, they finally sat, and Tony gazed about the hollow, dark-wooded chamber. He stared at the stained-glass windows and remembered the one thing he had liked about his childhood visit—these finely chiseled pictures, alive with color and light. The faces of the people in them were soft but certain, as if they didn't care one way or the other if life ended. They seemed to live in another dimension, one unaffected by endings or beginnings.

Granddad was guiding him to the front of the room now. He remembered this too. Mom had freaked when she heard about the wine, even though Granddad assured her that Tony hadn't partaken.

The priest had made a gesture in front of Tony's face. Now Tony stood beside Granddad, and Father Ricardo was stepping toward them, his vestments moving around him like a living thing. The lights around them were warm.

Father Ricardo stopped in front of Granddad. A small, happy smile invaded the priest's face. "Arthur," he said. Granddad nodded. Were there tears in his eyes? Tony looked away. Then he sensed Father Ricardo in front of him. He saw the priest glance back at Granddad.

"This is your grandson?"

"Yes."

The priest paused and looked at Tony intently. Then he made the same motion in front of Tony he had made years ago, the sign of the cross. "The Lord bless you and keep you," he said softly. Tony understood that he would not be given the wine or the wafer. He knew he shouldn't even be standing here. But it seemed that something had passed between the priest and Granddad. And the robes moved on. After a moment, Tony felt Granddad leading him away. They passed the uniform benches, a person here and there. They came to a small alcove in the back and to one side. Tony's feet stopped, and Granddad paused.

Against the wall stood a small stand of six or seven tiers, similar to the one in the living room that held a bunch of Mom's potted plants. But on this rack were rows of candles, some of them lit, all in short, blood red glasses. They formed their own warm halo of light in the dark church.

"What are they for?" asked Tony, not removing his gaze from the tiny bowls of flame.

"People come to pray. A person lights a candle and prays about a particular thing."

"Like something to help a wish come true?"

"Some people might see it that way. My mother used to light candles when she prayed for people who'd passed on."

"A lot of good that does."

Granddad lifted his eyebrows and looked at Tony. "Catholics believe in purgatory, you know. If you pray enough for someone, you can help them get out of limbo and into heaven."

"You think prayers for the dead do any good?"

They were silent as the flames danced, licking the sides of their glasses. When Granddad spoke, he tried without success to sound matter-of-fact. "I'd rather pray for people while they're alive. That way I know how things turn out."

They moved quietly out the door. Before they stepped into the bright world they had left outside, Tony looked back again at the stand of lights. The door closed heavily behind them, and they walked slowly toward home.

"Who puts them out?"

"The candles? Nobody does. They burn out."

"So if somebody blows your candle out, God forgets what you said, huh?" Tony found a tiny bit of energy in himself suddenly, enough to make a joke. To his surprise, Granddad chuckled.

"Well, I hope not, because when I was a kid I'd slip back there." Granddad was smiling a little. "I'd see how many I could blow out in one breath, then I'd relight them. The priest we had then was half-blind and nearly deaf; we could've played marbles back there, and he wouldn't have known the difference."

Tony laughed some at this. Then the daytime took them over, and silence with it. They said nothing else during the walk home. Once or twice Granddad took a breath as though he were about to speak, but didn't. As they neared home, Tony felt the weight of exhaustion overwhelm him. Just before they entered the house, Granddad pulled on Tony's T-shirt until Tony looked at him.

"I'll be watching you."

Tony searched Granddad's face for the first time, looking square at him. "They'll just freak out if you tell them."

Granddad's face had turned to stone again. "Then don't give me a reason to tell them."

Tony nodded, relieved. The thought of his parents knowing about the gun made him want to pick it up again. He had the feeling that Granddad really didn't know what to do. He was an old Italian who didn't put stock in psychiatrists or other people who claimed to be authorities on real life. Tony guessed that old Italians were, in the end, full of the religion they'd grown up on. And Granddad had done all he knew to do. Tony figured the blessings from a priest had as much power as anything to make things happen—or prevent them from happening. For what it was worth, he didn't feel as compelled to blow his brains out as he had a while ago.

Tony went to his room and lay across the bed. He could hear Granddad directly below him at the built-in bookcase. He was emptying the drawer. Tony couldn't remember where they'd left the gun. The back door slammed shut, and Tony lifted up to look out the window and see Granddad heading for the shed. His walk was the same as always; no one would have a clue what the old man had accomplished in the last hour. After a moment he reappeared wheeling out the mower, the sharpened blade lying across the top.

The bed felt comforting, and Tony didn't even bother to take off his shoes. He was pretty sure he could sleep for a while, and sleeping during the day usually worked better than at night. He pushed away memory of all that had just happened, except for one thing. Fresh sensations were playing with him. Closing his eyes tight, he waited for the dark alcove to come into view. The smell of hot wax entered the room, and he concentrated on a single candle, wishing its flame to dance just for him.

Part Two

JULY

The History:
Dissension Springs, 1890

Jake Meriweather rode through Thaddeus Seaton's gate on a Saturday afternoon. It had stormed earlier, and the sky was still a weighted gray, full of fast-moving clouds. The land below bore a dark yellowish tint, causing the farmland to glow at midday. Thaddeus sat on his chopping stump, smoking a pipe. The rain had put him in a mood. His two children, Samuel and Maryanna, were pulling weeds in Florence's vegetable garden, taking advantage of the ground softened by rain. Florence hadn't been able to tend her plants for several days. But that would change soon.

Thaddeus nodded in acknowledgement as Jake dismounted. The older farmer seemed out of breath.

"Saw Lewanda day before yesterday," he said, stretching his back.

Thaddeus raised an eyebrow and bit on the pipe. "Where?"

"Blue Horse Creek. Mile and a half north of the bridge."

"She set up there?"

"As set up as she gets. She's lookin' real thin."

Thaddeus sighed, feeling tired. "Would she talk to you?"

"Oh no. I'd hardly fastened my eyes on her, and she was back in the brush."

Thaddeus offered Jake some tobacco. Jake shook his head but moved the few paces to Thaddeus's cistern and hauled up a drink. "She ain't doin' no harm, I suppose."

Thaddeus watched a rangy chicken scratching near the vegetable patch. One of Lewanda's. Things had run wild for a while now. Her four pigs roamed between Thaddeus's and Jake's farms. "Well," Thaddeus said, "I should ride over there. Not that it would do any good."

"You never know, Thad."

An hour later, the sun was burning off the wetness, making Thaddeus's ride steamy. He followed the creek north and saw the lean-to—that familiar old tarp Lewanda hauled everywhere, along with a single pot for cooking, her hunting knife, and a bedroll and gunnysack. Thaddeus approached the little camp and saw some roots Lewanda had dug, washed and drying on a rock near the creek bank.

Lewanda's place had sat vacant since the finding of the spring two years ago. All the hard things that had happened because of it—the community's bursting apart, the deaths and mistrust—had taken Lewanda into a crazy time. She never came to the spring or within twenty yards of another person. And she couldn't sit still. One week her camp was at the creek, another time out in an unused corner of somebody's field or in a grove of scrub oak. She wandered in her tarp of a prison. A few times she'd left the area completely, only to show up again weeks later, crazier and quieter and more isolated than ever.

She had talked to Thaddeus all of three times. She talked all right but didn't listen when he told her things were better now. That nobody was dying for lack of water these days. That didn't matter, she'd say. It didn't take away the bloodguiltiness. When she talked about guilt and blood, Thaddeus went silent; he'd borne the burden of his own guilt, either for saving a few people or for making others afraid to live.

"What do you want, Thaddeus?" Lewanda sat just outside the lean-to, skinny arms sticking out of their sleeves. Her once-black dress was the color of dust and grass. Her hair hung to one side, dirty gray and tied with a rag. But her eyes weren't as flighty today as they'd been other times. And she didn't run when Thaddeus took a step toward her. He walked slowly, as though they were just passing the time of day and he needed to shift his weight.

"I'll be needing your help. Florence's time's almost here."

"I know *she* didn't send you."

"Meriweather's wife is away, at her sister's in Nebraska. Most of the others are not experienced."

Lewanda drew circles in the dirt with one finger. Her face looked hard as stone.

"Nobody knows more than you do," said Thaddeus. "She's had a bad time with this baby. I fear for her."

"Doc Parker can care for her."

"But I trust you more—" His voice broke, surprising him. He saw, suddenly, the sure willow stick trembling against a relentless sunset. He smelled water. He wiped his eyes.

"Come get me when the time comes."

"Where will I get you?"

"I won't move until after the baby comes."

"Let me bring you some potatoes."

"No!"

"We had a good crop."

"Leave me be, Thaddeus."

"I'll send for you."

Lewanda was still making marks in the dirt, not looking at him, when he walked away.

A few days later, Florence took to her bed. She gazed at the opposite wall, seeming fixed upon Aunt Ida's chest of drawers. She wouldn't speak. She placed her hands on her belly the way a preacher placed hands on the heads of the sick. She cried soundless tears.

The next morning Thaddeus was awakened by his wife's cry. He ran to the barn and didn't bother saddling his horse. He rode like a wild man to the creek, calling Lewanda before she could hear him. She climbed onto the horse behind him, and he dropped her off at the house before going on to Parker's place near the church. When he and Parker returned to the farm, Lewanda came out of the bedroom, then motioned the doctor in. Thaddeus searched Lewanda's face.

"I think the baby's dead. It can't make its way out into the world." She turned from him before he could ask any questions.

Doc Parker's arrival didn't afford the relief or the help they'd hoped for. He allowed Lewanda to assist him, but Thaddeus could see the man's mix of feelings about it. Doc Parker's well had not gone dry during the drought, and he had never touched the water of Lewanda's spring.

But Florence motioned Thaddeus to her, and when he bent close to hear her, the words she spoke were clear.

"Please make Lewanda leave, Thaddeus. She's not a Christian, and I fear for my baby."

Thaddeus looked into his wife's face. He saw not hatred but simply fear. "Sweetheart, Lewanda's got a good heart. She wants to help you."

"But the devil has a part of her—oh!" Florence's face contorted as a shock of pain went through her.

"Florence, try to push." Doc Parker's voice betrayed no panic or fear at all.

"She can't push anymore. The baby can't help her," said Lewanda. Thaddeus could see in her face that she had heard Florence's words.

"I'll be the judge of that," said the doctor. He didn't even look up from where he was working on Florence, blood and mucous up nearly to his elbows. His thin hair ran with sweat.

"I've seen this before," Lewanda said quietly, but no less urgent. "And I can tell by their look when the thing's gone bad. You need to get that baby out however you can."

"Thaddeus, please," Florence gasped.

At that, Lewanda moved up close to where Florence could see her. "I'm going, Florence, if that's what you want. But I'll pray for you."

Thaddeus was at his wife's head. He cradled her tenderly and begged her in a breathless voice: "It's almost over, darlin'. Almost over."

Lewanda started out of the room but paused at the doctor's side and said in tones too low for Florence to hear, "This has passed out of your hands. You need to see that."

She went outdoors then and walked through the empty yard toward the barn. Thaddeus had sent the children over to the Meri-weathers', and the place was quiet except for wind in the two small cottonwoods just east of the house.

Not many sounds were coming from the bedroom now. Florence had been trying to have this baby since early morning, and now it was nearly noon. Lewanda leaned against the far side of the barn, its wood rough and warmed by the sun. She murmured to all the powers she knew—to the strong sun, to the timelessness of the land that swallowed up individual concerns, to the tall grass that sang in half-voice in and out of season. She said the word *God* and shed a tear. This word had never come easily to her, and she wished that now, of all times, she was more familiar with it.

After an hour she saw Thaddeus emerge from the house, followed by Doc Parker. The older man clasped Thaddeus's shoulder. Thaddeus leaned against one of the cottonwoods as though he would collapse, but he managed to exchange a few more words with Parker before the doctor untied his horse from the tree and mounted. As Parker rode away, Thaddeus's gaze found Lewanda. He looked at her and shook his head. She followed him into the house.

On the kitchen table lay a tiny, perfect child, unbreathing. There were still smudges of blood on its wrinkled legs.

"Let me finish this, Thaddeus," said Lewanda. "Go tend to Florence."

"She's tended to," he said flatly. "Doc will send out Mrs. Harkness and some of the other ladies to lay out the bodies."

Lewanda jerked her head up at him. She walked past him through the bedroom doorway. Hazy, midday light shone across Florence's face. It was still damp with her sweat, reddish brown clumps of thick hair clinging to her ear and cheek. Her legs at last were flat on the bed, which was soaked with her blood. The gentle face was free of torment, perfectly still.

Lewanda found one tear left and blotted it from her cheek with a sleeve. Thaddeus sobbed in a man's harsh, broken way behind her.

"She was a dear woman, a good wife to you, Thaddeus. I'm eternally sorry."

"It was meant to be," he said, bringing his voice under control. "That's what they'll all say."

"It's their way of making sense out of bad happenings," she said softly. "But nobody knows what's meant by anything. I guess it would have taken more people's prayers than yours and mine."

She turned to the table and fingered the baby's soft form, tracing the creases of its elbows and knees, touching the tiny mouth and eyelashes. "A little girl."

"Her name is Deborah Elizabeth." Thaddeus sniffled and touched the ever-so-fine hair, the child's head contained in his large, callused palm. "We decided that before."

"Good." Lewanda looked at him with a firm smile. There was a glint of light deep in her eyes. "Nobody should die without first having a name."

They buried Florence and little Deborah in the same casket, in the churchyard not far from the spring. Florence had been well loved, and all of the community's sixty-three residents came to the funeral. Most farmed small stakes of land. A few were connected to the church, the general store, and John Saxton's saloon/boarding house.

That autumn, John Saxton stepped down from being mayor. He was only fifty, but a fatigue had set into him, and he felt that his business was all he could handle. The people decided to elect a town council, along with someone to replace John. Things needed to be done, such as hiring a schoolteacher for the twenty-some children who needed training. Doc Parker suggested Thaddeus be mayor, and the rest of them agreed that the young widower was a good choice. His involvement with the spring of 1888 didn't matter much to them now. And a man full of fresh grief needed to find a purpose to carry him through to better times.

So they elected Thaddeus, and he didn't protest. He wasn't anybody's husband now, but the town would look to him in a similar way Florence had—to make the hard decisions, to find ways to protect them, to take the blame if need be.

That summer was cooler and sprinkled with kind showers. Autumn brought the best harvest any of them had seen since settling there. But it was followed by a long, sharp winter that thawed out slowly. When all the ice had gone, someone noticed that the spring was dry. They dug it out, but it made no difference. No miracle was there anymore. It was just dry ground, looked upon by the church and the graves.

12

SARAH MORGAN:
THE SIGH

Sunday, July 6

Early on Sunday morning, Sarah took a walk while her husband slept. She couldn't remember ever doing this since she'd become a mother. But this weekend Jacob's parents were here for a visit because it was the Sunday before Miranda's fifth birthday. When Mom and Dad came, life changed for Sarah. She hadn't uttered a single in-law joke since she'd met the Morgans. There just wasn't much wrong with them that she had ever noticed. They had treated her like a daughter from the beginning of her and Jacob's courtship. They were both great with the kids. Mom took over the kitchen from the moment she entered the house, somehow feeding them incredible meals without making Sarah feel that she had been upstaged. Dad read to Miranda until his voice was hoarse, and he handed over advice without being pushy. Every time the Morgans came to visit, Jacob's stock went up on Sarah's scale.

This morning Mom had caught Sarah looking out the back door. It was five-thirty and daylight gleamed softly over the lawn.

"Do you still run, Sarah?" Mom asked. She stood behind Sarah close enough that Sarah could feel the heat from Mom's coffee.

"I had to stop running a couple of years ago. Too high-impact for my knees and lower back. I try to walk when I can."

"Why don't you go now? I'll do breakfast."

"You should come here to relax, not work."

"It doesn't feel like work. I don't get to cook for people much anymore, with just Dan and me at home. Go on. You'll have apple pancakes waiting."

Now Sarah smelled the worn-down pavements of summer as the heat pushed up from where her walking shoes hit. It was almost six now, and already the town was gauzed in at its edges, an unreal world of farmland and distant counties wavering beyond the perimeters of streets bearing names of trees and dead presidents.

She closed her eyes for a few moments to feel the sidewalk move underneath her. She was learning to appreciate sounds. If she closed her eyes long enough, she could hear trucks rumbling on the highway, a dog panting in a backyard, three or four distinct birdsongs, and the dim clatter of breakfast dishes. She heard conversations too, disembodied exchanges floating out of open windows.

She thought of Jacob's theory: that the most important things people said were the phrases they uttered in the privacy of daily maintenance—over sinks full of dishes or across the yard from one another, words having to do with dropping off the insurance payment or what to have for supper or what television program to flip to. He had often said that most of a person's life was spent dealing in the mundane rather than the extraordinary. And that probably God had known all along what the imbalance would be. Jacob suspected that God paid closer attention to what folks did with the mundane parts of their lives, the main parts.

Sarah wondered now if the God of the universe really gave a rip how many diapers she had washed this week or how well she edited *The Believer's Voice*. Did the Lord listen in with pleasure while Sarah instructed Miranda for the umpteenth time how to button herself or say something with correct grammar? Did he stand by and nudge the angels when she and Jacob compared notes on who would mail the bills and who would give Peter his medicine? She thought not. But she said nothing; her husband seemed to generate a lot of energy from these theories, as though he were going to crack God's code someday and know just what to do and when. He never spoke of "God's will" anymore, only of "living as God would have us live." This, he said, took the pressure off people to find the precise paths they were sure the

Almighty had mapped out for them. Jacob didn't really believe in those divine maps, but he didn't come out and say that, since Bender Springs types seemed to put a lot of stock in God's having a Plan for My Life. Jacob figured that until he could come up with something specific and practical to replace the Plan, he'd better leave well enough alone.

Sarah walked to the north edge of town, where a grove of oak trees provided shade just off the two-lane road. There was no fence keeping her from the trees, so she jumped the empty ditch and walked under the large, draping branches. Already the morning coolness was reduced to a few wisps of lower temperature in the air. The trees formed a windless silence of their own, and Sarah sat on a protruding root and closed her eyes.

She tried to be calm, not to worry so much. She tried to soak up the quiet and the morning and to push from her mind the hours of church that were fast approaching. She tried to think only of Sarah. But Jacob kept pushing in. Jacob and his theology. Jacob and all the talks they had had back in Chicago over coffee at the seminary. They had talked about God's plan, or lack of it. They'd talked about a new way to be Christians in a culture saturated with pseudo-Christianity. They had been so excited back then, so hopeful that they could give people a fresh glimpse of God. But now they were like those very people they had hoped to help. They were ordinary and tired and had no ideas left, and the few they had tried had not worked.

She left the grove angry. The road home was hot and gritty, and Sarah remembered that she had to sing in church today—with three other women. In fact, she needed to be at church a half-hour early to rehearse one more time. This would rush her once she got home. This stuff never ended. This summer would never end.

The apple pancakes did help. Sarah asked about Mom's volunteering at a community center in Hutchinson, and she was glad to get lost in Mom's answer. Mom and Dad weren't very religious, but they were supportive of Jacob's calling. They would be in the service this morning. They would hear Sarah sing and smile at her as she did so. This would help. She would ignore the congregation and just sing to Mom and Dad, Miranda and Peter. She knew Jacob would be seated on the platform behind her, looking pleased. But Mom would beam, and Dad would squeeze Miranda's knee and point at Sarah and grin.

Sarah headed out the door again at 9:20 to walk the few blocks to church and rehearse. An engine coughed on the street behind her suddenly, and she turned to see the Beckets, all six of them, waving delightedly at her. Mrs. Becket was the church's main pianist; she must be coming to rehearse also. The Becket's car was more than full, so

they didn't offer Sarah a ride, for which she was grateful. Their enthusiasm and naivete grated on her nerves.

When she entered the pale sanctuary, she nearly bumped into
Harold Becket, who was perusing the table in the foyer, always on the
lookout for new literature. Mr. Becket was a tract man. He kept evan-
gelistic tracts in his truck, lunch bucket, work locker, and shirt pockets. He gave people tracts whether they received them with gratefulness
or abused him for it. Harold was what Jacob referred to as a plodder—
not a bright star in God's constellation but a steady gleam nevertheless.
The Harolds of their churches could be counted on to keep their same
opinions, pray the same prayers, and support the same decisions
through years of membership. Sarah greeted Harold politely, trying to
edit her own thoughts of him. He held her there for a moment with his
glowing comments on the new booklet, *Having Family Devotions*.
Then Sarah retreated to her husband's study, just off the hallway east
of the sanctuary.

Jacob's study was the coolest room in the church, with windows
for a cross breeze and trees shading one side. The swivel chair at the
desk squeaked when Sarah sat in it, and it leaned to one side. She discovered that this was why Jacob had packed an ugly green pillow into
one part of the seat. The pillow and the chair maintained an imprint of
Jacob's body, even with Sarah sitting there.

She could hear Mrs. Becket practicing the numbers for church that
day. She was working on a newer hymn. Sarah could hear the woman's
murmurs of discontent as the arpeggio in the left hand failed repeat-
edly. Most of the music sounded the same to Sarah, but Mrs. Becket
often had new books of hymn arrangements displayed proudly on the
piano. Sarah could also hear the four Becket children calling to one
another from different places in the sanctuary. They were checking the
pews to make sure all the racks had the right number of hymnals and
Bibles and offering envelopes.

The study was quiet in spite of these outside noises. It occurred to
Sarah then that she was seated in Jacob's personal sanctuary. This was
his place. When he tired of her or the kids, this was where he came. It
stung Sarah to realize that she had no place of her own that even
approached this kind of retreat. It was quiet and cool and filled with
Jacob's books and thoughts and nearly everything else important to
him. The force of this hit Sarah for the first time in all the times she'd
been in this room. She cried some, then scrambled to find a tissue since
she knew Louise, Anne, and Ramie were probably waiting for her this
very moment. But Sarah sobbed some more, for the man who lived in
this study—the original Jacob—hardly lived at home anymore.

She heard the piano and the other women's voices and blew her nose again, put on some fresh face powder, and entered the sanctuary. They went through the song, a quartet version of "I Need Thee Every Hour," four times, with Anne directing and correcting. Sarah claimed to have no musical knowledge beyond a few terms she'd picked up in a music appreciation course in college, and she accepted Anne's comments without argument. Anne was an alto, as was Ramie. Louise's soprano was filled with vibrato and emotion, and Sarah's thin soprano voice seemed to offer nothing more than the glory of having Pastor's Wife help with special music. But these women were pleasant to work with and seemed truly appreciative of Sarah's efforts.

The church grew hotter as people came in. Mom, Dad, Miranda, and Peter preceded Jacob, who didn't even make it to his study, but stood outside in the bright sun, shaking hands and making conversation with folks as they filed in. Before long the small room was half full, Sarah sitting with her children and in-laws near the front, while Jacob took his place above them.

As it turned out, Mrs. Becket solved her arpeggio problem in the opening hymn by dissolving the left-hand part to rhythmic chords, sort of a pious "boom-chic-chic" that accompanied the melody in the right. The congregation didn't seem to notice. The same few voices took the lead, carrying the hymn in an odd mixture of vocal sounds. It had always amazed Sarah how people who would never sing for company in their own homes could give themselves so freely to music in a worship setting. In the midst of her many theological questions, Sarah sensed that part of her faith was held in place by hymn singing on Sunday mornings. It seemed to come from beyond the people who sang it, as though the hymns themselves were voicing something ultimately true and preexistent.

A south breeze panted coolly across the pews, ruffling up bits of hair around the faces of the people as they sang. Sarah heard Mrs. Murtle in the row right behind them. She glanced at Miranda to make sure the child hadn't turned around to stare. Mrs. Murtle wore a hat with silk flowers on it, and Miranda had noticed a couple of weeks ago that one flower bobbed when Mrs. Murtle sang. "It doesn't even stay in time with the music," Miranda had said in the softest voice she could manage, during a song last Sunday. At one point Sarah had caught her turned completely around, mouth on the top of the pew, studying Mrs. Murtle's loose flower. At the moment, Sarah wondered if the flower was keeping time with Mrs. Becket's boom-chics.

The only other woman who wore hats to church here was Beth Hodgerow. She wore a sleek navy blue satin cap with no appendages.

Beth had worn this hat to church for many Sundays now, probably because it matched her navy suit perfectly. This was just like Beth. She lived free of things that might bob out of beat. Her home was a shrine to the plastic slipcover. Her wordless husband, Horace, hosed down their cement drive every evening. Beth was a tidy alto, a no-nonsense parishioner, whom Sarah avoided whenever possible. She could hear Beth's unmistakable voice now and imagined it marching back and forth across the room in its own little navy hat.

When the hymn ended and Deacon Peters had given the week's announcements, Jacob stood and took his place at the pulpit. He made a point to meet a few gazes and said, after the usual greeting, "I hope you all are remembering to pray for our summer joint revival services. Week after next, July 18 through 25, is our second week, which will be held at the Methodist church. Please continue to pray for our sister congregations there and at First Presbyterian."

The next twenty minutes went by without touching Sarah in any way. She was still thinking about Jacob's study. Her mind ran over all the grievances again she had against him right now and all the spaces in her life that were not filled. She blinked back tears and sang automatically. At one point Miranda leaned against her, and she put an arm around the child and held her as closely as she could, hoping to draw some life from this little girl who possessed all the brightness Sarah had lost somewhere when she wasn't paying attention.

Then it was time for the special music. Jacob announced the ladies' quartet, and Sarah moved to the front with the other three. They took their places, Mrs. Becket played the introduction, and they sang the first stanza. It went all right. Sarah couldn't think of more than one line at a time, although she knew the piece well and the music was in front of her. She felt her voice drawn out of her by degrees, one measure after another, one note at a time. She had never felt so uninspired in her life. They made it successfully through the second stanza.

Mrs. Becket played a nice interlude, and the singers stood still during this, half smiling. Sarah knew she should try to make eye contact with the congregation, but instead she looked desperately to Mom and Dad. Their encouraging smiles were there as expected. Miranda, cuddled into her grandpa, sent a little wave.

Then, as Mrs. Becket led into the final stanza, Mrs. Castleberry, who always sat in the third pew on the south side of the room, sighed deeply.

Sarah closed her mouth and looked at Mrs. Castleberry. She was fanning herself madly with a church bulletin. Her sigh echoed inside Sarah's head. She had heard that sigh a hundred times in two years.

Mrs. Castleberry sighed as if she had been carrying the world on her back and had stopped to put it down and rest a minute. It was a full-bodied sigh. It had a beginning, a middle, and an end, just like a good sermon. And it utilized a wide dynamic range.

Sarah stumbled a bit on the lyrics, which had no meaning to her at all now. Her eyes raced across all the faces in the room, and she saw people who looked completely blank. They were drained from a week of work, from keeping homes intact. They sat dutifully with kids on their laps, listening to her sing as though this too would come to something in the end.

Suddenly, through Sarah's memory played every other sigh that had come from Mrs. Castleberry's bosom. She sighed when they turned to a hymn, whether it was a favorite or a new one. She sighed when business meetings went too long. She sighed when Jacob came to point two of his weekly sermon and when he got down to business at the end, asking people to apply the lesson to their lives. She sighed while the ladies decided who would bring salads and who would bring desserts to the monthly or special-occasion potluck. She sighed when Deacon Peters stumbled over an announcement. When they made decisions, took longer than expected, talked about finances, or shared personal prayer concerns, Mrs. Castleberry became a veritable fountain of tired air.

The song came to an end, Mrs. Becket brought the piece to a tasteful close, and the congregation murmured their amens. Sarah took her seat beside Miranda, and Mom leaned over, her eyes wide with concern. "Are you feeling sick?" Sarah nodded, then left her seat, and headed for the bathroom in the back. She didn't even look to see if Jacob had noticed or if anyone else could tell that something awful had happened.

She got to the bathroom but discovered that that wasn't far enough, so she slipped out the church's back door and stepped carefully through the scratchy summer grass to the small storage building. Of course it was locked. But on the west side of it a large wooden crate was overturned in the shade of a small maple tree. Beyond that were an alley and warehouses, and no one was around. Sarah sat on the crate while her heart pounded.

"I can't do this anymore, God," she said finally, after nearly five minutes had passed. She didn't close her eyes or look toward heaven. If God was around, he either wanted to hear what she had to say, or he didn't. But she had to say it. It was all exploding inside her, about to wipe out everything in its path.

"I can't do this anymore. I'm hurting these people just by being here. I don't add a single thing to their existence. I don't fit here; I don't have gifts anybody cares about. I don't think my husband loves me much anymore. My children need a better mother, and I can't be a better anything here."

The pain went too deep for tears. Sarah continued to talk at the maple tree, the summer air. "Jacob doesn't deserve this, but I've got to tell him that I need to leave now. I'm dying by inches, but nobody sees. I didn't see until just now. This minute it's finally clear to me. I can't do this. I can't do this."

She heard a dry sound in the grass and saw a slim green snake slip into a patch of weeds a few feet from her. A large grasshopper bounced and attached itself to one of the weeds, bending the shaft. It made her think of the plague of locusts in Exodus. "I'll wait until these revivals are over. I'll do that much. But no more. Don't ask me to do more."

She stood, dusted off her dress, and entered the back of the church. Jacob was almost to the end of his sermon. His words took a certain pace when he was getting ready to close and pray. Sarah sat on the end of the pew, next to Dad, gave a reassuring nod to Mom, and sang the closing hymn. She thought of the people she needed to contact—in Chicago, but also in Grand Rapids. That city had three Christian colleges that should be ripe with teaching possibilities. Chicago itself had to have something that suited Jacob's gifts. Her gifts too.

This decision held Sarah up through lunch at one of the nicer restaurants in Helmsly, where Mom and Dad treated them in honor of Miranda's birthday. Sarah held her daughter as much as she could. She stroked the beautiful chestnut hair and kissed the sweet little forehead. Afterwards at home, there were presents and a birthday cake and ice cream. Mom and Dad sat comfortably together, their granddaughter between them, for Jacob to snap a picture, and Sarah felt a pain in her heart. She would need to take Miranda up to Michigan to see her other grandpa as soon as they had a break from revival business. Sarah's father thrived pretty much on his own in a senior housing complex. He had an apartment of two rooms, three meals served every day in the common dining area, and he played cards and checkers with some friends in the afternoons. His wheelchair kept him from visiting anyone much, and some days he was foggy and didn't remember people's names. Since his stroke three years ago, Sarah was grateful for his peaceful, if uneventful, existence. But she wanted him here today. She even wished her long-dead mother could come alive again to see her grandchildren. But Sarah hardly remembered the woman herself. No point mourning a person she'd never known well and who had never seen Sarah's high school graduation or wedding or babies.

Kansas was entirely too far from her roots. She had thought this wouldn't matter. When she and Jacob had accepted this "call" to the ministry at Bender Springs First Baptist, she had thought a lot of things wouldn't matter. As it turned out, they mattered very much.

13

DAVE SEATON: LENA

Monday, July 7

Dust from a passing car hung in the bright evening sun. Dave's head still rang from the sound of the truck he'd driven all day. He blew his nose and black junk came out, one of the inconveniences of working with asphalt.

Now he turned his back to the west, to get the slanted sun out of his eyes and look over the garden. Somehow tomatoes, onions, peppers, squash, and potato plants still grew erect, although gray from their coating of dust and not as plump as usual. Dave licked his dry lips and tasted salt. Something tickled his head just behind his right ear, and he realized it was sweat. He kicked a clod of dirt at the edge of the garden.

"Are you mad at me?" Randy asked from the back stoop, just yards away.

Dave turned in surprise. "Am I what?"

"You act mad—just want to be sure it has nothing to do with me." She wore a green sundress and no shoes. Today's newspaper draped across her lap. She crunched on ice from her large glass of iced tea.

"No! Why would I be mad at you? You're the only good thing I have going." He didn't lie about that. Randy fit him like a favorite pair of jeans. He felt happy, in spite of everything else, just to have her sitting on his back stoop.

They'd been getting together for nearly a month, and she showed up at his place a couple nights a week. Dave felt that life was good. Except that the heat wouldn't end and the forecast hadn't changed. He'd never been one to think much about weather. He worked in all kinds of it, out on the crew, and usually didn't notice simple discomfort. But this summer felt more like a wild animal than a season.

Randy leaned with bare arms crossed over the newspaper. Her hair looked almost gold in the sunlight. "Are you really that upset about your garden? I mean, stuff is growing, isn't it?"

"It is, but it's a struggle this year. You know how long it's been since we had a real rain?"

She shook her head.

"Five weeks. And now the reservoir at Helmsly's getting low. We can't just hook up the soaker hose anymore."

"Can't wash cars either. I heard Dad griping about that."

"It just feels wrong." Dave walked past her and grabbed a bucket near the spigot. "Like something's stopped working in nature. Rain's just supposed to happen. Like the sun coming up or the weather getting cooler in September. Those things are supposed to happen without me worrying about them." He went inside to the kitchen sink and dipped dirty dishwater into the bucket.

"This is a real personal thing with you, isn't it?" Randy stood up when Dave stepped past her. She followed him to the garden. He handed her a tin can with one end cut out. He used a plastic cup. They dipped the water, a little at a time, onto the individual plants, working their way down the rows. "Just about half a can for now," Dave said. "We always had a garden. And it was always on this spot. I spent a lot of time with my dad out here. And"—he turned his head to smile at Randy—"I like to eat. And I like to feed you. And nothing tastes better than what you grow on your own. No chemicals. No other junk thrown in so it'll keep on a shelf for five years."

"I never knew a guy who could cook like you, Dave." She was reaching for another canful of water, and he took the opportunity to study her. Just a kid in some ways. He might have seen her a hundred times during her life here, just passing her at the post office or something. But she didn't have the kind of looks that would make a guy stop his course and start following her. She'd worked her way into his thoughts now, though, and it was making him nuts. She was beginning to make him expect good things in his life on a regular basis, when he'd figured he had run through all his good fortune during Karen's few years of love.

He had the feeling Randy could not be had completely. He'd always liked independence in a girl, but it bothered him now. She'd left some of her clothes at his place, but she refused to put them in a drawer. They were in a plastic grocery sack, in his bedroom against the wall, along with his old stereo and work boots. Dave woke up in the morning, squinted at the east window, and contemplated that tan-colored, wrinkled plastic bag, which contained a pair of cutoffs, two T-shirts, and two pairs of tiny, stretchy panties. It made him nuts.

He grabbed Randy's waist and pulled her in for a kiss. When they came up for air, he said, "If you like my cooking so much, why don't you move in?"

She pulled away and dipped the can into the bucket. "That would just spoil everything. It would be too much like marriage."

"You against marriage?"

"For now I am. You see my parents. I'm not ready for that."

"We wouldn't be like your parents. You're so different from them, I can't see how you're in the same family."

Randy sat down at the end of the pepper row. "Let's not ruin a good thing." In the hot breeze, strands of her hair lifted around the small face. Such tiny bones. She looked almost breakable. Her one crooked tooth made Dave want to protect her for the rest of her life.

"I heard your folks screaming all the way over here the other night." He tried to say this matter-of-factly.

"It hardly ever gets worse than screaming. I know it sounds scary, but I grew up with it. You learn to tune it out."

"It can't be good for you." He'd finished his row too and plopped down next to Randy.

"You never give up, do you?" She grinned.

"Well, I know we're right." He saw the look of panic cross her face and added, "I'm not talking about getting married, okay? But you spend most of your time here anyway. We get along. Why not live in the same house?"

She grabbed his hand and kissed it. "I've got to ask you something."

"OK."

She took a breath as though she were about to dive into water. "Do I remind you of Karen?"

Dave looked at her a long moment or two. He watched her growing concern as the silent seconds went by. Finally he smoothed her bare leg with his free hand and cleared his throat. "No. You're different from her in a lot of ways. She had a lot of anger. For good reasons I won't go into. I really loved her, but I love you in a different way. It doesn't feel as hard to love you, and I don't mean that in an insulting way to her."

Randy nodded. "I don't want to be too convenient, that's all," she said.

"Convenient?" Dave laughed. "Convenient is a quart of milk at two in the morning at the Get 'N' Go. Convenient is . . . ." He enjoyed hearing her laugh while he searched for a good one-liner. "Toothpaste that comes out in those little increments." He mimed pumping toothpaste onto a toothbrush, while she laughed harder. "Convenient is opening a can of soup 'cause you're too tired to cook real food. Convenient is . . . ." He looked at her while her giggles subsided, ". . . not you, baby." He allowed his voice to get husky. "Why, you're about the most inconvenient person I've ever met." She was smiling inches from his face. "Mainly you're inconvenient because you're not here." They kissed again while the low sun in the west burned at their backs.

An hour later, Dave was frying young summer squash with green onions while Randy watched from her seat at the kitchen table. She read Help Wanted ads out loud as he worked around her.

"Why are you reading those? You've got a job."

"It's not enough of a job. Being on my feet all day's killing my back."

A shadow appeared at the kitchen door. It was a slender woman in a wrinkled print skirt and a black T-shirt. Through the screen Dave could see her jewelry—large colored bands on both arms, and many rings. The gleam of early evening was at her back, lighting up her legs in the sheer skirt, and the woman's eyes and mouth looked like dark hollows in her face.

"Hey," Dave murmured, spatula raised above the skillet.

"I like your food smells," said the woman. "Too much butter, though. Poison to your blood, you know."

"Lena!" Randy stood and let the newspaper skid across the floor. A look of pleased familiarity came to her face. "Where did you come from?"

The woman opened the door and came in. Her hollows of eyes changed to two green marbles, ruffled with brown lashes. She was beaming. "I came from far away, on the wind," she said, raising her arms dramatically. Randy took two gigantic steps and hugged Lena. They laughed softly and moaned on one another's shoulders, doing an easy dance on the linoleum.

"This is Dave," Randy announced, reaching out to pull him closer to them.

"Hi," he said, trying to take in this creature who for some reason made him feel not at home in his own kitchen.

"Honey, this is Lena, my best friend since eighth grade. She moved away our sophomore year—to Denver, the lucky dog."

Lena offered a slender, tanned hand to Dave. Her arm was hairless, and the colored bands tinkled against one another. Her skin was cool. Dave met her eyes just long enough to be polite. He turned back to stir the squash.

"Let me fix you some iced tea," Randy said, pulling out a chair for Lena.

Lena sat at the table and crossed her legs. "Thanks."

Dave could feel her watching.

"So, are you the cook?" she asked.

"Sometimes."

"All the time," Randy broke in. "He cooks for me all the time."

"That's nice," said Lena.

The two women sat at the table and drank iced tea. Randy told Lena a summary of her life for the last two-plus years, including information Dave had never heard, so he tuned in, working with supper as quietly as he could. She'd traveled with her father to Tennessee to see some distant relatives. She'd sold some paintings at a craft show last year. She'd colored her hair a couple of times but liked it natural now. After a few minutes she ended with, "And now here I am with this hunk of a guy cooking for me. I did all right, huh?"

Dave knew she was joking but felt his ears get hot anyway. He didn't exactly like being presented like something she'd found at a great yard sale.

"I'm glad you're happy, Randy," said Lena, leaning toward the table, her back long and slim. Her voice was smooth like her skin. Dave watched the disks of squash grow clear and soft while he listened. At that moment he began to understand what made him so uncomfortable. The sound of Lena's voice wasn't just calm, but calm in a controlling way. He turned to look at her and Randy. Randy had practically scooted up to straddle a table leg in her eagerness to talk. Her arms were thrown across the table, the glass of iced tea in one hand. As always when she was happy, her eyes were large and her face open. Randy was a person who was always just what she appeared to be.

Lena looked posed, her shoulders straight, the skirt resting perfectly across her dark calves. Her hair fell down the T-shirt straight and shiny, no stray wisps, no strands oily from the heat stuck to her temples. Dave wondered if she were a model back in Denver.

"I'm glad I'm happy too," said Randy, then laughed. "About time, huh?"

"It doesn't surprise me," said Lena, sounding wise, handing down counsel to an inquirer. "I always knew you had inner power. We both knew it, remember? Remember the storm?" Lena's eyes glowed as though a lamp had been turned on behind the green marbles.

"Mmm." Randy nodded as she tipped up her glass. "Dave, I never told you about that, did I?"

"What's that?" Dave turned the fire off and reached for a pot holder.

"This really strange experience we had our freshman year. We were walking home from a softball game. It was something like seven in the evening, and it was really stormy, but it hadn't rained yet."

She looked at Lena for confirmation that she was telling the story right. Lena rested her chin artfully on an upturned palm. She nodded.

"And halfway home—we were taking a shortcut across Mason's pasture—it started raining like crazy. Like a wall of water all of a sudden. We were soaked in half a minute. But it was warm rain, like in summer, even though it was just the middle of May—"

"May 18," said Lena, not moving her head. She was gazing hard at Randy.

"How do you remember that? I can barely remember the month."

"It was important to remember. Tell him what happened."

Dave had dished up the squash and taken the chicken out of the oven. He set both on the table and sat down, looking at Randy.

"All of a sudden there was this gigantic noise, and a second or so later a bolt of lightning hit just behind us." She grasped Dave's arm. "It was so close we could feel the heat. I nearly wet my pants. And it crackled all around us. I could feel my hair standing up all over my body."

"You looked tremendous," said Lena with a small smile.

"That happened to me once," said Dave, examining a callus on his palm. "When I was helping a guy bring in his corn harvest."

Lena turned to him. "But she hasn't told you the most important part."

"You tell him," said Randy.

"After that first strike, we ran like devils," said Lena, her eyes pinning Dave, daring him to look away. "And the lightning struck again, just behind us, just like the first time. So we kept running." She paused and leaned back from the table, her arms resting easily in her lap. "It struck right behind us three times altogether while we were running across Mason's pasture."

Dave tried not to give away his skepticism, but Lena caught on and added, "Some other kids were on the street and saw us. They counted two after that first pop, told us that every time they were sure we'd been hit. But we weren't."

"Well, that was a real adventure," Dave said. He directed the words right at Lena. "I don't know that it says anything particular about Randy and life getting better for her, frankly speaking."

"Randy had been at a church meeting the night before, and she came back so upset I made her promise never to go into a church again. She was crying about how awful she was and that she knew God was angry, but she didn't know how to change. She was scared of hell."

The kitchen was quiet. Randy was watching the ice cubes in her glass swirl around in the bottom, her face thoughtful. Dave leaned back on two legs of his chair, staring at Lena, waiting for her to make a connection of some sort.

"And after that night she wasn't scared anymore. She'd beaten it," said Lena. She leaned back in her chair, too, spreading her long fingers on the tabletop. The rings looked large in the light that hung over the kitchen table.

"So that means?" Dave put up a palm, as a question.

"It means that she has the power to beat the lies. She outran the judgment. She conquered her fear. She laughed in God's face."

"Did you do all that, babe?" Dave looked playfully at Randy. She smiled a little and shrugged.

"Maybe so. It was pretty important at the time, anyway."

"It's still important," said Lena with an ultracalm voice. "Because it happened."

Suddenly the locusts began their piercing song out in the backyard. *Reee-oh, reee-oh.*

"Well, here's food." Dave waved at the chicken and squash in front of them. "Sorry about the butter," he said, turning slightly to Lena. "It's the way I like it."

"I'm glad you're sharing it with me, Dave."

Her use of his name made something in his mouth go bitter.

After supper, Dave left Randy and Lena at the table while he checked out the television lineup. Dissatisfied after surfing through all the channels two or three times, he left the volume on low and went to the bedroom to stretch out with a magazine and a smoke. He saw Mr. Kelsey across the street, examining his lawn. The old guy had declared war on crabgrass about twenty-five years ago. That and dandelions.

But he seemed pretty content. Dave thought about his own dad, who had shot the breeze with Kelsey a couple times a week. Dave made a point to at least say hi now and then. He'd helped Kelsey set out some trees last year, something his dad would have done.

The girls' voices rose for a few seconds. They were in the kitchen still, drinking wine, too far away for Dave to make out their conversation. Dave thought about how much he didn't know about Randy, how Lena's being here might bring up more things he didn't know. In some ways, Randy didn't seem to fit Lena at all, but what did he know?

A few hours later, he woke up when Randy crawled into bed beside him. She let out a long, contented sigh, then leaned over to brush his face with a kiss. In a moment her breathing was deep and regular.

He thought about how complete he felt when Randy was in his house. How happy she seemed to be from one moment to the next, but how sad she was overall. He would lay down his life to take that sadness away. In his half-awake state, this one thought rang clear and strong in his mind. He would lay down his life.

He heard sounds from the bathroom and saw light around the edge of the closed door. Someone was using the john, then the sink. He guessed that Randy had invited Lena to sleep on the couch. After a few minutes Dave heard the light click off and saw Lena's form move out of the bathroom, pause and look toward him and Randy in bed, and then flow into the living room, that long hair following her. He heard her settle into the couch and the sounds of the television cease.

When he walked out at six in the morning to water his garden, he found Tony leaning against a plum tree.

"Hey," Dave said.

Tony waved, not bothering to look up. He was staring at the garden.

"How long you been out here?"

Tony shrugged. "I don't sleep much. Been up since four. Thought you might be out here." This last sentence had a sad note to it. Tony's face was void of emotion. He could be talking in his sleep, for all Dave knew.

"Want a cup of coffee?" Dave asked.

The kid shook his head. "Is Randy here?"

"She's still asleep."

"You've got it made. With her I mean."

Dave kept his smile in check. "Did you and Randy ever date?"

"No. She's two years ahead of me."

"She can't be—she just got out of school."

"I was held back a year—fifth grade. I never went after older babes."

"You know the guy she used to date?—Jay?"

"Yeah. Kind of a burned-out guy. Doesn't seem like her type."

Dave looked at the half-closed eyes and slack face. Suddenly the eyes opened and focused, and Tony muttered and moved his legs to get up. He was looking toward the street. A station wagon idled there, and Tony's dad, Jake Gardino, was leaning out the window, shielding his face from the sun and looking toward them.

"Where have you been?" The man's deep voice felt disturbing on the morning air.

"Just stopping by to see Dave, my boss."

"Dave." The man nodded, then turned his attention back to Tony. "Tell me next time. Are you working now?"

Tony looked at Dave.

"Uh," Dave said to Jake, "he's supposed to go by Mamie Rupert's in a while. Seven-thirty'll be early enough though."

Jake turned to his son. "Get in the car. Your mother needs some help."

Tony didn't say anything to Dave. He just walked to the car and got in.

"Who was that?" Randy said softly from the kitchen door behind him.

"Tony's dad. Guy's a little uptight."

"They freaked out when Tony got caught at school with pills and pot in his locker. I don't think they let him out of the house unless it's to work for you."

"Are you serious?"

She nodded. She was wearing one of his T-shirts, her slim legs bare and sexy. He tried to touch her through the screen. "How'd you sleep?"

"Great. I'm making toast and eggs for Lena and me. You want some?"

Lena's name set him back. He'd almost forgotten she was here. "No. I had cereal already."

Randy smiled and pressed her lips to the screen. He touched them through it with his own. "In fact," he said, "I need to go a little earlier this morning. I'll see you this evening?"

"Sure. I should be here."

Dave looked hard at the scenery as he drove to work that morning. When he was a kid, he'd helped farmers work half these fields. One summer, Ed Hemmings's son had gone to Scotland as a foreign exchange student, and Dave, then just sixteen, had helped Ed most of the growing season and into the harvest. Going to Scotland had seemed like a thing only a chosen few would ever do. Yet when Sammie Hemmings returned, he told his Scotland stories for about a month and then finished school and got a job like everybody else. He lived with his wife and three kids out on Route 3. Dave often drove by and wondered how Bender Springs felt to Sammie since the Scotland thing. If maybe he looked at his wife and remembered some Scottish girl. Or if he looked at the soybean field at his back door and thought of Scottish countryside. It must have left a mark somewhere.

Right now, the soybeans were sick-looking, and the corn had hardly grown at all. A few miles over, the Rameys' place, mostly wheat and milo, was struggling. The lack of early rain had done a lot of damage to the winter wheat, and hadn't given the spring plantings anything to grow on. Dave slid by in his truck and saw yellow and brown everywhere. Even the few cattle, hanging around man-made ponds here and there, looked tired of it all.

He breathed in the smell of hot summer and crisp, dusty vegetation. Maybe this would be the best time to go somewhere else. Maybe if he got established farther north, closer to more civilization, Randy would want to come too, eventually.

Mark, the foreman, was early too, and they had fresh coffee in the office before the rest of the crew came in to load up the equipment and head down to the day's stretch of work.

"You still interested in working closer to the city?" Mark said suddenly. He was fifty, dark and leathery from too many summers bared down to the waist on road crews. His teenage daughter was in and out of the hospital with complications from a wreck she'd been in two years ago. Six surgeries so far. Mark's wife often came out and brought him lunch. She was good-looking but tired and teary sometimes. Mark looked tired all the time. He didn't put up with anything but hard work, but the guy was fair, and he actually remembered to think about other people.

"Yeah. Heard anything?"

"Johnson County may be hiring. Matt Hernandez oversees up there—good fella. I'll give you his number if you're interested."

"Yeah—thanks a lot."

Mark shrugged. "Anytime. Hate to lose you, but if you're wanting to move, now's the time. Later on you might not be free to do it."

"That's what I figure," Dave said. "Not much holding me here now." He thought of Randy but kept talking. "Mom's in Kansas City and won't go anywhere else. Dad's gone, and there's not much left of the place."

As if they'd been let off a bus, four other crew members walked in the door. They all punched their time cards and headed out to the trucks.

I'm telling you, Randy, the earth holds all the positive energy necessary for us to succeed, to be healthy. It's so natural." Dave heard Lena's unmistakable voice coming from the living room when he walked in the door at six. He entered the room and saw Lena and Randy crouched near the battered coffee table, books in front of them. Lena held a clear rock in her hand. From all the way across the room, Dave could see that Randy was not too impressed. This made him happy right away.

Randy was looking at the open book, what appeared to be a catalog of rocks. The three of them exchanged quick greetings. Randy grinned at Dave but didn't move from her spot. Lena didn't even look at him.

"I know they're called crystals," Randy said to Lena, "but my folks used to polish rocks like this and make jewelry sets out of them. They made loads of money at Silver Dollar City. These are *rocks*."

"Exactly. They're the earth. Creation. How in touch are you really with the earth?"

"We've got a garden out back that needs hoed," Dave offered. Lena hardly glanced at him. He got a beer from the fridge and sat down contentedly in the recliner across from them.

"You selling crystals?" Dave asked.

"Sometimes. Mainly, I want to buy a special one for Randy. You need all the help you can get in this town."

"I'm fine!" Randy waved her arms a little, making it seem to Dave that this friendly argument had been going on awhile before he arrived.

"But what if things change, and they aren't fine?"

"I'll adjust—like I have my entire sorry life." Randy propped an arm on the coffee table and made a kiss in Dave's direction.

Lena drew up and leaned very close to Randy. Dave could tell Randy was trying not to get a fit of giggles. But her expression changed slowly as Lena spoke.

"There's so much more to life than adjusting to the bad things that happen. There's such a thing as empowerment—taking some control over your life, and most people never learn that."

"Control only goes so far, the way I see it." Dave said this and took a sip of beer. The room was warm, not the slightest breeze coming in the windows. He noticed beads of sweat on the backs of Lena's perfect arms. "A drunk plows into me at four in the morning, my control over my own car means zero. A lot of things like that in this life."

"But we can set ourselves up differently so that we aren't always just reacting. This happens, so then I have to do this. That happens, and I adjust."

"Oh, excuse me. Shame my wife didn't know how to take more control over her leukemia. All those months of reacting just wasted." Dave knew he'd hit a mark when Randy gave him a reprimanding look. Lena chose the moment to shift positions, leaning against the couch now, her face visible to Dave. Her expression of calm and knowing had not changed but seemed more set than ever.

"See," Dave said, "all your religious philosophy—"

"I'm not religious," Lena broke in quietly.

"All your rock philosophy doesn't change the fact that bad things happen to people who do everything right, and good things happen to slobs who'll never deserve it."

"It never hurts to try something that may give you a new edge, don't you think?" Lena's green eyes were cool, and they rested on Dave with total confidence.

"It doesn't hurt. But don't make promises with your rock collection that you can't keep."

Lena didn't leave right away. They had bowls of butter pecan ice cream and talked about people around town. Randy had a story or two to tell from her hours with the regulars down at the Family Cupboard. Dave listened to today's tale without hearing much. He was wondering what Lena was afraid would derail Randy's life. Probably him.

"I'll see you tomorrow maybe, Randy," said Lena as she stood at the back door and put her hand on the knob.

"You be in town long?" Dave asked.

"All summer. At my gramma's. A break from Denver. Too many rich people." She smiled slightly and walked out the door. She turned orange immediately as patches of late light caught her. Her hair was tied up in a fashionable yet casual knot. Dave was sure she must model somewhere.

"She's actually related to somebody around here?" Dave asked Randy, after they'd kissed passionately for the first time since he'd come home.

"Her grandma's Alma Petersen. Her folks have split up. Her dad's got a girlfriend, and they're traveling in Alaska this summer. Lena doesn't get along with her mom at all. She'll be starting college in the fall, but her dad didn't want her living alone in Denver while he was gone. I think she had a boyfriend or something. I don't know." Randy took a breath, and her eyebrows bobbed up. "She's really bummed to have to be here. She never really fit in, even when she lived here."

"I wonder why."

"She always had to be different, but she's one of those friend-for-a-lifetime kinds of people."

Dave wanted to ask if Lena had said anything about him or about Randy's hanging out with him. But Randy had that look on her face that said she was changing gears already. The girl flew from one conversation to another like a bird with too many feeders to choose from.

Randy didn't stay the night. She didn't come over the next day, either. At least she called to tell Dave that she and Lena were going to Helmsly to see a show and do some shopping. She didn't know when she'd get back but had to help her mom with something that evening. Dave listened to all this and answered "OK" with a steady, no-problem voice, but his alarms were already blasting. He was feeling more and more like her present diversion. She would never stay with him. Having her here was just a stupid dream of his. Dave sat in front of a mindless cop movie and drank more beer than usual. He tried not to let his heart hurt over the inevitable. The way he felt now reminded him of the deadly ache that had hit him when he knew for sure Karen wouldn't make it. By bedtime, he'd decided he should break off the relationship before Randy had the chance. He couldn't go through this again.

He went to bed to the sounds of Mr. Kelsey across the street hacking and spitting near his garage. The cough sounded as if it had been around for a couple of decades. The old-man noises made Dave feel lonely, partly because they reminded him of Dad, but mostly because he felt old himself.

In the dark, he missed Randy. At ten o'clock he got out of bed, dressed, and walked in the warm, dark air down to Perky's. It would help to play a few games of pool. There were always two or three women hanging out at the bar, wearing too much makeup and trying to be angry and witty at the same time and cussing like men. They would be sure to put him out of the mood for sex. And he'd go home too tired to think.

14

MAMIE RUPERT:
THE CONVERSION

Wednesday, July 9

These days, Mamie couldn't find much comfort anywhere. The heat put everybody in a foul mood. Ruthie had a sick headache two card days in a row, and Liz was having car trouble. Alma's granddaughter from Denver had arrived for the summer, and so Alma was preoccupied. Mamie couldn't even find satisfaction in her little vegetable patch, because the weather wouldn't let it bloom into the tomatoes and peppers she depended on.

Mamie hadn't put out much garden for a number of years, but she counted on a few neighbors for staples: corn for the freezer, zucchini for breads and casseroles, and enough green beans to get her through the winter. As Frank Zorelli down the street began his dark predictions of a hot, dry summer; and as Ethel Hampton, usually full of updates on her various backyard crops, talked more and more of grandchildren, Mamie began to be agitated by feelings of insecurity.

She stood at the edge of a flower bed this morning and let dew soak into her canvas shoes. Never mind that it made her feet itch. Her tomato plants looked as though they needed to be put out of their misery, little hard knobs of green peeping through the ragged leaves. Those knobs should be large and red by now, at least some of them. Mamie wondered if the soap in the dishwater had stunted their growth. The town was under ordinance now—no watering of yards or gardens and no washing cars. The reservoir at Helmsly was lower than it had been in twenty years. Mamie figured that, in the larger scheme of things, she shouldn't be so concerned about a few tomato plants, but then it seemed easier to worry about them than about the entire area drying up. She noticed a fuzzy tomato worm of the same half-done green color as the tiny tomatoes, wiggling along a stem. Mamie bent over and picked it up with two fingers, regarded it with age-old disdain, and dropped it on the ground. The sole of her shoe was worn so thin that she could feel the worm squash under her foot. She would have to ask Arthur Gardino if he wouldn't mind picking up some plant dust for her. Maybe he had some extra he would give her; she knew for a fact that his several small outbuildings were bursting with garden paraphernalia. The boy, Tony, who was stopping by on Tuesdays now, could bring some over. Nothing rankled her more (besides unrestrained dogs) than her horticultural efforts coming to naught because of some spiky old worm.

With some delicacy Mamie stepped in odd patterns through her yard, examining this rosebush and that patch of mint. At certain spots she pulled up short and bent at the waist, as if leaning over an imaginary fence, her face wrinkled in horror at the dried-out lumps of dung that now seemed to be multiplying all over her property. She had the Gardino boy clean up every Tuesday morning, but that didn't seem to help much. Mamie tried her best to go on and make her next plant inspection, to tilt her head back and notice the family of robins in the maple and enjoy the silky cool of morning on her face, but each dung stop left her more distracted. By the time she climbed her back steps into the enclosed porch, she was groping wildly for her cane, which she left indoors in the mornings, when she felt more young and agile. Now she just felt breathless.

She ate breakfast stationed at the window, her usual spot now, allowing her eyes to scan the backyard while she made some effort to read the paper and choke down toast and margarine. The IGA's apples were mealy this month; she'd have to remember to catch a ride with Alma to Helmsly soon and grocery shop there for a change. She'd forgotten to thaw out the frozen orange juice overnight. So it was just toast this morning. After twenty minutes Mamie rumpled the front page in disgust. Where was That Dog?

She was beginning to hatch a plan. If she lured the dog to the back door with scraps of food, maybe she could lock it on her porch, and when Old Man Simpson came hunting around for the dog, she'd finally get to say her piece. She looked at a crust of toast still on her plate. In a rush of inspiration she crossed to the bread box and took out the heel. She tore it into pieces and put it with the crust on a chipped plastic plate. Over the bread she spooned some bacon grease from the can she kept on the stove. Then she sat at the window again.

Such a shame to have to spend her time like this, waiting for a mangy dog to make his appearance. She had other things to do. She had to find somebody to paint her house, for one thing. Ax Miracle had told her he didn't take her money. He'd walked over himself the day after Mamie had talked to Iris, said he'd never taken anything from her house besides a glass or two of lemonade, which she'd offered to him. Mamie had tried to believe him, but the money never showed up, and she just hadn't felt the same about Ax after that. Even if he were innocent, she didn't feel as secure, and she'd apologized to him for being sensitive that way but had dismissed him from any more work at her place. The entire experience had left her feeling bad, just one more thing to add to the summer's troubles.

The sun began to come in, raising the humidity in the small house. Time to close the east windows and put on a fan. Mamie wished morning lasted all day; it felt so new and gentle and quiet.

When she rolled out the electric fan on its stand to the far side of the living room, one side of the stand came loose and slipped with a screech out of its bracket. A butterfly bolt skipped across the tan carpet. Mamie squatted and reached with all her might, then finally lowered one arthritic knee to the floor to retrieve the bolt while holding up the loose side of the fan. Of course the bolt was stubborn, and sweat popped out all over her while she forced the bolt to do what it was supposed to. At the end of ten minutes, Mamie sat on the floor in a heap, the fan looming above her. Someone knocked at the front door.

"Just a minute," she called, scooting over to the sofa. She used it to hoist herself up off the floor. "I'm coming."

It was a young man—so young—and clean shaven. Even through the screen Mamie could see the brightness of his eyes and smell faint, agreeable wafts of soap and aftershave. Mamie had always had a keen nose, and she liked what she smelled now. Perfumed things had a different quality to them when they were on a man.

Mamie's pleased response to this visitor was stopped short. *Oh no, a salesman. They get around earlier in the morning these days.* She didn't unhook the screen. She stood on one side, he on the other, and let the silence get good and awkward. She knew how to handle these people.

"Good morning, ma'am," said the young man. What a sweet, deep voice. Mamie hardened her resolve not to buy a single thing.

"Good morning," she croaked, and cleared her throat. Another silent moment while she stared at him through the door.

"My name is Joe Travis, and I'm visiting around town to tell people about the revival that starts next Friday evening. You may already know about it, since your church is involved. Could I have just a few moments of your time?"

My church? I'm on the roll up at the Baptist. "Oh." She unlatched the door, and the young man smiled and waited patiently for her to let him in.

"Come into the living room," said Mamie, and she led the way, trying to be inconspicuous as she jerked her hemline a bit straighter. "You've caught me in a mess. Been outside working with my flowers."

"Why, that's quite all right. My mother has American Beauty roses too."

"She does?" Mamie glanced back at him and straightened a doily on the small table near the doorway as they walked into the living room. "You know, my husband Charles planted that bush on our twenty-fifth wedding anniversary. He died seven years ago."

"It's nice to have those reminders of him now, I'll bet."

"It certainly is. You're with the church? Sit down there." Mamie pointed to the sofa. She lowered herself into her chair and got situated to where she could look at him directly without crooking her neck.

"Yes. I'm a student at Midwestern Seminary. A couple of us have come down to help out for the revival meetings. Maybe you've heard about them—the Baptists, Methodists, and Presbyterians are doing joint meetings."

"I have heard something about it, yes. You're the first to come visit, though. The old pastor at the Baptist—that's where I'm a member—the pastor before this one, he used to visit regular, especially after Charles passed away. It was a real comfort."

"How long have you been a member, Mrs. Rupert?"

"Oh, about thirty years, I expect."

"Have you been to many services lately?"

"Well, not much anymore. Just got out of the habit. And my arthritis makes it hard to get around, you know. It's a long walk to the church from here."

"It must be difficult. Maybe someone could give you a ride. I'm sure we could find someone to come get you for one of the special services. Would you like me to line up a ride for you?"

His eyes were so honest and clear, Mamie found herself considering a special service a fine idea.

"That might be nice. I don't want anyone to go to trouble over me, though. I don't like depending on other people."

"I'm sure it won't be any trouble," said Joe. "We've organized rides for a number of people. Mrs. Gardino down the street might offer you some transportation."

Mamie tried to continue looking pleasant, despite her mental picture of Arthur's daughter-in-law, the only real Baptist in that family. The woman walked around so pursed up the religion leaked out of its own volition.

"Oh, I'd forgotten about her—" Mamie couldn't help that her voice landed with an awkward thud on *her*. "I've known the Gardinos for years."

"Mrs. Rupert, you just said that you don't like to depend on other people. I'll bet you've had to learn to depend on the Lord a lot since your husband died."

"I certainly have." Mamie nodded her head gravely. "I just couldn't have gotten through it without the Lord."

"Would you mind telling me a little about it? I love to hear what God has done in someone else's life. It's such an encouragement to me." The young man leaned close, expectantly.

"Well." Mamie snapped her mouth shut for a moment while she thought. She had to tell her story now. What was her story?

She ended up telling about Charles's heart problems and all the months she took care of him here at home, and the last stay in the hospital, and how lovely a funeral service the old pastor had preached. She told the young man how many people had come—more than she'd seen at any funeral in that town before or since.

And then, the young man looked so interested that she told about her experience after Charles's death. The dream she'd had about him standing at the foot of her bed, smiling, whole and healthy, letting her know he was better now. When she'd awakened the next day, she knew it had been more than a dream. It had all the feelings of a true memory.

"I felt so safe after that," she said. "Like he came to visit from time to time, just to see how I was doing. It was God's way of telling me Charles had made it to heaven."

The young seminarian smiled kindly. "Mamie, it's wonderful to know that Charles is in heaven now, waiting for you. Do you think that if you were to die at this moment you'd make it to heaven too?"

Mamie straightened her back. "Well, I've always been a good Christian, better than a lot of people who go to church regularly."

"But you know that the Bible tells us being good isn't enough. We need a personal relationship with God through faith in Christ. I'm sure you know all this, as long as you've belonged to the church."

"I do. I know that." Mamie couldn't breathe too well; she had that cornered feeling all of a sudden. Alice Gardino had shot a question like this at her several years ago, the one time the woman had ever come to Mamie's house. The whole visit had left a bad taste.

"Can you remember when you first trusted the Lord to save you?" asked Joe Travis.

"It's been so long ago—in a revival when I was a girl." Mamie leaned toward the young man, the memory perking her up. "My daddy and little brother and I would walk two miles down the road to the little one-room schoolhouse, every Sunday morning—two miles, mind you. The three of us would get there for Sunday school, while Mama got dinner going. She'd join us for church an hour or so later. Now, we were committed Christian people, my family."

"Mrs. Rupert," Joe broke in. "What's your relationship to God like now? Are you ready to see Jesus?"

"Oh, I am, I really am. I've been ready to see him since Charles passed away." Her voice trembled.

"But are you free from sin, able to stand before God, confident that you're saved?"

"I pray nearly every day." Mamie felt tears beginning to burn behind her eyes, making her nose tickle.

"Is there any unconfessed sin in your life, anything that might be standing between you and the Lord?" Joe said this very gently, and Mamie felt a single warm tear leak out of her left eye.

"Well, I—I'm not sure, but I've been wondering about something for a while. Maybe you can help me understand."

"What's that, Mrs. Rupert?"

"I've been having these terrible dreams lately. They're about my sister Cassie. She died eleven months before Charles did."

"What about the dreams?"

"Why, it's just so awful." Mamie took a quivering breath. She reached into her dress pocket for a tissue and dabbed the moisture from her eyes. "In these dreams, I kill her. I kill her in these awful ways, like I try to pop off her head with a broomstick, or I sit on top of her in bed and mash a pillow into her face. And always after she's dead, I feel sorry and try to fix her back. I do have repentance, Mr. Travis; I'm real sorry, but she won't come back to life. I'm afraid—" She paused to take a breath and blow her nose again. "I'm afraid I did something to Cassie that she's never forgiven me for, and now it's too late. I really loved my sister, although we had our disagreements." She dabbed at her eyes then and picked up the *TV Guide,* letting pages flutter down from her thumb. One young star—from one of those new sitcoms—had developed serious smudges on his face, a water ring slashing through his right eye.

"Mamie, the Lord understands why you're having these dreams, and he knows that you can't talk to Cassie now and make things right. But you can confess anything to him, and he'll forgive and heal you of these bad feelings."

The seminarian waited while Mamie flipped to the end of the magazine, her eyes stuck on the fleeting glossy images. She could feel the young man watching her, and pressure mounting. Finally she put the *TV Guide* back on the end table. She straightened in the chair and said, "If you think I need to pray, then I can do that. I mean—I do pray all the time, but maybe I'm not doing it right. I think if I were saying the right things, I'd stop having these terrible dreams."

Joe Travis went into action. His Bible—in a zippered leather cover— was out and spread open across his hand. He leaned as close to Mamie as he could. He cleared his throat. The Bible came open in the Book of Romans. From there he read several verses, explaining each of the vital points: every person has sinned; we deserve to die for our sin; God sent Jesus to die on our behalf; we have to accept this gift consciously, purposefully; we need to pray, asking God's forgiveness for our sin and thanking him for the gift of eternal life through Jesus Christ.

Mamie felt her mind begin to wander. She'd heard all this before and wondered what she'd done to indicate that she no longer believed or practiced it. Joe stressed once or twice that Mamie had to accept the Lord's salvation for it to take effect. At that point she felt something inside her give, sort of like pent-up gas, but she recognized it as the dark emotion of guilt. Maybe she'd been fighting the Lord on this. Maybe she hadn't been sorry enough about the hard things that had passed between her and Cassie. Or even between her and those Miracles. Now seemed a good time to take care of it. Mamie clasped her hands together, stared at the open Bible on the lap across from her, and said in a rather timid way, "Could we pray now?"

A wonderful smile moved across Joe Travis's face, growing so large that it seemed to reach out and touch Mamie. He reached over a strong, young hand and squeezed Mamie's arm. "Of course we can pray now. Would you like me to start?"

Mamie nodded. They inched a bit closer to one another in the intimate posture of prayer, heads bowed and eyes shut tight against the room around them.

"Father God, I thank you for Mamie—for her steadfastness through the years, and for her searching heart now. . . ."

Mamie tried to hear him and think about each phrase, as though she might get quizzed later. These church people made her feel a little off balance no matter how kind they were. She tried her best to follow the logic of what the seminarian was praying, about her sin and about God's forgiveness, about Jesus on the cross, a figure she had known well since earliest childhood. Strung together in a prayer like this, they all seemed rather artificial, as if they were being rushed along in some logic she wasn't quite used to.

A strangely familiar sound brushed her ear just then. A rhythmic, outdoor, antagonizing sound came from the open window behind them. A panting—a wet, slurpy panting. Mamie cracked open her left eye, her face turned slightly to the window. She saw the shaggy form, and it shattered her senses. That Dog was just yards away from where she sat. It was near her front walk, and of all things, he was on a leash. On the other end of the leash was Bill Simpson, being dragged so mercilessly that his arm seemed about to dislodge itself from his suspendered shoulder. There they were, the two of them, owner and culprit. And culprit had lifted its leg and was dousing her American Beauty with a yellow stream.

Mamie felt her eye freeze open and her heart palpitate. A cry rose in her throat and stuck there politely, for the seminarian was in earnest soliloquy.

"So I ask you, Lord, to hear Mamie's prayer now, to give her heart peace and her mind understanding of your wonderful gift of grace."

Joe Travis stopped praying. Mamie opened the other eye to see if the prayer was over, but the young man sat inches from her, an expression of patience and peace rooted into his features. His eyes remained closed.

Was she supposed to pray now? What were those five spiritual steps? From her peripheral vision she could sense that the dog had moved on to the next flower bed. The old man mumbled under his breath, "Slow down, dang it." Mamie could see the perturbed look half-hidden under the straw brim of Simpson's hat. Someone must have complained enough at least to prompt Gideon to lay down the law. That leash couldn't have looked more unnatural with Simpson if it had been a hula hoop.

"Would you like to repeat after me, Mamie? Would that make you feel more comfortable?" The blue seminarian eyes came awake and searched Mamie's face just as she tore her eyes from the sight of full-blown desecration out in the peony bed.

"Well, yes, I suppose that would be fine." Mamie's fingers felt like ice in her palm as she tried to maintain the posture for prayer. She bowed again, about the time the leash rattled again, signaling yet another stop near the northwest corner of her yard.

"Jesus, I admit that I'm a sinner." The seminarian waited to be repeated after. Mamie took a labored breath and repeated the phrase, quickly, hoping he would make this a fast, down-to-business prayer.

"And I'm sorry for my sins."

Another rattle of the chain outside. *Dear Lord, they're in my mint patch! I've been putting those leaves in my iced tea.* "And I'm sorry for my sins," came her tremulous reply.

"I understand that Jesus paid the penalty for my sin."

Mamie shot the phrase back at him, her voice low to mask the fury that was rising. If she could only rap on the window—was it completely out of line to interrupt a prayer?

"And I accept that you have forgiven me through his shed blood."

"And I accept . . ." *Old man, I'm going to have that Gideon on your front step waiting for you when you get home!* Mamie's voice prayed automatically, while the rest of her felt each step That dog made, imagined the damage being done while they sat so quietly there in prayer.

"Thank you, Lord, for saving me and making me your child."

"Thank you, Lord, for saving me and making me your child."

The rattling outside grew faint. Mamie squeezed an eye open and could see the pair moving east, nearly to the corner. That Dog trotted as though he had been freed of a great burden, his master puffing and stumbling behind him.

"Amen." Those young blue eyes came up to grab Mamie's, and he grasped her hands. "Well, Mamie, the decision you've made today has given you an eternal place with the Lord."

Mamie nodded and felt a gush of tears come into her eyes. They surprised her but didn't seem to concern Joe Travis. He only smiled broader as the river flowed higher and wider and poured out of its banks. Mamie sobbed for a minute or so. As the torrent was drying up, Joe took a small, glossy booklet from the jacket of his Bible. He handed it to her.

"This book has special devotions for every day for a month. I think it would be a good thing for you to go through it. It will remind you of God's promises."

Mamie looked at the book in the man's hand. The picture on the cover was of a deep blue pond in the middle of a deeper green meadow. There were white mountain peaks glistening in the background and shimmering clouds above with the silver words emblazoned: *God's Word for Today: A Bible Study for New Christians.*

"Okay," Mamie said quietly. They stood. Joe Travis zipped up his Bible and stepped toward the door. "I'll get in touch with you about a ride to church next week, all right?"

"That would be fine," said Mamie. She was feeling pretty tired. The young man slipped out the door and stepped lightly to the sidewalk that ran along the street. He waved to her before setting his face for the next house.

Mamie leaned against the doorjamb and looked up and down the street. By now she didn't expect to see That Dog. The frustrations of this life. Oh well, the cry had done her good. She checked the clock and saw that it was high time to give Alma a call and catch up on the last half of yesterday.

The study booklet was still in her hand. She gazed about the room for a safe place to keep it—such a pretty cover. When she finished with the book, she might frame the picture and hang it up. She stopped in front of the narrow china cupboard and carefully turned the small key that let the glass door sway open. She found that the booklet propped against Aunt Edith's bud vase quite nicely.

15

TONY GUARDINO: LENA

Friday, July 11

Tony tried to spit the grime out of his mouth. He was bent over a row of beets, and the dew on the plants made his legs itch. Probably he should have listened to Granddad and worn jeans.

Actually, Granddad had told him to try a pair of overalls, because loose clothing was cooler, but Tony had to maintain some sense of autonomy. It was bad enough that the old man had him out here every morning at the crack of dawn, puttering over the scrubby mounds of dirt. Under normal circumstances Tony would have smirked and retreated to his bedroom.

The understanding between them was unspoken and edged with desperation, if not a whacked-out version of compassion. Granddad hadn't said a word to anyone since they returned from Mass that day, but his gaze had traveled often across the dinner table or living room and held Tony in its clench. That first evening he had said to Tony, just as he was about to retreat to his room, "The door stays open." Tony left it open and slept in fits; twice he awoke to see Granddad's sleeping silhouette in a chair against the dim hall light.

Next morning, Granddad had jostled Tony out of bed. "It's time you went to work," he mumbled and handed Tony some clothes. Too sleepy and surprised to protest, Tony had done what he was told. He hoed until 10:30. Near lunchtime, he heard in the background faint mutterings from the kitchen: "What's Tony doing in the garden?" No one was sure. Was he under some kind of punishment? Granddad stated in a louder voice than he ever used that he needed help and Tony wasn't getting much yard work yet. Mom smiled approvingly and said some words of appreciation when she handed Tony a sandwich. Dad reminded him that he still had other responsibilities around the place. Annie asked if he was into organic things now. For once, Tony had no smart answer for her. He was still feeling worked over, the memory of cool metal quite acute. It was a relief to have Granddad explain.

So Tony had worked every morning, except Tuesdays, when Dave Seaton sent him to Mamie's to do whatever yard work she had for him. Tony had pulled a few weeds in her flower beds and taken an old lamp out to the junk pile for her. That was after he cleaned the dog dung out of her yard; she seemed really intense about that. Thursday Tony was supposed to work at Adam Jones's place, but the old guy went into the hospital the day before.

For the first few days after getting caught by Granddad, Tony had slept with the door ajar and had awoken a few times to that old-man shadow in his room, usually in a chair near the doorway. Granddad claimed that sometimes he slept better sitting up, and the breeze was better in Tony's room. The family accepted this, but Tony knew better. Once after a nightmare, he'd discovered Granddad sitting on the bed, a hard hand pressing on the sheet over Tony's arm while he said, "It's all right, son. Just a dream." Tony couldn't remember if he had cried during the dream or not. He was afraid that Granddad might hug him or something; the thought of it made him want to run. At the same time, Granddad's presence held him in place. Every morning out in the grit with the sun bearing down. Every night his room open to the world, his bad sleep on display. And then there was the Mass.

They attended every other morning, at the early service, when only a couple of devout farmers and some old people who couldn't sleep did their religious business. While practically everyone else in town slept, Tony and Granddad went to early prayers, Father Ricardo blessed Tony, and they paused at the mountain of flame-filled glasses at the back of the church. Some mornings Granddad stayed behind to talk with the priest—old acquaintance chat, since the farmers didn't linger, and one old lady stayed in her pew to pray a moment longer. Tony stood and let the candle scent fill his lungs and the dipping dancing lights sear his eyes.

Granddad never explained why Mass was so important all of a sudden. Tony hadn't known him to attend regularly for a long time. But there was no getting around it now. Tony figured it couldn't hurt to pacify the guy's need for religion, for feeling that he was doing something, maybe using his Catholic prayers to chase the suicide demons away. Granddad kept any of his intentions hidden, his concern at a comfortable distance. Tony himself felt little attachment to the words and the prayers, the order of the small book, the priest's motions. The only thing that made an odd kind of sense to him was the pyramid of light at the back of the room. Then there was the light from outdoors he watched turn to color as it came through the figures in the windows. It had occurred to him that all forms of light—sunlight, campfire, flame of candle, or the embers of a cigarette—came from one source. There was an energy there that made him feel that maybe he could catch the tail of a universal power. Fire made the sun burn, and fire could be held in the hand. Fire in the back of the church never went out. It came from the cosmos, through the hands of unimportant people making their wishes known to Something Out There. They called it God. Tony didn't know about that part of it, but he liked the flame. That he could keep matches at his disposal, carry them in his pockets, and store them in the dresser drawer gave him infinitely more comfort than all the words being flung around rooms and churches and streets. Words were just noise that got in the way. Flame didn't make a sound. And it smiled while it burned at you.

He liked the candles so much that he'd provided a few of them for himself. There were always some extra candles and glasses around the stand of lights. It had been easy enough to lift a couple every few trips. By night before last, Granddad, evidently sure that Tony wouldn't be making any middle-of-the-night trips to the shed, went to his own bedroom, and Tony was left once again with his fear of the dark and with the Feeling that was always at the edge of his life. He discovered that the candles helped.

After lunch Tony was allowed off the property. Granddad didn't need his help, and Dad seemed OK when Tony announced he was going over to Dave's. As much as Tony didn't like this yard job, it was convenient to have an adult in town that his father trusted him to be with. As far as Dad knew, Tony had been to Dave's several times lately. Tony had actually been over there only twice. Now he walked down the street in that direction and didn't veer to the north until he was out of sight of his house. He cut through Alma Petersen's yard and to Mr. Timms's back lot. There were a couple of trash barrels and an old mower leaning against a shed. Between the shed and the alley was a large pear tree. A tree old enough that the branches were large and some of the thinner ones drooped toward the ground. Tony crawled under the tree and smoked some weed. Then he just leaned against the trunk and shut his eyes.

He'd discovered some time ago that there was something good about lying underneath a tree. If he lay still long enough, flat on the grass, with leaves directly above him, he could feel vibrations in the ground. Maybe the earth was breathing. Or maybe it was just all the activity of living things under the surface: seeds germinating and roots reaching down and small animals burrowing and insects of all sorts going through the motions of their lives in whole, tiny universes, just a foot or so below him. Sometimes he thought he could feel the earth revolving, sort of like when he used to spin around and around when he was little, spin around and around until he fell down, and then he could feel the earth spin as he sat there in the grass. He would reach out and touch clover flowers, and they were moving too. Now he didn't spin around, but the earth spun for him anyway, softly and so gradually that he couldn't feel it unless he held his breath and stayed very still for a while.

For the same kind of reason he liked to walk in the fields in back of the high school. They were just vacant lots, overgrown with long grasses. The railroad tracks ran through a quarter of a mile away. Several times a day, Tony could hear the freight trains chugging. Since the fields weren't farmed or grazed, the grasses grew wild, and on most days, when the wind was blowing, the fields themselves seemed to move. Tony would stand in the middle of them and feel the ground lift and shimmer around him.

This tree of Mr. Timms was a particularly friendly feeling tree. It was out of sight of nosy people on the lookout for a dopehead enjoying a smoke. Mr. Timms didn't venture farther than the chair on his front porch, so his backyard was out of range. The tree's branches hung close to the ground. Mr. Timms's garage hid it from the house, and a hedge shielded it from the alley. No one ever walked through there. Out to one side of the tree and shed was a large, bare yard that ran into the side street just down the yard's gradual slope. Tony could lie under the tree, safe under its branches, close his eyes and stay cool in the shade—while the ground underneath him hummed.

The day was so hot already that it buzzed, but the shade over him made it seem not so bad. When he first got under the branches, his heart was speeding, and the Feeling was breathing close by. The pot helped. It also helped for Tony to stare hard at the white sky behind the leaves. Finally he closed his eyes completely, lay down, and placed palms down on the ground at his sides. He took three deep breaths. It freaked him out to be afraid of things in broad daylight.

He had the sense, suddenly, that something was blocking his skyward view. He opened one eye and saw a girl's face above him. Very green eyes. She was bending over him, and her long hair waved like a curtain. Black hair. Green eyes and black hair.

"Are you meditating?" the girl asked. She didn't budge when Tony raised up to an elbow.

"No."

"Were you sleeping?"

"No." Tony stared at her. She stared back.

She straightened and slung her weight back on one hip, folding her arms. "So you, like, just like the ground?"

"I like this tree." Tony sat all the way up and draped both arms over his knees.

"You like the tree." Her eyes told him absolutely nothing. "Are you a pantheist?"

"A what?"

"A pantheist—a person who thinks God is in everything—trees, rocks, you know."

"I'm not into God, and I don't care where he is."

"How do you know God's a he? Maybe she's in this tree right now, and that's why you're drawn to it."

Tony laughed. Who'd directed this loony-tune to his spot? "He or she—I don't care. I just like hanging out here, OK?"

"Mind if I sit down?"

Tony shrugged, and she sat down across from him.

"I'm Lena."

"I'm Tony."

She regarded him for a while without saying anything. She tugged at the brown grass by her foot. "Do you spend a lot of time on the ground, around trees? Is this a hobby?"

"No."

"I think maybe you have a spiritual connection to this place."

"I already told you I'm not into that."

"Spiritual doesn't have to have anything to do with God, Tony." She tilted her head and gazed at his face. He scratched his arm uncomfortably. Suddenly Lena reached over and grasped his arm, and he looked up. She was smiling.

"I didn't mean to bother you. But it's kind of interesting, finding a guy under a tree. I'm stuck here for the summer and expected to die from boredom the first week. But here you were, and I couldn't help myself." She squeezed his arm, and her green eyes glittered.

Tony took in a sudden breath of realization. "Oh—are you Mrs. Petersen's granddaughter?"

Lena nodded.

"You used to live here, right?"

"Yeah, moved away a few years ago."

"I heard something about you being here. Didn't make the connection right away."

Now he took some time noticing what she looked like. Smooth brown skin. Crazy green eyes. Nice body, and plenty of it in the right places. She wore pink sandals, and her toenails were painted silver. Tony couldn't remember her looking like this before. He didn't really remember much about her being in school; he thought she was probably ahead of him by a couple grades. She was smiling at him now, like she was still waiting for him to recognize her and couldn't wait until he did.

"You're here for the summer, huh? Lucky you."

"Neither parent had room for me in their wicked hearts this summer."

"Bummer. Who needs parents if they're going to act like that?"

"That's how I look at it."

Those green eyes were making Tony's heart speed up again, only this time it felt pleasant.

"I'm staying over there." Lena pointed in the direction of Mrs. Petersen's place.

"Yeah, I know where it is."

"Good." Suddenly she stood up, keeping her neck and shoulders bent just under a low hanging branch.

"You don't need to leave."

"Enjoy your tree. I hope you find what you're looking for."

"Hey—" Tony raised a hand, hoping to keep her there with him a few more minutes.

"I'll see you again." She said it with the tone of authority, but it only intrigued Tony more. She turned and walked down the alley, not looking back at him. Her hips hardly swayed—she was thin like a boy in that way—but a sexiness filled the space around her.

The encounter left Tony shaken. He hadn't felt anything positive racing through his body in a long time. All of a sudden, life was stimulating in a good kind of way. Already he was looking forward to being in this spot the same time tomorrow. And tomorrow was a subject he'd kept out of mind as much as possible for the past several months.

He enjoyed a while longer the ground breathing underneath him and the leaves moving slightly, like pieces of crepe paper above him. Then he walked to Dave's, replaying his and Lena's conversation. No one was at Dave's place. As Tony left the yard, he imagined Lena's face watching him out a back bedroom window. He actually thought he saw her as the curtain slipped back over the opening. He shook his head at his own craziness. But his heart was crashing around as though something—or someone—had jolted it awake at last.

Tony walked in the door at home and was met by his sister. There was fire in her eyes, as usual, but also an energy about her that was not the norm. She put herself in his path as though Tony were an ogre kidnapping the village's children and she were Xena.

"Tony, I've got to ask you something."

"What?" He didn't bother to cover his irritation. They had been irritated at one another for at least three years.

"Come with me." Tony reluctantly followed her up the stairs. She stopped in front of his bedroom door. "Let's go in."

"Nobody goes in my room but me." Tony slouched against the hallway wall.

"This is important. You have to let me in."

He gave her his most deadening look, but she stood ten inches from him, working her chewing gum, hands on her jeans-covered hips and skinny arms looking dangerous at the elbows.

Tony let out a breath of disgust and opened the door, allowing her to go in first.

"I want you to explain this." She said it as she crossed behind him to shut the door and give them privacy.

"Explain what?"

"All of this." Annie's hands indicated the small collection of candles that marched in front of his CD player. "What is it?"

Tony didn't answer right away. Annie popped her gum, appearing to have all day to wait.

"Well, Annie, they look a lot like candles. What do *you* think they are?" He folded his arms.

"You've never had candles before. And now they're all over the place. There's some more on your dresser over there."

"I know. I put them there."

"What do you do with them?"

"Sometimes I just let them sit there. And sometimes I light them. And then sometimes I get really creative and blow them out."

Annie seemed to suck in enough air for a major speech, but all that
came out was, "Are you a satanist?"

Tony laughed. "What?"

"Just tell me, so I'll know."

Tony kept laughing and sat on the wad of sheets and dirty clothes
that covered his bed. "No. You need help. You and Christy consulting
the Ouija board again?"

"I don't do that stuff. I don't do candles either. But satanists do
both."

"Mom uses candles too. Have you asked her if *she* worships the
devil?"

"I just don't understand why all of a sudden you have so many. It
looks like . . . like a church or something. It's totally weird. And you're
doing this Mass thing with Granddad. Did you know satanists do the
Mass backwards?"

"I don't know anything about those freaks. I like candles. If I
change religions, I'll let you know. Would you get out of my room
now?"

"Some people are saying that Craig Thorner is a satanist."

"What—because he painted a pentagram on his van? I don't think
so." Tony flopped back onto his pillow. "Craig's a flake. It's all just an
act."

"I heard Jason did heroin the other night."

Tony hadn't talked to Jason since the night he'd turned down
Jason's party invitation. "Who told you that?"

"Carrie. She's really freaked. I mean, you can't blame her. I'm not
a moralist or anything, but heroin's scary, you know?"

"Jason hangs with Brian Giddings. They'd snort nuclear waste if
they could find it."

"So you're not doing heroin?"

Tony just looked at her.

"OK, OK," Annie slowly unfolded her arms and turned to leave.
She didn't ask about pot, and Tony figured she knew he'd lie anyway.
If the family knew how much crazier he'd be off reefer, they'd be sup-
plying him themselves.

Annie shut the door behind her, and Tony wiped off the sweat
along his hairline. He studied his private arrangement of lights. He
actually only lit them one at a time, to make them last longer. He
couldn't risk copping them from the church very often. Maybe he'd
pick up some at the mall. But he had the feeling they wouldn't work as
well as the church ones.

As evening came, Tony lit a single candle set in one of the church glasses. He sat cross-legged on the floor beside the stereo and stared hard at the flame. After a while he undressed and crawled to a clear spot on his bed. He fell asleep, knowing that the fire would last late into the night.

16

SARAH MORGAN: JOURNEYS

Saturday, July 12

Sarah squinted at the digital glow on her night table. Two in the morning. Jacob snored softly beside her. She closed her eyes and tried to reenter her dreams, but all her nighttime antennae were out. Sounds came at her from all over the house. She couldn't even identify most of them; she assumed they were by-products of the soft breeze that traveled through the house, in and out of rooms and windows like a restless ghost.

After ten minutes, she got out of bed and brushed her teeth. The water from the cold tap was lukewarm. She splashed her face with it anyway. Her eyes looked small, staring back at her from the mirror. Her upper arms were getting flabby. She turned off the light and walked down the hallway as quietly as she could.

She went to Miranda's room and watched the child sleep for a few minutes. These nighttime awakenings sometimes seemed to be warnings for Sarah to check on her children. She watched Miranda and then Peter and wondered if she truly was unraveling. It was a crazy thing to be full of fear at this time in her life and with no real threat except the Bender Springs threats of always staying the same and the rain never coming again. After a few more minutes, Sarah made herself leave the children.

She had developed a pattern lately on these hot nights. She went through the same motions: put on her shorts and T-shirt, drank some juice, surveyed her kitchen, and contemplated whether she was up to giving the entire room a good cleaning, then decided against it. Then she walked to the hall closet, opened the door, and stared at her art boxes. She had sworn to herself that she would never box up her life like this. Before the children she would often paint at night. But now the thought thudded against her like a demand too large to fulfill. She shut the door, put on her walking shoes, and slipped out the back.

It was stimulating to be out in darkness, vulnerable, but out here of her own will. Her legs started moving automatically—out of the yard, down the alley, to the side street, past Main Street. She stood at the intersection and considered her options. She'd gone the length of Oak Street and liked the interesting old house where the street dead-ended. Someone told her it had been a boardinghouse when the town was young. But Oak only extended three-quarters of a mile, and she felt the need for a long walk—maybe three miles—tonight. A quarter moon peeked out intermittently as small clouds slid across it.

Jefferson Street dead-ended, too, but on the other side of town, and it spilled into a pasture. Beyond the pasture, what? Sarah couldn't remember, but decided it was a good night to find out.

As her own home fell away behind her, Sarah thought of her children, asleep in their rooms. Miranda slept like a dead weight until seven in the morning, like clockwork. Peter sometimes woke up at about 4:00 A.M., but Jacob had worn him out playing last night, and he hadn't closed his eyes until nearly ten. If the baby cried long enough, Jacob would wake up and tend to him. Sarah was safe. Safe to be by herself, to feel out the dry little town as it slept. A nice feature of Jefferson Street was that it seemed free of dogs. She had learned the hard way which streets had self-appointed sentinels, yowling and growling invisibly from behind hedges, patio walls, and other backyard enclosures. At night, the small town belonged to canines and a few stray cats. They sniffed and whined and padded through the alleys and beyond streetlights. They made up an entire other universe that existed within the human one.

This was her third walk since last Sunday, the day she had made her decision to change her life's course. Now it seemed that her subconscious mind wouldn't leave her alone, kept waking her to walk and think and make plans.

Once out and walking, though, the plans would not form, and she was filled with something between dissatisfaction and anticipation. She had a strange sense that she was searching for something—or someone?—specific. Her legs would move, her eyes would open wide, and she couldn't stop herself from looking in windows and down alleys. She hadn't felt so compelled to action since her first pregnancy, when she had read at least two novels a week. Kept reading other people's stories, hoping to see her own future in them. After Miranda arrived, the compulsion had gone away.

She wasn't pregnant now, and she didn't know what she was looking for this time. But for some reason she felt better to be out of her house and walking.

The pasture at the end of the street (and of the town) looked like a still life in the moonlight. Sarah made a mental note to come back sometime with her easel, when the moon was full. She happened onto a footpath, a slightly worn down swath through the knee-high, scratchy grass. Each of Sarah's steps seemed to set into motion a series of small, reactive noises—she guessed field mice, rabbits, and insects and maybe a snake or two. The experience made her giddy. Her old friend Miranda would be very proud of her, exploring the world she'd been given for now. Sarah felt like an inquirer after mysteries—or at least some peace of mind.

The pasture ran into a small hill covered with trees, but the path went to the left and right, around the hill. Sarah went left and came around the hill to find another. The path cut between them. After forty yards, it ended at a large water hole.

Strip pits. What had been left after the gargantuan shovels had skimmed off layers of earth years ago to get at the coal below. In these parts, the veins lay too close to the surface for deep-shaft mining to be efficient or safe. The deep mines, open over half a century ago, had closed when the big shovels arrived. They scooped up whole fields, mining the coal and leaving the farmland upturned on itself. Now mining companies were required to return the land to its original state, but in the early days it had remained torn open, the deep gouges eventually filling with water. In the years since, small ecosystems of trees and animals had sprouted on the leftover mounds of dug-up earth.

Sarah had seen the small wooded hills as she and Jacob drove down the highways in this part of the county. But here she found a whole other world at the edge of her feet. The water shone in the moonlight, and Sarah heard the soft flop of a fish on its still surface. The trees around her were tall and surrounded by underbrush. She sat on a fallen limb near the water. The air around her felt peaceful, but inside her legs were still moving. She had imagined finding a quiet place to sit, out here in the night by herself, but once here she didn't feel that she'd arrived at the right place. She decided to go around the pit to where it seemed to branch into an adjoining one.

Voices grated suddenly on the warm air. Sarah jumped, not knowing which direction they came from, and backed into the covering of trees several yards from the bank.

A ragged car engine came close, echoing within the small canyon. Sarah could see then across the pit from her a large, clear spot. Two cars and a van had just rolled out of the trees, probably on some small road, and idled next to each other close to the water. Several people got out. Looked like teenagers. Sarah stayed hidden in the brush, although she doubted anyone could spot her clear across the pit. The kids were laughing and swearing. A couple of them were stripping off their clothes. In a moment they were in the water, calling the others to join them.

Sarah heard familiar conversations. There were the sexual innuendoes, the invitations to share a joint or a beer, an argument that sounded vicious one moment, just-kidding the next. The laughter was rough, full of anger. Like kids everywhere, they were blowing off steam and showing off everything they could think of. In the end, they sounded lonely, Sarah thought.

She thought then of the Presbyterian church parlor, its space almost completely filled with a large wooden frame and a quilt stretched tightly across it. Along the four sides, women sat on folding chairs and talked and stitched. A coffeepot perked in the corner, and two oscillating fans turned rhythmically.

Rona Carruthers had invited her, and she'd stopped by before grocery shopping. She'd walked slowly around the quilt, enchanted by the pattern that was forming, stitch by careful stitch. They'd given her a cup of coffee, and she had felt at home. She had stayed over an hour, happy to listen to their quips and stories. Happy to be there. When she left, they had all urged her to come again. Please come back when you can stay longer, they had said.

How could it be so? Now that she knew it was time to leave, her heart had found a small resting place. It was the first time in two years she had actually longed to go back and learn about the people she had met.

Of course, they weren't from her church.

But she couldn't take back what had happened, her walking through the parlor door. It had been such a simple act, to step through that passageway and say hello, but it had taken her further than she had intended. Her heart had made immediate and genuine connections without even consulting her.

Once long ago she had taken a train up to Wisconsin, for some weekend retreat the church was sponsoring. On the train she met a young woman, and they started talking. The woman was going to a movie at the Art Institute in Chicago later in the week, and she invited Sarah. Sarah met her at the Institute steps two nights later, and they watched the film and had coffee afterward. Sarah invited Denise to dinner with her and Jacob the next weekend. After that Denise invited Sarah and Jacob to a series of meetings about art and religion, held monthly in people's homes. From those meetings had grown several friendships, some that had influenced the course of Jacob's seminary study. All from a conversation meant to kill time, on a train ride through north Chicago. All because Sarah had put away her magazine and ventured to say hello. It was frightening to live in a world where a single event could change your life. Sarah gazed across the water at the kids and the cars, wondered what decisions they had made tonight that would turn their lives onto paths they couldn't even see yet.

She noticed then which van it was. From the centennial parade. The Demons, or something. Heather Walker had called Jacob one evening, informing him that those kids with the van were in the occult. Heather had no more than hearsay knowledge, but she assured Jacob that kids at the high school were sure a satanic group was in the area. Sarah felt prickles along the back of her neck. Satanic groups had never come up in her seminary studies. She watched the teenagers across the pit and tried to see if they were doing anything that kids wouldn't do ordinarily when left to themselves off in the woods. If she were a true Christian soldier, she would sneak closer and spy. But she wasn't sure what to look for, and it hit her suddenly that she was exhausted and had more than a mile and a half to walk back to her house and her bed. She had to be out of her mind, out like this at four in the morning.

She quietly skirted the water and made it back out of the little pit canyon. She walked faster going back and didn't slow down until she had hit Maple Street. There, a light in someone's window caught her attention. She paused at the hedge and looked in the window. Through sheer curtains she saw a man, early thirties, bare-chested, sitting in a chair by the lamp, an open paperback in one hand. In the other he held a cigarette. In spite of everything evil about tobacco, Sarah had always liked the way young men looked when they smoked. At ease and friendly. Thoughtful. Sarah stepped into the shadow of a large for-sythia bush not far from the man in the window. She studied his face and wondered why he was up reading. He wore no rings. He had straight, masculine lips that seemed to caress the cigarette each time he took a draw.

Back before Jacob, Sarah had loved a man who smoked. She could still remember the taste when they kissed. She hadn't liked it then, would probably like it less now. She watched the man a few moments more. She and Jacob were good together, but there was so much baggage between them now that the simple act of sex carried more than its intrinsic weight. Sarah had never in her life had sex without relationship, but she played with the idea now, gazing at the handsome smoker. Then she laughed a little at herself and continued along the sidewalk. Maybe irresponsible sex was what her soul was searching for, wandering silent streets at night in a town she didn't even like. In the same way she craved Almond Joy bars nearly every day. Stupid, unhealthy cravings.

She checked on the children when she returned. They were perfectly still, and their faces had the look of untroubled sleep. Sarah microwaved water and had a cup of tea on the front steps. Her legs were still restless, as was her heart. She had never known feelings like this, not since before her Christian days, years ago. A gigantic inner restlessness had forced her in God's direction to begin with. Having such emptiness return made her wonder if it was possible for a found person to get lost again.

17

DAVE SEATON: JULY EVENING

Saturday, July 12

The week after the Fourth of July was so hot and so intense that Dave spent more time in Perky's than usual. Randy hadn't been around much, and the beer at the bar seemed colder and more satisfying than what was in his own fridge at home. He'd drink a mug, play a game of pool, and then go back for seconds. He was getting pretty good at pool; Arnold Schwartz was about twelve dollars poorer these days. Dave couldn't remember feeling so little purpose in life. He was drinking and eyeing his next shot or dozing off at home in front of the TV. One evening he'd turned to his favorite cookbook and tried a couple of new recipes. But then he'd ended up with a cucumber soup he didn't care for and enough pasta salad to feed a road crew. And that reminded him that he didn't have Randy around to share it with. He might never have her around again. On the other hand, he could have this pasta sitting in his fridge for the next month. Well, maybe he *would* take it to the road crew. They'd stopped making comments about his hobby some time ago, partly because he fed them sometimes.

Actually, the snide remarks had let up right after he'd brought in the barbecue beef sandwiches.

He'd made a point not to call Randy or keep asking when she'd be over again. Maybe it was better this way. Just sort of let it all slide away with nobody blaming anybody else.

At four-thirty Saturday afternoon, he was changing the oil in his truck when a racket brought him out of the garage. He looked toward the front yard and saw two cars idling at the curb. One was an old Camaro, the other the same beat-up Cavalier that had dumped Randy on his lawn that first evening back in June. One of the radios was going full blast. Randy, Lena, Jay—he guessed—and Craig Thorner gathered between the front end of Jay's car and the back end of Craig's. Lena, long and tan in a skimpy tank dress, stood apart from the rest, one hand on her hip, the other tapping ash off her cigarette. Randy's arms were folded, and she was shifting nervously from one foot to the other. Jay was talking in earnest to Randy, while Craig looked at Lena from several feet away, smiling and talking to her.

Dave started across his front yard. As he approached the four, he heard Randy saying, "You always say that. But I'm not seeing anything different."

"Hey, Dave." Craig nodded. "What's up?"

"I don't know. What's up?"

"I don't know. I guess we're dropping them off."

"What about the movie?" Jay asked Randy, ignoring Dave.

"I said I don't want to go."

"You were saying ten minutes ago you wanted to see this movie."

"I do, but I don't want to go now."

"Why not?"

Randy turned away from him. "Hi, Dave."

"Hi."

The five of them stood around the cars. Craig seemed to notice suddenly that the music was blaring. He reached through the open window and turned down the volume.

"Randy, why don't you want to go?" Jay sounded more insistent this time.

"You know why."

Jay sniffed and looked down the street. "I've got stuff to do."

"Thanks for the ride." Randy didn't smile or move any closer to Jay. Her arms were still folded in front of her.

Jay got in his car. Craig managed to walk close to Lena and brush her arm as he walked back to the Camaro. The two cars pulled out and then rushed away. The music came up again.

Dave kicked at the grass where it edged the street. "You two want a beer or anything?"

"Sure," said Lena. "Thanks." She walked toward the house. Dave walked up beside Randy, who finally looked at him.

"Good to see you," he said. "Was there some problem?"

She shook her head. "He's stoned."

"Didn't look it."

"He hides it well. But I can tell. And Craig has his own pharmacy, just carries it around in his car."

"They trying to push some of it on you, or what?"

"Not really. But I tell Jay I don't like being around when he does it, and that doesn't make any difference."

"You been seeing him?" They were almost to the front porch.

"No. Have you missed me?"

"Yes."

"You didn't call or anything."

"You didn't either." He brushed a long strand of hair away from her mouth. "Come in and cool off."

The three of them sat at Dave's kitchen table with their drinks.

"Hey, you hungry? I've got pasta salad."

Lena sighed a little, but Dave couldn't tell if it was about his offer or things in general. Randy perked up right away.

"Real food! Yeah."

Dave felt some relief from the familiar sound in her voice and the look on her face that seemed just as open to him as ever.

"Get out another plate, Dave," said Lena. "I see Tony walking up."

Dave looked out the back door. The kid was nearly to the porch. "Hey, Tony. C'mon in."

Tony didn't say anything, but his look changed completely when he saw Lena.

"You guys having a party or something?" he said.

"No, Dave's feeding us," said Lena. "I suppose it's a pasta party." She sounded bored, but Dave decided not to think about her. He set a full plate in front of Randy and kissed her lightly on the lips. She put a hand on his shoulder and kissed him back.

Tony sat next to Lena and said thanks when Dave set a plate in front of him.

"You can't find anything to do either?" said Lena.

"Why should today be different from any other day?"

"Well, we know about a party you can go to," Randy said. "A real kegger. Probably some of your little cigarettes there too."

Tony picked at his food. "Don't think I'll get clearance from the old guy for that."

"You need to clean up your act, kid, and get him off your back for a while." Dave sat down with his own plate.

"I could never have an act that clean."

"Lions are doing a picnic thing in the park," said Randy. "Charlie's Country Band and a pie bake-off."

"Oh yeah. They're dragging this centennial through the summer," said Dave. "Wouldn't want to miss that excitement."

"You're so cynical, Dave." Randy's eyes were playing with him.

"What was that I heard about a movie?"

"Oh, there's a matinee playing in Helmsly—*Jerry McGuire*. But it started half an hour ago. Doesn't matter."

"We could go to a later show if you want."

"No, let's go to the picnic. I'm hungry for pie."

"Clean your plate first," said Lena. "Pasta before pie. Clean your plate, Tony."

A look close to anger passed over Tony's face, but he gave a little laugh. "Yes, ma'am."

As they walked toward Shawnee Park a while later, Dave couldn't help seeing Tony stare with acute interest at Lena, who walked a step or two ahead. The tank dress showed off her slim figure. While Dave didn't feel any responsibility for Tony, he hated to see the kid get sucked into Lena's force. But he could hear her calm-as-iron voice doing its work, Tony practically attached to her shoulder so he wouldn't miss a word. Dave speeded up his steps to get past them, taking Randy gently by the arm.

"Hey, where's the fire?" she asked.

"Behind us," Dave muttered.

"What?"

"Never mind. I just want you to myself for a minute."

They heard music as they came within a few blocks of the park. Sounded like bluegrass. "Old Charlie's got it going already," Randy said.

"Hey—pie and music—we've got it made."

Randy stopped and turned on him suddenly. "What's with this mood? Are you just mad at me or the world in general?"

"I'm not mad."

"Yes, you are."

"It just gets to me." Dave looked at her and saw that she didn't understand. "This puny park with its old-timers. Lena putting the moves on Tony back there."

"What business is that of yours? They can do what they want."

"That's right. But I get bad vibes from her."

"I know that." Randy started walking again; this time Dave had to run to keep up with her. "I don't know what your problem is with her, but she's my best friend, so you just need to deal with it. She's a little weird around the edges, but just about everybody is."

Dave caught her arm as they came into the park. A couple hundred people were milling around among the trees, which were lit crazily by the lanterns that had been strung throughout the park. A soft haze of smoke lingered around them, loaded with smells of hot dogs and burgers, popcorn, and homemade pie. Dave looked at the anger in Randy's eyes and wished none of this Lena stuff had come up. This was the kind of evening when they should be able to sit back against a tree together and enjoy everything.

"Listen, I'm sorry I opened my mouth. Let's just be together, OK?"

Her look didn't change, but she said, "You have money for pie?"

"All the pie you want." He took out his wallet and opened it under her nose. He pulled out a twenty and put it in her hand. "I'm sorry, babe."

Randy took the money and headed for a booth fifty yards away. She tossed a comment back to him without looking. "Just don't talk to me for a while, all right?"

That was the last Dave saw of her. He looked everywhere for an hour or more, while people around him relaxed on blankets, ate, sipped beer, and enjoyed the music. He spotted Lena and Tony snuggled against someone's station wagon at the edge of the park lights. They thought Randy was with him.

"Give her some space, Dave," said Lena, all-knowing. "Don't get freaky. She's probably run into somebody."

"She could have said something." Dave marched away from them. He bought a hot dog and ate without tasting it. Lorna Doveland, an old classmate, stopped him midfume, and he was distracted for a while, catching up with her and her husband. It was amazing how many people he knew who had nothing much to do with him anymore. He looked around and could name nearly every face he saw. But the face he wanted had vaporized.

He had decided to go home when a series of loud pops echoed at them from the south. Dave stood up to stare in that direction and saw a stream of fireworks shooting into the sky, he guessed near the high school. It looked as if someone had tied about thirty fireworks together and lit the bundle. People stopped in surprise, and a slow commotion began to form itself in the midst of the food and music. Dave heard shouts from voices he recognized—guys around town who volunteered as firemen. The music stumbled to a stop, and Gideon's voice piped out at them. The sheriff was so short he was hardly visible on the makeshift stage.

"Folks, we've got a fire hazard over near the school. If your house is in that area, we'd like you to go home and check your yard and buildings." His words were met with an immediate shift in the celebration. The town was so dry that the fireworks show for the Fourth had been canceled last week.

Dave jogged home and got in his truck. It had to be Craig's bunch. Was Randy over there, just to irritate him? Along the way he picked up Ralph, owner of Ralph's IGA, who was with the fire department. They eased close to the high school, eyes peeled for fire, and found a number of vehicles parked at the edge of Mason's pasture. Dan Wheeler was hosing down a smoldering spot about twenty yards from the road with his own garden hose. Other volunteers walked the pasture carefully, looking for anything else.

Doc Lawrence got out of his car and walked up to where Dave and Ralph were standing. "I saw that painted-up van down a ways, where the road turns off into the pasture."

"Just tryin' to start up somethin'," said Ralph, pulling out a smoke. "Pretty stupid, though. This whole place could go up. Least the wind's calmed down today."

"You mean Ted Thorner's van? With the graffiti all over it?" Dave looked down the road and searched the windbreak of trees near the railroad tracks.

"Yep. Don't know whose it is. It and an old Camaro roughed up Iris Miracle's tail feathers about a month ago."

Ralph decided to stop at his mother's before returning to the park. She lived just a block or two from Mason's pasture, so he told Dave to go on without him. Dave took the truck for a slow ride around the town's outskirts. Maybe he'd see the kids. There wasn't much he could do but call Gideon. The Demoniacs traveled in a pretty big group, and Dave felt too hot and beat to try to bluff all of them at once.

When he turned off the main highway and onto Rural Route 2, he saw Randy walking near the deep, weed-choked ditch. She was walking fast. Dave's heart gave a thud, and he was angry and relieved at once. He pulled up beside her and rolled down the passenger window. At the sound of his voice, Randy jumped but she didn't stop walking.

"You know, it would have been nice if you'd let me know you were leaving. I could've enjoyed the pie judging a lot more." He tried to joke, but even he could hear the irritation in his voice.

"I just didn't feel like doing anything all of a sudden." She barely looked at him. The truck shuddered, and Dave shifted it into a lower gear, keeping pace with Randy's determined walk.

"So, were you in on all the excitement back there?"

"What excitement? I've been walking."

"Just some fireworks." He did his best to keep the truck even with her. "What's going on?"

She didn't say anything. She didn't look at him.

"Are you just tired of me—is that what this is?"

She shook her head.

"Is it Lena? I don't like her much, but I'll learn to get along better if that's what's bothering you."

"No. It would be nice if you were nicer to her, but I can't be responsible for all that."

"Then what? Are we breaking up, and I just don't know it yet?"

Randy stopped and looked at him finally. He stopped the truck and put it in neutral. The idle sounded loud. Dave noticed irregular twinkles happening behind Randy. Fireflies. They floated in the dim evening over the field behind her.

"Don't ask me questions like that. I don't think that way, OK? I can't think about us right now. I've got stuff to deal with."

"Why can't you let me help you deal with it?"

"I don't know." She raised her arms and let them drop helplessly. For the first time Dave heard tears in her voice.

"Babe, just get in the truck."

"No. I'm all right. I want to be by myself right now." She started walking again. Dave watched her fade several yards into the colorless landscape before pulling up even with her again.

"Stop by if you need to. You don't have to talk. But I want to be sure you're OK."

She nodded and waved him on.

He didn't drive home but stopped at Perky's. The place was alive with the evening's gossip. Dave listened absently to as many versions of the day as there were people around the bar. It all made him want hard liquor, but his stomach didn't handle the stuff, so he stuck with beer.

"I don't know what I'm doing here," he said on his second beer, speaking to the mirror behind the bar. In the reflection he saw Ax Miracle stationed at his booth near the men's room. Ax saw Dave looking at him and nodded slightly in acknowledgment.

Dave rubbed his eyes, supporting himself on the counter with both elbows. "I need a change of scenery."

"You still trying to leave us, Dave?" Gabe was suddenly right in front of him in all his bartenderly glory.

"Yep."

"Job not going well?"

"It's all right."

"Girl not working out?"

"I don't know."

Ax Miracle gave a grunt, and both men looked at him. He returned their looks but didn't say more.

"I think girls have changed a lot," said Dave, staring into the mirror again. He could see Ax still eyeing him from the booth. "Used to be they were happy to have a guy, to settle down. Most of them were waiting for Mr. Right." Now they don't know what they want."

"What do *you* want?"

"A woman full time. I'm tired of this dating crap."

Ax grunted again, and Gabe let out a low whistle.

"What I really want is to be someplace else."

"Just as long as you take everything important with you." Gabe moved toward the other end of the bar, and Dave could hear him laughing.

When Dave got back to the house Randy was on the front porch, reading a magazine by the yellow porch light and having a Coke. One leg hung over the edge, and she leaned back against the porch post, stretching her back when she noticed him coming. He parked the truck in the back and walked around.

"Hi," he said.

"Hi." Randy wasn't smiling. Her face was calm but closed and dark. Dave smoothed her leg as he sat down on the step.

"You don't look so good," he said.

She shrugged.

"What's wrong?"

She flipped through the magazine, not looking up or responding to his touch. When she got to the end of the magazine, she took it in both hands and studied the cover.

"I can't live at home anymore," she stated.

"What happened?"

"I'm fed up with it. And I can't live with her. Daddy and I have an agreement; he stays out of my way and I stay out of his. I think he likes me more than she does. She hates me, and I hate her."

She looked up at him. Her eyes were dry.

"It's about me, I bet," he said.

"She knows I'm over here a lot. She decided a long time ago that I'm makin' it with every guy who stops at the house to ask directions."

"But you aren't. You're a decent person." He touched her cheek affectionately.

"So? She thinks what she wants." Randy's eyes were fastened on some point in the distance.

"What will you do if you don't live there?" Dave asked. A loaded silence followed.

"I haven't figured that out yet." Again, there was that slight waver in her voice.

His hand moved across her skin, and he grasped her hand. She leaned back, still focused on that something in the distance Dave couldn't identify.

"You don't deserve to be hurt so much," he said softly.

"I'll be all right."

"Let's go inside." He rose, her hand still clutched in his, but she made no move to go with him.

"Let's stay out here awhile," she said.

He sat down again and looked at her. "Don't you want some comfort, baby?"

"I need to think. I can't think when we're doing that."

A silence took them over. It closed off the porch from the rest of the neighborhood. Dave could see Mr. Kelsey wandering in and out of his garage, but there was no sound at all.

"I don't know if I can help you much," Dave said finally. "I'm not making a lot of money, and I don't know what's going to happen. I may talk to this guy who manages a crew near Kansas City."

Randy bit her lip and nodded, watching a car go by them on the street.

"As far as I'm concerned, you can move in here, and we'll do what we can. You—" He let out a frustrated breath. "You can sleep on the couch if you want."

"I never said I wanted that."

"Well, I just want you to feel free. I want you to do whatever you need to do."

Two tears had escaped, one down each of Randy's cheeks. She wiped at them with impatience.

"I won't cost much," she said. "I make enough at the café to keep up my end. That's what I've been doing at home. Would you believe she's wanting to charge me rent? I've been out of high school two months. She just couldn't wait to make things harder for me."

"Don't pay her rent. Bring your things over here."

She reached over suddenly and wrapped her arms around his neck, her face in his hair. "You're my best friend, Dave."

She smelled like Ivory soap and the green leaves of peppermint. Dave kissed an ear. "You want some comfort now?" He felt her nod against him. They went inside and pulled the bedroom shades against the gaping glass panes of Mr. Kelsey's house across the street.

When morning came, Dave drove his truck to the Kluvers'. He backed into the yard all the way up to the sagging back porch. This brought Lorene Kluver out in her bathrobe, hair uncombed, to cuss him out loud enough to wake the neighborhood from its Sunday sleep.

"Get out of my yard!" she hissed. She grabbed at Randy as the girl walked past her, but Dave was at the bottom step of the porch in half a second. He pointed a finger at her, just inches from her face.

"Don't lay a hand on her, or you'll answer to me, Lorene."

She drew her hand back from Randy, who stepped into the house. Lorene leaned close to Dave's finger, as if she were going to bite it off. The way she looked, kind of evil in a crazy way, he half expected her to try. She spat words at him. "You have no right, you—"

"I'm not here to cause trouble. Randy's of legal age, so just back off. She'll get her things and we'll be gone in ten minutes. Don't—" Dave held up both hands as Lorene opened her mouth. "Don't cause a scene here."

Lorene closed her lips tight, pulled the bathrobe into a knot around her, and watched with narrowed eyes as Randy and Dave walked in and out of the house several times, loading the pickup. Lorene lit up a cigarette and smiled as they put the last boxes in.

"Well, sweet stuff," she said, pointing the cigarette in Randy's direction, "don't plan on walking through this door again. And don't think this is over." She looked at Dave. "When Charlie gets back from this trip, he'll be coming to see you, Mr. Can't Keep It in His Pants."

"I'm just down the street. He's welcome anytime." Dave waved his arm in the direction of his house and opened the passenger door of the truck for Randy. Then he got in himself and drove out of the yard.

They unloaded the truck without talking. Dave was pretty sure Randy was crying, but there was sweat on her face and the heat had reddened her complexion, so he couldn't be sure.

Tony and Lena showed up within the hour. Lena and Randy stayed in the bedroom, Randy crying and Lena sounding more gentle and kind than Dave could imagine was possible. Tony shifted uncomfortably in his chair at the kitchen table and sucked Coke through a straw. "What happened?" he asked.

"I don't know. Maybe nothing. Randy's just tired of dealing with it."

"Mrs. Kluver likes to fight. I've seen her mix it up with my grand-dad a couple of times. How'd Randy turn out so nice is what I'd like to know."

"So were you and Lena in on the fireworks last night? I didn't see you around."

"No. We were busy somewhere else."

"Watch your back, kid."

"I am. I'm fine."

Dave paused to look at him. His eyes didn't look right, and he was thin as a rail. But the eyes came to life a moment later when Lena entered the kitchen to get Randy some iced tea.

"She OK?" asked Tony.

"No. But we're working on it." Lena poured the tea without look-ing at either of them.

"Thanks for coming over, Lena," Dave said, wishing he meant it more.

18

MAMIE RUPERT: NEW LIFE

Saturday, July 12

As the summer got hotter, Mamie's dreams got more and more violent. She killed Cassie a different way every night. It didn't matter what she ate or didn't eat before bedtime. It didn't matter if she prayed especially to be a better person. What was most disappointing was that her prayer with the young seminarian didn't seem to have much effect either. And, like a furry demon, That Dog continued to find a few minutes in each day when—Mamie was sleeping or at the grocery store or simply had her back turned or the TV—on to do his dirty business. Mamie called Gideon again, and again Gideon assured her that he would talk to Bill about keeping his dog on a leash. But the dung was still there, fresh every day.

Mamie got up every morning, feeling older and stiffer and guilty as sin itself; there must be something evil in her for these dreams to go on this way. She had to admit that she had never been very close to Cassie, and Cassie's being so difficult had caused Mamie not to hear her sometimes when she was going on about her problems. Ultimately, though, it was easiest to blame it all on the emotional upset caused by the dog. One evening Mamie rummaged around in the basement closet and located Charles's hunting rifle. She would kill That Dog dead the next time she saw him; it was all that was left to her. But she couldn't find any shells, and the gun seemed stiff. Knowing her luck, the thing would explode in her face. She put it back in the closet and tried to think of the next best thing. Rat poison maybe, in some raw hamburger. But she wasn't sure how much it would take, and some innocent animal might come across it.

On Saturday morning Mamie decided that since she was a true Christian now, she should give Sunday school a shot. She hadn't done Sunday school for over twenty years, and the materials had never been terribly interesting to her. Mamie really wanted to do her churchgoing with Alma to the Methodist class, but she'd pretty much signed on with the Baptists. Liz snorted when Mamie brought up the subject, but Ruthie volunteered to go along to the seniors' Sunday school class. Mamie figured that was better than nothing. And having Ruthie there would guarantee that Mamie had little time to open her own mouth and embarrass herself. She'd heard church lessons all her life, but none of it stuck much, and she reckoned she would be one of the most ignorant people in the class. Ruthie would cover for her nicely.

The next morning Ruthie pulled up in her '82 Celebrity. She looked rattled already, but she mustered a strong smile when Mamie got into the car. "Beautiful morning for church, isn't it? As beautiful as we get these days anyway. How'd you sleep? I just kept waking up sweaty, even with my air conditioning, although I think the filter needs cleaning. Were you wanting to stay for church too?"

Mamie sat quietly until the questions ceased. "We may as well stay for the whole show since we're dressed up."

"You know, that's exactly what I thought." Ruthie slammed on the accelerator to back out of the drive, and Mamie's head flew dangerously close to the windshield.

"Easy on the gas, Ruthie. You're about to kill me where I sit."

"Oh, I'm sorry. Don't drive much anymore. Just doesn't feel safe, all those wild young people out in their fast cars and satanic vans."

"Believe me, Ruthie, they're no match for you. Just go slow; the church is only eight blocks from here. If we died in between, wouldn't that be pathetic."

They lurched to church and were on the lawn in time to be greeted by Pastor Morgan. His face brightened, even while he perspired. A nice-looking young man, although he was beginning to gray a bit at the temples. Beside him was an adorable child who took Mamie's hand energetically.

"Good morning! Welcome to church, and please be seated. The sermon today is about Jesus." The child looked up into Mamie's face with full confidence.

Mamie laughed. "Why, where did you come from? Are you preaching?"

"No. Daddy is. That's his job."

"Mrs. Rupert, I'm so glad you've come. Joe Travis told me he had a good visit with you the other day." Mamie recognized the same bright warmth in the pastor's eyes as she'd seen in the little girl. "This is Miranda, my daughter. She's helping me greet people."

"And what a little greeter she is!" said Ruthie. She began to say more, but Mamie broke in quickly: "Where's the senior citizen Sunday school class? I think the rooms have changed around since I was here last."

"Down the first hallway on your left. Ask anybody inside. But we have a little opening service first. Just have a seat in the sanctuary."

The service was sort of an announcement time—talk of the revival services, people who were in the hospital, and a youth-group trip coming up. They'd changed the carpeting and put in seat cushions since Mamie had been here last. She couldn't recall her last visit. It was when Charles was alive, and he rarely went after he and Deacon Peters got into it over something; Mamie couldn't even remember what the fuss had been about. Charles had never claimed to be a saint, but he was real straight and narrow when it came to religion. Always talking about people not being respectful of holy things anymore.

Mamie recognized a number of people, most of them young. There were lots of children who seemed to be antsy to go to their classes. They sang songs, but Mamie didn't recognize those. They were out of a little paperback book and not the hymnal. Real repetitive and way too fast for her to keep up with. She could hear Ruthie's voice twitching frantically beside her and felt relieved when they were all dismissed to Sunday school.

Mamie figured out later, looking back on the day, that her real problem with Sunday school was Louise Filcher. Louise, who'd done most of the centennial planning without asking for anyone else's opinions, even Mamie's, and Mamie had been city clerk for forty years and knew a thing or two. Louise Filcher evidently liked to be the voice of authority elsewhere too. When Mamie and Ruthie walked into the Sunday school class, Louise was there at the front of the room with her reading glasses on, welcoming people and suggesting where they might sit.

"Don't tell me she's the teacher," Mamie murmured close to Ruthie's ear.

Ruthie's eyes got big. "That's what it looks like. I figured for older people they'd have the pastor do the teaching. Or at least a man."

The lesson was about one of Jesus' parables, the ten virgins and their lamps and the wedding about to happen and the groom being late. Mamie could remember it from other lessons long ago. She'd never understood the importance of pointing out that the ten women were virgins, like it was anybody else's business. But Louise seemed to put a lot of stock in it. She spent a full ten minutes going on about how young people today had no morals whatsoever, and a person would be lucky to find ten virgins at any wedding ceremony these days. Finally some old man in the corner asked if she wanted them to take turns reading the lesson from their Sunday school quarterlies, and Louise giggled a little and said, "Of course, that's what we always do."

So they took turns reading. Really, the lesson was all explained right there in the quarterly. As they went around the room and read a paragraph at a time, Mamie was convinced that Louise was totally useless, sitting there so precious in her reading glasses. With the book explaining things, who needed a teacher? As it turned out, the main point of the lesson had nothing to do with whether a person was a virgin. It wasn't even about weddings but about being ready for Christ's Second Coming. And, since she'd prayed with the young man from the seminary, Mamie assumed that part was taken care of now. She was ready. *My, was she ready*, she thought as Louise cleared her throat and corrected some comment a woman next to Ruthie had just made.

"Well," Mamie said as she and Ruthie made their way to the sanctuary for the real church service, "can't say that I got much out of that. You'd think they could find someone better qualified to teach."

"Yes, you would." Ruthie looked tired. She had been strangely silent throughout the Sunday school hour. Mamie guessed she felt unqualified to say much, although that certainly didn't stop her any other time.

The church service was more pleasant than Mamie expected. They sang real hymns, and the pastor's sermon was encouraging. He talked a lot about how people often thought that God was just interested in the big things, but a person could turn to him anytime for anything, no matter how small or how silly. Mamie thought then about her Cassie dreams. Maybe this pastor would have something to say about that. She hadn't even considered bringing it up in Sunday school, but she could imagine young Pastor Morgan listening to her and pausing to think and then saying something that would make her feel better. In fact, she felt better just being here, in the sanctuary, singing hymns and being encouraged. She kicked herself for waiting so long to come back. When the service was over, she made a point to shake the pastor's hand again and tell him how good the sermon was. She even stopped outside the church under the shade tree to talk with Ethel Hampton for a few minutes. And there was Ludie Meyers with her daughter nearby; Mamie hadn't talked with Ludie for years, it seemed. When Mamie and Ruthie climbed back into the car and waited for the hotter air to escape out the open doors for a minute, Mamie turned to Ruthie.

"That was nice, wasn't it?"

"Oh, it was, it really was. I think I'll just come up here again. I don't suppose they mind that I'm really Lutheran. I mean, they wouldn't question me about it, would they? I've not stepped into a Lutheran church since I visited my eldest son two years ago. He and his wife are religious, take the kids to church every Sunday. Their youngest, Avery, can recite Bible verses by the yard. He was Joseph in the Christmas pageant last year—never saw such a smart little man. But they're Lutheran, straight as arrows. I didn't have the heart to tell Clive that I haven't been attending. Of course, he knows the closest Lutheran church is in Helmsly and I don't like to drive, what with all the wild young people out on weekends. But you know, I don't think there's really much difference between Baptists and Lutherans, do you? Maybe some of the hymns are different. It's hard to say."

"Start the car, Ruthie, before I melt."

In early evening, Dave Seaton came by. He called to Mamie through the door of the screened-in porch.

"Tony told me your handrail was loose. Want me to check on it?"

"Oh, yes. It wobbles so much I lose my balance." Mamie stepped onto the porch and let Dave in. Then she walked up the steps that went into the house, grabbed the old pipe banister, and shook it.

"I see where the problem is. Just take me about ten minutes."

"It's so nice of you to stop by."

"We don't want you doing any nosedives down your steps. Go on inside where it's cooler. I've got everything I need here." He tugged at the tool belt that hung on his hips. Mamie went back inside. She heard him clanking around while she mixed up fresh lemonade. By the time she'd poured it into glasses and set out chocolate-sandwich cookies, Dave was inside.

"I think that'll do it," he said, his back to her while he washed his hands at the kitchen sink. "Just let me know when it gets loose again."

They sat at the kitchen table and sipped cold lemonade.

"Do you think you could paint my house? It needs to be done by August 6." Mamie had decided just to dive right in. She looked into the young man's gray eyes. He set down the glass.

"Sam Hays paints houses, doesn't he? It's not something I've got a lot of experience with."

"It just needs a coat or two slapped on it. Sam's too expensive, and I don't know him. You've done work for me for two or three years." She offered a little smile and got him to smile back. At her age it was shameful to flirt, but Dave Seaton just brought it out of her. He was too sweet for his own good.

"So, you and Sam have a disagreement or something?"

"What would make you think that?"

He cocked his head. "Oh, ol' Sam has a way of getting people mad at him. Just wondered."

"Why should I ask him if you can do it?"

"Mamie, you have the will of an ox."

"I just know what I want. Can you do it? By August 6?"

He smiled at her then, and she knew it was a deal.

"All right. Tell me what color, and we'll see what we can do. I'll get Tony to help me."

"That'd be fine. I've known him since he was in diapers, not that I'd tell him that." She poured more lemonade into Dave's glass, although it was still mostly full. "That Miracle fella started, but he's dishonest and isn't too fast. I fired him before he finished scraping."

"I can see that somebody started at least."

"I bought the paint already, though the trim paint's on order at Frank's."

"Sounds like you're all set."

"Ruthie and I drove by your place today. My, what a garden you've got."

"Think so? Kind of puny this year."

"But at least you have one. It's two feet taller than everybody else's."

"Really? Hadn't noticed."

"What have you got growing now?"

He shrugged. "The usual—tomatoes, peppers, corn, green beans, squash, onions."

"My tomatoes aren't worth anything this year."

"I'll bring you a ripe one, how's that?"

"You just read my mind." Mamie thought for a while before speaking again. "Have you seen those old piles of dung in my yard?"

Dave drained his glass. "Can't say that I have. Tony says you've had him clean up some."

"It's that Bill Simpson."

"*Bill's* going to the toilet on your lawn?" Dave's eyes glinted.

"You know what I mean. His dog. Goes out there every morning. I've called Gideon, and he just won't do a thing." Mamie paused again. She watched Dave wipe his mouth with a napkin. "Do you think," she started carefully, "you could go talk to Bill?"

"Nope." Dave shook his head and continued shaking it after he'd spoken. "I'm not getting mixed up in your feud with Bill."

"Well, Gideon's not much help."

"I can't help you there, Mamie."

"But you'll paint the house."

"I'll paint the house. But no dog-dung negotiations."

"All right then." Mamie sighed as she watched Dave walk out of her house and get in his truck. Maybe this summer would be manageable after all. She'd gone to church and was feeling more like a Christian than she had in a long time. And the house would be painted fresh by Charles's seventy-fifth birthday. The dog trouble was still with her, but with Dave around painting her house for a few days, who knew what could happen. Mamie picked up the phone to bring Alma up-to-date on how Sunday had gone.

19

DAVE SEATON: THE EVIL IN THIS WORLD

Tuesday, July 15

Tony looked as if he hadn't slept for days when he trudged up to Dave's garage Tuesday morning. Dave was having a smoke; he'd already done what he could for the garden today, Randy was at the café, and he needed to hit the road for work in about ten minutes. But he called Tony's name and took an extra long drag while the kid came out of the garage and walked over to him. Tony sat on the other side of the wide stoop.

"Two things I've got to say, Tony."

"Yeah." The voice sounded uninterested.

"I can't have you showing up looking like an addict. You're spooking people. I was on the phone with Mrs. Bitano last night for half an hour. She said you acted like you couldn't understand what she was saying, that you nearly knocked over her flowerpots."

Tony shifted his weight and swore. "She's got 'em balanced along that skinny porch railing—"

"That's not the point. You're gonna lose me business. I don't care what you do on your own time, but you gotta have some focus when you're working."

The kid nodded.

"You okay? I mean, is this stuff under control?"

"I'm not an addict," Tony said hotly. He was frowning out at the sunshine.

"You look like crap."

"I don't get a lot of sleep."

"Maybe you should take a break from Lena."

"That's not what I mean. I mean . . . I don't *sleep* much."

"Maybe you could see a doctor or something."

Tony looked at Dave. His eyes were scary—or scared. "There's not a problem."

"There's a problem if you're falling asleep and operating machinery."

"I'll figure something out. Have you seen Lena?"

"It's six in the morning; where would I see her?"

"She's not at her grandma's. Thought she stayed the night here."

"No. Haven't seen her for a couple days. Things really picking up with you two?"

Tony acted as if he didn't hear at first. "We're okay. I think she's got a guy back in Colorado. It's kind of weird."

"I think she's got guys in more places than that. Don't let her get to you. She's only here for the summer."

"Well, we've got to get through the summer too." Tony got up and started for the garage. It seemed to Dave like a strange thing to say, but he didn't comment.

"Hey—you interested in helping me paint Mamie's house?" he called after Tony.

Tony turned and shrugged. "I've never painted a house. But, yeah."

"We'll probably start next weekend. I'll let you know."

Randy worked late that evening—some wedding rehearsal dinner the café was doing, and Dave wandered around the house for a few minutes before landing in front of the TV. He was beginning to feel as though his evening couldn't get started without Randy in the house. The bachelor inside him nagged that this was not a good sign.

During a commercial he went to the kitchen to make a sandwich and found Lena sitting at the table, reading a magazine.

Dave planted himself in the doorway and looked at her with a deliberate lack of emotion. "What's up?"

"I thought Tony might be here," she said, just as flatly. "Have you seen him?" There was that perfectly controlled posture, like a cat's.

"No. He was looking for you early this morning." Dave got himself a Coke without offering Lena any.

"And Randy's at the café late tonight?" Lena tossed her hair over one shoulder and pulled a pack of cigarettes from her back pocket. Her cutoffs were so tight, Dave wondered if the smokes came out flat. The shorts were barely there. Lena crossed her legs and lit up. Dave shifted his gaze to the backyard window and took a drink.

"He's kind of unstable," Lena stated after tipping back her head to exhale.

Dave raised a questioning eyebrow, barely.

"Tony. He's fun to mess around with, but I wonder if he's going to freak out sometime. He's that quiet, wired type—who might take a gun to the mall and start shooting people. Like in another ten years he'll be living by himself and burying body parts in the basement."

"You talk about all your friends this way?" Dave leveled a look at her until she looked back. "He probably smokes too much dope, but I hardly think that makes him the next Jeffrey Dahmer. I think this town's too boring for you—when you start turning regular people into psychos."

Lena tilted her head and examined the collection of rings on her right hand. "You're the one who's bored, Dave." Her eyes traveled to meet his as she brought the cigarette slowly to her lips. "That's what Randy's all about."

"You don't know anything, you know that?"

"I know more than she does. You're just a town guy. You'll hang out and drink beer with the greasy old men at Perky's for another forty or fifty years. And you'll suck all the life out of Randy. And then you'll be clueless when she hits thirty-five and goes into deep depression for the rest of her life."

Dave felt anger burn his gut but said softly, "You're just out of sorts because I haven't tried anything with you." He smiled. "I think that's what Tony's about."

She shook her head, closing her eyes, ever superior to him. "You are so wrong."

"I saw your green light the first time you walked up here. How many of us you figure you'll rack up by the end of the summer? It's time for you to go, Lena babe." He nodded toward the door abruptly and then turned his back to her and walked into the living room. His heart was pounding, a surge of adrenaline charged by the familiar sore spot she had struck. *Town guy.*

He heard the back door open and close and knew he'd just screwed up big time. Once Randy heard about this, it was over. He grabbed a beer out of the refrigerator and sat on the sofa to drink it. But then a vision came to him—of him in fifty years, nursing his beer in front of the television, passing gas, and eating Cheetos for supper. He threw the can across the room and didn't even move to clean it up when the beer foamed onto the floor.

Randy didn't come home that night. She called from Lena's grandma's house, sounding strained and tearful, to let him know where she was, but she insisted that she couldn't talk right then. She hung up before Dave could say anything.

She wasn't home when Dave got in from work the next night either. He could picture her sitting cross-legged on the floor next to Lena, talking about important things, laughing at him as though he'd been something to help her kill time.

All this came at the worst time. The foreman had called his friend upstate that very day, and Dave had an interview lined up for mid-August. He needed to talk about this stuff, and Randy was the only person on earth any of it affected.

He delved into the fridge for a beer, picking up the last one. The shelves were pretty bare. Randy was going to grocery shop today—no, yesterday, the day she hadn't come home. Dave sat in his beat-up easy chair and sipped, scowling at Dan Rather. Then he checked around the house one more time for any signs of what was going on with Randy. The last thing she'd said to him—before their very short phone conversation last night—was that she planned to grocery shop and then make herself a sundress. She figured it would take her two evenings to do the dress, unless she had to work late at the café. Dave stood in the bedroom doorway, the beer sweating in his hand, and looked at the untouched sewing machine. Not a thread trailing anywhere.

Lena sprang to his thoughts again. If he'd just not let himself argue with her yesterday. He knew she liked to pick fights, and he'd felt all along she'd love to have a knock-down-drag-out with him. Would Randy just go back to Colorado with Lena when the summer ended? Were they already gone?

Dave stopped in front of the old desk and looked at the one picture he'd left up of Karen. Karen had been harder to live with, but at least she'd stick around to argue. Randy just kept disappearing on him. He really didn't know her that well. He knew what she liked to eat and watch on TV. But maybe there were too many important things he didn't know.

By the time Dan Rather checked out, Dave had finished his beer and was steaming in spite of it. He went to the kitchen and raided the fridge of its measly contents. He'd come to enjoy cooking for her too. He chopped up a leftover half potato to fry and turned on the radio station that had the least talking.

He sensed movement behind him and turned to find Randy beside the cabinet near the back door. She held a plate of food with plastic wrap over it. Her face was swollen, a pinched white with red blotches.

Dave turned down the radio.

"I brought some supper for you," she said quietly and averted her face from him as she set the plate on the counter.

"Where have you been?"

She held up her hands. "Just don't be mad, OK?" Her voice was weighted and weak.

"I'm not mad." He turned back to the skillet of potatoes, knowing that he was mad and they both knew it. He looked at her again. "What's wrong, babe?"

She burst into tears, covering her face with a dish towel. He was over to her in one long step and gathered her close to him. He smoothed her hair, pressed her face into his neck. After a few moments she settled down. She ripped a paper towel off its dispenser and blew her nose.

"I've been at Mom's."

"What's she done now? I don't know why you even go over there. Every time you come back upset—"

"She's sick." Randy drew in a shuddering breath and spoke with effort. "She's real sick. She has cancer."

The evening rang quietly around them, the air heavy with heat if not humidity, and the insects had tucked themselves up and made no noise. Dave finished the warmed-up spaghetti from the plate Randy had brought him. He looked at her face for the twentieth time. She seemed to be dazed, like a boxer who had taken too many blows. Her mouth opened in a strange, crooked line he hadn't seen before.

"What can we do for your folks?" Dave asked softly, afraid he would startle her.

"I don't know yet. She won't say. She just crawls up inside herself and tries to be strong." Randy's eyes were set on a shaft of orange light that slid over the floor and table. It was a few inches wide and seemed to cut the kitchen in half, Randy on one side and Dave on the other.

"We'll have to figure out what to do and just do it," said Dave.

Randy stood up and took Dave's dish to the sink, her back to him. "Her voice was real gentle," she said. "Or maybe it was just tired. But it sounded gentle to me."

Dave came up and hugged her from behind. "Let's go to bed."

"Your fights are on tonight."

"Doesn't matter. Let's just lie down and be quiet."

"I can't do much but be quiet."

He led her to the bedroom. They undressed in silence. She put on a long T-shirt, and he slipped some early Linda Ronstadt into the tape deck. They lay together, touching shoulders.

"I know this is a bad time to bring this up," said Dave, "but my boss has set me up to see the guy near Kansas City. I'm supposed to have an interview in about a month."

"That's great, hon. Go for it."

"I'm thinking it would be better to wait, see what happens with your mom."

"That's a bad idea. You've wanted to get out of this town for a long time. This is your chance."

"I don't want to go without you." He turned to face her silhouette. "You know that, don't you?"

She let out a long sigh. "Yeah, I know. This is just too much to think about right now."

"OK. Why don't you sleep." He bent over her and kissed her gently on the mouth. They lingered there, the kiss long but without any movement forward. Dave wanted to stay there the rest of his life, covering her life with his, taking care of those soft lips, brushing away tears with his fingers. The kiss ended, and he touched her cheeks and eyebrows with kisses, too, then lay back down. He turned on his side away from her and barely heard her when she spoke.

"I'm sorry I run away sometimes."

"Don't worry about that. I'm not mad at you. Just want to know you're OK." He cleared his throat, sounding like an authority. "So I'll stay put for now."

"Aunt Bess will come stay with her if it gets too bad. What can I do, anyway? She won't let me do anything. She's such a stubborn b—" Dave heard another sob come and go.

"Well, she's your mom, and we'll do what we can." He turned back over to face her. "When my dad passed away, he'd been in the hospital three weeks. Something happened in his brain, and he got real mean toward the end. But when he was going, he squeezed my hand like he used to when I was little. We'd walk downtown holding hands and send messages to each other with squeezes." Dave laughed, remembering. "One squeeze meant 'car's coming'; two meant 'fat lady ahead.'" Randy giggled, still sounding tired. "Three meant . . . let's see, 'the grocery store,' four meant 'the café,' and five meant 'you're my buddy.'"

"So he squeezed you a message when he was dying? Which one was it?"

"It was just a long squeeze. I don't think he was strong enough to do it more than once. But it felt like he was going to take me with him, like he'd never let go. I took it as five squeezes. You have to make allowances for what people become when they're sick."

"It would be easier if the rest of her life had been better. I feel like it's all my fault, like I should make everything good for her now."

"That's not up to you, babe."

"I love you, Dave."

"You've never said that before."

"I know. Scared, I guess." He rubbed her tummy, and she put both her hands over his one. "I'm scared of bigger things now."

20

SARAH MORGAN: SUMMER'S END

Thursday, July 17

The woman standing on the Morgans' front porch looked all of one hundred pounds, but her knock resounded through the house. Sarah looked slyly through the sheer curtains of the bedroom window, which gave her a side view of their front door. She didn't recognize the woman. Whoever she was, she looked capable of standing on the porch all day. Sarah traveled through rooms and opened the heavy inner door. She and the thin woman regarded each other a moment through the screen.

"Can I help you?" Sarah asked.

"This the Baptist preacher's house?"

"Yes."

"I need to see the pastor."

Sarah dropped her hand from the inside of the screen door. "He's not home right now."

"When will he be home?"

"I can't say for sure. Sometime this afternoon, I guess."

"He doesn't have a schedule, so that you can find him when somebody needs him?"

Sarah shifted her weight. "Have you tried the church?" she asked.

"This place is closer to my house. I'm on foot, and I'm sick. I can't go chasing all over town. Can I come in out of the heat?"

Sarah got the same feeling from this woman she'd often had around street people in the city. They were always desperate and often pushy. You wanted to help, but no matter what you did, it wasn't enough—for some of them. This woman had that quality that made Sarah want to shut the door fast. But she stepped back, and the woman walked past her and into the living room. She sat down on the sofa, moving some of Peter's playthings out of her way.

"Sorry it's such a mess. We have a baby."

"Where there's kids, there's mess. You just have the one?"

"We also have a five-year-old."

"I came to ask your husband about the emergency fund."

"Excuse me?" Sarah balanced herself tentatively on the edge of the easy chair.

"The emergency fund for people who need help."

"Oh. Well, I don't know much about the church finances."

"That's why I need to see your husband. I need some money."

"Oh." Sarah reached for a magazine covered with ring marks left by several glasses of cold beverage. She picked up the pen she had used to do the crossword puzzle in the magazine. She turned to a page that had a little space on it and thought suddenly that a pastor's wife should have coasters, so her magazines wouldn't have rings on them, and pads of paper all over the house. "If you give me your name and phone number, I can have him call you as soon as he gets in." Sarah held the pen hopefully.

"See, I have cancer, and they have to do a lot of tests on me. We don't have health insurance. Me and my husband are self-employed, and we just can't afford insurance."

"So what you need is a large amount of money." Sarah rested both pen and magazine on her lap. "What you need is public assistance."

"We don't believe in welfare. That's for people who don't work." The woman's eyes seemed to have angry little sparks flying out of them. "Me and Charlie work hard—harder than most folks in this town."

"But Mrs. . . ."

"I'm Lorene Kluver."

"Well, Mrs. Kluver, our church may have an emergency fund, but it's for people who have sudden, temporary emergencies."

"Cancer isn't an emergency?" Lorene leaned back, her arms folded tightly across her small chest.

"It's an emergency, but it calls for long-term treatment. We don't have nearly that amount of money."

"I thought you didn't know anything about the finances."

"I don't know the specifics, but I do know we're not a rich church. We do well to keep utilities paid." Sarah felt like an amateur boxer, hands helplessly at her sides while the champ pranced around her, delivering little jabs here and there, biding time for the kill.

Mrs. Kluver leaned forward, wiry hands pressed into her bosom. "I'm sick. We need some help. Churches are supposed to help people." Her voice was becoming strident.

Sarah leaned away. "Are you and your husband members of our church, Mrs. Kluver?"

"What does that have to do with it?" A crackling silence passed between them. Then a wail filled the hallway. Peter's cry had never been more welcome.

"Excuse me." Sarah got up and hurried down the hallway. Peter was flailing in his crib, face red and unhappy. Sarah grabbed him up and changed him, wondering if it was a good idea to leave Mrs. Kluver alone. She reprimanded herself; the woman was needy but probably not a criminal. Sarah wondered when it was that those two categories of people had merged in her mind. She carried Peter down the hallway and found that Lorene hadn't changed her position on the couch. She looked ready to stay a long time.

"I'll have my husband call you when he gets home, Mrs. Kluver." Peter bellowed into Sarah's ear as she moved toward the door. Lorene didn't budge.

"Are you sayin' that if I don't have membership in your little church club, it's just tough luck?"

"I'm not saying that at all. But I'm sure we can't offer the kind of help you need. There are lots of programs you can look into—"

"They're not for people like me." A deep frown had taken over Lorene's face. "I *work* for my money." She pointed her chin at Sarah. "Do you know what it means to work for a living?"

A trembling went through Sarah that no other person would have seen. She felt heat rise through her hands, neck, and face. Peter continued to cry, balanced on her hip, which gave Sarah reason enough to raise her voice. "Yes, Mrs. Kluver, I know a lot about work." Peter squirmed, and she hitched him up more tightly. She swiveled at the waist and bounced him a little.

"You know, I raised two children and worked full-time. I didn't have any church payin' for *my* groceries."

Sarah shook her head a little, struggling to comprehend what she was hearing. "What?"

"You heard what I said. It's real easy for you to sit and judge. You don't have a worry in the world."

"Mrs. Kluver, I am not judging anybody! All I've told you is that our church doesn't have the kind of funds you need. And I resent being told that I don't work. What do you know—"

Lorene stood, and despite her small frame seemed to fill the room. "I'm a sick woman. I'm dying, Mrs. Pastor's Wife! And you're sayin' you won't help me! What is a church supposed to do if it doesn't dig into its pockets and help people out?"

Sarah walked to the door. She couldn't keep the tremor out of her voice as she said, "I think it's best if you go now. I'll tell my husband just as soon as he comes in. I'm—" She had to swallow suddenly. "I'm sure we can do something. I'm sorry we can't pay all your bills for you, but this is a little town and a little church and—" She turned to the woman, the anger finally breaking through her polite pretense, "Everybody's having a hard time making ends meet. We have farmers about to lose everything because of this drought. We have elderly people who don't get enough Social Security to live on from month to month. You're not the only person in the world with a problem, Mrs. Kluver!" Sarah opened the door wide. Her sudden shift in volume had shocked Peter into silence. She glanced to see him looking at her intently, sucking on four fingers at once.

Lorene moved slowly. "You're just the way everybody says you are," she said calmly, walking out the door. She had gone all the way to the edge of the front porch before turning, a smirk narrowing her eyes and nudging her mouth into a smile. "This whole town knows how you are—selfish and unsociable. I may not hang around church ladies' circles, but I hear. We all hear. Nobody can figure out what you're doin' here. You just sit in your house all day."

Sarah slammed the door. Even as she slammed it, she imagined what people would say about a pastor's wife slamming a door on anybody, no matter how obnoxious they were.

Sarah and Jacob looked dully over the dirty dishes on the table in front of them. Jacob took a last bite of bread and butter, then tossed the rest onto his plate. Sarah knew he was looking at her. "There's always somebody around like Lorene Kluver. She talks like that to everybody," he said.

Sarah stared wordlessly out the window above the sink.

"Sare, you can't take it personally. I'm really sorry I wasn't here to deal with her."

"Don't take it personally?" Sarah turned a look on her husband that she knew had the power to beat him up. "How am I not supposed to take it personally when the whole town is talking behind my back about what a worthless pastor's wife I am? Tell me that."

"We've talked about this before," Jacob said softly, moving a crumb around the plate with his finger. "Some people have impossible expectations. And those are the people who talk. The ones who count—" He looked searchingly into her face. "The people who care about you know all that you do. And anybody who's been a parent knows what it's like to deal with a baby full-time. Those people respect and love you."

"Tell me their names."

A silent anger slid across Jacob's face. "I'm not going to play this game."

"Tell me their names."

They stayed locked in horrible stillness. Finally Sarah rose from the table.

"I can't take this, Jacob," she said, her face away from him. She began stacking dishes in the sink. "I've been telling you in every way I know how. This situation is not working for me. I'm sorry I'm not stronger and wiser and more loving and—" she turned to him. "And just a better person. But I'm standing on a ledge here, and we've got to do something more than have these stupid discussions."

She turned back to the sink and heard a familiar sigh escape her husband. It was the sigh that told her how helpless he felt and how angry it made him not to be able to please her.

"I'm sorry," she said.

Madison Carruthers looked surprised when Jacob and Sarah appeared in his office doorway. His surprise changed to pleasure immediately, and he got up to greet them.

"Sorry to barge in without an appointment," Jacob said.

"Appointment!" Madison's eyes widened, and he seemed to have a tickle in his throat. Sarah realized he was chuckling. "I'm a heretic, son. Don't even own an appointment book."

"How can you do that?" asked Jacob, real wonder in his voice.

Madison showed them to the sagging couch on the other side of the room, floor-to-ceiling bookcases towering over it from behind. "I don't plan for any more than I can hold in my head for one day. Keeps life manageable." His look changed then, as he viewed the two of them. "What's on your mind?"

Sarah's throat tightened, and she heard Jacob take in a careful breath. "I want you to read this and tell me what you think of it," he said. He took a folded paper out of his shirt pocket and handed it to Madison.

Madison unfolded the paper, and his eyes shifted to bifocal level. The room became still as Jacob and Sarah watched him read. He looked up slowly, at Jacob and then at Sarah. "When did you decide this?"

"Just lately. Although . . ." Jacob glanced at Sarah. "I guess some of it's been going on for a while. I'm worried about the wording. I don't want them to think it's anything they've done."

"They'll think that no matter what you write," Madison said grimly. He refolded the paper and gave it back to Jacob. "Churches are like children; they read rejection into any weakness or problem Daddy has. They see it as their own failure. I must say, I didn't see this coming." He was looking at Sarah in much the same way he'd studied her over a month ago when they met for the pastors' meeting.

"They can put the blame on me," Sarah offered, unable to remove the bitter note in her voice. "They've thought all along that I wasn't doing my job."

"Don't be so hard on yourself, Sarah." Madison's voice was gentle. "I don't know which job is more impossible, that of the pastor or that of the spouse. But I don't like the feel of this. I'd like to see the two of you work through some of it before, rather than after, you leave. I think you need to work through some of it with the people you're leaving, so everyone's a little more clear about it. You aren't resigning from your marriage too, I hope."

"No. We're trying to save that." Jacob didn't sound hopeful. Sarah hurt for him, suddenly and so acutely that tears formed in her eyes.

"You seeing a counselor?"

"We haven't gone that far yet."

"My view is that counseling should precede a major decision such as this one. I've got a friend at Helmsly College I recommend highly."

"Thanks. I don't know if we can manage counseling and the pastorate too."

"You're in a crisis now, aren't you?"

Jacob nodded.

"Can you tell me about it? Can Rona and I help you hang on until you can make this a better transition?"

At the mention of Rona's name, Sarah began to weep but managed to say, "Oh, we don't want to burden you and Rona."

"I thought we were Christians here. I've always believed that helping with burdens was part of what we do." Madison's voice came closer, and Sarah looked up to see him standing in front of her with a box of tissues.

"Thank you," she said, taking one.

"Would you like to bend Rona's ear while Jacob bends mine? She's at the house now."

"I don't want to interrupt what she's doing."

"Sarah, dear, it's high time you interrupted." He touched her lightly on the shoulder. "I'll give her a call so she'll know you're coming." He offered his hand and helped Sarah up from the couch. She didn't look back at Jacob.

The sight of Rona at the back screen door, looking concerned and wearing an apron, was more than Sarah could bear. She was crying before she crossed the threshold. Rona led her to the worn and friendly sitting room, where Jacob and the other men had sat all those weeks ago.

Rona sat next to Sarah and made comforting sounds while the tears flooded and finally subsided. She got up long enough to get some lemonade. When she returned, Sarah was blowing her nose.

"This is all so screwed up," Sarah said. "Jacob and I have always been good at things. We've been good together. But this summer everything has disintegrated. I don't want to be here anymore. I don't know if I want to be with him anymore."

"This won't help much, but I know exactly how you feel. And I can tell you it won't always feel like this."

"But we can't survive until it feels different."

"Is there any particular thing that has been the final straw?"

Sarah began about Lorene Kluver. She'd only said a sentence when Rona touched her gently.

"Honey, you need to know that half the people in this town have had run-ins with Lorene."

"Well, would she just make up that everybody was talking about what a failure I am?"

"She's very good at picking up little pieces of gossip and innuendo and turning them into testimonials. You really can't take what she says to heart. I don't mean to make light of how it feels to you. But please don't give it more weight than it deserves."

"It's not just that." Sarah sniffled. "I really thought I could overcome who I was and be what Jacob needed me to be. Why would God call us to a place we don't fit? Where *I* don't fit?"

"Maybe God would rather you be who you are."

Sarah was silent.

"That takes more courage," said Rona.

"People here can't make room for who I am."

"They can, but that takes courage too."

The tears started again. Sarah wadded up more tissue and tried to catch the flow.

"I think this is an important time for you, Sarah. I could tell you about some important times of my own, but that's not what you need."

"You're so much better suited for the job."

Rona leaned back against the sofa cushions. When Sarah finished blowing her nose again, she looked up to see the older woman watching her.

"Would you want Miranda to try to change who she is?"

"I know where you're going with this." Sarah smiled a bit as she shook her head. "But I still can't reconcile the difference between what I do best and what I'm required to do just by being here."

"I know. Do you need aspirin? You look like you've got a whopping headache."

"No. I frown these days with or without the headache."

Rona leaned toward her. "I just don't want to see you make any decisions out of fear. You seem ready to run away."

"Oh, I am."

"Please don't."

"I won't right away—not and spoil these revivals. I can do that much for Jacob."

"I'd like to pray for you, Sarah. May I do that?"

Sarah shrugged. "That hasn't made much difference lately. But go ahead if you want."

Rona prayed. She kept it short and didn't fill it with clichés Sarah didn't believe anymore. After the amen, Sarah looked straight into Rona's eyes.

"Rona, do you think it matters at all to God—how hard I've tried? Does that mean *anything?*"

For the first time, Rona's eyes filled with tears. "Yes. I think he hates to see us trying so hard."

"I wish he'd help out a little more, then. It would take the pressure off."

Rona dabbed her eyes. "I don't have a thing to say to that one."

An hour later Sarah and Jacob sat at their dining-room table. Usually they had discussions in the kitchen, but something had changed this afternoon. This talk was different from all the others they'd had.

"Madison has some suggestions," Jacob said, sounding weary. "I think we should consider them."

"All right." Sarah was numb. She heard Miranda singing to her dolls in the backyard.

"First we see this counselor. Sort out exactly what's happened with us."

"Is he expensive?"

"I don't know. We'll have to work out the money."

Sarah was quiet.

"Then after the last week of revival is over, we make the decision whether to stay or to go. Leaving right now would be too damaging for everyone involved."

"We need to move in time to get Miranda started in first grade. I don't want her starting late in a strange place."

"We'll do whatever we have to do. The last week of revival is the first part of August. That'll give us a little time."

"Very little."

"If we have to, you and Miranda can go ahead of me, and I'll pack up the house."

"If we decide to leave."

"If we still think that's what we need to do."

Jacob stood to look out the east window where he could catch a glimpse of Miranda in the yard. "For what it's worth, Madison wasn't too easy on me. He's really concerned about you. I know I haven't handled this situation very well. I'm sorry."

"Let's not apologize right now. My brain is too tired to process it."

"Do you want me to contact this counselor?"

"Yes."

They ate supper quietly, allowing Miranda's monologue of her day's events to carry the time. For the first time in a long time, Sarah felt that her pain was one with Jacob's, that they were actually in the middle of this together. It brought little comfort now.

The next day Sarah readied the extra room for Joe Travis. Of all times, they *would* have company for the week. Well, that might make it easier for her and Jacob to put a lid on all this trouble and just do what they needed to do to finish out these ghastly revivals. After she worked on the spare room, Sarah spent the afternoon making calls to the women who had volunteered to provide refreshments all week.

Sarah decided, for the first time in weeks, to cook a decent supper. Her emotional investments were all full up, and it felt good to get lost in something that didn't matter. She did her orange-almond chicken recipe, with fresh vegetables and an applesauce cake for dessert. Jacob's eyes widened slightly in surprise.

"This is nice. You didn't need to spend so much time over a hot stove."

"I wanted to do it," she replied quietly.

"Thank you."

"You're welcome."

"Do I have to eat the orange rind?" Miranda wanted to know.

"No, sweetie, that's mainly for decoration."

"Cool."

"Isn't Mommy a good cook?" Jacob asked.

"She's exxx-cellent," said Miranda.

Sarah wanted to explode. *A little late to try to flatter me, Jacob.*

"What time will Joe get in tomorrow?" she asked.

"About noon. I got in touch with Dr. Nieman. She can see us Thursday at two. Is that all right for you?"

"A woman professor in these parts. What a surprise." Sarah was actually pleased, but her words came out sounding sarcastic. "Yes. Two is fine."

Later, they lay in bed together, hardly breathing. Sarah hated feeling so uncomfortable around the man she'd been married to for nearly seven years.

"I don't really want to keep Joe Travis in the dark," Jacob said into the air above them, "but it's probably best that he doesn't know about this stuff with us right now."

"I agree. It really has nothing to do with the services. We're going to be so busy this week, I don't expect it to be very hard just to go on like nothing's wrong."

She felt him shift slightly. She didn't know if he was moving closer to her or farther away.

"I can't believe this has happened. I can't believe I've been so dense," he said.

"This is mostly about me, Jacob. I'm not cut out for this business, and I should have figured that out before I signed on."

"Signed on with the ministry—or signed on with me?"

"I really don't want to talk about it now, OK? Maybe we should both take some notes so we can get more done with the doctor on Thursday."

"OK. Good night."

"Good night."

Their words stayed in the air like a vapor. They didn't move. Sarah knew that Jacob was wounded deeply. He was already loading blame onto himself. She was exhausted and knew she couldn't reach out to him. But it would be the right thing to do.

She gathered her last ounce of strength and placed one hand on Jacob's bare chest. The coarse hair was as familiar to Sarah as her own body. She rested her hand there, feeling totally incapable of living up to what she was saying with the gesture. When Jacob's hand came up to cover hers, the pain of his love made tears jump into her eyes. She heard Jacob sniffle, and in the next instant they were holding each other, weeping.

Sarah knew these tears were unlike making-up tears of the past. This time, she wasn't at all sure tears would be enough.

21

RANDY KLUVER:
THE JULY REVIVAL

Wednesday, July 23

W hat's gotten into you, anyway?" Dave asked. He was stretched out on the bed, twirling a Kansas City Royals cap on one finger. Randy glanced at him in the dresser mirror. She looked back at herself, makeup brush lifted. She had already applied and washed off one face.

"Nothing's gotten into me. Just thought I'd go to church." She wiped off most of the blush she'd just put on.

"You've never wanted to go before." Dave tossed the cap into the air and caught it.

"Not since you've known me. I used to go all the time when I was a kid."

"Everybody goes when they're kids. Most people grow out of it."

She gave him a look. "I don't see why people have to grow out of God. It's not like he's Santa Claus."

"Ol' Joe was by a couple days ago, wasn't he?"

"We asked him to visit next time he was in town."

"Yeah, but this was a church visit. I saw the revival thing on the counter. Does he get extra credit for getting you to come to one of their meetings? Graduate from seminary with honors or something?"

"Don't be mean. He visited, that's all."

"And now you're going to church. Some tubby preacher boy's gonna steal you from me. I should have left him and his sorry car in K.C."

She threw her eyeliner, unused, at him. "I don't think so."

"It's about your mom, isn't it?"

She turned around to face him this time. He looked sorry that he'd made that last comment. "What do you mean by that?"

"I'm just saying that this guy's got you thinking about eternal souls and heaven and the like. And it's easy to think about that stuff with somebody sick in the family."

"I'm going because I haven't been in a long time."

"Lena going along?"

"Oh, right. She's more antichurch than you are." She turned back to her reflection. Lipstick or not? She thought church people probably weren't as hung up on makeup as they used to be.

"I'm not antichurch. I'm just—" Dave stopped while she slipped out of her T-shirt and put the sundress over her head. She caught him looking at her with that smile. It was a smile she liked to see, but she pretended not to see it now.

"You want to come along?" she asked.

He rolled onto his stomach and heaved a sigh. "Churches make me nervous. You never know what people expect you to do."

"For cryin' out loud. Just because you haven't been around church enough to know anything. Coward."

"Go by yourself." He swatted at the skirt as she passed him on her way out. She walked out the door without saying anymore. Church-going wasn't something she'd expect from Dave, but it felt lonely going down the sidewalk all dressed up and by herself.

Maybe that's the way life would always be, facing important things without any company. It seemed that every time in her life she had needed to sort something out nobody had been around to help. Like when she'd lost her virginity to Jay. It was the type of thing a person wanted to talk about afterwards, but there hadn't been anybody. When Jay had dropped her off at home later, she'd been full of emotions that needed expressing. But Dad was on the road, and Mom was on the phone harping at somebody who'd crossed her. Randy had tried to sit on her bed and think about what had just happened, but Teri had turned the room into Barbie Town with cardboard boxes set up everywhere and dolls in the middle of their own love stories. Randy had ended up in front of the TV, eating leftover tuna salad, trying to figure out what she'd just done and if there was a reason for her to feel as empty as she did.

Well, Jay hadn't worked out, and now it looked as if Dave would. But who could say? And Lena was back, bringing the New Age with her, and most of that felt like clutter in the brain. And now Mom was really sick; she might even die. But nobody would talk about it. That made Randy want to scream and shake people.

This revival meeting seemed important. Joe Travis did have a lot to do with it; there was a peacefulness around him that made her feel able to think clearly. Dave was peaceful too, but a girl had to have a place where she could just think, without noise anywhere. So Joe's talking about God's love and how Jesus went through all that he did so that people could experience peace—well, it had sounded like a thing to look into for herself. She wasn't sure she'd ever felt peace for more than a few minutes.

When she entered the Methodist church foyer, a lot of people were standing around talking in little groups. A middle-aged man greeted Randy with a big smile and pressed a church bulletin into her hand. She stood there feeling conspicuous, wondering if she should break away from the crowd and find a pew to sit in. Just then music started from the front of the sanctuary, and people started heading for the pews. Randy found a spot four rows from the back. She took an aisle seat and made herself busy by reading the bulletin.

The singing part went all right. Randy had sung all the songs at one time or another. Reverend Dancey welcomed them all, and they sang some more; then a woman with gray hair stood up at the podium and sang a solo. Randy noticed Joe Travis sitting in the front row. He was watching the soloist and never turned around to see Randy. It made her feel better to see him, though. She recognized a lot of people here, but Joe was the only one who had ever talked to her about matters of the soul. Other people would just ask, How's business at the café?

About twenty minutes into the service the guest speaker got up to deliver the sermon. He looked close to Dad's age, maybe a little older. His short hair was gray, and he had a huge neck and a wide, red face.

The man began reading from a large Bible that draped across his thick hand. "'But you are a chosen people, a royal priesthood, a holy nation, a people belonging to God, that you may declare the praises of him who called you out of darkness into his wonderful light. Once you were not a people, but now you are the people of God; once you had not received mercy, but now you have received mercy.

"'Dear friends, I *urge* you, as aliens and strangers in the world, to abstain from sinful desires, which war against your soul. Live such good lives among the pagans that, though they accuse you of doing wrong, they may see your good deeds and glorify God on the day he visits us.'"

The preacher wiped his mouth with a handkerchief and cradled the book on his arm as he walked to one end of the platform, looking out over that side of the congregation.

"*Chosen!* A *chosen people!* Did you hear that? *God chose you* to belong to him, to speak for him, to be—what does it say? 'A royal priesthood'! *You!* A priest of the Lord!"

He turned and headed for Randy's side of the church. "And you say, 'Well, Brother Arnold, how can *I* be a priest? I'm not educated. I'm not all that religious. I'm not even *good* most of the time.' But Brother Arnold didn't call you a priest; *God did!* How did he make you a priest? Let's just look here and see—"

The open Bible slipped back onto his wrist, and he used the forefinger of his other hand to point to a place on the page.

"'That you may declare the praises of him—' listen now—'the praises of him who *called you out of darkness into his wonderful light.*' Did you know that you're living in the light? If you know Jesus you are—just like we talked about last night, that Jesus is the Light of the world, and when you accept him into your heart, you've what?" He cocked his head. "What have you done when you've accepted Jesus into your heart?"

"Walked into the light," came the answer from a pew close to the front.

"Lord bless you, that's right." A great smile stretched across his moist face. "You've walked into the light. And *because* you've come from the darkness to the light, you have credentials with God. You've got the only credentials it takes—knowin' the difference between darkness and light. That's all it takes to be a priest." His voice had softened, like that of a father explaining some truth to a small child. He raised the Bible again and found his place on the page.

"'Once you were not a people, but now you are the people of God; once you had—,'" His voice fell to a strong whisper, his body bent toward the people in the front pews—"'not received mercy, but now you have received mercy.'"

Randy could feel her heart beating. It seemed that every tiny sound was going directly into her ears, as if the volume of everything had been turned way up. She could hear the preacher breathing and someone fanning with a bulletin in the pew behind her. Somebody across the room coughed. Inside Randy's head, words were echoing: *Now you have received mercy.*

The preacher straightened up and gave them all a hard look. "This passage isn't talking to unsaved folks. No, it's talking to people who know what's up—just like a lot of you know what's up. You've known for a long time, some of you." His index finger trailed over them. "I've been around these little towns. I know." A shake of his great head. "Lord knows I know—that many of you have known the difference between the darkness and the light since you were yea tall." He held a hand waist high. "But for whatever reason you've tucked that knowledge away—I don't know, maybe for a rainy day, maybe for an emergency." He dropped to a whisper again. "You're children of the light, but you're walkin' in the dark."

Randy leaned back, unnerved by how quiet the room had become.

The preacher raised his Bible again. "'Dear friends, I urge you, as aliens and strangers in the world, to abstain from sinful desires—' Live in the light, is what he's saying here—'sinful desires, which war against your soul.' Now." He put the Bible on the pulpit and loosened his tie. "I imagine a lot of you are here tonight because you have serious problems. You're in *pain.* You're *confused* or *afraid.* Why do you think that is? Well, if you've never accepted Jesus Christ as your personal Savior, that's your *only* problem right now, and we'll review that in a minute. But my guess is that I'm staring at a whole roomful of *children of the light.* And the reason your lives are so full of trouble and pain and confusion—is that there's war going on in your souls!" He sucked in a great breath and raised his arms above his head, then brought them down with each emphasized word: "You're living in the *dark,* not abstaining from *sinful desires,* and there's *war in your souls!* Am I right?" He looked to the other side of the congregation. "Am I right?" The question was met with dead silence.

He walked off the platform then, stood in the center aisle, and paused a long moment. When he spoke again, his voice was calmer.

"The horror of this passage is that it tells us the other results of not walking in the light. It says that we should 'live such good lives among the pagans that, though they accuse you of doing wrong, they may see your good deeds and glorify God on the day he visits us.' What does it mean—'pagans'? It means those people who've never seen the light. It's that husband or friend or mother or little sister who doesn't know the Lord. This verse tells us that if we would just live in the light, they'd see it too. And *that's* what it means when it says we are a *royal priesthood.*"

Randy sat, numbed, and followed the preacher with burning eyes as he explained what it meant to see the light and accept Jesus. He talked about some forms of darkness—about family strife and personal pride. He even mentioned the satanism that some teenagers in town claimed to be involved with.

"See, God just leaves us in the dark, to stumble around until we get tired of stumbling. Don't expect him to shine a flashlight on that dark path if it's a path leading you in the wrong direction. No, sir. Darkness isn't fun, it's not what the good Lord intended, but he'll make your darkness serve a purpose too. After a while you'll get tired of stumbling into rocks and trees, gathering bruises. You'll get fed up with that war inside you, and you'll turn to the light. And friends—" He held up a hand, as if to stop all other motion. "When you walk in the light, other people can see what a light-filled life looks like. God doesn't call us priests because we're better than other people. He calls us priests because we can't help but minister to others when we're walking in his light."

The preacher walked down the aisle a few steps. He stopped three or four feet from the pew Randy was sitting in. For a second his gaze locked onto hers, and she saw, in the midst of the large, sweaty face, two gray eyes filled with pure kindness. He sounded tired and hoarse when he spoke, his hands clasped as reverently as large, callused hands could be, and his voice fell to a softer, ending note. "The Lord Jesus is light, and he wants *you* to live in that light. It's your choice. It's God's gift to you, but he won't force it. The only choices that count are the ones we make freely."

Those last words shot straight into Randy's soul. Of course. Peace had to do with choices. Choices that came out of a free heart. Choices a person made for herself that would change the course of her whole life.

A hot fountain bubbled up from her heart then, and she was crying, just like that. While the evangelist repeated his sentence a second and third time, breathing close to all of them, probing into their heads, Randy thought of Mom and Dad, of Teri, and of her dead aunt from Branson. She thought of Dave at home in his own darkness, and of Lena who had left long ago and now lived in such a different world. Randy knew right then that her friend—Lena, who was always so together and confident—was stumbling around and didn't even know it.

As Randy listened to the preacher talk on about darkness and light, she felt pieces of her life falling into an order finally, one she could understand. He had explained in just a few words all the hurtful things that had come and gone, stealing whatever peace she had tried to hold onto.

A few people were walking up the aisles to pray at the altar railing up front. Randy felt her body vibrating, needing to move forward, needing to make that good choice. But at the same time her legs felt too weak to make the journey. She bowed there in the pew, tears running off her face and onto the sundress. She felt a warm hand on her shoulder and looked up into Joe Travis's face. He bent toward her and said gently, "Randy, may I pray with you?"

It was a pale night sky that spread above her when she made her way home. Behind her she could hear voices of people parting in the churchyard and car engines clearing their throats, little grates of human sound against the summer noises of frogs and crickets. She walked toward home but couldn't hear her feet. Her head was humming.

She'd been washed out—by regret, then by gratitude. With each step toward home she could almost feel the burdens fall away, burdens she'd been loading up almost since birth. There really was a right way to go, and a truth large enough to dispel the lies that had piled up for years. In the center of her soul rested a satisfied and long-needed relief.

Dave's house came into view. The porch light was on. A fuzzy television dialogue met her at the front steps. She paused, wanting to spend another hour or so in the night air, where she could still hear her memories of "Love Lifted Me" and "Softly and Tenderly." She leaned against the porch post and looked up through black branches. The speech she'd made up in her head, about finding peace with God, felt timid now, too far back in her private self to bring out. Maybe it would be best not to say much tonight. Right now she was feeling pretty worn out.

She opened the door and walked in. The room felt outdated to her suddenly, as part of the life she'd had before. The bill of the Royals cap turned in her direction. Then the scene on the television changed from a city street at night to a sunlit beach somewhere, and Dave appeared in the recliner, glowing with ocean colors.

"Hi, babe. How was the revival?" His voice was light.

"Really good."

"Oh yeah?" He found her skirt and tugged on it gently until she sat in his lap. He kissed her, his hand resting on the top of her dress.

"Meeting went kind of long, didn't it?" he said.

"Oh, you know, revivals aren't like normal meetings."

"I wasn't worried or anything."

She nodded and let her head rest on his shoulder.

"You OK?"

"I'm fine."

"You sound like you've got a cold."

Gunfire popped out at them to the sound of running feet and guitar music.

"What are you watching?"

"Some cop show rerun."

"Yuck."

"Want to turn in?" He squeezed her shoulder.

"I suppose." She let him guide her into the bedroom. She needed to tell him about what had happened. It seemed almost unfair to sleep with him when she felt like such a different person.

They undressed and took their turns in the bathroom. She was last in bed and had hardly touched the sheets when his arms encircled her, clasping her body against his. Any other summer night, with the scent of flowers outside their window and a soft breeze coming across the bed, this would have been her favorite thing to do. But there were the words of hymns in her head and new rhythms rocking her heart. Dave didn't seem to notice that she wasn't as enthusiastic as usual, and after a while he snuggled next to her. He would be asleep in a few minutes.

"Dave?"

"Mmm?"

"A wonderful thing happened to me tonight."

"Really?" His words were sluggish, giving way to sleep.

"I finally got some peace of mind."

"Good." He squeezed her arm. "I know how upset you've been lately."

"Everything's going to be OK now."

"That's right."

"Because I'm new inside."

Silence followed. She wondered if he had drifted off. But then he shifted, turning onto his back. "That's good. You don't want to hang on to the bad stuff."

"But I couldn't just let go of it. God had to take it—and then give me something to take its place."

Dave was quiet.

"I guess this doesn't make much sense to you," Randy said, resting her arm across his chest. "It's a pretty personal thing."

"Yeah, religion's personal."

"I prayed tonight. And for the first time I *felt* somebody listening. Has that ever happened to you?"

"Can't say that it has. I don't think about that stuff."

"Well, a prayer got answered tonight that I hadn't even gotten around to praying yet. It's the most incredible thing that's ever happened to me." She squeezed his hand and looked into his face for some kind of signal that all this was OK. He just smiled at her and patted her arm.

"A lot of things make sense to me now," she said. "I've spent so much of my life being mad about the things that were wrong. I never stopped to think about the choices I need to make for myself."

"What choices?"

"The choice to live in the light or live in the dark, for one thing. I've been looking for the light, but always in dark places."

"Well." Dave seemed to be measuring his words. "From what I can see, you *are* living in the light. You're honest and loving and good to people."

"But you can be those things and still be in the dark. And the dark is sin. I don't know why I didn't just see it before now."

"Sin? Don't get morbid on me, Randy."

"It's not morbid. It's the truth."

"The truth for who?"

"For all of us."

"I can't buy that. Look, I'm glad you had a meaningful experience and all that, but don't preach at me."

"Who's preaching? I'm just trying to explain something that happened to me."

"That's fine."

"If it's fine, why are you upset?"

"I'm not upset." He was making circles with his hand as he talked, the way he always did when he'd been put on the defensive. Randy decided to let them both sleep.

"Good night." She leaned over and kissed him tenderly on the cheek. "I love you." His lips brushed her face in return.

Randy turned over, her back against Dave's. She clutched the folds of sheet in a fist. Her insides were roaring with spent tears and new hopes and the ominous feeling that life was about to get harder in some ways.

She whispered into the still air what she couldn't say directly to Dave just yet: "God loves you too."

22

TONY GARDINO: RESCUE THE PERISHING

Friday, July 25

Tony sat on his bed, breathing hard. He could hear Mom crying outside his door.

You just hide behind your religion so you don't have to see what kind of a life you have! He could still see her dodging back as though he'd taken a swing at her. The pain was all over her face. Had he really said that? Yes. He'd called her a hypocrite. He'd said that he hated her. How could he say that? Mom was pushy and pathetic, but she didn't shut off like Dad or ridicule and walk away like Annie. But Tony had said he hated the sight of her.

Tony's inner blackness was heavier by the minute. It made his stomach burn. He should just apologize. Now.

He heard something screech and looked out the window to see Granddad moving garden equipment around. He'd been somewhere in the house, if out of sight, when the argument happened. Tony figured the old man had been close enough to hear everything. He didn't know how Granddad had reacted, if he had reacted at all.

"Tony?" It was Mom, outside the door, with a congested voice, a frightened voice full of pain. "Honey? I want to talk to you."

Tony sat like a stone. At least Dad was at work. But Tony had to get out of this house.

"I want to understand why you hate me so much." The tears in her voice flooded him, but he didn't move. He might talk to her later, but the way he wanted and when he wanted. Not like this. Not like a trapped animal.

"I just wish you'd talk with Pastor Jacob," Mom was saying. "I know there's something bothering you. He has a degree in counseling."

Tony hated the way his mother sounded when she was pleading. He hated how weak she was. But why did he have to tell her he hated her? She would always think it meant something it didn't.

A plan came to his mind then. "See if the pastor can talk to me at four this afternoon. I'll talk to him then if he wants."

"OK, honey. You just stay there. I'll call." He heard her hurrying away. Better to be in a pastor's office than here when Dad got home. No one would get hurt. Dad hadn't tried to whip him since Tony was thirteen. But Tony was beginning to be scared of what he might do to Dad.

He stepped into the hall and stood at the top of the stairs. Mom was giving the pastor a real rundown. She managed to make things sound three times as bad as they were. Why, Tony was about to run away. She was afraid he'd join a gang—or that satanic cult. He'd never, ever used such language before, and she was so afraid of what he might do. Tony wasn't a bit surprised when Mom came to the bottom of the stairs and called up to him that four o'clock would be fine. Pastor Jacob would meet Tony in the pastor's office at the church.

"I'm going over to Dave's," Tony said quickly as he walked down the stairs and past his mother.

"OK, honey." She touched his shoulder, and he ducked away from her.

He went to the pear tree but kept going. He may as well hang out at Dave's. Nobody would be home. He could sit on the porch. Or maybe knock around in the shed, sharpen a tool or something.

Dave's back porch was flooded with midday heat. Tony started around to the front porch and remembered that Dave never locked the place. He probably had beer in the fridge. The kitchen door opened, and Tony stood in the quiet for a minute, wondering if he should really be inside the house. He found the beer and sat down at the table. The opened package of cookies there didn't appeal to him. He remembered that the whole fight with Mom had started because she was trying to get him to eat something. He hadn't been excited over food for a long time. The cookies in front of him had double cream in the center, but he just looked at them and gulped the beer.

"When did you come in?"

Lena—*Lena*—was standing in the doorway to the living room.

"Hi! I, uh, just stopped by. Didn't know anybody was home."

"Does Dave know you drink his beer while he's away?"

"This is the first time. Had to get out of the house for a while. What are *you* doing here?"

"I'm borrowing a pair of Randy's sandals." She turned out a foot for him to see. Perfect, tanned feet in black cloth sandals, laces going around the ankle. Black toenails.

"Gramma wants me back for lunch," she said. "Want to come?"

"Sure." He gulped down the last of the beer.

"Eat a mint or something. Gramma will smell that."

Tony smiled at her and pulled a pack of gum out of his pocket.

"So what happened at home?" Lena asked as they walked out the front door and down the shaded walk. She wasn't looking at him and sounded curious mainly.

"Mom gets hyper. I yelled at her, and she cried."

"Eww. Messy, huh?"

Mrs. Petersen's house was only three blocks away. They entered the back door. Mrs. Petersen was setting sandwich stuff and what looked like cut-up fruit on the small kitchen table. She grinned at them as though she'd been waiting all month for their arrival. "I'm almost ready here. Go sit in the front room where it's cooler. I'll call when it's ready."

"C'mon," said Lena. Tony felt the soft hand take hold of his and pull him into the next room.

"Come on out here." Lena brought him into a small side room that was practically all windows. Probably a porch once. Plants were everywhere—on little stands and in large pots on the floor. Hanging from hooks. There were so many plants the air looked green. The room smelled of clean dirt and plastic watering cans.

"Your grandma's into plants."

"This is the feel-better room." Lena sat on a couch glider under the row of windows. The glider was covered by a quilt and loaded with pillows. "Here." Lena patted the space beside her.

"The feel-better room?"

"Yes." The smile on her face looked like a little girl's.

Tony ducked beneath the small jungle of hanging plants and sat down. The mattress gave like a marshmallow. Lena wrapped an arm around him; her skin was cool on the back of his neck, like a scarf. The sensation slipped down his spine. He reached up and held her hand where it rested on his shoulder.

"When me and my cousins were little, we'd visit Gramma all at once—six or seven of us camped out for the weekend. And somebody always had a stomachache or nosebleed or something. Gramma'd put the sick one out here on the daybed under the plants and give us aspirin and peppermint tea."

Tony liked how soft her voice had become suddenly. "Did it work?" he asked.

"Most of the time—yeah."

"Maybe she put something special in the tea," he said, slipping his other arm around her waist.

"I think it was just being treated special." Lena's voice was thin. Tony expected her to start crying, but she twisted around to pull a dangling vine out of her hair. "You know—kids want attention. Our parents were always busy. Lie down." She stood up and took hold of his feet, lifting them up to the bed. "Sometimes I pretended to be sick just to have this room to myself." She stretched out beside him and snuggled into his side, staring up into the tangled variations of green.

Tony couldn't remember ever wanting something the way he wanted to possess Lena right then. Her hair smelled like peaches, and every part of her that touched against him felt so soft. He thought if he hugged her too hard she would collapse like a feather pillow and his hands would meet each other in her middle. She was sad, like him, but in a strong, beautiful way. He wished he could press her into him until they were the same person. Then he could be strong like her. Her sweet hair and skin would soothe that constant pain that beat through him every day and through every sleepless night. He bet he could sleep after making love to her. He could probably sleep by just having her beside him like this.

"Don't hold me so tight—you trying to choke me?" Her voice had no anger in it.

"No. I just like it when you're close to me." He kissed the back of her head, strands of her hair sticking to his lips.

"I like it too," she said lightly and relaxed. She turned toward him and pulled his face close to hers. "See—this really is a feel-better room." She kissed him long and hard. He was about to get lost when Mrs. Petersen's voice cut through the air from the next room.

"OK, kids, lunch is ready."

Lena unwrapped herself from Tony. "Sure. We'll be right there." She saw the look of disappointment on Tony's face and shrugged.

"Later," she said, standing beside him and smoothing her jeans, tucking in her shirt. He followed her into the kitchen and ate the food Lena's grandma put in front of him. He didn't taste much of it. He listened to Lena and her grandma talk about things, nothing in particular, and he enjoyed watching this incredible girl. *Later,* she had said.

After lunch they walked to the video store and checked out *Fly Away Home.* They lounged on Mrs. Petersen's living-room floor, a fan near them moving the air-conditioning faster, pillows under their heads. It was a lame movie for the most part, because they'd chosen one that wouldn't offend Gramma. But it was enough to be in the cool living room in the middle of the stifling day outside, the green feel-better room within sight.

At three-thirty, Lena's grandma had to run some errands. Lena led Tony outside. They started walking.

"She won't let me have boys in the house when she's not here."

"Not paranoid, is she?"

"No. Just old-fashioned. Decent girls don't have boys over when there's no adult around."

Tony laughed. Lena didn't.

"I can respect that. Gramma's really clueless about a lot of things, but she's got more dignity than my mother ever had. And a *lot* more than any of Dad's babes have."

Tony watched her face. It didn't really look sad, but he worried that maybe he'd made her mad by laughing. "Sort of like my granddad," he said. "Right out of the old country. Never talks to anybody. But when he does, wow. Like, the world stops to listen."

Lena nodded. "They have dignity. From not being scared because so much has happened already and they've lived through it."

"Yeah. I can see that. I hardly know anything Granddad's lived through."

"Well, you know a lot of it had to be bad. I mean, he and Gramma were our age during the Depression. I get ticked when somebody else has checked out the video I want. But I come home and Gramma's fixed lunch for me. There's never a question if there's going to be lunch or not. You know?"

"Yeah." Tony couldn't think of anything else to say. He looked up then and saw someone waving at him frantically from down the block. Mom. He groaned. "Uh, I've got something I said I'd do for my mom. See you later maybe?"

Lena shrugged. "Who knows? In a town this big, we may never see each other again." She smiled a tired smile.

Mom's eyes were wide with intent. Tony was barely within hearing when she started talking.

"You're supposed to see Pastor Morgan in ten minutes." He could feel her right behind him as he went into the house and splashed some water on his face from the kitchen sink. He heard the sound of the big knife on the cutting board near him.

"I want you to tell Brother Jacob why you're so unhappy. A lot of times it helps to talk."

Tony could tell she had been working up just the right tone of voice for this statement. Mom never said anything without considering it hard for about ten minutes. Tony glanced at her back, bent over the counter where she was cutting up a chicken. Sometimes she looked as if she were expecting someone to start hitting her, her feet planted a bit apart, shoulders rounded in to protect her, head cocked so that she would see or hear the first sign of trouble. Tony suddenly felt really sorry for his mother.

"I don't want to be a Christian right now."

Mom turned around, a profoundly sad look in her eyes. "You're already a Christian, honey. You accepted the Lord when you were eight years old." She smiled weakly. "I was there."

"I don't remember what I did when I was eight years old, but none of it means anything to me now. I know that makes you feel bad, but that's just the way it is." He felt exhaustion fill his head and turned to leave the room. He heard Mom sob before he'd reached the door. "Don't cry!" he shouted. "I hate that!" She cried louder, and he walked away from the house as fast as he could.

Pastor Morgan's office was cool and quiet when Tony tapped at the doorjamb. The man looked up from some letters in front of him. It took a moment for the busy look to leave his face and a smile to replace it. "Tony." He rose and walked over, holding out a hand. Tony took it briefly. "I'm glad you came. Have a seat."

"I'm here for Mom's sake, all right? I don't want to talk with anybody, but she freaks every time I tell her I'm not a Christian and don't want to be. So let's just talk about football or something, and you can say a prayer over me, and I can tell her we did this."

The pastor's eyebrows shot up as he took a seat in a nearby chair. "I like an honest person. I'll be just as blunt. You're scaring your mother half out of her mind."

Tony looked at the set of eyes in front of him. They looked back without flinching.

"She's scared about everything. I can't help that," said Tony.

"Do you think you could find at least one thing you do that makes her scared and do it differently?"

"I said a bunch of stuff I shouldn't have. I won't do that again."

"Good."

"So, we're finished?"

"Have you been sick?" Tony jerked his head up at the sudden change of subject. "You look like death warmed over. What's going on?"

"Nothing."

"Your mom said something's bothering you."

"It's bothering her, not me."

"What is it that's bothering *her?*"

Tony's heart had speeded up. "Everything bothers her. Like, I don't want to eat much, and she takes it personally."

"Looks like you haven't eaten much for a long time."

"I'm not hungry."

"Do you know why that is? My little girl weighs as much as you do. Seen a doctor lately?"

"I'm not sick."

"Just not hungry."

"Right."

"Are you ingesting some things on the side?"

"No."

"If you need some help, it's time to say something, Tony."

"I don't need help. I just need for people to stay off my back." He stared at the pastor, determined not to blink first. It was time to get out of here. "Look, I'll apologize to her for what I said. And I'll force down a little more food, OK?"

"That's a good start." Pastor Jacob leaned toward Tony just a little. "But I think there's a lot more we should be talking about right now."

"I don't think so."

"Will you come by when you feel like talking?"

Tony sniffed. *Just save the rest of the world, all right?* "Can I go now?"

The pastor lifted a hand toward the door. "I won't try to force it. But I want you to know I'm concerned. Your body may be trying to tell you something, with this no-appetite business. You hear what I'm saying to you?"

Tony slumped toward the door. He turned just enough to catch the pastor's eye. "It's no big deal."

"Thanks for coming by. Door's always open."

The sidewalk outside was hot through the soles of Tony's old sneakers. It made him think about hell. He wished he could go back to childhood and erase all the sermons he'd heard about it. Even now that he was old enough to know better, all those sermons kept coming after him, like nightmares that happened during consciousness.

They had been scraping Mamie's house for about four hours. They'd drunk at least two gallons of iced tea in the process. Finally Dave got off the ladder and stood behind Tony, who was working on siding closer to the ground.

"This is insane, man. It must be a hundred out here. Let's knock off until the afternoon's over. Can you come back this evening?"

"Yeah, I think so." Tony stood back to look at their progress. "Randy at the café today?"

"She works some Saturdays. I don't think she's sorry she's missing this."

"Call me at home when you're ready." Tony followed Dave to the back porch, where they washed paint chips off their arms in an old work sink.

Tony headed for Alma Petersen's. As hot as it was, he figured Lena would be working on a big bowl of ice cream. The minute he knocked on the door, Mrs. Petersen would dip some up for him too.

Lately his head was full of Lena, as if he were a fifth-grader going through his first crush. These days, Tony was able to face his room at night with just memories of the way Lena looked and walked and talked. His candles had sat, unlit, for about a week. This was beginning to feel the way summer should feel.

Lena was at her grandma's kitchen table looking through a box of junk, mainly jewelry. She had already picked out quite a load for herself. A pile of rings, bracelets, and other decorations glittered at her elbow.

"Hey, look, Tony. Gramma's giving me a bunch of her old costume jewelry. They don't even make some of this stuff anymore."

Tony took a seat at the table and nodded when Mrs. Petersen offered him a Coke. "Pretty nice," he murmured. "I can see you wearing it."

"I'm glad there's somebody who wants it," Mrs. Petersen said. "I've got too much stuff in this house—need to start getting rid of it. And I'd rather give it to family. Here you go, sweetie." She set a huge plastic cup full of ice and soda in front of him. Tony thought for a split second that it must be nice having a grandma still alive. On the whole, older ladies seemed easier to get along with. Even Mamie Rupert, particular as she was, followed up her worst criticisms with food and drink. She'd told Tony a couple of days ago that she thought he had a nice haircut. That it was different than anything she'd ever seen, but that just made him more interesting. Mom would never say a thing like that, and probably nobody else Mom's age would either. But grandmas had learned to loosen up. This made it extra pleasant to come visit Lena.

"I think that's all I want, Gramma." Lena scooped the jewelry into her hands but couldn't get it all, so she gave some of it to Tony. They carried it to the bedroom Lena was using. "Just put it on the dresser. I'll sort it out later." She sat on the bed and smiled at him. He came close and kissed her, bringing a hand up to stroke her arm.

"There's something I want to do. Will you come with me?" Her green eyes had something in them Tony couldn't identify. She was gorgeous. Everything about her was perfect—her eyes, her skin, her face, her hair, her body.

"Sure," he said.

"Gramma, we're going for a walk," Lena called as she pulled Tony down the hall toward the front door of the house.

"Oh, honey, it's too hot to be outside now. Why don't you stay in for a while. You kids could get a video."

"No. We'll be fine."

"Wear a hat."

Lena laughed but it wasn't necessarily a mean laugh. "Okay. Can I take your floppy straw one?"

"That's the best one for keeping off sun." Mrs. Petersen's voice got louder as she came into the foyer with the hat in her hand. "Good. Tony's got his ball cap. Except you need to turn the bill around the right way." Tony turned his cap around. "Once your head gets hot, there's nothing that will cool you off. You kids stay out of the sun as much as you can."

They both promised to do so. Lena's long legs carried her down the street almost too fast for Tony to keep up. He turned the bill of his cap to the back again.

"You look good in the hat," he said, just behind her.

"Hats usually look good on me. Some people look goofy in them."

"Where we going?"

"It's a surprise. I'm glad you're coming. It's the type of thing I want to share with somebody."

Tony felt something swell up in his chest. He tried to get her to talk more about it, but Lena wasn't in a talking mood. He'd figured out already that there were times she was just going to clam up and nothing could get a word out of her.

They walked all the way out of town, to where the paved street turned into gravel, and a pasture lay just beyond a straggly barbed-wire fence.

"Hold the wires up so I can get through," Lena said. Tony obeyed. Lena stepped through the fence, then held the top wire up for him to go under.

Insects were sounding off all around them. Heat gathered around their bare legs and faces as they stepped through high, brown grass. Tony was hot and itchy all over. Even Lena, a couple steps ahead of him, had visible sweat on her bare shoulders. Her body was perfectly tanned, slim, and sleek. Tony wished she would say something. They'd been walking for nearly half an hour.

"Exactly where are we going?" he asked.

"You'll see." She didn't turn or look at him.

"Will I see before or after heatstroke?"

"Don't be a wuss."

"A what?"

She did stop then, long enough for him to come up beside her. "You don't know? Well, this *is* Bender Springs. You know, *wuss*, like a wimp."

"OK, OK, I'm a wimp. It's only about a hundred out here."

"We're almost there. You whine sometimes, you know that?"

Tony looked around. Anything within "almost" distance was nothing at all.

"See?" The brown, perfect arm extended to their left. Tony didn't see, but he followed her through waist-high weeds. They stopped at a small ridge that extended far beyond them in both directions.

"Train tracks," he said. "What do I whine about?" He gave her as harsh a look as he dared.

Lena didn't answer. She stood with arms crossed, surveying the single set of tracks as if she'd built them herself. "Oh, you don't really whine. But you let things bother you too much. You're sort of short on personal power."

"Oh, I feel better now, understanding that about myself. Thanks."

"You just *give in* so much. To life. All the little irritations. Your folks."

Something knotted up in Tony's stomach. "Well, are you going to explain that statement?"

"If I have to explain, you're not ready to understand it."

He blew her off. She laughed at him. White sun flooded over her. He heard her laugh and wished he had it in him to make love to her then and there. Tony climbed the small rise and sat on one of the rails. It was hot through his cutoffs. "You talk like you know everything, but I don't believe you half the time, Lena."

"I don't care," she said, bending to pick up a handful of small rocks that filled the rail bed. "I say what I want and you believe what you want." She leaned over again, and Tony reached with his hand and touched the hollow of her throat with one finger. Her skin was like warm, live silk.

"In a few minutes the train will be through," she said, ignoring his advance.

"So?"

"So, that's what I'm here for."

"You gonna throw rocks at the train? Is that our big afternoon entertainment?"

Lena sat her tiny seat on the opposite rail. "No. That's too easy."

"Gonna jump on the train?"

"Too easy."

Something rippled through Tony's gut again. "What are you going to do?"

"Jump in front of it."

Tony looked into her eyes and waited for her to laugh. She looked straight back and didn't say anything.

"Jump in front of it," he repeated.

"Yes. I've been planning this for a couple weeks now."

"And what will I do?" he asked quietly.

"Watch. Or jump, too, if you want. I don't think you want it bad enough, though."

"How would you know what I want?"

"You're so easy to read. I've known all about you almost since I met you—under the tree, remember?"

"Did you know I've tried it already?"

"Really? I didn't know you had a thing for jumping trains."

"No, I tried it with a gun. Got caught though. You're only the second person who knows."

She peered at him from behind her veil of dark hair. "A gun?"

"Yeah. Never thought of doing it this way."

She shrugged, her face still hidden by her hair. "To each his own, huh?" She looked eastward down the tracks.

"Maybe now would be as good a time as any. Why wait till summer's over?" He wasn't really asking her.

"So, aren't you going to try to talk me out of it?" Her green eyes peered at him, teasing.

Tony swore. "Lena, you are so full of—"

"Full of what? Wanna find out? You'll see in a few minutes."

"I'm out of here." He jumped down from the ridge and headed across the pasture. "Invite me along to watch you off yourself! Friends don't do that to each other!" He heard her laughing at him. He walked a hundred yards, trying to make his brain work. He should stay. To hold her back. Or maybe to join her.

"Tony, the train!"

He turned around and heard the sound at the same time. It was a half mile away, emerging from a stand of trees and not coming too fast. A dirty freighter engine, hauling empty boxcars. Tony saw Lena drop down into the high grass beside the tracks. He calculated the distance he'd walked away from her and how fast the train was coming.

"Lena!"

She didn't answer.

He started back toward her. He started running. The train was a quarter mile away. "Lena!"

He saw her rise out of the grass. The wind caught her hair, and it danced in slow motion. He saw her spring up in slow motion. Tony was in slow motion, too, like a bad dream where no matter how hard you try you can't move fast at all. He heard his own heart and breath in his ears. He heard screams come out that sounded like his voice. He saw the train come up not far from where Lena ran in the grass, toward the rails. Tony was a few yards away, and his arms couldn't reach her in time. He turned his head as she jumped, felt the roar of the train and bits of dust and grass fly into his face.

The train hitting Lena's body made no sound at all. There was no whistle or screaming steel brakes. The engineer hadn't seen any of it.

Tony knelt in the grass and felt darkness creep in around his eyes. He was making sounds but wasn't sure what they were, if he was crying or just breathing hard from running. Then he heard the screaming. It filled the sun-drenched air like wind. It wasn't his voice. The train had gone by, and the screams continued.

"Lena!" He jumped up and ran toward the sound. When he got on top of the tracks, he could see her arms flailing in the high grass.

By the time he could see Lena's body, the screams had turned to crazy laughter. "What a rush!" Lena shrieked. "Did you see how close it was?" She screamed again.

"You're crazy!" Tony shouted, moving closer to her. There wasn't a scratch on her. She rolled around on the ground, the skin of her legs brown against the yellow weeds. Tony picked up dirt and grass and threw it at her. "You crazy—"

He was cut off by a fresh blast from Lena's lungs. She laughed hard, shaking all over and holding her sides.

"You let me think you were going to—" Tony gave up trying to put a sentence together. So he screamed again, this time leaning close to her. "You're crazy!" He followed with every name he could think of. He shouted and kicked dirt at her.

She stopped laughing suddenly. "Let's do it right now, Tony." She panted like someone who had just finished a race, and her eyes were wild with light. "Do it now!"

Tony couldn't move.

"That's what you want, isn't it?" Her eyes were wide behind the strands of hair blowing across her face. "Well, you have your wish."

"What are you doing?" Tony was able finally to move. He shifted from one foot to the other. "What are you doing to me?"

"I'm not doing anything to you. Anything that gets done to you, you do to yourself. You've got the power to do anything you want."

"You're crazy." He turned and walked away from her.

"And you're a victim," she called after him. He closed his eyes. His body felt weak. The high grass gave way in front of him. After a while, Lena's laughter had faded in the distance.

M om was washing dishes when Tony came in. The air-conditioning chilled his skin as he walked through the door. He felt hot and cold and wiped out and completely wired. He saw suds on his mother's arm and thought of sweat on Lena's skin.

"Tuna-salad boats in the fridge," Mom murmured. "Dad wants to talk to you."

Tony wandered into the living room, where Dad sat on his throne, the recliner that had all his stuff around it that nobody could touch.

"Where have you been?"

"Scraping Mamie's house."

"You weren't there when I stopped by."

"We quit for the afternoon, and I walked over to Lena's grandma's. Then we went for a walk."

"You're supposed to tell me where you are. Dave Seaton called nearly an hour ago, asking if you could come work."

"Oh." Tony slapped his forehead. "I didn't know it was this late." He reached for the phone.

"Where were you with Lena? Put the phone down and answer me."

Tony put down the receiver slowly. "Just walking around town. There's not much else to do."

"You watch yourself. I know what goes on."

Tony liked to deliver a particular kind of sigh after Dad had said something like this, but he really wanted to get out of the house and decided to let the old man fume and say what he wanted.

"We just talk. She's interesting because she's from the city. We talk about music and stuff. Is it OK for me to go over to Mamie's? Dave and I want to get some more work done while it's cooler."

Dad seemed a little shocked by not only the length of Tony's speech but that none of it was hostile. "Go ahead. I'm glad Dave's helping Mamie with her house. But come straight home." His voice was almost friendly.

"I will." Tony grabbed a tuna boat and ate it on the way over to Mamie's. Dave looked at him a little longer than usual.

"Thanks for coming over."

"Sorry I'm late. Got busy."

"Got some sun." Dave pointed to Tony's face. Tony knew that by now he looked pretty red. He was beginning to feel it too.

"Yeah. Went for a walk with Lena."

Dave turned back to the section of siding he was scraping. Tony was glad not to be asked any more questions. He didn't know how to describe this afternoon to himself, let alone to somebody else.

23

Dave Seaton:
Love Your Neighbor

Monday, July 28

When Dave got home from work, he found Randy stretched out on the couch. Light from the window shone through the page of the book she had propped on her stomach.

Dave tapped her foot. "We going to Kmart?"

The foot wagged away from him. "Just a minute. I'm almost to the end of this chapter." Her usually uncomplicated features were showing worry and a strain for comprehension.

"Is it worth all the energy you're throwing into it?"

She spoke without looking at him. "You're just irritated because this is a book from Lena."

"Exactly. I thought the two of you had a falling-out."

"I wouldn't call it that. She's hyper about me going to church the other night."

"That's no surprise. She'll have a harder time turning you into a New Age freak now."

"You know, she makes me think about life. This book makes me think about life. There's more to it than Kmart."

"You Miss Above the Rest of the World now? Too good for real people who run out of milk and masking tape?"

"Dave, don't argue with me, please."

There was that tone again. That Lena condescension traveling several blocks down the street to be embodied in his once-pleasant lover and friend. Dave kicked the back door open and marched out to examine his truck. There was always some new dent in it, and he sometimes walked around and around it, meditating on how those marks got there without his knowing about them. He ran his hands over the body now, taking in the irregularities in paint, the nicks in the trim. But he was thinking about Lena. She was floating in a yoga position out over one of the strip pits at the edge of town. In his fantasy, Dave shouted her name, and her concentration broke, a worried look came to her always-in-control face, and she began to sink, pit scum sliding over her tanned limbs, catching in her hair. She sank until her perfect nose made dirty bubbles on the surface. She could levitate, but she couldn't swim.

"I'm sort of worried about her." Randy was suddenly on the other side of the truck, gazing at him so that he would finally look back. The book was still in her hand. "This book is about channeling—you know, when dead people speak to you through somebody else."

"Sounds right up Lena's alley."

"How would you know? She's *my* friend!" The two of them regarded one another and after a moment came to an unspoken truce. Randy continued. "I admit she was into dope back in school. Most of us tried it at least. And Lena wore funky clothes, and everybody thought she was a witch or something. But she was just Lena. At least that's how I looked at it then. I mean, half of it's for show. She'd have a new philosophy every other week." Randy raised the book. "I think this stuff is for real. The Bible talks about people calling up the dead. We're not supposed to be involved with that."

"So tell her." Dave wasn't feeling too charitable toward the Bible lately, but at least he and the Good Book agreed on something. He leaned on the truck and toward Randy. "You're her best friend. Just tell her. Not that she'd listen."

"She'd listen, but then she'd just talk all around it and confuse me. She's so good at words and ideas. I've never won an argument." She gave Dave an emphatic look. "Never."

"Let's go for a walk," Dave said.

"It's too hot."

"We'll go to Perky's."

"I don't want to hang around there."

"We won't hang around, we'll just go in and get a couple of Cokes. How 'bout it?" He peered at her like a little boy. She came around the truck and they linked fingers.

At the corner, she pulled him westward. This happened more often now, the unplanned side trip to her parents' house. Dave had been coming with her for the past week. It had turned out not to be so hard after all for him to be there. He didn't receive much from the Kluvers in the way of niceties, but they did show him where he could sit and asked if he wanted iced tea. They hadn't murmured a word of approval, but Randy's dad had darkened the door once with a pound of bacon he'd bought in a buy-one-get-one-free deal. After a short conversation he left, and Randy burst into tears. It meant something that he'd done that.

Lorene was on the couch, the television on, when Randy and Dave called out and came in the back door. She turned enough to see that someone had entered, picked up a remote control, and turned down the volume. Randy and Dave noticed at the same time that not only was it a new remote but a new TV, with a larger screen than the old one.

"Your dad bought it for me," said Lorene. "Since I'm stuck on this couch so much now."

"Have you been sick today?" asked Randy, trying to get into her mother's field of vision.

"Threw up first thing this morning."

"Oh Mom, I'm sorry."

"You need something?"

"I need to know if you want me to pick up anything for you. We're going over to Kmart in a while."

Lorene wrinkled her nose. "Can't think of anything I need."

"If they have bathrobes on sale, you want me to pick one up for you? You've had this one forever."

"Whatever. I like cotton. Don't get me any of that silky crap—it's too hot. Sticks to me."

"I remember. Anything else?"

"There's iced tea in the fridge."

"No thanks," said Dave. "Just had some at the house."

Randy walked to the couch and kissed Lorene as though she had done it every day of her life. "We'll drop by later."

"Not too much later. I'm pretty tired—turn in about nine tonight."

"OK."

They left the dim house and got to the sidewalk as a van rumbled by. They turned to the side to avoid a dust bath. Dave reached to grab

Randy's hand. He looked at her face and saw resolve only. Sometimes he thought she was the strongest person he'd ever met. The first few days after she'd heard the bad news about Lorene, Randy had done all her crying. They would go to Kmart and buy a cotton robe and drop it off later. Lorene would respond with a cool "Looks like it'll do" and never say thanks or return Randy's kiss.

Dave squeezed Randy's hand and waited for a return squeeze. He got it after a few steps.

"You okay?" he asked.

"Yeah. I hope she's taking her medication and doing everything they tell her to do."

"Why don't you ask your dad?"

Randy sighed, and her hand turned limp in his. "He can't take this. Cries every time I try to talk to him about it."

"Huh. I didn't know that."

They were at Perky's. Randy turned to him as he reached for the door. "Promise we won't stay long."

"Just a few minutes."

Coolness from the dark room brushed their faces and arms when they entered the doorway. Only a few customers were in. The wood of the bar shone in the light that seeped through the tinted front window. Gabe appeared in front of them, at the bar. "A cold one today?"

"Just a Coke for me, please," said Randy. "Lots of ice."

"You've got it."

"Ah, same for me, Gabe," Dave said, glancing at the tap. He remembered the evenings not that long ago when Randy would come in here with him and help him drink a beer. She was underage, and Gabe knew it, so he never put more than one glass in front of them at a time. But the revival meeting had changed that, thank you very much. Now they sipped their Cokes while the ancient fan spun over their heads. It didn't seem to be catching much of the air-conditioned air from the front window.

"I've been wrong all this time." Randy's eyes were looking at themselves in the mirror behind the bar.

"What's that?"

"I thought all these years they didn't love each other." Her eyes pooled up suddenly. She blinked and kept the flood contained. Dave leaned closer so he could hear the small voice.

"But it's killing him to watch her suffer. He told me he'd take her place if he could. If that isn't love, what is?"

Dave didn't answer. He looked past her to the street outside, cars going to the grocery and beauty shop, glaring white figures of people stepping through sun and dust to keep up with all that was asked of them, to carry out their duties, do what they needed to do.

Later, when they returned from Kmart, Randy took a new robe to Lorene. Dave watched her walk down the street, large plastic sack in hand. He took in the other bags and thought about dinner while he put things away. He wanted to do something special for Randy. He had some trout in the freezer. That, and fried zucchini—as always, with fresh tomatoes—might make her smile. It was nearly seven-thirty. He carried a new window fan to the bedroom. There hadn't been much breeze lately, and the small air conditioner in the kitchen kept that part of the house cool enough, but it didn't make it around the corner to the bedroom. Randy hated to be cold when she slept, so they'd decided on a fan rather than another air conditioner. Dave smiled as he raised the window and dusted out the dirt in the sill. He considered it a good sign that she was helping him buy things for the house. Maybe she was really feeling that it was her home too.

Dave could see through the open window that Mr. Kelsey was sound asleep on his porch just across the street. The old guy seemed to sleep a lot. Now he was right in the sunshine, not even a hat over his face. The high porch roof didn't prevent the evening sun from covering the front of the house.

"You must think I can't cook." Randy sounded as if her feelings were hurt when she returned and saw him at the kitchen counter.

"Why do you think that?"

"You'll hardly let me near the stove. I haven't made one meal here. This is, like, your domain or something."

He sat in the chair next to her and reached to touch her arm. He thought awhile before coming out with what was on his mind. He wasn't even sure he'd thought of it himself until just now.

"I never cooked for Karen," he said. "I'd come home every day and expect her to have dinner on the table. I'd get mad if I had to wait. Even after she got sick I was worthless in the kitchen. Neighbors were bringing food over all the time."

Randy shifted a little and looked at him, those eyes that seemed open to anything or anyone.

"One time I just went off on her. I came home after a twelve-hour day, and she was sick on the couch, and there was no food in the fridge. And I just went off." He shook his head. "I couldn't believe I was yelling at her for being too sick to fix me supper."

"Oh, Dave," Randy said, massaging his hand, "you were just mad because you couldn't make her better."

He looked at her, feeling a small sting of relief and hoped she would say more.

"You know," she said, "like, maybe if you ordered her around and had to have your supper, that would be enough to make her well."

"Where do you get this stuff, Randy?"

"I'm mad at Mom all the time. The sicker she looks, the madder I get. It feels awful, but I think it must be natural."

"I just want you to know you're important to me, babe."

"You don't have to cook big fancy meals to do that. I thought I'd do burgers for us tonight. But you'd have to teach me how to use the grill."

"OK." He got up from the table. "I'll just throw this trout back in the freezer. Let's do burgers."

They fired up the grill just off the back porch and made hamburgers together. They sliced Dave's fresh tomatoes. Then they decided to eat on the front porch, facing east and out of the glare of the sun. They rounded the corner of the house with TV trays and their plates.

"I'll get the drinks," Randy said and went in the front door. "Do you ever lock this? People could just walk in."

"Who? What would they steal?" Dave swatted at her behind and missed. He sat in the lawn chair and brought up the burger for his first bite. His eyes came even with Mr. Kelsey's front porch. "Oh, man." Dave put down the burger. "Randy?"

"Yeah?" She came out the door and handed him his beer. He put it down, his eyes fastened on Mr. Kelsey, who was still on his porch.

"What is it?" Randy asked.

"Just stay here." Dave was up and off the porch.

"What?"

"Just stay there." He was across the street. He came up to Mr. Kelsey's front porch. It blazed from the western sun, beginning to go orange. Mr. Kelsey sat quietly, in the same position he'd been in when Dave had last noticed him. Dave said the man's name—once quietly, then twice more, louder. Dave couldn't hear or see breathing.

"Is he all right, Dave?" Dave heard Gideon's voice and turned to see the patrol car idling at the curb and the five-foot-five sheriff on his way across the yard.

"Man, I don't think so. He was like this over an hour ago."

"Yeah, I passed by just now and thought he looked like he hadn't moved. Guess we better look."

Dave was already at the old man's side. He gently felt the wrist. "He's still warm."

"He's been in the sun." Gideon pressed two fingers to the wrinkled throat. "Yep. He's gone. Poor old guy. Heart probably just stopped."

Dave stayed beside Mr. Kelsey while Gideon called the coroner from his car radio. Randy came over and sat with them on the porch steps while they waited. When the county came, they carefully gathered up Mr. Kelsey. It seemed strange, their putting arms and legs and head in place without even asking the old man how he felt, without even trying to make some life rise up out of him and talk to them. It hit Dave how, once he stopped taking that next breath, he'd have no power at all. That others would come to haul him down his own front steps.

It was eighty degrees and the sun was still out, but Dave shivered a little. He'd seen dead people before, had pulled corpses out of a bad wreck once. But seeing Mr. Kelsey get wrapped in a dark bag and carried off like a dried-up Christmas tree filled him with a sick discomfort. After everyone left, he and Randy took their supper into the kitchen and ate.

Part Three

AUGUST

The History:
Dissension Springs, 1893

In the third year of Thaddeus's reign as mayor of Dissension Springs, a man named Bender settled into the short row of buildings that was the town. Joe Bender was a blacksmith. He was a quiet, brooding man, never very clean but so intent on his work that a person had to be in his line of vision before being noticed at all.

Joe Bender had a wife, several years older than he, rumored to be the sister of his first wife, who had died of influenza a few years back. They had a son, sturdy and busy at age six. The girl, Corrie, was sixteen when the family arrived in Dissension Springs. The daughter of Joe's first wife, she held no resemblance to him at all. She was thin as a sapling but looked more ready to break than to bend. Corrie's voice was light and childlike, and she could be heard singing in the church on Sundays. Folks regarded her as a child, more or less, particularly when it became clear that she was ill. The girl caught every ailment that went through the community, and she would struggle with it longer than anyone else. She was forever weak and tired and pale. Several boys of marrying age approached her, one after another, and one after another abandoned their quest. She was a weak thing who often coughed for weeks on end. And, in the only way she was like her father, she had little to say to anyone. No chattering with other girls. No bright-eyed gossip from those faintly pink lips. Her hair appeared to have no color at all.

And her passion was not for men but for God. She spent entire nights at the church, coughing violently in the cold space, entirely involved in a relationship others would never comprehend. She seemed to dwell just barely with the rest of the people. Some invisible fire kept her fueled, her thin body full of life that was both ecstatic and ghostly.

Folks grew accustomed to Corrie, quietly accepted her after a fashion. They stood back when she spoke about God and God's concerns. She was a preacher and a pray-er, embodied in a voice that lit on a person like a hum close to the ear. When she spoke at prayer meeting, squeezing her eyes tight and kneading one hand with the other against her stomach, people grew quiet, as ones who were witnessing insanity. But the girl's thoughts were wise and clear. Sometimes she walked over to another parishioner and placed hands on a head or a shoulder. A few people claimed to have been healed by her. They feared this kind of power in such a strange one, and they resented her weakness, which was always in front of them, as if to remind them that life was a gift that could be snatched away at any moment. But they were compelled to listen when she spoke.

The year Corrie turned seventeen, there was a sense of death about her. Doc Parker could find nothing he could attach a name to, but he shook his head and told Joe Bender that it probably wouldn't be long. Corrie spent many of her days in bed, but when she could, she wandered the edges of the town like a sad but friendly spirit. She could no longer come into the church for fear of giving others her disease, whatever it might be. Sometimes she sang weakly outside a window. But even the first few notes of singing collapsed into wracking coughs.

Thaddeus watched the girl's failing with more than sadness. Her dying would be a loss of hope for him. For some reason he had believed that spring this year would bring healing to the healer. He didn't fear her as others did. Her spiritual bearing was a welcome thing. Since the night he and Lewanda had found the spring, he'd had a tendency to think often about power outside of himself. He had hoped to ask for her hand when early summer was at its fullest bloom. She would keep living, and he would join himself to that delicate beauty.

His heart made a sudden jump when Corrie appeared at his door one morning. They greeted one another briefly, then exchanged questioning gazes.

"I need to see Lewanda," the girl said finally.

Thaddeus swallowed. "Haven't seen her for near a month."

"But you generally know where to find her. You haven't seen her because she hasn't come around. But she never goes far from you." The girl brought up a handkerchief and coughed into it. Thaddeus thought he heard her very insides rattle. Corrie finished coughing and looked up at him expectantly.

"All right," he said. "I'll locate her and come get you."

"I'd like to wait right here." The girl backed up a little. "I can stay on the little rise behind your chicken house. I understand how you'd not want me near the children."

"No need. They're fishing. I'd be pleased if you waited in the house."

It took Thaddeus the better part of the day to find Lewanda, who had wandered a good distance from her camp near Blue Horse Creek, and then into the evening to convince her to talk with Corrie Bender. Lewanda despised being around folks, let alone a girl said to be of a particularly spiritual nature. But Thaddeus prevailed upon her, saying that, after all, the girl was hardly a woman and near to dying.

It was past sunset when Thaddeus came back to his home. He convinced Corrie to share supper with him and the children. Then he sent the children on to bed and hitched up the wagon. He took Corrie down the creek and off to the east, where Lewanda had her camp. As she had promised, Lewanda was there. She stood in front of her lean-to, arms crossed.

Thaddeus watched the two women meet. There weren't any stars or moon, and Corrie Bender's dress glowed above the ground where she stood. Lewanda, in her black work dress, was a patch of deeper darkness next to the young woman.

Thaddeus could hear faint sounds of words as the women spoke quietly. Then they turned and walked together toward Blue Horse Creek. Thaddeus waited for some time, growing sleepy. He stretched out in the wagon and slept. When he awoke, the eastern horizon was gray with predawn and Corrie Bender was touching his shoulder. "You can take me back to town now," she said. They took their seats on the wagon bench.

"Is everything all right?" he asked.

"Yes. Thank you for helping me."

Some impulse moved Thaddeus to take hold of her hand. It was cold and small. She didn't seem frightened or angry—or even startled. But she looked straight at Thaddeus, seeming to wait.

"Lewanda's been misunderstood," he said. "She's not a bad woman."

"I know that, Thaddeus." Corrie placed her other hand over his. "I can see you've been a good friend to her. God remembers such things."

Thaddeus felt an ache in his throat. "I've heard about God all my life. But when you talk about him, I find myself believing it more."

Even in the darkness, Corrie's smile was visible. "Good. We need to believe. It's what we were made for."

"I just wish you weren't so sick," Thaddeus said, and choked. "It breaks my heart to see you so."

Tears glittered in the girl's eyes. "You have a precious heart, Thaddeus. And I shall always remember you."

They held hands, like old lovers, all the way back to Dissension Springs. Thaddeus could have married her then and taken her home with him forever, but as the girl stepped down lightly to the ground outside the smithy, Thaddeus knew it would never be.

In early May, Corrie Bender died in her bed. Her face was full of peace, and her eyes, wide open, looked wiser than the eyes of a human. At least that's what Doc Parker said. This statement traveled the community until the story was that the dead eyes had looked at the doctor as though alive still. Some said the small body glowed like heaven itself. Others thought there was the sign of the cross on the front of her gown. But the sign was in fact a stain, blood-tinged spittle that had dried before morning when old Joe found her.

Lewanda appeared at the smithy long after the other folk in the community had come and gone. Her silhouette appeared against the wide, pale sky of evening. Thaddeus had come midmorning, having grieved in his cornfield earlier. When he saw the girl's body all laid out, he remembered Florence, dead at twenty-nine, just four years before. He looked at the girl, not even eighteen, and thought about how much power a woman had over a man even after she was dead. He still did things around the house the way he knew Florence would want them done. And he remembered Corrie telling him about believing being what people were made for, and he tried, from time to time, to think of what he should be believing, and believe it better.

They buried Corrie in the churchyard with Florence and those who had died during the drought and since that time, now six years past. There were ten in all, marked by small wooden crosses. Thaddeus made certain the markers never leaned or sank. He came by every Sunday morning early and pulled weeds and straightened the small graveyard. He did not go to church. The building was still full of too much that hurt him—memories of Florence's alto voice and the minister's strident one, the songs and prayers that still sounded like other languages to Thaddeus. And the feeling of bloodguiltiness that just seemed to jump onto a person once he walked through the door. Thaddeus had never entered the church when he hadn't left it feeling worse.

He forced himself to think about believing, for Corrie's sake, and he brought the children to church on Sunday mornings because he figured they might be stronger than he was, and because Florence would want them to be there. But the small building, filled with hymns and wailing, did not seem like a friendly or helpful place to him.

A few days after they buried Corrie, Lewanda appeared at Thaddeus's cistern. She had a bag of her things and her pot and knife on a leather strap, lying in the dust at her feet. The bright morning light brought out the woman's pale features.

"Your daughter's of the age she needs a woman here," Lewanda said. "And you can tend your crops better with me here to cook and such."

Thaddeus sat down next to her. "That's mighty kind. It'll be good not to have you out in the weather so much. You're welcome to stay." He didn't ask questions. This was probably just a spell she was heading through; no telling how soon she would change her mind and take to wandering again. But she seemed happy for the moment, and Thaddeus certainly needed her help.

Joe Bender moved his family to Springfield, Missouri, that autumn, once harvests were in and most of the farmers had paid off their debts to him. Not long after, Jake Meriweather took his family up to Nebraska to buy into his father-in-law's large farm, and the Harveys, who owned the general store, took their business west to Wichita. Doc Parker went to St. Louis, and Rev. Harkness died of a cold just after Christmas. The few remaining families left quietly during the winter, for their own reasons, to towns far away and bigger. By spring, only Thaddeus and his children remained.

And Lewanda. She had made herself a place in the loft with the children and never offered to leave or wander again. She learned what habits Florence had built into Samuel and Maryanna and made sure they continued in them. This included reading from the Bible in the evenings after supper. Thaddeus was most surprised at this, especially since Lewanda listened with interest and never moved from her place until the reading was through.

Thaddeus thought a number of times about moving his children to a better place, but his farm was doing all right. And it seemed to him that all of them—he and the children and Lewanda—had wounds still, from the losses they had suffered, and uprooting any of them to start over again would not be a good thing. It relieved him that Lewanda's crazy, wandering times were over, and he feared that a move might set her back.

Samuel and Maryanna had created special places for themselves— a little camp by the creek when the weather was warm enough, and a gully off the cornfield that had two large trees strong enough to attach ropes to. They spent afternoons swinging and shrieking. Maryanna was becoming a young woman now, and her emotions were often unsettled and tearful. Lewanda stayed close to the girl at those times and seemed to know what to say when Thaddeus felt helpless.

Dissension Springs, a ghost town now, was still a familiar place, and it was the last place where dear Florence had sung and tended vegetables. Her rosebushes were flourishing, and her garden still fed them well.

24

Two Pastors

Friday, August 1

The heat reminded Iris of her seventeenth year, when her father had led the town in prayer for rain. He had been a tall, bony man, severe and glaring one moment, awash in passionate tears for the lost the next. And she could recall him striding across the brown grass in his three-piece suit, the white shirt underneath showing through at the elbows, his large Bible curled up in his hand. His righteous stare had cut straight through the shimmer of dust hanging in the afternoon sun.

Iris and Ax (they still called him Maxwell, then, after their mother's missionary brother) avoided Preacher Papa when the suit came on; he didn't belong to them then, but to the Lord. He had no children or wife, owed nothing to anything but that book, and nothing distracted him. If someone broke an arm, it would just have to wait. If his dear wife was sick or called away to Tennessee by a death in the family, so be it. The suit stayed on, and the mission clung with it. His eyes saw past them all to that wider world—the one painted for them in color illustrations scattered through the family Bible, skies in pinks and lavenders, people with eyes like Preacher Papa's and skin that seemed translucent. Earthly life crumbled away before the panorama, the vision, even if only a few saw it. They were only pilgrims, after all, he often said.

That summer the congregation had gathered around him like migrants looking for work, a wary hopefulness present there in the tiny church. A few townspeople of other churches had come in, sitting by themselves or with other members of their congregations. They had sung two hymns. Then Preacher Papa came down from the pulpit platform and said simply, "It's time to pray, children. Time first to confess our faults and transgressions to the Lord and to ask his forgiveness. Then we must stay on our knees and ask him to have mercy and give us rain." To Iris, there in the front right pew, he looked suddenly like a wise statesman; it occurred to her how much he looked like Abraham Lincoln, with that gauntness, that intensity and sadness in his eyes.

His righteousness made her lonely sometimes; when she was small she had hated God because he kept Preacher Papa from loving her. All his love was for God. There were no hugs or storytelling, no walks together unless she was allowed to tag along, mouth closed, while he practiced his sermons. But the Holy Spirit helped her understand by and by. The attention she wanted from Preacher Papa would not be hers.

She didn't need to worry about a man's attention anyway. Billy Drake came by on a regular basis these days, young and awkward and bursting with music for the Lord. He was a fine singer, and Iris played piano for him at church and sometimes when he traveled a county or two away. She felt in her soul that their spirits were being knit together, moving toward holy union. She could see it in Billy's eyes when he turned to her during a song. They would love the Lord together, praising him with music. Billy had a quiet manner, gentle and respectful— and yes, even admiring—of her. When the Lord had given her so much, it seemed petty and selfish to resent Preacher Papa's lack of warmth or time.

That evening they prayed for she didn't know how long, as sunlight shifted through the room. The wailing, the hallelujahs, and the weeping were familiar to her ears, and the heat had been so ever present that even it had no power to distract. They had all grown accustomed to it, moving slower and not minding much that the air was so warm it was hard to feel it enter their lungs. The whole town had learned to breathe and to move on faith, thus proving Preacher Papa's theory that the Lord worked even through summer droughts to grace the lives of unbelievers.

Iris could remember how straight and pure her prayers had been that day. She had never experienced such jubilation and surety of having her words reach the throne. She sensed that the confession cleansed her to the bone, and her praise was as genuine as a child's. Her petitions were reasonable, praying for others and not for herself.

And while the white sun splashed over the altar, the Lord called her name. "Iris," he said, "I want you to preach my Word." There in the midst of prayers for rain, he anointed her to follow Preacher Papa. She knew it as surely as she knew what year it was and what color dress she wore. God's call was unhalting and dazzlingly clear.

It rained the very next day. And Iris told Billy that he mustn't court her anymore. She was the Lord's alone. A man could be a prophet and a husband too, but a woman who must tend a house and bear and bring up children could not preach and do both callings justice. She knew what she must do.

Preacher Papa had wept with joy.

It felt like that long-ago summer today, oppressive with heat and dust, a scorching, stripping day that could bring one amazingly close to the almighty God. Iris looked out the kitchen window at the burned yard and murmured, "Dear Lord, work in this desolation." She felt that day when she was seventeen hovering near her. The room seemed to ring with distant music, and she could feel herself transported for a few moments. She floated for a while, above the dingy floor and stained cabinet tops, listening for a Word. Dry bushes rattled against the house, just under the kitchen window. *Lord God, work in this desolation.*

There was no word, but no matter. All she really longed for sometimes was the sense that God might speak, that God *could* speak if he wanted to. A moment of that sense was enough to get a person through a wordless day. She would open her Bible in a while, and the pages would feel cool against the suffocating atmosphere. The meanings of the verses would perk up, and there would be comfort for all the hard things.

She moved to the dining-room table and lifted a few papers off the mountain of ideas and inspirations that lived there. As she was reviewing an old worship bulletin, a movement caught her attention. Out the front window she could see Madison Carruthers, the Presbyterian pastor, making his way down the sidewalk. His gait was slow and careful, as though he were pacing himself for a long journey. His face was bright pink.

Iris stood at the window, hidden from view by several years' dust in the once-sheer curtains. The sidewalk was a number of yards from the house, but she could make out that Carruthers was talking to himself, looking down at the walk. From this distance, Iris couldn't hear what he was saying.

He was a fairly old man—not a good thing for him to be out in the sun like this. Had his car broken down? But in a second Iris recognized the shape of his lips, the posture of his head. He was praying.

Her first inclination was to snort; a Presbyterian muttering at the sidewalk held little resemblance to prayer in her mind. Those people stifled the Spirit, their singing old and ragged, their prayers long and distant. She had never heard Carruthers preach, but she could imagine it, the old fellow shuffling newspaper clippings and articles from *Reader's Digest,* clearing his throat to intone some bit of worldly wisdom. There would be an Old Testament reading and a New Testament reading, both of them formal and short, without passion or depth. She had visited churches during her twenties, just to see. She'd seen enough—the poor, dried-up bunch of them.

Rev. Carruthers had moved up the street, the sun glaring off his sweaty neck. And Preacher Papa's words entered Iris's mind: *For what purpose has this come?*

She shook her head with a start. She had heard him say those words hundreds of times—when the money ran short, when gossip made its vicious way around to his children, when a troublemaker passed through. For what purpose has this come?

"Well," said Iris, folding her large arms. She pressed her lips together and looked at the pastor, who faded into the day like a mirage. "Well. Maybe I should wonder what he's praying about."

She knew there were revival meetings going on—the last of them, she thought. They hadn't asked her help, of course. They didn't like Pentecostals; they were afraid of the Spirit, that the Lord might actually move. She knew that, so she had allowed her pity for them to override the anger she felt. But the meetings must be what Rev. Carruthers was praying about. Maybe she should too. That must be the purpose—God telling her to pray. Why else would the man walk this way? He never had before.

Iris moved away from the window and held two fingers to her temple. She felt a headache coming on, but that followed to reason too. Satan had all his darts ready. With sudden energy she fell to her knees by the sofa and raised her hands. She wasn't sure how to pray for those people but counted on the Spirit to help her out.

It took only half an hour for Iris to know what she must do.

Rona escorted her husband to his wicker chair when he came in, saturated and breathing with difficulty. She turned the fan on him and set a bowl of green seedless grapes on the lamp table next to the chair. She had finished long ago with scolding him for these unreasonable treks into the weather; by now she had learned to be quiet and just pick up the pieces. Walking was how he worked out his thoughts. He wrote his sermons at the old maple desk, scuffed by the years, and he conducted church business door-to-door or in their family room, she hovering close with refreshments. But what he called the "gut-level meditation" got pounded out down alleys and dog paths. He had that look now, the look she knew Jacob must have had after wrestling all night with the angel—fire and fatigue.

"I've turned it over and over," he wheezed.

"What's that, dear?"

"The eighth chapter of Amos."

"What is it you're working on?"

He chomped a handful of the grapes, catching the juice before it dribbled down his chin. The color in his face was already calming down. "It's about famine," he said. "'Not a famine of food or a thirst for water, but a famine of hearing the words of the LORD. Men will stagger from sea to sea and wander from north to east, searching for the word of the LORD, but they will not find it.'"

Rona sat in the chair opposite him and waited. The fire in his eyes had risen.

"'In that day "the lovely young women and strong young men will faint because of thirst."'" Madison was gazing at her. "They faint because of thirst. Makes you wonder if this drought is symbolic, doesn't it?"

"Most physical things do turn around to mean something else, don't they?" Rona was pretty accomplished at following her husband's exegesis. After nearly forty years, she could get up and preach for him. Not that she would want to, of course.

"True," said her husband. "We need the Word as well as water. Except that the people in this town have had the Word, haven't they? Maybe the famine is in their understanding. As Jesus said, they have ears but don't hear."

"It must be that. They've heard their share of it from you."

He waved her off, wrinkling his nose. "It's rare that I can tell them as much of the truth as they need. The closer the truth is, the harder it is to keep them listening."

Rona looked at her husband a long time. He seemed more beaten than usual. "I think something else is bothering you."

His eyes met hers. They were full of sadness.

"Are you worried about the Morgans?"

"Heavens, yes. This is his first pastorate, and already he's decided he can't cut it."

"Do you think he's right?"

"No, I don't. He's got a heart for people. A good head too. And I believe he really loves his congregation. That kind of love is a spiritual gift."

"But Sarah has struggled from the beginning. The best pastor in the world can't make up for a neglected marriage."

"I'm not sure it's neglect. But I don't know what it is."

"They're seeing Jaymee?"

"Yes."

"She'll help."

He reached for her, and she crossed the few feet between them. She sat on the little footstool in front of his chair, and they held hands.

"I hate seeing people so disappointed," Madison said, emotion in his voice. "I don't know how so many have gotten to be this way. What are they missing? What have we forgotten?"

"Maybe it's not disappointment. Maybe it's just weariness from fighting the battle. Keep praying for rain," she said, pressing the softness of his palm to her face. "Of one kind or another."

25

TONY GARDINO: THE PAINTING

Friday, August 1

M an, are you sick?" Dave's voice came through running water, in a tunnel. Tony guided his head toward the sound. He could feel Dave close by, above him.

"Tony?" A hand clutched Tony's shoulder.

"Yeah?"

"You OK?"

It took the words forever to die down.

"Ummm." Tony struggled to put a sentence together. "Took something for a headache. Too much, I guess."

"What did you take?"

"Painkiller. Had codeine in it."

"How much?"

"Double dose, I think."

Dave muttered something as he left Tony's side.

The early evening burned around him. Tony crept over to the shade under the oak tree near Dave's shed. It was nice to float while the sun dodged around his spot. He stayed turned toward the house where Dave and Randy were. The day felt light and peaceful.

When he looked toward Dave's back porch again, the sun was gone, and yellow light from the kitchen spilled down the three back steps.

Tony got off the ground and walked toward the light, feeling heavy. He trudged up the steps and leaned against the screen. Randy was at the kitchen table, looking at a magazine. A bluish flicker from the living room indicated that Dave was watching television.

"I'm going home," Tony said. Randy jumped and then cursed him for startling her.

Dave appeared in the doorway. "You get home okay?"

"Sure."

"We'll start painting trim on Mamie's house tomorrow." Dave said this more like an announcement, not a reminder that Tony was going to help.

"I'll be there," Tony said.

"I called your folks and told them you had supper with us."

"Oh. Thanks." It was beginning to dawn on Tony that he'd been out of it for several hours and Dave Seaton had just saved him from who knew what. He took a detour home to buy some soda and chocolate at Ed's.

He dragged his feet down the sidewalk, staying hidden in leaf shadows as much as possible, and tried to figure if he'd taken too much of the Vicodin or too little. Mom had used it after her surgery over a year ago and would never miss it. Tony had figured year-old pills wouldn't pack much punch, and so he'd doubled up. Or maybe he'd tripled. The evening was warm, too warm probably, but everything felt very pleasant at the moment. There were still ten pills left in the bottle, which was buried under Mr. Timms's pear tree. Maybe he could find more somewhere.

Mom looked at him too hard when he came in the kitchen door. "That Dave is wearing you out, isn't he?" She seemed happy about this.

"We're working on Mamie's house. Then I had supper with Dave and Randy."

"I know. You look so tired, honey. You feel okay?"

"Yeah. Think I'll go to bed."

His room was dark. It felt old and unused. He hadn't spent much time here lately. Now, with the narcotics wearing off, the familiar hollow feeling hit him full force. He closed the door and got candles out of his sock drawer, where he'd kept them since Annie noticed and made such a scene. The candles sputtered a bit when Tony lit them. Instead of lying in bed, he put a blanket on the floor close to the window. He opened the window, letting in the outside with its sounds. He set the three candles in front of his CD player. He sat on the blanket and hugged himself and watched the flames.

This was the first week of August. A little over a month ago he'd put the gun in his mouth. Somehow this time had gone by. Granddad had worked him and watched him, Tony had found the candles, Dave Seaton had given him work, and Lena had come to town. Tony had managed to fill the summer with things that made it bearable. He hadn't fought with Dad at all. He couldn't believe he'd managed all this time without tangling with the old man and ending up punished. Dad had actually loosened his grip lately. Tony could spend all day hanging out at Seaton's, and that seemed to be okay.

Tony told himself all this, but the whole thing was unraveling there in his room. He needed Lena. Now. He jumped up and went downstairs to the telephone in the living room. Dad was there, half asleep in front of the TV. But he didn't listen in on conversations nearly as intently as Mom did. And she was still in the kitchen, where the other phone was.

After two rings, Lena answered.

"Hi," said Tony.

"Tony?" She laughed a little, and he couldn't tell if it was a mean laugh or not. Her voice sounded uninterested.

"Yeah. I'm home. Just thought I'd call." He saw the train coming through the field suddenly and Lena running toward it. "Uh, we'll be painting over at Mrs. Rupert's tomorrow."

"Really? I think I'll skip that."

She was still running. He panted to keep up with her.

"I thought maybe we could get a Coke, you know, when I'm finished."

"Maybe. I've got to see some people. Might go tomorrow. If I'm here, sure." She sounded as though she couldn't wait to get off the phone.

"Right. Well, maybe I'll see you tomorrow. 'Night."

"Good night."

He went back to his room and watched the candles. He stared straight into the flames, but darkness sloshed around him anyway. He turned on the radio and leaned against the bed. By six he could be out of the house and at Dave's. That was only eight hours away.

Mom woke him up, knocking loudly on his door. He'd decided that she knocked that loud to give him time to hide anything she didn't want to see. His clock said 7:30. When he'd last noticed, it had been 5:15.

"Honey, Dave's on the phone."

Tony crawled off the bed and wandered to the phone in the living room.

"Hey, Tony. Hope I didn't wake you up."

"No."

"Listen, I need to go over to Randy's mom's, help her move some furniture. Would you stop by Frank's and pick up the trim paint? Mamie ordered it, and he's got it waiting for us."

"Sure."

Mom was already planning breakfast for him. Tony tried to shake her off at first but then remembered Pastor Jacob and thought better of it. He asked for a banana.

"On some cereal?"

"No. Just a banana."

"That's not very much. You'll be painting all day. At least have milk with it. You want toast?"

"I'll take the milk." Tony slouched at the table and forced down the banana, watching the clock. Frank's opened at eight. He finished the fruit and milk, rinsed the glass, and put it in the dishwasher. About then, Granddad came in for his second cup of coffee. Today wasn't a Mass day. They were keeping to Mondays, Wednesdays, Fridays, and Sundays, and sometimes Granddad let Tony off the hook Friday mornings. Granddad lifted his eyebrows at Tony, the closest thing to a morning greeting the man ever offered.

At 8:05, Tony found himself at the counter of Frank's Hardware.

"What can I do for you, Tony?" Tony guessed it was Frank who stood at the cash register, smiling at him. It was kind of nice to be called by name. Tony realized that hanging out with Dave Seaton had earned him some respectability around town. Couldn't hurt.

"Mrs. Rupert's paint. For the trim."

The man brought out a brown paper sack and stacked several small cans of paint on the counter before putting them in. He lifted one of the cans. "Here it is. Thunder Gray. I put the bill inside."

Even though he was relatively happy to be away from home and with Dave and Randy, Tony's steps slowed as he got to Mamie's. The house looked really big. And it had way too much trim; this kind of trim was for mansions somewhere.

"Thanks for getting this," Dave said, taking the sack from Tony. He and Randy had just pulled into Mamie's drive. "Lorene needed her dresser and bed moved, and Charlie's away for a couple days."

Tony silently took his brush and a can of the paint and went to where Dave directed him. He felt like he hadn't slept at all. At least Dave had brought a radio. That would help.

Randy, in her cutoffs and a halter revealing pale skin, decided to start at the top and climbed onto the ladder a few feet from Tony. They didn't say much. The heat was heavy, and no one was in a very good mood; the painting stretched out like several miles through desert. Tony could tell Dave and Randy had been arguing, mainly because they didn't find stupid little things to joke about. He never thought they were that funny, but he liked them better that way than mad and silent.

At 9:30 Mamie appeared at the side of the house, where the closest shade tree stood like a plastic statue in the windless sunshine. "There was a sale on oranges," she puffed, setting out a little patio table with a tray. "This Tupperware has orange sections in it. The green thermos is tea and the pink one is lemonade." Then she nosed around for about ten minutes, leaning close to see their work. She and Dave conferred while she fanned herself with a newspaper. Their voices sounded loud against the house. A car pulled into the drive then, and an older, thin woman got out. Mamie called her Liz. The two of them went into the house.

Tony waited until they'd been painting awhile, then asked Randy, "Have you seen Lena?"

"No. She said something about going to Wichita with Craig and Fred. They've got some buddies up there."

"You think she's OK?"

Randy didn't answer for a minute. "I used to think she was fine. But you know, I'm seeing things in a different way these days, and I worry about her."

Tony thought he heard Dave sigh over by the porch on the back of the house.

"Yeah. She'll try anything, won't she?" Tony said.

"She just might. But that was always Lena."

Tony glanced up at her and couldn't tell how she felt. She didn't look judgmental at least. Dave had said she'd gotten religion now, but she seemed all right in spite of it.

"She's always pushed the limits, you know?" Randy said. "And she nearly always gets away with it. But she wants everybody else to take chances with her. And I've got other things to think about now."

Tony thought about taking chances. He thought of the train. "How's your mom?"

"Sick a lot, from the chemo."

"Sorry."

The radio played some Deep Purple, and Randy muttered something about Dave and his classic rock. They could hear Dave singing along from around the corner.

"I think she got to know too much about me," said Tony, loud enough for only Randy to hear.

"You know, Tony," Randy said, "Lena sort of comes and goes. She's never been what you'd call dependable."

"That doesn't sound like something you'd say about a friend."

"Oh, she's my friend," Randy paused, tongue out, as her brush maneuvered a tight spot, "but I have other friends I depend on."

At noon, Mamie fed them tuna salad and ice-cream bars. Then she told them she'd be taking a nap and could they not play their music so loudly. But within an hour Mrs. Petersen came roaring up in her Ford Escort. She hardly stopped to say hello but went straight to Mamie's back door and began pounding. Tony watched her and thought about Lena some more. About the feel-better room and how it would feel to be there now. Almost before he could picture it, Mamie and Mrs. Petersen were getting in the car, looking in a hurry. As the car backed out of the drive, Mamie smiled distractedly and waved.

"What's going on?" asked Randy.

"Who knows. Must be some new intrigue in the pinochle club," Dave said. He came over to view the progress on Tony and Randy's side of the house.

"Hey, wait," he said, standing behind the ladder Randy was on. His face registered confusion.

"What?" said Randy.

"What's this paint?" Dave came closer to inspect her work. "What *is* this?"

"What?"

Dave picked up the can. "Where'd this color come from? It's some *blue* crap!"

"Isn't that what it's supposed to be?"

"No! She wanted gray trim." Dave stepped back to get a better look at that side of the house. Tony and Randy had done nearly a third of the trim already—all a nice greenish blue.

"Man!" Dave started swearing and wiping sweat from his neck. "Tony, how'd you get blue? Come here." Tony's chest ached as he followed Dave around to the back of the house. The trim Dave had been working on was a soft, steel gray. Dave picked up the can he'd been using. He held the two cans side by side: Thunder Gray and Soft Teal. Dave looked ready to crush Tony's head between the two paint cans.

Tony tried to shrug. "I'm sorry. I thought they were all gray. The guy at the counter thought they were. I'm—I'm sorry. I'll take it back and buy more gray."

"That doesn't help much, buddy. You've wasted our time. What'd I tell you about coming to work with half a brain? Can't you keep clear long enough to do this job!" Dave backed away as if to stop himself from going on.

"Dave," Randy followed him, and Tony could hear them, Dave cursing and Randy trying to come up with a solution. Tony heard his own name at least twice. He sat on the hard ground and put his head in both hands. He'd read the label of the first can but not the others. His brain just didn't work anymore. No wonder everybody thought he was a dopehead. He couldn't think or remember things. It was getting harder and harder to do simple things. He heard Dave's and Randy's voices coming closer again.

"Maybe you should just go home," Dave was saying, not as angry. Mainly he sounded tired. "I'll pay for your time up to now."

"No—don't pay me for anything!"

"It was probably Frank's fault anyway, Tony," Randy said, and Tony could hear Dave sighing again. It was over, his working for Seaton. Lena was over, and this was over. Fine. He had the solution; it had been waiting for him all summer.

"Why don't we paint it both colors?" Randy said. Her comment was followed by silence.

"What?" Dave looked at her as if she were crazy.

"Paint it both—you know, two-toned. A lot of places are doing it now. I saw it in a magazine. We saw some in Kansas City."

"Two tones." Dave seemed to be considering it. "I don't know. Mamie wanted gray, and she'll make a big deal out of this."

"Well, we can paint one side of the house that way, and see if she likes it. You know—a test. And if she does, we'll finish, and if she still wants gray, we'll redo it. If we have to redo it, we would have had to anyway."

"We could do the test on the front, where there's blue already." Dave seemed to be considering the idea.

"I'll stay and help," Tony said miserably.

Dave glanced at him. "May as well see what happens."

Randy had picked up the gray paint. "Give me your brush." Dave handed it over. She went to a spot Tony had been painting on the lower part of the house. She slowly painted a strip of gray on the upper half of the trim.

"This actually works," she said, still concentrating on making a straight line. "Because this trim has a ridge in it anyway. Only the old houses in town have this kind of woodwork. Dad has a name for it, but I can't remember."

"Well, I hope this works. It's too hot to be out here in the first place." Dave's mood hadn't improved much. Tony picked up his brush and paint can.

"Where do you want me to paint, Randy?"

She pointed to a place that didn't have any paint yet. "You keep up with the blue, but only paint the lower half of the trim. I'll come along behind you."

"You gotta paint a straight line to make this work," said Dave.

"I can paint a straight line. I was working on my dad's wood carvings when I was eight. Used to paint clothes on the dolls. Just chill, Dave."

Dave raised both arms in resignation. "All right. We'll see what happens."

Tony took in a long breath and started painting again. He glanced over at Randy's sweaty face, the tongue out as she worked over the trim he'd left a while ago. He'd never noticed her much when they were in school together. He wished he had. She was all right. Not a real pretty type, but the kind of friend a person could probably count on forever. A friend unlike Lena, who was with somebody else now. In Wichita or something. He wouldn't think about her now. He would just paint and paint. That's all he had to do. Not think about anything but a straight blue line.

26

MAMIE RUPERT:
THE PAINTING

Saturday, August 2

That scarf looks a bit much."

Liz's mouth quirked this way and that as she appraised Mamie's selection of clothing. The first revival meeting at the Baptist church was still a week away, but Mamie wanted to be prepared. Since she'd been converted and prayed that prayer with the young seminarian, she was feeling substantial pressure to look just right. So she'd given Liz a call, Liz who wouldn't set foot in a church but had good fashion sense for occasions both religious and regular.

The pale yellow dress with short sleeves, pleats in the torso, and white collar and cuffs had made the grade. The yellow-and-green silk scarf that Mamie kept manipulating into her hair had slid out three times now, and each time Liz had snatched it up as if to say, "Well, you don't really need it anyway," and each time Mamie grabbed it back, set on making it work.

"No old women wear those scarves in their hair anymore," Liz said.

"The color's just right—shade matches this dress like it was made for it."

"But the style's all wrong. You look like a flapper from the twenties whose head got stuck on the wrong body."

Mamie puffed and ran the silk along the pale of her arm. The phone rang, and she took up the receiver with a grunt. "Yes?"

"Mamie, this is Ruthie. Do you have any lids? My niece from Missouri brought over a mess of corn and beans, and the tomatoes from Arthur Gardino are beginning to go bad. I'm running out of canning lids."

Mamie pursed her lips. The scarf was wadded in her fist like a hankie. Liz muttered, "Who is it?" and Mamie formed Ruthie's name with her mouth. "Yes, I think I have one small box. You want the standard size, don't you?"

"Well, I'm doing some pints and some quarts."

"Pints or quarts, they all have the same size opening, Ruthie."

Liz had taken a seat and lit up, legs crossed. "Do you still take *Ladies' Home Journal*?" She looked through the magazines on the coffee table.

"Do you need them now?" Mamie used the scarf to mop her forehead. Covering the receiver with her hand, she spoke in Liz's direction.

"Can you run some lids over to Ruthie's for me?"

Liz waved distractedly. "I can't stay all morning."

"Just run them in and run out."

"All right."

"Liz says she'll run them over. OK? I've got to go."

She hung up the phone and looked at the material in her hand. "I won't wear this scarf. It's got pulled places on it," she announced to Liz on her way to the kitchen. After some hunting around, she came back out, wiping the dust off a small box with a dish towel. "Here. It's all I have. Hope it's enough."

"She has a car. She can buy her own." Liz snuffed out the cigarette and stood up. She never smoked while she drove. Said it looked trampy.

"But driving makes her nervous."

"Living makes her nervous."

Mamie laughed.

"I mean it, Mamie. You should see her house."

"I've seen it. I'm over there two, three times a week."

"She's always sorting—her kitchen drawers, her yarn, magazines, rearranging knickknacks. The woman never sits still, and she never gets anything done. Just like a car stuck in neutral, I swear."

"Her daddy was German. They like things organized."

Liz held two magazines under her arm. "I'm borrowing these." She preceded Mamie into the kitchen. Her car was in the back drive. "The other day I went in to drop off her prescription. She had all these greeting cards on the living-room table. Cards people had sent her. She was sorting them by year and by occasion." Liz pointed to imaginary piles to illustrate. "Over here were birthday cards from 1978, here were birthday cards from 1979, and on up to the present. And then there were Christmas cards. She'd divided up cards that came from relatives and those from nonrelatives. Those with letters inside and those with just a signature. Mamie, the woman needs help."

Mamie gave a little laugh.

"I mean it. There's a real good psychiatrist in Hayward. My granddaughter went to him after her miscarriage. Real down-to-earth. Doesn't take any nonsense. He'd probably tell Ruthie to have a ceremony to burn all her cards—in whatever order she wanted. She'd do it if a doctor told her to. We should take her in."

"Liz, how your mind works." Mamie waved as her friend got into the car. It made a racket when she started it. Liz said something over the noise—about the one mechanic she trusted being on vacation for another week.

Mamie heard familiar swishes and walked around the back to where Dave Seaton was painting trim. He and the Kluver girl and the Gardino boy were real quiet and working away. How wonderful it felt to leave this painting business in trustworthy hands. At about noon, she made tuna sandwiches for the three of them, then surprised them with ice-cream bars. Lunch was a small price to pay to get the house done by Charles's birthday.

On her way back into the house, she noticed her BB gun resting against the wall of the screened-in porch, next to the kitchen door. That Dog had not made an appearance lately, which made her think that Sheriff Holt had actually paid a visit to Simpson. Yet evidence of the mutt was still fresh every day. The old man must just wait until he knew she was gone, then turn the dog loose to do his damage. The thought of it all made her stomach knot up.

At 1:15, Mamie heard a loud rapping at her back door. She had been napping on the daybed, dreaming that she was driving tacks into Cassie's fat toes. It was something of a relief to wake up and discover that the real sound of nails being driven was coming from across the street. But then she realized that someone was at the door. She had risen, straightened her housedress, and was halfway to the kitchen when she heard Alma's voice.

"Mamie? You there?"

"I'm coming, Alma. You woke me up, and I'm a little fuzzy." Even through the screen Alma looked stricken, almost as though she knew what Mamie had been doing to Cassie in the dream.

"I'm sorry," she said, as Mamie unhooked the screen and let her in. "But it's an emergency. Has Ruthie called you?"

"Not since earlier, when she wanted canning lids. What in the world is wrong?" Mamie grabbed at a renegade bobby pin hanging near her ear and fumbled to repin it while Alma stood there in her going-to-town clothes, smelling of Moon Mist.

"She called me ten minutes ago and just sounded beside herself. Wasn't making any sense at all."

"How confused was she? More than usual? You know how flustered she gets."

"Oh, this isn't normal. I was on my way to town, but the more I thought about it, the more I thought we should check on her. You know all those prescriptions she takes. Maybe something's mixing together wrong."

"She goes to three different doctors," Mamie said over her shoulder as she walked into the bedroom to find some knee-highs and her everyday low heels. "Lord only knows what she's taking."

"I know. And some of those drugs can make a person disoriented."

All Mamie could find was a single suntan and a single nude knee-high. She put one over each arm and decided they would have to be close enough. She grabbed her pocketbook and followed Alma out the door.

"I'm picking up my aunt in Helmsly to go grocery shopping," Alma said as she backed out of the drive. "I should have called her. When I'm late, she thinks I've forgotten her address." She laughed. "She's lived there three years now, but she still sends me little notes about her address change."

"How old is she?"

"Ninety-two."

"Sounds old, doesn't it?"

Alma nodded. They were bumping along, the windows rolled up to keep the dust from sifting in. "'Course, I used to think that sixty-five sounded old, but I passed that mark a couple years ago. Seems just middle-aged now."

"Don't be foolish. It *is* middle age."

"Ruthie said something about Mrs. Markham's cat. She started crying, and I couldn't understand her. Then she jumped off to something else—how much corn she's canned. And then she started crying again and said her sister's found another lump. I *think* it's her sister."

"Elda?"

"Yes. That's who she said."

"Elda's always finding something. She's been trying to get cancer for the last fifteen years."

They pulled up Ruthie's drive. The square green house seemed to sit crookedly on its lot, the front wall not quite parallel to the road that passed by. A profusion of plants, domestic and wild, sprang out from the base of the house, its front porch draped in hanging pots of begonias, their leaves and dusty blooms statue still in the heat of afternoon. Alma parked the car in the drive, and they walked around to the side door. For a moment they stood wordlessly and peered through the gray of the screen. A cuckoo clock, stuck on ten o'clock on the opposite entryway wall, had its cuckoo half in, half out of the little window. Kitchen noises drifted through the next room to meet them—that, and the sound of frantic puffing. From where Mamie and Alma stood, they could hear Ruthie's anxiety, little dismayed noises in her throat, snatches of words she said to herself.

"Ruthie! It's Alma and Mamie."

They heard a scurry of soft-soled shoes across linoleum, then silence and the swish of pantyhose rubbing together. Ruthie appeared before them, hair pinned in ringlets to one half of her head. Her eyes were rimmed in moisture. "Well, mercy! Come in!" She noticed Alma's clothes and pocketbook, and a look of horror came over her face. "Are we going somewhere?"

"No. I'm going to Helmsly to shop for Aunt Bernice, that's all." She and Mamie came into the hallway. Before they had a chance to say anything, Ruthie turned on her heels and hurried back toward the kitchen. They looked at each other and followed.

"Ruthie, you sounded so upset on the phone. Is anything—"

"Oh, mercy!" Ruthie jerked around to face them, a pot holder in one hand and tongs in the other. Ears of corn bounced against one another in a large pot of boiling water on the gas range. On the burner next to it tomatoes were stewing in an equally huge kettle. "Elda has it for sure now! It showed up in her tests from last week. *And Luticia's been murdered!*" She grabbed ears of corn out of the pot with the tongs and put them in a colander. "I've got to have new locks put on my doors. There's too much meanness; it didn't used to be this way. I've never had to lock a door in my life. Mamie, could you look up the number of the hardware store? But be quick; I've got to call Elda's son Cleaver and let him know which bus I'll be on. And then get Celia's number; she's taking me."

Mamie struggled to follow instructions. The phone receiver was in her hand. "The hardware store? Why do you want me to call them?"

"Who's Luticia?" asked Alma. "I had the news on at noon and didn't hear about any murder."

"Tell Frank I want new locks put on *today*. And I'll be out of town, so he needs to come by and pick up my extra key. Oh, they wouldn't put anything about Luticia in the news. They probably don't even know about it yet." Ruthie had her back to both of them, working on the corn. She ran cold water over the ears in the colander, then dumped more fresh ones into the pot. Hot water splashed onto the floor, and she and Alma jumped back.

"Be careful, Ruthie! That's boiling water! Who's Luticia?" Alma tried to put herself into Ruthie's field of vision without success. Ruthie was at the freezer. She bent over, her upper half fairly disappearing as she dug through frozen foods.

"She's Mrs. Markham's cat. You know, the pretty longhaired one? Murdered, I swear. What's this town coming to?"

"Oh, that's all. I thought you were talking about a person."

"Well now, that's *not* all!" Ruthie straightened up, red faced, to look at Alma. She had something square in her hand, freezer frost all over it. "Luticia was all Mrs. Markham had, since her son went to Australia. Her only living relative is a cousin up in a rest home somewhere in Omaha. Luticia was like a child." Tears dribbled down Ruthie's face. She held the package under the faucet long enough to clear it of ice.

"How do they know it was murder? Cats run in front of cars all the time."

"Yes. She needs it done today," said Mamie from the telephone. "She's going out of town, so somebody needs to get her house key." Ruthie stared at Mamie.

"Tell him I can leave it under a potted plant on the porch if he can't come get it. I'm leaving in an hour." Then she turned back to Alma. "Her little throat was cut. It was an *execution*. Trina Bitano's sure it's those satanic kids doing rituals. Mrs. Markham is just going out of her mind. Could you warm this up in the microwave?" She thrust the frozen item into Alma's hand. "Poke a few holes in it first."

"What is it?"

"Banana bread. I want to take something over for Mrs. Markham before I go."

Alma started to say something but seemed to think better of it. She stabbed some holes in the cellophane with a fingernail and put it in the microwave, fiddling with the buttons until she figured out how to set the time and temperature.

"What other number did you need?" Mamie stood with phone in hand.

"Celia. It's inside the front cover of my address book under 'C. W.' Ask her what time she's picking me up to go to the bus station."

"Ruthie, I don't even know the woman!" Mamie exclaimed, but she saw that Ruthie was now stirring the tomatoes and didn't hear her.

"Oh, my hair. I've got to finish pinning it." Ruthie started to cry again. "Oh, Elda. I just knew it. I knew when she didn't call over the weekend that the tests were bad." She was engulfed in the steam from both pots, stirring the tomatoes frantically while tears ran down her chin. She dabbed at her eyes with the edge of her apron.

Alma had put down her pocketbook. "Mamie, would you give my Aunt Bernice a call while you're at it? Tell her I'm coming, but I'll be late."

Mamie made a little sound of protest but knew she was beat. She angled a look at the women in the kitchen and jabbed at the buttons on the phone. "You'll have to wait till I've talked to Cel—Hello, Celia? You don't know me. I'm a friend of Ruthie's, and she can't call right now. She wanted to know what time you'd be picking her up for the bus station."

"Where are the pins, Ruthie?" Alma waited while Ruthie pondered the question and pointed hopelessly toward the dining-room table. "I think I set them down there. The comb's in on the lid of the toilet, I think."

Alma found the pins and comb. She stood at Ruthie's side and began working on the unpinned side of her head.

"Oh, thank you. Hair's probably dry by now. You want me to wet it?"

"Are you kidding? All this steam?"

"Oh, I guess that's right. You know, Elda's had these lumps before, but I think it's more serious this time. I told her I'd be on the next bus out."

"That's so good of you, Ruthie," Alma said soothingly. She twirled a strand of hair around an index finger and slid a pin through it, holding the curl fast to Ruthie's head. The microwave beeped.

"Where's Cleaver's number?" Mamie asked.

"In the *B* section. His name is Benson. When is Celia coming?"

"2:30."

"Ohhhhh." Ruthie wilted between the two funnels of steam. "I can't get this canning done by then." She slipped from Alma's reach and searched a lower cabinet for something.

"Are you canning? You've got to sterilize your jars still." Alma sounded panicky for the first time.

"No. I ran out of jars on the first batch this morning. There was so much more than I thought. I'm cold-packing these. If I can just find my freezer bags and boxes." She went down on hands and knees, pulling out canned goods and plastic containers. "I had some left over last year."

"Where'd you get all this? Nobody's garden has been worth a thing this year."

"My niece in Springfield. They've had rain there, you know. She loves home-canned food. She provides the vegetables, and I put them up and keep what I want."

"Cleaver wants to know which bus you'll be on. There are two arriving in Kansas City this evening," called Mamie.

"Whichever one transfers from the bus that leaves Helmsly at 3:15. I have no idea. He'll have to call the bus station for himself." Ruthie's voice was muffled inside the cabinet.

"If you're cold-packing, you can just set the tomatoes in the refrigerator and freeze them later," said Alma.

"But I don't know how long I'll be gone. They could spoil before I get back. Mamie, call Liz and see if she has any freezer bags and boxes. I can't locate mine."

Mamie turned wordlessly to the phone. Finally, a number she didn't have to look up.

"Is the bread thawed? The banana bread?" Ruthie struggled to her feet and was tonging corn from the pot into the colander. She gave the tomatoes another stir.

"Yes, the beeper went off a minute ago." Alma was back to pinning hair.

"I'll take it over to her right before I go."

"I can do it for you," said Mamie, as she waited for Liz to answer her phone.

"No. I need to do it in person."

"Ruthie, it's just a cat!" said Alma. "You take food over for condolences when a *person* dies."

"Luticia was like a child to her." More tears mixed with the glaze of perspiration on Ruthie's face.

Mamie left the phone finally. "Liz is coming over," she said, surveying the kitchen. It looked as if somebody was preparing for Thanksgiving dinner.

"You called Bernice, didn't you?" asked Alma.

"How could I? I don't know her number."

"It's 445-3276." Alma directed Mamie back to the phone. "I've got to go in the next ten minutes."

"Liz has half a box of boxes and bags. Will that be enough? She's on her way over."

"That should do fine. What's left over, the three of you can divide up and take home."

"I've finished your hair, Ruthie, but it won't dry in here. Don't you need to pack?"

"Ohhhh. I knew there was something else." Ruthie handed Alma the corn tongs and hurried from the room.

B ye, Ruthie. Hope the trip goes well," Mamie called from the back step as Celia hoisted Ruthie's suitcase into the backseat of her car. Ruthie marched to the car, fresh pin curls jiggling, and hardly turned to wave. In seconds they were gone.

Mamie went back into the house. She approached the kitchen doorway to be met by a hard stare from Liz, who was at the gas range in a tomato-spattered apron. "That's just like Alma, to get us committed and then leave for Helmsly," she said, a cigarette dangling from one side of her mouth.

"She couldn't help it. You know she would have stayed if she could." Mamie took her station and resumed rolling single ears of cooked corn into aluminum foil to go into larger plastic bags and then the freezer.

"So Elda's finally got it, has she?" Liz dipped stewed tomatoes carefully into freezer-bag-lined boxes.

"Maybe. Ruthie thought it was more serious this time."

"And the satanists are after old people's cats now."

Mamie shook her head. "I don't know about that. Seems kind of extreme to slit a cat's throat when a bullet would do just as well. I *could* imagine it being part of a ritual."

"I wish those kids would call me. I could direct them to a few cats nobody would miss."

"Liz!" Mamie put a hand on her hip. "I don't think it's anything to joke about."

"I think the whole thing's a joke. Why would devil worshipers take any interest in any of us? A bunch of old widow women. I'd think they'd set their sights higher—Oral Roberts or Billy Graham or something."

"I don't know. Let's not talk about it."

They worked in silence. Mamie decided she should probably go to church again this Sunday and ask around about this devil business. Maybe somebody could tell her something that would ease Ruthie's mind.

"Did you see her piles of Christmas cards?" Liz nodded toward the dining-room table.

Mamie nodded. Then she gave a start and said, "Oh boy."

"What?"

"The banana bread is still on the table. She forgot to take it over."

"Is that the bread for the cat?" Liz did not even try to hide her sarcasm.

"For Mrs. Markham. I guess we should take it over."

"I'm not taking food anywhere for a dead cat."

"I hardly know the woman. I can't go by myself."

Liz dipped tomatoes fiercely, her lips tight together.

Mamie had picked up the bread and was standing in the dining room. "She'll be upset when she remembers that she forgot."

"Mamie, I'm not going over there. The whole idea is ridiculous."

"It's not like *we'd* be giving it. We could just say that Ruthie was going to and had a family emergency."

"Well." Liz let the dipper drop into the kettle. "Let's get it over with." She took off her apron and walked over to Mamie.

"Oh, look," said Mamie. "She even got out a sympathy card to go with it."

Liz took the card from Mamie's hand and set it back on the table, then picked up the bread. "Come on."

Mamie removed her apron and followed Liz out the back door. After a moment of discussion, they decided that the Markham home was across the street just west of there. Liz went first, with Mamie behind her, as they made their way across the burnt grass.

When Liz brought Mamie home from Ruthie's, the world had shifted into another orbit. Dave and Arthur's grandson and Dave's girlfriend were painting away, music pounding from out of a boom box thing near the front steps. Mamie hadn't really viewed the house from a distance since early this morning, and now, with so much of the trim painted, it was looking newer than she had expected.

"Hi, Mrs. Rupert," the girl said from where she stood at a front window. She wore a bikini sort of top. The poor child looked thin. She raised her brush and smiled. There was paint on her chin; as Mamie got closer the smudge seemed to get bluer.

"Hello," Mamie said tentatively, taking another step. "Is that *blue* paint?"

"To tell the truth, I think it's what they call teal."

Mamie noticed the strip of blue—or teal—on the window trim. "Honey, you got the wrong color of paint, didn't you?"

"Well, we need to talk about that." Dave was off the ladder. He walked over to her, and for a split second she saw her Charles, sweaty, shirt partly open, those clear eyes.

"We made a mistake, Mrs. Rupert. Painted the trim on the back of the house a different color than on the front. We were all three going at once and didn't even know the paint was different till we were halfway through. It was really the store's fault, but anyway . . ." Mamie listened carefully as Dave explained what they intended to do. In the meanwhile, Liz got out of the car and joined them, her eyebrows arched quite high.

When Dave Seaton finished his explanation, Mamie felt that what had happened probably wasn't a bad thing. She looked at the neat strips of double color all along the front eaves. She turned to Liz for an opinion, for she always had one.

"Oh, I don't know, Mamie. This looks kind of . . . snazzy. Can't hurt, can it?"

"Looks nice," said a voice quietly from the front walk. The three of them turned to see Sarah Morgan, who stood there, baby in hooded stroller. Under her bright orange sun visor, the pastor's wife was smiling. She was in shorts and a T-shirt, light green, splashes of faded color on it. When Mamie greeted her, she rolled the stroller tentatively onto the grass and squinted at the paint job. "I like the combination."

"You paint houses, Mrs. Morgan?" asked Mamie.

"Oh, no." The young woman blushed a little. "But I was an art major years ago. I've studied color quite a bit."

"So you think it looks all right?" Mamie moved a bit closer. Mrs. Morgan's little boy looked up at her, a hand in his mouth.

"Yes. It's fine. Will you just have the two colors?"

Mamie looked at Dave, and he laughed. "Should there be more?"

"Well, a lot of people use three when they do the multicolor trim. For instance, to separate the darker colors you might use a rose pink. But—sorry—I don't mean to tell you what to do."

"Pink?" Mamie leaned closer to be sure she'd heard correctly.

Sarah Morgan was nodding. "The third tone would set off the rest perfectly. You're going to do the porch posts too, right? And the railing?"

"Mmm." Dave was cocking his head and eyeing the house. Mamie moved closer still. It seemed that this thing was getting out of her reach again. She tried, there in the midst of the people and the late afternoon sun, to imagine what Charles would say to all this. Charles was so sensible. You could never hurry him or pressure him into a decision. And here was a small crowd of people on her lawn, making all kinds of decisions and changing her life's color scheme. She couldn't just let it happen, could she?

"Do you really think all those colors will look all right, Mrs. Morgan?" Mamie put herself between Sarah Morgan and the house until the pastor's wife looked her in the eye.

"Oh, yes. It'll be a showplace!"

Mamie felt a laugh escape her, and covered her mouth. "That's really not what I had in mind!"

"Go for it, Mrs. Rupert," Arthur's grandson said from where he sat cross-legged in the mint patch, doctoring the basement window.

"Go where?"

"Go ahead and do it," said Sarah Morgan. She reached out and gave Mamie's hand a squeeze. "It will be beautiful."

"Well." Mamie surveyed all of them. "You need to find pink paint now? You'll need some more money, won't you?" She craned her neck at Dave.

"No. This is on us, since we made the mistake."

"I made the mistake," mumbled the boy in the mint patch.

Dave looked at Sarah Morgan. "Could you find the right shade? I'm willing to try this, but I don't know much about color combinations."

"Sure." Sarah smiled broadly for the first time since she'd come into the yard. "Frank's Hardware?"

"I don't know if he'll have pink, but you could start there."

Sarah was looking over the paint paraphernalia. "You have a stick I can take samples of this other paint on?"

"Over there."

She bent beside each can of color and dabbed a bit on the paint stirrer. "I'll be back as soon as I can."

Mamie and Liz watched the pastor's wife fairly spin the stroller around and rattle off down the walk toward Bender Springs's several blocks of downtown. Then Mamie turned back to the others and said the only thing that came to mind: "Would everybody like some iced tea?"

The three painters groaned a yes. Mamie could see sweaty strands of hair sticking to their necks and faces.

"Give me ten minutes."

"I'll help you, Mamie," said Liz. When they got in the door, she turned to Mamie, eyes wide. "You need to find out if they'll charge you more. It's bound to take them a lot more time. Have you asked them?"

"I just got here and saw it myself! They cooked all this up while I was gone." Mamie tugged at the kitchen curtain worriedly, peering out at her yard.

"You want me to ask them?" Liz had her determined look.

"Well . . . if you think that's what we should do. Wouldn't they come out and tell me if they were going to charge more?"

"Huh!" Liz was already out the door. From the window, Mamie could see her come around the corner of the house and look up to Mamie's left, where Dave Seaton was painting. Mamie could hear the soft swish of his paintbrush. The sound stopped when Liz spoke up, in a voice so loud Mamie covered her own mouth.

"Excuse me. Mamie never contracted for all this extra fancy stuff. Do you plan on charging extra for it?"

"No, ma'am. It was our mistake. Price hasn't changed." The swishing resumed.

"Oh." Liz looked at Mamie through the window screen and shrugged discreetly with one eyebrow.

Mamie leaned into the screen until her nose touched it. She motioned at Liz and said in as loud a whisper as she dared, "Ask them if they want their tea sweetened or plain."

"Excuse me."

"Yes, ma'am?"

"You like your tea sweet or plain?"

"Ask them," Dave answered.

Mamie saw Liz look up toward the girl and down at Arthur's grandson. The boy mumbled something about it didn't matter. But the girl—what was her name? some boy's name—said quite clearly, "I like lots of sugar in mine, thanks."

"All right." Liz marched back around the house, and Mamie heard her come up the back porch. "Sweet," said her friend, putting her pocketbook on the kitchen table.

"I heard. I guess I'm gettin' a real deal."

"I guess you are, Mamie. Your ship has come in today." Liz disappeared into the living room. "You know, if it's going to be so snazzy on the outside, you ought to think about replacing these curtains."

"The curtains?" Mamie walked into the living room, stirring the pitcher of tea as she went. She'd just dumped over a cup of sugar into it, and it was taking forever to dissolve. "You think I should change the curtains?"

"You've got blues and grays and—pink, is it?—on the outside. Nice fresh coat of grayish white all over the house. These old pinkish tan drapes don't quite come up to snuff, you think?"

"Well, I suppose something with blue would look better." Mamie stirred the tea thoughtfully. "I've got several other sets of drapes in the chest in the back bedroom. Don't remember half of what's there."

"Let's look through them." Liz looked bright eyed, particularly for someone who had been spooning hot stewed tomatoes against her will for half the afternoon. It could be a pleasant thing when Liz experienced a mood shift.

"I thought you were in such a rush to get home."

"My day got shot when you dragged me over to Ruthie's. I may as well be a busybody the rest of the day too."

"Help me with the tea tray, and then we'll get into the chest." Mamie felt herself warming up to the rest of her afternoon. She and Liz got out the old, wide wicker tray and loaded it up with the tea pitcher, glasses full of ice, and some napkins. Just before they headed out the door, Mamie reached for the cookie tin, which still had nine or ten sandwich cookies in it. She threw them on a small plate and added it to the tray. They were nearly to the door again when she remembered she still had some white grapes in the refrigerator. Liz put the tray back on the table and gave a little moan of protest while Mamie washed off the grapes and arranged them on another plate. She tried to put all of it on the tray, but it had suddenly become too small for the load, so she found a larger tray under the sink, with a faded oriental design on it, brushed it off carefully with the tea towel, and reloaded.

The dishes and glasses clinked together softly, a refreshing sound on the sun-soaked air. It was gratifying to see her painters' faces light up when they saw her and Liz come around the corner. She pulled the lawn chairs and small aluminum table from the screened-in back porch and waited until the three were seated and sipping before leaving the tray on the table and heading indoors. Liz couldn't help but comment on the girl's bikini top when they were out of earshot, but her high mood was unchanged as they opened the old chest and began to examine its contents.

"I forgot I even had this!" Mamie pulled out a sheer lavender tablecloth.

Liz took out two more cloths and dug out some faded pink napkins and a set of brand-new, queen-size sheets, still in the package. "You don't have a queen-size bed."

"Those were a gift. Thought I might get a bigger bed someday."

"Why would you need a bigger bed? You got a boyfriend I don't know about?"

They both giggled. Mamie's giggles brought tears when she imagined herself in a slinky nightie, bedding down with some man. "That would be a sight!" she said, trying to catch her breath.

"I don't know, Mamie, there's always that handyman."

When the sudden vision of Ax Miracle, trousers half off, came to mind, Mamie found herself gasping for air. Liz's eyes were tearing, too, but she managed to add, "With a last name like Miracle, you never know!"

They hooted, covering their mouths with embroidered tea towels that smelled of mothballs.

"We'd need to hose him down first," Liz got out.

"I don't know that I'd want him sober. I wouldn't look as good to him!"

Liz bent over and caught Mamie's arm. "Shut up, Mamie, or you'll make me wet my pants!"

There were three sets of drapes in the chest, two the right size for the living-room bay window. One was a loose gold-and-orange weave, from when the room had been painted some other color, years ago; Mamie couldn't even remember that phase. The other was a cranberry print, large, satiny, dark blossoms of some sort. They'd been in the back bedroom in the seventies, as she could recall, but had made the small room look too dark; she had replaced them with sheers.

The two women examined the material for moth holes or other major flaws. They spread it out on the bed and looked at the blooms from every angle.

"It's not really the right color, is it?" Mamie remarked.

"It's better than what's up now, but I think you could do better."

"If I change the drapes, I'll have to get new throw cushions and everything."

"Those throw cushions have been around since before I had grand-children. I think you could manage a change." Liz had lit up, and it occurred to Mamie that possibly her friend had been waiting for twenty years for the excuse to suggest changes in the house's decor. Maybe Liz had never liked a single cushion or curtain in the entire place. Maybe she was already compiling a list in her head of new colors for Mamie's walls and kitchen appliances, her bathroom even. That bathroom had been pink for going on thirty years. Some things a person just got comfortable with.

"Alma has blue drapes in her dining room. Maybe she'd trade," said Liz.

"I wouldn't want to ask her to do that. Then she'd have to redo *her* color scheme."

"She doesn't have a color scheme. There's nothing else blue in the room."

Mamie eyed her friend with new suspicion. "I'll bet Ruthie has several sets of drapes packed away somewhere," she said.

Liz blew a furious puff of smoke. "That would mean unpacking all her drawers and boxes. It would take her ten years to re-sort it all. I don't think I could bear to see her scattered out for that long."

"I'll bet she knows exactly what she's got and where it is. She wouldn't have to unpack everything. I'll give her a call when she comes back to town." It gave Mamie some satisfaction to have made a decision contrary to Liz's direction. Liz liked directing too much; it was the one thing, besides the cigarette smoke, that had irritated Mamie down through the years.

They carefully repacked the chest, but not before Mamie took everything else out of it. A china teapot belonging to her Great-aunt Jessie, a packet of postcards from a trip she and Charles had taken in '62 to South Carolina, a sweater she'd knitted for her mother and had taken back after the funeral so it wouldn't get auctioned off with the rest of her mother's belongings, spare sets of towels and sheets. A perfect, miniature, pink lacy dress, puffed sleeves and petticoat stitched right in. For the little girl who had died right on the threshold of this world, forty-odd years ago. This treasure was no surprise; Mamie knew the very corner in which it was packed. Her hand had gone right to it. She unwrapped it from a bit of plain muslin and spread it in her lap. There had been another dress, heaven-white, in which they buried tiny, perfect Eliza Marie. This Mamie had saved, a bit of grief and hope preserved forever, tucked away safe in her house. She allowed herself two or three tears while Liz, unaware of anything, took a break at the window, observing the painters. Then back into the muslin, into the corner. They shut the lid.

"Pastor's wife just brought the pink, gave instructions to Miss Bikini. Oh, she's heading home already; kid's squalling." Liz nodded toward the window. "She's a different one, isn't she?"

"Seems nice enough."

"City girl. Louise Filcher said she'd heard her go on about how wonderful Chicago is. She didn't come right out and say what a hick town this is, but everybody knew that's what she meant."

"It's a big change for a person," said Mamie, leading the way back into the living room. "I'd feel pretty funny about moving to a big city after being here all my life. You know, Alma or her daughter could *make* me a set of drapes and cushions to match. Her daughter's a whiz at that sewing machine. I'll bet she wouldn't charge much more than the cost of the material. Let's go look at those colors again."

Looking through old things and feeling the pull of old years had given Mamie a push into her future. She had to keep living in the here and now, somehow. Maybe new drapes would chase her Cassie dreams away. Maybe she just sat on her haunches and thought about all these things too much. Why, she was about to have a house that was something akin to modern art, right smack in the middle of town. She had to keep up and move on. She unlocked the front door and stepped onto the porch. "Dave?"

"Yes, ma'am." He was way over at the north corner. She peered at his work and got her first glimpse of the third color. Anything but a gaudy pink, the dusty rose color snuggled right into the gray and teal. Yes indeed, she was on a new road here. Her heart pounded a bit louder and faster, but she sort of liked the feel of it. She smiled up at her painter, admiring the strong look of his legs. Legs told you a lot about a man. "What color drapes do you think would go best with these new colors?"

Something just short of panic crossed Dave's face, and his mouth opened for a moment before anything came out.

"Drapes? Hey, I didn't mean to make you change—"

"Oh, I'd been wanting an excuse for years. Blue, you think?"

Dave Seaton shook his head, a slow, deliberate movement. "I'm not about to give interior-decorating advice. No, sir. You just do whatever you want to the inside."

"Teal's a good color," said the girl with the boy's name.

"Randy—" Dave started.

"It would go with the outside colors, and it's real easy to work into colors inside, too, like your sofa and the carpet and all."

"Teal. Hmm." Mamie thought she noticed a sharp look pass between Dave and Randy. Bikini or not, the girl sounded as though she knew what she was talking about. "Well, I'm not deciding today. Just wanted some opinions."

"The drapes you have look fine, Mrs. Rupert," Dave pleaded.

"No, they don't. Not if she's wanting to coordinate," said Randy.

"She doesn't have to *coordinate* if she doesn't want to," Dave said.

"I'd agree with my daughter. She's right once in a while."

Mamie spotted a woman in one of the lawn chairs, seated with her legs crossed and holding an umbrella against the sun. She was a shriveled-looking thing, a hard mouth and sharp eyes. Mamie introduced herself.

"I'm Lorene," the woman said.

"Randy's mother?"

The small head barely nodded. She was watching her daughter carefully. Randy was high on the ladder, adding pink to the center gable. Lorene swore and said, "Randy Mae, if you twist another inch, you'll fall off that thing."

The girl didn't reply but kept the careful line going. Mamie stepped back a bit at the profanity.

"Would you like some iced tea, Lorene?"

"I'd rather have hot coffee—if it's not too much trouble."

Mamie noticed then that the woman was wearing a cardigan. "Are you *cold?*"

"Right now I am. Changes on me though. It's from my chemotherapy treatments. I'm dying of cancer, you know."

"Oh no, I didn't know. I'm so sorry. I'll bring you some coffee." Mamie headed for the house but turned suddenly, noting the woman's bare feet. "Be careful of the dog dung."

"Dog dung?"

"Yes. One of my neighbors lets his dog run loose, and he's done his business all over the yard."

"No wonder your roses look so good." The woman shifted in the lawn chair, as though she were trying to get more comfortable. "Send 'im over to my place. I've gotta *pay* for my fertilizer."

Mamie gathered up the tray of empty glasses, pitcher, and cookie and grape remains. They'd cleaned it all up. Climbing the front steps, she realized how tired she felt and that she'd never gotten her full nap time. It had certainly paid to miss some sleep today, though. She put on her apron and fired up the coffeepot. She came close to starting dinner for the whole crew, but it was only four-thirty. That Lorene looked like she needed a lot of food. But somebody with cancer, you never knew what they could eat. Mamie would be obligated if she offered to cook and then found out she didn't have a thing anybody would want to eat. A person had to draw the line somewhere.

She took out Lorene's coffee and avoided conversation. The daybed was calling to her. Her bones hurt. She lay down for the second time that day and hoped the dreams would be better. She hoped Cassie's ghost would flit by and see the house and be too preoccupied to make her appearance in dreams.

When she awoke, it was nine-thirty. She'd missed the evening news and dinner. The clock on the far wall was strangely bright. Then she realized there was a light outside, in the yard. She blinked in the brightness, straightening her hair as she tried to see out the window. There were voices out there. And music, some of that rock music. She saw a glint of skin and bikini pass by through the beam of light. Goodness, they were having some sort of party in her front yard. She knew all this today couldn't be completely good. A female voice laughed. She heard a man cough. How many were there?

She wasn't still dreaming, was she? She turned on a light and placed her hand on the wall. It was her house, and herself. She put on her yard slippers and ventured into the light outside.

"Hey, Mrs. Rupert, we're almost finished!" Dave Seaton hurried over to take her arm and help her down the front steps. Once out of the bright beam, she focused slowly on Arthur's grandson and on Randy. Lorene was gone. But Abe Perkins from next door was standing close by, grinning, hands shoved into his overalls. "H'lo, Mamie."

"Is something wrong? I woke up and saw the light and thought maybe the police were here."

"Oh, no, no." Abe reached to take her other arm, and he and Dave turned her around so that the light wasn't so bright on her face. "They were running out of daylight. Jake lent them the beamers from his truck." Jake was Abe's son, who had moved back home after a divorce last year. He'd been a help to Abe and Thelma. By now Mamie had turned around and seen the meaning of it all. The entire front of the house was lit. Tony was working on the porch railing. Just then Mamie spotted Arthur himself, standing close by, watching the boy.

The colors were almost indescribable. The place looked as if it had been dropped out of the sky, brand new. Never in a million years would she have come up with such a plan. The trim was three colors all around. The porch posts and railing posts were teal; the railing itself was steel gray, and the caps at the top were rose. The three colors played in the fancy woodwork at the peak of the gable, as well as the latticed window frames along the top of the bay window. The trellis at the east end of the porch was teal. As she moved closer, Mamie saw delicate painted gray vines twirling around each porch post, tiny rose blossoms peeping out here and there. Even the slats over the porch crawl space were a fresh gray. In all her years, Mamie had never seen so much color on a single house. But when a person stood back, it looked perfect. It was a carnival without the noise and dirt. It was a perpetual decoration, apart from Christmas or the Fourth of July. It was like a picture you'd see in a magazine from some other, more important place. Mamie stood there between Dave and Abe and couldn't say a word. She heard voices of two or three other neighbors who had been summoned out of their homes and off their porches by the strange light. She could feel them gathering at the edges of her yard. "I've got to call Alma and Liz," she murmured and broke from them to enter the dark of her front room. She could look out the window as she stood by the phone and dialed the numbers. From this window the light wasn't so direct, and she could see people moving about, hands on hips or folded in front of them, or scratching their heads, as they took in the sight before them.

Within ten minutes, Liz and Alma arrived in Alma's car. They made little sounds of wonder and approval as they walked over to join Mamie. She had pulled up one of the lawn chairs to sit in, so she could look it all over more carefully. She couldn't take her eyes off the clean, perfect lines, the flourishes, the gleaming gray-white, and the bold colors. She placed her hand on the chair next to her. If Charles were alive, why, he'd be sitting right there, puffing in a satisfied way on his pipe. She could see his stubby finger pointing out different features to Abe, or the pipe stem being jabbed in Dave's direction, making comments, nodding in that way that said he was pleased, very pleased.

"You know, it's getting hotter," Dave spoke up. "It was cooler an hour ago. Anybody heard the weather report?"

"Eighties all night. May be hotter tomorrow. No rain in sight, of course," Abe answered.

Mamie noticed a beer in Dave's hand. Near his feet was a Styrofoam cooler, no doubt full of bottles. The music she'd heard seemed to be coming from Jake's truck, parked across her front ditch so that the set of large lights across the top of the cab could shine on the house.

"Heat wave." Dave sighed. "All we need. We're all gonna dry up and blow away."

"At least Mamie'll blow away in style!" Abe said with a grunt. The laughter of several people lingered in the close night air. The crickets were beginning to rev up. The bright, unnatural light made Mamie's house look like a stage waiting for its characters to make their appearances. Mamie settled back and was aware of Alma and Liz sitting on either side of her. There was hardly anything left to say. They all stood or sat, wiping moisture from their faces, and watched the front of Mamie's house as though the play were about to begin.

27

DAVE SEATON:
DORIS, HIS MOTHER

Wednesday, August 6

Since being grown, Dave hadn't made a habit of resenting people. But when his mother's Buick LeSabre pulled into the driveway early Wednesday evening, old feelings pulled in with her. Dave couldn't say that he'd ever hated her. But he'd never liked her either. He stood at the back door and watched the car come to a stop and Doris gather things from the passenger seat and pull down the mirror on the visor to check her hair and face. Then she got out, purse on her arm, and dusted something imaginary from her jacket sleeve. She was heavier and looking older, but everything matched. As usual, she wore a pastel suit, something that looked as if she'd picked it up from the dry cleaners that morning. This suit was yellow. Her hair, dyed to a soft silver, glistened in the sun. She was smiling when Dave stepped out on the porch.

"Hi, hon." She gave him a light hug. He gave her a light kiss on the cheek.

"Come on in, Mother. Didn't expect you."

"If you'd buy an answering machine, I could have left a message." Her tone was not angry, just a "you still haven't done what I've suggested" tone.

"Don't have need for one. Most of the people who would leave me messages I see every day anyway."

"I'd forgotten all about this." Doris was lifting a slim blue vase from its dusty spot on one of the tiny kitchen shelves above the sink. She had begun her touching routine. From the moment she stepped into the place she was roving from room to room, putting her hands on surfaces and objects. The paint job on the living-room trim, the knickknacks on the desk, the magazines on the coffee table, the dishes on the cabinet, the pictures on the wall. It was a Doris inspection, but not really an inspection. It was Doris getting in touch with the place she'd left ten years ago. It had been her house once, before Dad got sick and she'd used the stress as an excuse to visit her sister in Overland Park more frequently. Then had come her own ailments, caused by stress, the doctor up there had said. So she'd had to leave Bender Springs. She'd cried and carried on and called a lot, at least at first, to check on Dad, but it had been pretty clear to Dave that his mother had finally gotten what she wanted.

When she did visit, it seemed as if she had to check and make sure, once again, that she'd taken everything she needed from the place. She always left with something—a sugar and creamer, a book, a picture—acting as if she'd missed it when she packed and certainly Dave would have no use for it anyway.

Dave watched her now, putting her polished fingernails all over a set of horse-head bookends on the desk. "Dad kept his Louis L'Amour collection between those," he said. Doris put them down. One way to loosen her grip on anything was to connect it directly to Dad. And she wasn't walking out of this place with those bookends.

"Have you had your dinner?" she asked, examining the curtains of the front windows.

"No. Want to go to the Cupboard? I don't have much around here." Randy was going straight from work to the midweek church service tonight. Dave was glad the two women weren't in the house at the same time.

Doris wrinkled her nose, just a little, just enough. "There's a new steak house in Helmsly, somebody told me."

"Let's try it out then."

"Why don't you drive my car. I'm tired of driving—the trip gets longer every time."

Forty minutes later they sat at a booth over steak and salad. "Have you been here before?" she asked. Dave leaned back and enjoyed the air-conditioning.

"No, can't say that I have. Not a big steak eater, I guess. But this is good. You didn't have to treat."

"Of course I did. I'm not going to come see my only child and not take him out to dinner!" He had to admit that her smile was beautiful. At fifty-nine she was an attractive woman. A few years ago she'd remarried, but the guy had died of a heart attack within the year. Dave tried to feel some compassion for her, but she didn't inspire much. She'd bought into her sister's retail businesses in the Plaza district of Kansas City, and she had more money than even she could spend. She was perfect in every way, to look at her—full of big-city poise—but it was all bought and paid for.

"How are you doing?" she asked, cutting up a large piece of leaf lettuce.

"Fine. You?"

"Are they paying you anything?"

"Sure."

"I'd like to take you clothes shopping. I think you were wearing that shirt the last time I visited."

"I like it. I don't need any clothes, Mother. I'm fine."

"You look unhappy."

Dave watched her hack up more lettuce, then returned to his steak. "How's Aunt Eleanor?"

"All right, considering. That granddaughter of Cheryl's is driving everyone crazy." Dave made his eyes focus on Doris while she gave him the rundown on family members he'd never had anything to do with. They were all snobs with snobs' problems. He'd met Cheryl's granddaughter and actually thought she was a pretty cool kid. That had been two years ago, when the girl was fifteen and excited about things like going to West Virginia for two weeks to help fix up old people's houses. No wonder the rest of Doris's family couldn't deal with her.

"So have you thought any more about moving up closer to your old mother?" Suddenly, what Doris was saying came through the fog clearly to Dave. He looked up and tried not to seem surprised.

"Was I ever thinking about it?"

"We talked about it the last time you came to see me—last fall sometime. If you're interested in selling the old place, I've got an idea you might want to hear."

"What's that?" Dave looked over at the dessert bar, a few yards from them. He didn't have dessert very often.

"My nephew, Pete, knows a man who owns a company not far from here that builds these prefab homes, moves them onto lots. Nice homes—I've seen a couple of them. And if you decide you want to get the place off your hands, we could have a new house brought in, bring up the property value—I'm talking about *way* up—and then sell the whole kit and caboodle for a very nice profit."

"Bring a new house onto the property?"

"Yes."

"Tear down the one I'm living in."

She waved her fork at him. "It's practically falling down already. Never was much of a house. Too small for more than one person."

"The three of us lived in it all right."

Old anger entered her polished features, just for an instant. "It may have seemed all right to you, because you were just a little guy. But believe me, it was crowded. Anyway, what do you think?"

"I can't afford to have a house built and moved in."

"I'd pay for that. The place *is* still in my name, remember, and I'm responsible for it."

"Doesn't have to be that way. I told you a long time ago just to sign it over to me. You wouldn't have to worry about it again."

"Your father had the chance to sell that place years ago but passed it up. I've always regretted it. Actually, when your granddad sold off the back lot to the Steepses, we could have made a good profit on the whole place. That was in '65. It might have made the difference in the kind of care your father got later—if he'd been closer to decent hospitals." She clamped her mouth shut in an irritated expression while she added more sour cream to her baked potato and pulverized it with her fork.

Dave's steak was settling on his stomach badly. He told himself every time she showed up that he wouldn't argue, wouldn't get mad. And every time she brought up Dad's illness in one more attempt to exonerate herself. It had been Dad's fault, after all, for not moving to the city with her. If everyone had just done what she wanted, everything in the universe would have worked out better.

"I'll let you know if I decide to move," Dave said tightly. He would not say more. Not this time.

They finished the meal with her chattering about her various family members "up there" who were succeeding in this business or that profession. She had begun, in recent years, to talk of her investments, as if Dave knew what she was talking about. He hardly knew a mutual fund from a savings bond, and he didn't care. He didn't need to care. Yet she kept talking as if he wanted to know everything about her life.

As they drove back to Bender Springs, she couldn't seem to help herself.

"I worry about you, hon. It's not natural for a man your age to be living alone."

"I'm not living alone."

Her head fairly spun in his direction. "Really. Why didn't you say something? Where is she? I want to meet her."

"Her mom's sick with cancer, so she spends a lot of her time over there right now."

"Oh, what a dear. Do I know her?"

"I don't think so. Probably know her folks—or know of them. Remember the Kluvers?"

The car became very quiet. Dave thought the cornfield they were passing looked a foot or two too short for this time of the year.

"Oh. Yes, I remember them. He's sort of a hillbilly artist, isn't he?"

"Works with wood and metals. Gone a lot to shows around the area."

"I didn't know he had a daughter. The way the two of them always fought, I'm surprised they have any children."

"Her name's Randy. She just moved in a few weeks ago."

"Is she pregnant?" Doris tilted her head downward to look over her sunglasses at the farmhouses they were passing.

"No. We haven't made those kinds of plans yet." He didn't look at Doris's face but knew from memory the expression that was there—as if she had indigestion but would die before belching in front of anybody.

"Well, I'd like to meet her." She didn't sound convincing. Dave smiled at the stunted cornfield.

"Need to stay the night, Mother?" Dave asked as they pulled into the driveway.

"Oh no, hon. I'm going now to visit an old girlfriend."

"Around here?"

"No. In Helmsly."

"Why didn't you say so? I could've driven the truck, and you wouldn't have had to come back here at all."

"No trouble." They got out of the car, and she came around to the driver's side. She paused to stare across the yard at Harry Steeps's place. "Mr. Steeps has done a good job over there."

"Yeah. He's pretty handy—built the garage and deck himself."

"Old Crazy James is probably spinning in his grave."

"You mean Great-grandpa James?"

"When your Grandpa Hank decided to sell off those back lots, James threw fits. Going on about his hollyhocks." She turned to Dave. "As far back as I can remember, he had nearly half the lot planted in hollyhocks. Nothing else, no real flower beds or landscaping. But he'd go mutter to his hollyhocks and practically have a nervous breakdown if anybody acted like they were even going to walk through them."

"Hollyhocks wouldn't harm anything."

"Well, he was a sweet old man but crazy as a loon. He'd worked in the mines, you know, and they had to dig him out of a cave-in when he was twenty-two. Never was the same after that. Probably the reason Hank was such a mean one. Ran off when he was sixteen and showed up twenty years later—no wife, but a son nearly grown."

"Dad, you mean."

"Yes."

"I hardly remember Grandpa Hank."

"I'm afraid you're not missing much. He was a good businessman, I'll give him that. Sold off those lots to Harry Steeps's dad when he could get a robber's price for them. Them and those silly hollyhocks."

They stood quietly, staring toward the Steeps home, beyond Dave's garden.

"Sure you don't want to stay awhile, Mother? Randy will be back by eight or so."

"Oh, I really have to hit the road. Maybe next time." She smiled her beautiful smile once again and patted Dave's cheek. On her hand were three large, expensive-looking rings. "Had to see my boy." She got in the car, and Dave leaned in the window.

"Thanks for dinner," he said.

"Come see me, next time, and I'll *really* take you out. There's this Greek restaurant just a mile from my house—oh my, you'd love it."

"I'll think about it."

"Think about the house too. We could really do well. Even if you didn't want to sell right away, you could have a bigger place—for you and Randy."

"I doubt I'll be interested, but we'll keep it in mind."

Dave sat in the kitchen later as evening turned to nightfall. He sat at the table, in front of the air conditioner, and worked a crossword puzzle. It helped him not think about Doris. He'd decided a few years ago that he wouldn't let her bother him so much, and most of the time he succeeded. But it always took him a while right after he'd seen her. By tomorrow he'd think of her as a successful woman in her senior years who had problems in herself she'd probably never see.

Randy came in at nearly ten o'clock. Dave turned when he heard the door open behind him, and he watched while she put her purse on the cabinet. Tonight, she put a Bible there too. It looked new.

"Hi, babe. Missed you."

She came up and hugged him from behind, kissed his ear. "Did you really?"

"Yep. How was church?"

"Pretty nice. They talk a lot. Hardly leave any time at the end for prayer, and it's supposed to be a prayer meeting. Go figure."

She sat down across from him and stared at him for several seconds. "You OK?" she asked.

"Oh, my mother was here. I'm never OK after that."

Concern wrinkled Randy's forehead.

"Don't even ask," he said. "I'll tell you all about it sometime. She and I have never been in the same universe."

"I'm sorry. I didn't know that."

"Mainly, it's the way she was with my dad. He was a real decent guy. Worked hard, but she always said he didn't 'have ambition.'"

"What did he do?"

"Janitor at the high school—until he got too sick to work."

"So, she has something against janitors?"

He shrugged. "He wasn't any big-time professional, but he liked his job OK. Liked being around kids. Liked coming home in the evenings and working in his garden. But it was never enough for her. It makes me mad when I think of how much she didn't respect him."

"She probably doesn't think much of you shoveling asphalt for the county, does she?"

"She's had sense enough to keep her mouth shut about that. But she comes around here once or twice a year and hints about the jobs I could get in the city, and all that. Wanting me to sell this place now."

Randy's eyes got big. "Are you going to sell it?"

"No. Or if I do, it'll be when and how I want to."

"Good for you." She grinned but looked really tired. She was spending more time with Lorene, and Dave knew that wasn't easy. He walked over to her and lifted the brown hair to one side so he could massage her shoulders and back. He thought about how Doris would think what a common girl Randy was, and he was glad all over again that the two women hadn't met.

When Dave got home from work Friday, Joe Travis's car was in the drive. Actually, it was backing out of the drive. Joe waved at Dave as they passed each other, him going out and Dave going in.

"Hey, Dave—good to see you!"

"You want to come in?"

"No, I'm leaving. Was talking with Randy. Got a meeting tonight at the Baptist church."

"Hope it goes OK." Dave made himself smile.

Randy was at the kitchen table, the new Bible in front of her, when he walked in.

"You and ol' Joe have a good talk?"

She stepped up for a kiss. "All this stuff is new to me. He was just explaining some things, getting me started."

"You going to the meeting tonight? It's revival, right?"

"First night of the final week. I've got to check on Mom first. Want to come along?"

"To your Mom's or the meeting?"

"Well, either or both."

"Don't think so. I figure you can pass on Bible teachings to me now; I don't have to go looking for them."

"But it's not the same that way, you know."

"Maybe I'll go to Perky's. Haven't been up there for a few days."

"Whatever."

"I hope you're not going to get weird about beer and all that."

"No. I'm not having any, but you go ahead."

"You mean you're not having any from now on, or just tonight?"

"I don't know. Is it that important?"

"I just don't want you getting fanatical on me."

She stared at him as if to say *I can't believe you just said that.* "Why are you so against this?" she asked, raising the Bible.

"I'm not against it. I just don't believe it."

"You don't believe in God?"

"Nothing's ever convinced me there's anybody up there looking out for me."

"Just because he's not looking out for *you* doesn't mean he's not around."

"I'm just looking for evidence."

"Good things have to come from *somewhere.*"

Dave suppressed a sigh.

"Look," said Randy, "I'm beginning to see how I've depended on some things to help me cope. I've found a new way to cope now, and I'm wanting not to depend on the other things so much, at least until I know what's what. Beer's not a big deal, but I really looked forward to it at the end of every day. Maybe I looked forward to it too much. So give me a little space, okay?"

"I don't like how this is changing stuff between us." Dave saw Randy's face and wished he could unsay that last remark.

"Something happened in me," she said. "Like after all this time, I've got words to explain me to myself. I wasn't trying to be spiritual, but a spiritual thing happened anyway."

"You've got a lot of stress with your mom and all. Religion helps sometimes. I've got nothing against it."

They were quiet. The air around them felt ready to do something.

"But . . .?" Randy said.

"What?"

"*But.* You've got nothing against religion—but? I'm waiting for you to finish the sentence."

"Crap, Randy."

"Tell me what you really think."

"I really think that religion is OK. It's just not for everybody." He paused but felt some strange momentum keep his mouth going. "And . . . I think most people who push religion are a bunch of operators. I'd rather you have your spiritual experience without bringing a churchload of preachers and do-gooders along."

"Who else am I gonna be spiritual with?"

"Why do you have to be spiritual *with* anybody? You can be spiritual right here." He tapped the tabletop.

Randy rubbed her eyes with the heels of her hands. "Maybe I'd rather be spiritual with other people who know what I'm talking about."

"All right, all right, just drop it. I—" He let out a breath. "I don't understand this, but never mind."

She twisted a strand of hair near her ear and looked at the floor near his feet. "It's not like I'm running around with other guys. I don't understand what's making you so crazy all of a sudden."

"I just feel things changing, like I'm not good enough for you anymore. Like your schedule's all filled up. I mean—," he slapped his hand on the table—"it's like you're a lot of places besides here. Even when you're with me, those wheels in your head are flying off somewhere else."

"You aren't the only thing in my life," she said, and folded her arms. "You think my whole life should just revolve around you."

"No, that's not what I meant."

"It's too bad I've got a mother dying of cancer and friends I've had longer than you."

"Would you just cool it?"

"And then I become a Christian, and that really did it, didn't it?"

They regarded each other, lips tight.

"Some people think I should move out, since we're not married. But I'm still here. Does that mean anything to you? Do you know what that means to me, to have people think I'm living in sin?"

"Well, maybe you should move out, then. It's only a matter of time before I lose. There are more of them than me. I was just convenient for a while."

She kept staring hard at him, eyes bright. He saw then that she was shaking. He decided to speak before she had a chance to.

"I can see how things are going with us. I'm just tired of all this, Randy. I'm going north if I can get that job."

She didn't say anything, but he thought there were tears in her eyes.

"Why do you say you know how things are going with us?" she said finally.

"You tell me."

"You know, Dave, I've spent my whole life just having things happen to me. My parents happened to me, and I had to deal with it. Then Jay happened to me. Then you happened to me."

"Then Jesus happened to you."

"And Jesus happening to me has made me think about how a person has choices. Can be moving in a direction; you know, taking steps. I never did anything like that before—sat down and decided where I wanted to go or how I wanted to do it. Nobody's gonna make those choices for me. Everything'll just keep happening to me, and before I know it . . . ." She was crying now; it seemed to be more out of frustration than anything. She stood up and walked out the back door. "I'm going to check on Mom."

Dave slumped against the door. Every time he got honest, he got into trouble. As he watched her leave across his backyard, he couldn't feel much anger toward her. Even as she stomped past the garden, her thin body and wispy hair broke his heart.

Dave looked over the garden. Tomatoes red and green. Pepper plants, corn—it looked better than he'd realized. It looked as if the summer hadn't been hot and dry and relentless. "Plant sense," Mamie had called it. A special gift of his.

Something crazy happened to him then. He would look back later and still not be able to explain it. All he knew was that one minute he was admiring the greenness that was his handiwork. And the next minute he hated it more than he'd ever hated anything. After all that work through the hot summer, he had nothing really. Every day he'd been out here caring for those rows of plants, he'd really been caring for Randy, giving to her. But it didn't matter, all that he'd done. Didn't matter at all.

He started walking through the garden rows then, systematically pulling up every stake, string, or wire that held the green leaves and vines in place. Then he went into the shed and brought out his biggest mower. It roared into action, and he made path after path through the garden, watching colors fly out to the side—vegetables, leaves, and dirt went together. He ran the mower back and forth and up and down. Then what it hadn't been able to handle, he chopped down with the hatchet and hoe. He finished with the tiller, mixing the cut-up remains with the dry dirt. In an hour's time, the garden was gone, and Dave sat on his back stoop drinking a beer. He finished that one, went in to look at Randy's things in each room of his house, then drank another beer. Harry Steeps from across the alley ventured through the yard and up to Dave.

"Hey, you OK?"

"Yep. Just got tired of the work. Garden's a lot of work."

Harry laughed nervously. "You're right about that. Well, I guess you did what you wanted to do."

"That's right, Harry. A person's got to look out for himself, you know what I mean? Got to figure out what you want and just get it somehow. And get rid of what you don't want. Life's too short. You know what I mean?"

"I hear ya."

"Want a beer, Harry? I've got plenty."

"Oh, I don't know about that," said Harry, keeping his distance. "Looks to me like you don't have near enough."

Dave laughed at that, hard, and a little too loudly.

"I'd be happy to get sloshed with you, but Jeanne Anne's got people coming over. You want me to bring you some grilled chicken in a while?"

"No. I'm fine. I'm great."

"I can see that. Give me a holler if you need anything, OK, buddy?" Harry walked back across the yard, glancing at the raw garden spot as he went.

If the evening had ended that way, Dave could have chalked up the garden thing to being mad and too hot and tired for too many weeks in a row. He'd had four or five beers by six-thirty, and the heat was still with him and Randy wasn't. And the garden was gone, and by then he didn't know whether that was a good thing or a bad thing.

Then, for no reason that was reasonable, she came walking into his yard. She was by herself. She was wearing a gauzy dress, her body shining through it. She floated over the lawn toward Dave.

"Hi, Lena."

"My, my. Hello, Dave. You're in bad shape tonight. And Randy's at her mom's crying. What did you do now?"

Dave wasn't focusing too well. It had been a long time since he'd drunk so much so fast.

"Can I get you some coffee?" The dress and body came closer. She was on the porch. She touched his face with her hand. "Maybe you should go inside. Maybe you can sleep if you lie down."

He followed her into the house. He stumbled a little when his shin hit the footstool in the living room. "I'm fine," he said. "You can leave now."

"No, I think I'd better stay. Till I'm sure you're OK."

"When did you get concerned about *my* well-being?"

"I've never *not* cared. But we just always get off on the wrong foot."

"Just go." Even as Dave said it, pointing toward the door, he was gazing at those green eyes. Her face was flawless. And for once she was smiling at him. He felt an illogical desire taking him over.

"You want to lie down? You might feel better. Sure you don't want coffee?" That smile again. Dave recognized it suddenly for what it was. She was mocking him. She was enjoying this.

"No. I don't want coffee. I just want to be left alone."

"I don't think that's what you really want." She moved closer.

In the heat of the moment, Dave remembered later, he'd made a decision to come on to Lena. But he decided it because he hated her so much and wanted, if just for a few minutes, to put her in her place. He suddenly wanted to do anything that would force that perfect composure to leave her face. When it was over, Dave couldn't tell if he'd accomplished what he wanted. He knew something had gone really wrong when Lena finally said something.

"Well, I'm sure this will help Randy decide whether she wants to stay or leave. Coming on to her best friend. You're in top form tonight, *Dave.*"

"Get out of my house." He called her the most vile names he could think of. "In fact, just go back to whatever planet you came from."

She smiled then, as though she were very pleased with her work. She smiled and floated out his front door. After that, Dave didn't remember much. He doused his panic and anger and sadness in a couple shots of the bourbon he had way back in a kitchen cabinet. His last memory of the night was the TV making a single blue glow in the living room and the recliner spinning around.

28

SARAH MORGAN:
THE AUGUST REVIVAL

Wednesday, August 6

Sarah gulped at the cool night air. It was like drinking water. She
found the moon in its low three-in-the-morning spot. She was
already a mile from the house, having zigzagged her favorite route
through town. She'd stopped to watch the young man read in his window. She'd done a little detective work and knew that he worked the
late shift at a grocery warehouse the other side of Helmsly. His name
was Jimmy Durham. She'd laughed inwardly when she heard that; the
name came right out of a cheap novel. Knowing that name had helped
to cool her curiosity and her fantasies. She'd never talked to him or
even heard his voice, but she knew at some point, no matter how handsome he was bare to the waist early in the morning, he was bound to
be a disappointment in one way or another.

Nearly at the edge of town, she made her second stop. Mrs. Weisel
was also reading tonight, in her small bed beside a low window. Sarah
had been surprised, walking the streets, at how many people weren't
sleeping these days. Mrs. Weisel read magazines and drank hot chocolate.

Sarah loved to watch her face. There was a soft motherliness in it that made Sarah want to know the elderly woman. Mrs. Weisel had never shown up at the Baptist church; someone had said she attended the Lutheran church in Helmsly.

It was four-thirty when Sarah quieted her steps slightly and strolled up her own front walk. Jacob was sitting on the porch glider. Peter slept in his arms.

"Hi," she said.

"Hi. Took a long walk tonight."

"Weather's beautiful. It's so quiet this time of the morning."

Her husband was looking at her, and she couldn't read his expression, but she knew something wasn't right.

"Peter been fussy?"

"He woke up. I fed him some formula. That's OK, isn't it?"

"Sure." She sat on the glider next to Jacob. "I give him formula for at least one feeding now. Is he all right?"

"Yes. You do this walking every night now?"

"Not every night. More like every other."

"I don't think it's safe."

She sniffed. "Even the criminals go to bed by ten around here."

"Don't be so sure." Jacob inhaled the way he always did when he was ready to say something important. Sarah looked at him and waited. "Sarah, what's going on here?"

"What do you mean?"

"This wandering around town in the middle of the night. What are you doing?"

"Walking. What do you think?"

"I don't know what to think. You've never done this before."

"When or where could I have done this back in the city?"

"But why do you feel so compelled to wander the country in the middle of the night?"

"I don't know why," Sarah said after a moment. "It's hard to describe. I feel as if I'm searching for something. I don't know what it is. But it relieves the feeling to walk."

"Are you searching for something else or for someone else?"

"Oh, Jacob, please."

"I need you to answer me."

"I just said I don't know what I'm looking for. When I find out, I'll let you know."

"Will you?"

"Yes. I'm going to lie down for another hour or so."

"Go ahead. I'm wide awake now."

"You want me to put Peter back to bed?"

Jacob carefully handed the baby to her, and she slipped inside the house. She walked into the nursery and then stood there looking at the crib. She turned and went to her and Jacob's bedroom instead. Still holding the baby, she managed to get her walking shoes off. Then she lay on the bed with her clothes on, the baby pressed against her. When Peter had been an infant, sometimes she and Jacob had put him in bed with them. When the colic had been at its worst, Sarah had slept with him a lot in Miranda's bed, sending Miranda to sleep with Jacob. Being close to Sarah had been the only thing that seemed to calm Peter in those days. Now that he was settling into an easier routine, Sarah found herself needing his little presence next to her at odd times. She didn't know if it made her feel safer or if she felt that the baby was safer. Now he snuggled into her and gave a sigh that sounded grown-up and full of meaning. She stroked the barely existent eyebrows with one finger and fell asleep.

She and Jacob hardly spoke at breakfast three hours later. Then she found him rummaging through the hall closet later, seeming agitated.

"Where's my box of books from seminary?"

"They're all at your office."

"No. There was one box I never unpacked. Books I don't use as much, and my shelf space at the office was already full. I'm sure I marked it *seminary*."

"Well, it's not in that closet, because I've straightened it lately and I didn't see it." She walked away from him. "Look in that little space under the stairs."

"Tomorrow's day camp, I hope you remember," he said, appearing in the nursery doorway ten minutes later. Sarah stopped in the midst of putting Peter's undershirt on him. She saw Jacob get irritated at what she knew was a surprised look on her face.

"We've had it on the calendar since March," he said.

"Oh." Once again, Sarah felt her daily failures piling up on her. "I forgot. I'd planned to take Miranda to a matinee tomorrow. They're showing two Disney things."

"We can rent them. She'll enjoy day camp. Kids from all over the county will be there. She'll be in her element."

Sarah set her jaw and didn't respond to any of his statements. After a moment she asked, "It's all day?"

"Yes."

"And she'll just be with staff—I mean, you're not going to be there."

"The pastors have a meeting on the campgrounds; I'll be tied up most of the day. She'll be fine. They've got plenty of staff there to watch the kids and lead the activities."

"I don't know."

"What do you mean, you don't know?"

"I've been planning this day out for a while. It was going to be a special day with Miranda and me."

"Why don't you just go to day camp? It might be good for you to be there, get acquainted with women from other churches in the county."

"You're not getting my point. I just—I'm sorry, Jacob, but I'm not crazy about these little camps. I get these visions of some good-ol'-boy evangelist screaming at the children in King James. If these camp teachers knew anything about child development, I'd feel a lot more comfortable leaving Miranda with them for hours on end."

"I don't believe this. You are such a city snob. I can't believe I'm hearing this coming out of you." Jacob had taken a few steps into the nursery. His face was white.

Sarah put up her hands. "OK. That's it. Miranda's not going to camp. And I'm not going to town. She and I are going to visit Dad up in Michigan for a week or two, starting now!" She felt rage stinging behind her eyes and rushed down the hallway to their bedroom, hearing him pound after her.

"Sarah!"

"Leave me alone!" Sarah heard her own scream ring through the old house, bouncing off its high ceilings and narrow hallways. She took a suitcase out of the closet and started throwing clothes into it. She watched herself doing this and wanted to laugh. This really was like some bad movie script.

She sensed him standing behind her.

"Sarah." His voice was softer now. She'd expected the rage to grow, but it seemed to have turned into something else. "Sarah, please. We've got to work through this a better way."

"I just don't want Miranda at day camp. Not this time. I need for her to be with me tomorrow. I *need* this, Jacob. Please, if you don't understand, just accept it for now." She sat on the bed, suddenly weary and ready to cry.

"You're scaring me, Sare," Jacob said. He moved toward her cautiously. "This wandering around at night."

"I'm not having an affair."

"I've never thought that. But you're not acting like yourself." His hand was raised toward her in a helpless gesture. She didn't reach for it, and he left the room. She finished dressing Peter, then followed Jacob to the kitchen. He was at the cabinet, pouring himself a cup of coffee. He looked ten years older than his age.

"Don't leave now," he said hoarsely.

"I won't. You couldn't drive me to Michigan and be back in time for the meetings. I've—," She waved at the kitchen—"I've got all this food stuff to coordinate for the revival. But I do want to see Dad as soon as we can."

Jacob nodded. "I'm sorry we haven't been able to visit him much since living here."

He poured another cup of coffee and handed it to her. They sat down at the table.

"Uh, we're supposed to do this stuff for Dr. Nieman," Jacob said, daring to look her in the face again.

"I know. When do you want to do it?"

He shrugged. "Maybe this evening? I haven't had much time to think through family history."

"I don't know if the doctor is on the right track here. I've got no deep, dark family secrets."

"Let's give it a try anyway."

"I really don't want Miranda to go to camp tomorrow."

"Go have your day with her. If it's that important to you, I'd rather you do it."

"Thank you."

Sarah's sadness and panic deepened through the afternoon. She wept for missing her father. She watched Miranda play and wanted to run away with the child. When she and Jacob sat down in the living room after dinner and the kids were in bed, she wanted to run. She looked at him and knew she still loved him, but he felt dangerous to her now. Their life felt dangerous, and she didn't have a clue why.

On Friday, the day of the first revival meeting of August, Sarah was with Jacob in the church, figuring out the best location for everything. They'd settled where the refreshment tables would go and made sure there was a fresh pitcher of ice water and a clean glass at the pulpit.

Alice Gardino came in that afternoon. She would be the pianist for all the services since the main pianist, Mrs. Becket, was at a family reunion. Jacob and Sarah walked over to her now, where she was sorting out sheet music at the piano.

"I really appreciate your playing this week, Alice," said Jacob, his warm, pastoral self. "It's a lot to take on, I know."

The woman looked at them both, and a grim but glorious set came to her mouth. "I've been practicing since April, Brother Jacob. It won't be anything fancy, but I can play the week."

Jacob patted the woman's shoulder, and Sarah was reminded suddenly of an old movie about an understudy who became a star because someone had fallen ill at the last minute. The thought of Mrs. Gardino taking bows at the end of offertory made a tiny laugh rise in her throat.

That evening, Sarah had to admit to herself that the revival plan had worked pretty well. With three sets of meetings at three different churches, and with new speakers and musicians each week, it almost seemed like a new revival every time. And the services were actually well attended. Sarah had noticed a few faces reappearing at each church, people who'd caught the ecumenical spirit the pastors had tried so hard to generate. She was glad someone, at least, possessed enthusiasm.

The weather was as uncooperative as ever. Jacob had turned the air conditioning up early in the day so that he could shut it off just before the service, to cut out noise and not freeze the older folks. Sarah watched the elderly parishioners come in, panting and red faced, their hankies already damp. A pang of sympathy went through her, seeing their faithfulness, and she found herself going up to them one by one and helping them get settled in their seats. She even offered to get a cool glass of water for a couple of them. Most of them looked too relieved just coming out of the heat to care about anything other than sitting still to cool off. Thus they sat, in states of contemplation, while the musicians tuned up and unsnarled microphone cords and other folks of Bender Springs came in and found their places.

Joe Travis, looking hot but pleasant, was greeting guests on the other side of the sanctuary. Thank goodness, so far he'd been an easy guest to have in their home. He stayed quietly in the spare room, studying. He made visits with Jacob, and he'd even taken time out to be entertained by Miranda. Sarah watched him and thought that in about ten years Joe would really be something. Jacob had been sort of awkward, like Joe, when she had first met him. Awkward but fervent about ministry, as Joe was. Sarah thought that marriage could have been easier if she'd married Jacob later in life, could have skipped so much of their strife that had been due mainly to immaturity—hers and his. But maybe marriage was part of what had grown them up. Still, she looked at a man like Madison Carruthers and wished that husbands just came that way, fully developed and wise and at ease with themselves.

It occurred to Sarah that maybe she should stand at the front door beside Jacob and greet people from there. "Miranda, do you want to stand with Daddy and welcome people into church?"

"Yes! Can I?"

"Let's both go." They held hands and walked past pews and to the open double doors. So much for keeping in the air-conditioning.

Just then Sarah saw a strange procession half a block away. She nudged Jacob. About twenty people seemed to be marching toward the church, black Bibles under their arms, heads held up with holy purpose. Their leader was Rev. Miracle of the Pentecostal church. They came down the walk and then up the steps to where Jacob and his family stood.

Jacob put out a hand. "Hello, Rev. Miracle. So nice to see you."

"Good evening." She nodded to him just as cordially. "We've decided to cancel our own evening meetings this week to come and support the revival. It's a tremendous thing you're doing, Brother Morgan."

Sarah stared with great interest at the preacher and her crew. They were mainly women, many with the beehive hairdos that seemed in these parts a direct, natural result of being baptized with the Holy Spirit. Some of them wore long sleeves. None wore makeup. Instead of feeling distanced from these strange Christians, Sarah was suddenly awed by them. These were not movie characters. They were everything they appeared to be—sober about life and serious about faith. She didn't know exactly how they had achieved this, but for a moment she envied them. She doubted she could carry on a long discussion with any of them, but being near them made her skin tingle a little.

Jacob gestured toward the sanctuary, and the line of Pentecostals filed in, smiles on their faces, and walked up to the fifth row on the north side. Within moments they had filled three pews and nodded to one another as they conversed quietly and waited for the service to start.

"Why, hello, Mamie!" Sarah said to Mrs. Rupert, who, cane in hand, was navigating the several steps to them. Jacob turned in pleased surprise.

"Evening, Mrs. Morgan, Rev. Morgan." Mamie and her friend, Alma Petersen of Chris Dancey's church, both looked slightly frayed, as though they had barely gotten into their good dresses before being whisked out the door and through the streets to stand here in front of the church.

"Looks like a nice crowd," said Mamie. Her yellow print dress brought out the shine in her white hair. Sarah thought of Mamie's house, all painted now. Mamie had started coming to church only lately, but she had a straightforward way about her that Sarah liked.

"I'm sorry about Ruthie's bad news," said Jacob. "Be assured we'll mention her in our prayers this evening."

"Thank you. I know she'll appreciate it, Reverend," said Mamie.

In spite of all the ill feelings Sarah had struggled with over these revivals and the people of First Baptist, she felt some excitement now as the sanctuary filled and people waited for the evening to begin. Sarah thought suddenly that God just might do something here tonight. It had been a long time since she'd suspected something like that. She thought maybe now that she felt certain they would be leaving she could afford to relax and enjoy the moment. As Miranda scooted in beside her and Jacob took his seat behind the pulpit, next to the guest speaker, Sarah took a deep breath and allowed herself to smile and be expectant.

Mrs. Gardino started the evening with a complicated arrangement of "His Eye Is on the Sparrow." It sounded so good that Sarah turned to watch her. The small woman's face was glowing. *Why have I never noticed her before?* The church grew quiet, visitors and members alike shuffling to a stop, rearranging hymnals and Bibles and offspring so that they could view the small pianist, her permed hair bouncing as she emphasized octave jumps. Then the piece slowed and grew soft, whispering in poignant chords to an end. A moment's silence hung until she lifted her hands and the piano stopped its ringing. "Amen!" sounded across the room. Sarah was surprised to feel a lump in her throat.

For people being so tired and worn out, they sang with spirit, substantially aided by the Pentecostals, who soon had the whole room clapping. Jacob was clapping as much as anyone. Sarah tried to hold the image of her husband looking happy and in the midst of work he loved.

The musicians played through six or seven choruses, Alice Gardino taking a break on two of them and letting the guitarist do most of the work. The room was buzzing by the time Jacob rose to introduce the week's speaker, Gerald Raymond from Philadelphia. Raymond's polished, east-coast appearance had the congregants somewhat in awe. The people watched him carefully through the remainder of opening songs, prayers, and announcements.

But once Gerald began to preach, Sarah perceived a tangible relaxing in the pews. She'd never met Gerald, but Jacob had known him since they'd been in college together. Sarah sat up a little to hear him as best she could. Miranda watched, like a little adult, beside her.

"Once a woman and her young son were thrust out into the desert of Arabia," Gerald began. "It was a jealousy thing, an intense family conflict, that put her there. She was the powerless person in that situation, and she had to leave. She had her son with her, her only son, only child. And when they had been out in the wilderness a while, I'm sure they knew what it was like to know thirst and heat and desolation."

Sarah smiled and settled back. A storyteller. Her favorite type of preacher. Gerald already held his audience. He talked softly enough that they had to strain, just a little, to hear him. In the stillness of the full room, he painted a story, word by word.

Ten minutes into the story, a burst of music—electric guitar and strident voices—shattered the atmosphere. Everyone jumped, jarred out of concentration by the heavy-metal sounds from the street in front of the church. Ed Heddingsworth, a teacher at the high school, headed for the door. Madison tensed a bit in his chair, as did Jacob, and they looked at one another but stayed put. After a few moments the volume on the music went down, and Ed reappeared and took his seat.

"And, while we're on this point, let's stop to spend a moment before the throne, shall we?" Gerald was saying, not having skipped a beat. Sarah smiled. She liked a minister for whom prayer was a natural pause in any sermon or conversation. Gerald, hardly changing his voice, began praying that each person would understand what they needed to understand tonight, in order to make the next good step in their lives. Sarah noticed that Iris Miracle was nodding in approval.

Heads bowed around the sanctuary. The Pentecostals' hands were up, and Gerald spoke a gripping prayer, sounding as though he were speaking to a dear, dear friend. The Pentecostal rows punctuated his sentences with "hallelujah" and "praise the Lord." Meanwhile, the music outside was slowly coming up in volume again. Sarah saw Jacob's eyes open and Ed Heddingsworth shift nervously.

Then Iris Miracle stood straight up. At first Sarah wondered (with apprehension) if she was about to speak in tongues. But Iris did not say a word. She stepped in front of the other people in her pew and strode down the aisle to the front door. When she opened it, more music blared in, and the lyrics were enunciated too well to be ignored. Gerald, for the first time, raised his own volume and threw in a prayer for the kids outside.

Sarah could barely hear Iris's voice outside, able to make out her tone but not her words. The music came up a bit more, then went down considerably. In her peripheral vision, Sarah saw Jacob shift. He was grinning and whispering something to Madison, something about Iris taking command of the situation, Sarah guessed.

Gerald finished his midsermon prayer and started in where he'd left the story hanging. A woman near the front was dabbing her eyes.

The music came up again.

Ed came out of his seat and disappeared out the door. A moment later, they heard a cry of alarm. Sarah clutched Miranda and watched her husband hurry off the platform and down the side aisle.

Gerald stopped for a moment. There was scuffling at the back of the church, and Sarah heard Jacob tell someone to call the police. At the same time, she heard a woman's gasp just outside the front door. "Oh, my Lord! Oh, my Lord!"

It took only a few moments for Sarah and Miranda, along with many others, to make it out the door to view the street below. It took longer for Sarah to make sense of what she saw.

Jacob and Ed and a couple of other men were struggling with several teenagers. The kids were in a strange knot beside a gaudy van, from which the music spilled out. The kids were resisting and filling the air with their profanity.

Sarah saw a flash of motion and recognized two boys she had seen at church. Howard Sheffley, a newcomer to First Baptist, was pulling at a girl in the knot who seemed to be hitting someone on the ground. Sarah looked hard. Was it Rev. Miracle? The girl pulled away from Howard, but he grabbed her arm and tried again to pull her away. Another boy grabbed him from behind. It was Alice Gardino's son. He landed on Howard, and they both fell to the ground, and the Gardino boy started beating Howard.

"Tony! Stop!" Jacob rushed to the two of them and pulled Tony off, and Sarah let out a pent-up breath, relieved. The rest of the small mob seemed to be under control. Gideon the cop had just pulled up. In a moment the music stopped.

"What is *wrong* with you? There's no excuse for this kind of behavior!" It was Jacob's voice, an octave higher than Sarah had ever heard it. He was in Tony's face, face red and fists clenched.

"Mommy, what's wrong with Daddy?" Sarah was suddenly aware of Miranda, who was clutching at Sarah's skirt, real fear on her face.

"These boys were causing some trouble—"

"Who do you lowlifes think you are, huh? These are decent people here." Jacob's voice was still out of control. He pointed toward the church, and Sarah could see his hand shaking.

"Oh, no Jacob, no," she murmured to herself.

Tony held up a hand and started to say something.

"You just shut up! Shut up! In fact, get out of my sight!" In the early evening air, with the music shut off, Jacob's rage echoed down the street. Sarah could feel the crowd of church people behind her. She watched Tony Gardino back away and then take off through the yard across the street. Jacob loosened his tie, face still red, and said to Gideon, "You lock every one of 'em up. We're pressing charges. We're tired of this."

A woman's voice rang out then, sounding hysterical. "It's Rev. Miracle!"

Sarah could see then, behind Jacob, Iris Miracle on the ground. Her dress was ripped and her face gashed, blood streaming from her mouth and scalp. She drew up her legs and huddled, saying over and over, in the shocked silence, "Help me, Jesus, help me, Jesus. O God, forgive them." The weakness in her voice sent a shudder through Sarah. She turned to a woman behind her.

"Please keep Miranda here." The woman nodded and reached to pull the child back into the crowd and away from the scene.

"Marie, we need an ambulance down here at First Baptist. Call St. Bartholomew's," Gideon was saying into his radio. "There's a woman here who's been beat up pretty bad."

Suddenly Iris was surrounded by people, mainly women who reached to smooth her hair and straighten her dress, sobbing softly and telling her to lie still, that an ambulance was coming. They found welts on her legs and arms, and a long scratch down the side of her throat. One eye was swelling rapidly. A flutter of summer hankies came down to dab at her blood. Someone brought out a pitcher of water and a clean tea towel from the church kitchen. Slowly the men backed away.

The waiting silence of the crowd in the summer evening was a heavy presence of its own. Locusts suddenly began droning their high pitch into the brassy light that slanted toward them from the western end of town. Then, as if by signal, timid discussions began here and there.

Gideon had used up all his handcuffs and relied on some of the church men to keep the rest of the kids from running off. There were four boys and two girls. Alma Petersen was down there, too, looking distressed and trying to talk to one of the girls. Sarah heard from somewhere in all the voices that the girl was Alma's granddaughter. Two of the boys were older, and they stood and laughed while Gideon lectured them.

"What you kids did here was plumb evil. There's no excuse for this."

The other two kids were younger, probably still in high school. Alma's granddaughter wouldn't meet anyone's eyes, a cool, almost bored expression on her face. The other girl was crying, saying they didn't mean for this to happen.

Periodically a man or woman would step out to look down the street for the ambulance. Sarah had lost track of Jacob. Maybe he'd gone back into the church. She wanted to go to him but felt helpless to find him—and especially helpless to know what to say.

The crowd stood for twenty minutes, growing more subdued as the sky in the west turned a violent red. The ambulance came then, and the paramedics attended to Iris, who had fallen strangely silent. They shooed away the people and rolled her into the ambulance, making adjustments and finally closing the doors. As they drove away, the siren wavered on the air.

Madison's calm voice reached them then. "Folks, let's go back inside where it's cool." Sarah looked up to see him and Gerald Raymond in the middle of the crowd on the church steps.

"I think we should continue the service, don't you?" Gerald said. He lifted an arm to shepherd people back inside.

Sarah could see Chris Dancey and Joe Travis in the faces around her. Jacob wasn't anywhere. She felt her legs trembling beneath her, and she murmured a thank-you when Mamie Rupert gripped her arm to help her up the steps.

29

TONY GARDINO: AFTERMATH

Friday, August 8

As he faded back into the hedge by the alley, Tony saw the ambulance pass behind the houses of the next block. A few cars followed the winking red lights. Tony recognized the car of Jacob Morgan, and his heart started crashing again. The man's red face was like a nightmare in front of him. And the way his whole body had shook. And the things he'd said. So much for God being loving and understanding. Tony had never felt so hated by another human being. He felt Pastor Morgan's hatred for him was even greater than his own hatred for Howard.

Howard, who had gotten in the middle of Craig's business like a fool, trying to be a hero or a martyr or something. If Howard would just stop showing up in Tony's life, things would be better. But Howard's jumping on Lena had been an open door, and Tony had walked through it with pleasure. He finally had the excuse to beat the crap out of Howard, who had deserved a beating all his life and had never gotten it. It had felt good to land on Howard, to feel his fist meet

Howard's pasty, stupid face. Then Morgan had to show up and start screaming.

Eventually the street got silent and empty of cars, and Tony was aware again of soft leaf sounds at his back. His breathing had settled down, his legs were in a cramp, and the sweat had dried from under his arms and around the waistband of his jeans. He came out of the hedge slowly. In his head a little square of film was presenting itself. Inside it appeared layers of chin with ribbons of blood chasing down them, the raw red shining between her teeth. Tony heard sounds, too, whimpering, shocked noises, the short bleats each time Craig and Lena had struck her.

It had actually been Ted's idea to start the music up right outside the church. When Craig opened the van doors and cranked up the music, Tony had felt exposed and a little worried, but the three or four beers had dulled his restraint. Lena was having a good time, egging Ted on to turn up the volume. They knew that before long Gideon would come around and shake his nightstick, lecture them; they would play with him awhile and then move on.

If the lady preacher had left well enough alone, Gideon would have gotten his call and everything would have taken its course. It was her own fault. If she had just shut up and stopped preaching at them. *Craig looked like he couldn't wait to hurt her, like he'd been waiting for a chance like this.* Anybody would go off for someone telling him he had a devil. She had no right to pray and scream at them. She was probably a mental case. *They kicked her where she lay on the ground. Ted kicked her in the stomach. Craig was pulling out chunks of long gray hair. There was blood on the ends where the roots came out.* The woman was so crazy she expected Jesus to come to her rescue. She was saying, "Lord, forgive them. Lord, have mercy!" What right did she have to come straighten them out? It was Gideon's job. *They pulled up her dress. They laughed at her fat legs. They poured beer all over her and wouldn't stop when she begged them.*

Tony knelt in the grass and hunched over in dry heaves for the third time.

He walked home through the alley. All the lights in his family's living room were on, as if the brightness would keep evil from coming in. Tony walked in the front door.

Dad glared at him. He sat with Mom on the sofa. Her face was puffy and red from tears. Annie sat sullenly a few feet away, looking more alert than she had been in a long time. Granddad stood in the doorway to the kitchen. He had a bottle of aspirin in his hand, and he was glaring, too, at Tony.

"Where have you been?" Tony thought Granddad said it but realized that he was looking straight at the old man and his lips had not moved. He turned to Dad.

"Where have you been?" Dad was startlingly present, his face animated, resembling old vacation pictures taken when someone surprised him from behind.

Tony couldn't figure the best way to answer, so he said nothing.

"You'd better answer me."

Tony raised his arms, a gesture between helplessness and exasperation. "Well, I was at the church for a while. Then I was walking around."

"Why were you beating up on that boy?" Mom asked, her voice hoarse.

"He was beating up on my friends."

"And your friends were beating up on a woman," said Dad in a tight voice.

"I wasn't in on that. I didn't know that was going to happen."

Dad came up close to him, and Tony felt the man's eyes lock onto his own. The air felt of static, distant sounds fading in and out. "I guess you didn't try to stop it, did you?"

Granddad was a few feet from them, the aspirin bottle lifted as though he were ready to offer some to them. The old gray eyes were fastened on Tony, and when his own look met them, it made Tony feel like asking for help of some kind. But they just stood, the three of them, in an odd triangle, tongues and minds on hold. Tony heard his mother begin to cry again. In the muddle of it all, he heard Annie say, "Tony's not *mean*. He wouldn't beat up a woman."

"That's not the point. He was part of it, and he's not supposed to be hanging around with drugheads."

Granddad put his hand on Dad's arm, and that seemed to release Tony to back away. Mom was still sniffling. Tony backed away into the kitchen. "I need a drink of water."

At the kitchen sink, he could feel coolness from the backyard pressing at the screen of the window. The air smelled of rain, the atmospheric belch from another county probably. The tapwater was lukewarm. Tony held a finger under it and waited for it to get colder. The hum of it through the faucet gave him the same sense, suddenly, of a larger power somewhere, the source of all waters that came churning and moaning through pipes and into houses, all over the country. All over the continent, being pumped up from some dark underworld, coaxed around mountains and redirected into the veins of cities, of small waterless towns. He could turn it on and off, just like that, and stop the force. He turned the knob, and the fountain squeaked and gulped back its flow.

He could hear Annie and Mom talking in the living room about satanists. "The only way you can fight them is through Jesus' name," he heard Annie say, and he wondered where she'd heard that. Tony couldn't recall it having had much effect. The woman preacher had chanted *Jesus* over and over as she was losing consciousness. At the end her voice had sounded small and disappointed.

Tony stood at the sink, pressing himself into the counter and away from his family's sounds. He really wanted to get out, to walk around town now that the air and the event had cooled down. But Granddad was peering at him from around the doorway, and he knew that he would not leave the house again tonight. He realized then that Dad was standing right behind him.

"I don't know what to do with you anymore, Tony." He didn't sound angry for once, just intense.

"You could start by believing me."

"What do you want me to believe?"

"That I'm not on drugs. All I ever had was some pot."

Dad nodded, slowly. "All right. But that doesn't explain the way you've been acting."

"How have I been acting?"

"Spacey. Out to lunch."

"I'm just tired. I've got insomnia."

"Maybe you should go to the doctor."

Granddad, still in the doorway, cleared his throat. "Sounds like a good idea to me."

Dad glanced at his father, then back to his son. "I don't want you with those kids again. Not after what they did tonight."

"I don't want to be with them."

Dad made a slow turn. "All right." He went back into the living room, followed by Granddad. Tony watched them, but he was seeing another scene entirely.

I don't want to be with them. Not even with Lena. He tried to stop the tape that was replaying in his head, the tape of Lena saying "You psycho paranoid!" That made his chest hurt.

Before the music had been cranked up, and before the lady preacher and the beating, Lena had stood there in the heat, with a drink in her hand. Craig had leaned close to her. He'd grabbed her. She just looked at him, with that smile she had, the smile that never let you know where you stood.

Craig didn't let go. He just moved closer and tipped his beer so that it dribbled down her shirt. That's when Tony said, "What's your problem?"

Craig had laughed at him. "I don't have a problem. What's yours?"

"Get your hands off. Have some respect."

Craig had answered by throwing some beer on Tony. Lena laughed at that, and Tony looked at her in surprise.

"What's with you? You want him to paw you like that?" Tony asked.

"I do what I want. Back off." Her tone of voice was different from what it had been the other times with him. She looked at him in a way that made him feel foolish.

"All I'm saying is that he should show you more respect than that."

"Don't be jealous, Tony."

"I'm not."

Then she had turned away from him slightly and walked toward the front of the van. Tony barely heard what she said, but he was sure he heard right. "Psycho paranoid. Hey, Ted, crank it up. Those people are getting too quiet in there."

Maybe because she had shown so little regard for Tony, it had been even more important for him to let Howard have it when he grabbed her and tried to pull her away from the preacher. It was all Tony had left, something to prove to her that she was important to him, that he had strength of his own, that he would fight to protect her. It hadn't worked. He'd messed Howard's face up pretty good, but then Pastor Morgan had jumped in and added his own insults to Tony's evening.

Dad and Mom didn't try to talk to Tony for the rest of the evening. Everybody seemed to know that it was better not to talk anymore, just to be quiet. Everybody except Annie. She knocked on Tony's door. He opened it, remembering how she'd stood up for him in front of Dad.

"I hope you stay away from Craig and those guys. They're not like you. I think they're evil." Annie's face reached out to take hold of him. "I know you like Lena, but she seems like bad news too."

"Don't talk to me about her. Just don't talk to me."

"OK. Are you all right?"

"Yeah."

"You really got Howard. What was that all about?"

"I hate him. Don't ask why. Just believe me, he deserved it."

Annie shrugged and looked more like her normal self, sort of awkward and sassy at the same time. Tony watched her walk to her room. In a moment the door closed, and he could hear her on the phone. Because Annie didn't get into trouble at school or do drugs, she had a telephone. She went to it like a best friend ten times a day. Tony wondered for the first time if she felt as desperate as he did—desperate to make it through living here, or desperate to get away from here.

He lit some candles, but the evening's events intruded on his mind every few seconds. He saw the crowd up on the church steps. He saw Gideon put handcuffs on Lena. He saw Howard's bloody face. He saw the pathetic, dumpy woman on the ground, talking about Jesus.

He didn't sleep. He watched the flames. He took the last of the pain pills. They made the room soft and slippery, and they made him not care so much that he'd lost Lena and that everybody hated him.

30

SARAH MORGAN:
THE VISIT

Friday, August 8

Jacob came home late, having sat with Iris Miracle until she'd been treated and put into a room for the night. He'd called Sarah from the hospital. She had talked with him cautiously, trying to sound supportive, trying not to demand much from him.

Jacob would never know this, but Sarah had spent some time with Alice Gardino, settling her down after the ambulance had left and she had been told about the pastor's scene with her son. The woman had crumpled like a paper cup. Sarah had promised that Jacob would come by to patch things up as soon as he was able.

Sarah listened from their bed as Jacob entered the bathroom and brushed his teeth. He crawled into bed and didn't say a word, although she knew he knew she was awake.

"How is she?"

"Pretty beaten up. They'll keep her at least a day."

He lay on his back; she could trace his noble profile against the pale streetlight shining in their window.

"What scares me, Sarah, is that I don't expect anything from God anymore. I don't expect a thing."

Sarah turned toward her husband and stared until her eyes adjusted to the dark and she could see his face clearly. Everything but his basic bone structure had changed over the past few years. There were bags under his eyes, and the skin on his face was not so taut, bulging slightly with added weight. Above his ears, his hair shone as though someone had taken a single swipe with a paintbrush full of silver. The whole of him was looser, heavier, darker, and bearing creases that had sculpted a different, more burdened person out of the original.

Sarah thought about the Old Testament couple, Sarah and Abraham. They had set out to parts unknown, had left everything to follow God. The Bible made it sound like a glorious thing, this partnership of pilgrimage and faith. But present-day Sarah intuited that the journey had surprised the ancient couple too. She felt sure that the other, faithful Sarah had lain in bed with Abraham and looked at what the journey had done to his face, his eyes, his hope—and wondered what both of them would look like when it was all through.

"Oh," Jacob said, interrupting her thoughts, "I thought of something today. It may be nothing, but as long as we're seeing this therapist, maybe it'll help."

"What's that?"

"I'm thinking you told me that your mother died when you were five."

"Yes."

"And Miranda just turned five."

Sarah waited for him to say more, but he didn't. She listened for him in the darkness. "And?"

"Well, sometimes people relive an early trauma when their own child reaches the age they were when it happened."

Sarah heard the room ringing, like in a black-and-white movie when the heroine is exploring the old house and the soundtrack has gone silent.

"Like I said, it may not relate at all. But I remembered something from the pastoral counseling class I took, back in that other life I had when I showed great promise as a minister and all that bull."

Sarah tried to put together what he was saying. She was having difficulty processing it for some reason.

"I guess what made me think of it was the way you reacted when I wanted Miranda to go to day camp. I mean, when you were six months pregnant you were tutoring kids in one of the scariest housing projects in Chicago. You were always fearless. And now you're freaking—excuse me—now you're concerned because Miranda's going to be out of your sight for a few hours."

Jacob turned his back to her then, which usually signaled that their discussion had ended. "I'm exhausted."

"I hope you can sleep," she said. It was odd for him to open a subject and drop it like that, but it seemed that he was talking without really being present. And he hardly ever said, "I'm exhausted." She decided to leave him alone.

"I can't believe I lit into Tony like that."

"You can patch it up."

"He'd barely talk to me before. I guess it's really time we moved. It's time I found another job."

"Oh, Jacob, it's just the summer. It's this awful, unending summer. Let's try to sleep. Good night."

"Good night."

Sarah listened to his breathing, which grew deep in just a few moments. After that, she stared into the odd night shadows of their room. She couldn't move. Something Jacob had said. She felt as though she were waiting for a conversation to finish or for an answer to come. After a time, just before she fell asleep, she saw her mother's face, young and clear, against the window. Sarah stared into the almost forgotten eyes and felt a hot tear slide down one cheek. A lost little girl, wandering all over town. Needing Momma.

The next evening, Sarah heard Jacob come in the back door quietly, as he always did when meetings at the church ran late. She had attended tonight's service, mainly to be there with him, supporting him from the pew, while he apologized to the congregation for his display of anger the night before. He did a good job, and people were quite understanding. The beating had unnerved all of them. Sarah had gathered the children before the service ended and come home because she had promised Miranda that she could go next door and watch *101 Dalmatians* with the Andersen kids. Peter was down for the night. Already darkness was coming earlier; it was barely nine o'clock, and the sky was running out of light.

When she heard Jacob creep in the back door, it occurred to her that she'd never figured out if he did this because he thought she and the baby were asleep or because, at some level, he was ashamed to be away from home at night. He knew she thought there was something intrinsically wrong with what his schedule did to their life. Maybe that was the real reason his late entrances were so timid. She met him in the kitchen.

He stood at the counter, near the two rows of ripening, sunburned tomatoes that the Greshams had dropped off on their way out of town. Week before this, the Thomases, also en route to vacation, had unloaded four monster zucchini, the only vegetable in the county that seemed to have evolved into a drought crop. Sarah had done what she could, frying up pale slices of the stuff, even using Betty Bloom's squash casserole recipe. Still, she was left with two and a half zucchini. She'd grated the half and frozen it, having heard it made a great quick bread. But no one would ever know that the last two had gone in the garbage. Sarah knew by now that this was one of several unpardonable sins in Midwest farm communities everywhere. She hadn't even told Jacob.

Now he surveyed the tomatoes and finally looked at Sarah directly. Neither of them smiled or spoke. He rubbed his eyes.

"I thought it went well," she said.

"Thank you for being there." She knew he meant it, but his voice had no emotion in it.

"What's the latest on Rev. Miracle?"

"They're releasing her tomorrow, and she's not happy about it. Wants to be out right now. Madison had some flowers sent." The information came out of him automatically, as though he had been asked the same question ten different times on his way home. Then he added, "She'd asked me last night to be sure and check on her brother today, but he wasn't there when I went by late this afternoon."

"I didn't know she had a brother."

"You wouldn't guess they're related. He's soused most of the time. Works at the brickyard when he's able. He was probably at Perky's today."

"Perky's Tap." Sarah tried the name out slowly, turning it over as she poured him a glass of iced tea. "Bet there are a lot of interesting stories in those walls."

"Whatever." Jacob looked into his glass, eyelids low.

"Are you going to look for him down there?" She tried to look past his anger for the moment, knowing it must have something to do with her, with them.

"No, but maybe I should stop by the house now."

"Maybe you should go to Perky's and have a drink with him." She smiled and tried to pry open his closed face with her eyes.

He laughed—more of a sniff, really—and shook his head, pulled out a chair, and sat at the kitchen table—all while sipping the tea. "Don't think so. People around here like their preachers and their drinkers in distinct categories."

For a moment Sarah missed the neighborhood sports bar she had watched a hundred Bulls games in, back home, where normal, decent people could go into a bar and get caught up with neighborhood gossip. Jacob had even gone with her during the playoffs. He hadn't been so uptight back in seminary.

She sat down across from him. "I know. I was kidding."

When he didn't speak for several moments, she poured herself a glass. "You want to talk about last night?"

He looked at her blankly.

"The meeting?" she said.

"What's to say?" He shrugged. "Except that it seemed to be the appropriate culmination of all my work here."

Sarah felt her husband's discouragement descending upon them, oppressive and inescapable as August fatigue. She'd heard it over a year ago when Jacob and the other pastors were desperately trying to find a way to inject new life into their congregations. She'd heard it when Peter wouldn't stop crying and when she herself had done so badly in the beginning. He'd never been an idealist, but even his educated cynicism hadn't been ready for this town. She was tempted not to speak but heard her voice respond, out of some duty to encourage. "Those kids acting up had nothing to do with your work, Jacob."

"But it all seemed so . . . representative. The supposedly climactic revival week of the summer degenerates into total chaos." He raised his arms helplessly. "There's nothing here, Sarah. You were right all along." His voice broke slightly, but he didn't lean toward her or meet her gaze or use any of the other connecting devices that had worked themselves into their relating over the years. "It won't feel bad to leave here after all."

Sarah chose to say nothing. Trying just seemed to make it worse. When Jacob rose to go back to his study, she felt her arm move toward him to graze his leg as he walked past her, but she didn't reach quite far enough, and he never sensed her intention.

As Sarah sat alone, trying not to think too much, she heard a soft rap on the door. Joe Travis was on the other side, smiling.

"Oh, come on in. You don't have to knock."

"Doesn't feel right, just walking in," he said. He looked incredibly young, so young to be in such a rough profession.

"I know I've said this already, but raid the refrigerator anytime. Scout around the cupboards, too, if you want to. It's all for common consumption."

"Thanks. That's really nice." Joe sat down at the table across from her. "I really appreciate your having me here. I know it's an inconvenience to have houseguests, and . . . ." He suddenly seemed to lose his train of thought, or he had decided that what he was about to say wasn't appropriate.

"You're a very easy guest to have around. I'm just sorry we're not better organized." Sarah tried to think of an excuse she could give to leave the table. She didn't have the energy to chat, and she didn't want last night's service to come up.

"Sarah, is there anything I can do . . . to . . . make this week easier for you?" Joe's blue eyes reached out to grab her. His sincerity made her want to cry. But her mind clicked in instead.

"Actually, there is one small thing. Could you hang around here awhile, in case Peter wakes up? And Judy will bring Miranda home about ten-thirty, but we should be back by then."

"Sure. That's no problem at all. Your kids are fun to be with." He smiled again. "I'm in love with your daughter."

"Get in line."

Jacob stood in the bathroom, combing his hair. Sarah appeared behind him in the mirror. "Going to see Iris's brother?"

He sighed. "May as well."

"Can I come along?"

"What?" She knew he'd heard but didn't quite believe what he'd heard.

"Joe said he'd watch the kids."

"Oh." He searched her face for some explanation, but she simply smiled and asked, "I don't look too frumpy, do I?"

"Oh no." He smiled a little at that. "I've never seen you frumpy. Uh, yeah, come along if you want. I have no idea what we'll find."

"An adventure. Cool."

Is it this way?" She pointed south as they stepped out of their yard. He nodded, and they walked silently under the oak that bent over the buckled front walk.

The house they stopped in front of was a dull, dirty yellow, and the boards of the front porch gave a little too much when they walked across them to the door. Jacob knocked, and the windows on either side rattled. After the third tap, a thick voice growled from somewhere deep in the house: "Come around to the back." So they worked their way through the weeds and reached the driveway, avoiding the stalks in the center of the drive by staying on one of the gravel ruts. The door was tucked into the far end of the side porch. As they approached it, the screen swung to, a bleary-looking man on the other side of it.

He stepped back wordlessly, allowing them into the dark room. It smelled of bacon and mildewed newspapers. Sarah found herself groping with her eyes; the only light on was a fluorescent bulb above the kitchen sink. She sensed a heaviness of spirit, old drapes pulled shut, outdated magazines stacked in corners, neglected plants, and lots of dust. When the man turned on a lamp, she found that her senses had been startlingly accurate, except for the plants; there were none.

"I know you—Baptist pastor." The man glanced at Sarah but directed his statement at her husband. He was heavyset, and the whites of his eyes were pink.

"Jacob Morgan. This is my wife, Sarah."

"Hello." Sarah put out her hand, and Ax took it carefully.

"Wanna sit down?"

"Thank you." Jacob followed Ax's nod and sat on the sofa. Sarah joined him. The seat was so soft that it seemed her knees came up to chest level. She tried not to stare at the room, but the clutter was intriguing. After a moment, she forced herself to look at the man who sat across from them.

"I just called the hospital," said Ax. "They said Iris'll be released tomorrow." He paused. "You need some kinda information from me?"

"No." Jacob gave the man what Sarah had dubbed his "pastoral, affirming, show-no-teeth" smile. "We just thought we'd look in on you."

In on you. Sarah tried not to notice the phrase, but her sarcastic self butted into her thoughts: At what point had these people begun to multiply their prepositions? The voice proceeded to rattle off phrases gleaned from conversations: In on you, go on down to, went on over to, it's over by, looked around in . . . .Conversation in this town was something like the Amplified Version of the Bible—multiple choice. And her husband was soaking it up like a cultural sponge.

The drunk was shrugging. "Nothin' to look at here. Gideon's filled out all the reports. Just have to wait, I guess."

"Wait for what?"

Ax sat there on the sofa, mute. He sniffed loudly and seemed to forget that he'd been asked a question.

"It must be rather hard for you to see that kind of violence done to a member of your family," Sarah said quietly.

"When kids are allowed to run loose, this type of thing happens. Shouldn't've happened to her, though." He met Sarah's gaze for the first time. "Iris is strong willed, and she talks too much, but . . . ." He seemed to shake his head a bit and then looked at the old blue-green carpet worn smooth at his feet. The dining-room window was open, and they could hear cars driving by on the street in front of the house.

After a moment, Jacob cleared his throat. "Would you like us to pray with you?"

Ax's eyebrows jerked upward. "Pray? For what?"

"For your sister's recovery, for one thing. For your daughter, who's been through a real trauma."

The drunk's eyes darkened. "She wouldn't have been through anything if she'd stayed home with me. That kid spends her whole life in church meetings. It's time some of the real world came to her."

"Where is she now?"

"Over at Lana Beth's. I don't reckon she'd want to be with her old drunk dad."

Jacob straightened his back. The sofa cushions were incredibly soft and deep, and Sarah could see him trying to work his way out of them so that he could lean toward Ax while he prayed.

"I'd like to offer a prayer for you and your family, Ax. Would that be all right?"

The man didn't move. He seemed to have trouble focusing his eyes. Jacob didn't wait further but clamped his eyes shut and began to speak. Sarah could feel Ax's restlessness and objection, and her jaws clenched, and her fingers grew cold. Her husband's prayer was short. He didn't say "amen" right away but asked quietly if Ax would like to add anything. Sarah carefully opened one eye to see the man's reaction.

Ax clamped rough hands on his knees. He shook his head a bit in what looked like resignation. "I can't pray." The voice was full and gruff with something like regret and old, old pain. "The words don't even come out no more."

"I don't believe they have to come out," said Jacob. "God hears unspoken things too."

"What if I don't want to say anything?" The drunk looked steadily at Sarah's husband, tired but unwilling to yield. The yellowish light near him lit up the top of Ax's head, single strands of greasy, gray hair combed back in bent spikes, the scalp shining through. His eyes lost their color in the dull beam. Sarah could see that the man before her was completely empty.

She expected her husband to finish then and make as graceful an exit as they could. But he stayed where he was. "Why don't we just sit here awhile," he said, "and let God figure it out. I don't have much to say either."

Ax pursed his lips as though humoring the young pastor-type in front of him. He rubbed his eyes and coughed. "All right."

The three of them sat in the thick air of the room. After the moment of initial awkwardness, Sarah appreciated the silence. She leaned back into the massive sofa and closed her eyes. It was so unlike Jacob not to fill silence with theology. She had feared her husband would try to explain all that had happened, to put it into some religious overview. Something had clearly snapped in him this time. Here they were practicing meditation with a man too far gone to appreciate it. Maybe Jacob figured that Ax Miracle really had heard it all.

After several minutes, Jacob closed with, "We're at your mercy, Lord—amen," and stood up. Ax and Sarah followed as he made his way around the jumble of mismatched furniture to the door they'd come in. "Would you like us to check on Leah?" he asked, turning to Ax.

The man shook his head with a jerk. "Naw. Lana'll do fine. Thanks, though."

They reentered the outdoors, the atmosphere unusually silent and laden with humidity. She wasn't sure, but it seemed to Sarah that everything with life moved more slowly than usual—one or two other people on the street, someone's Irish setter; even the shrubbery seemed to exist in a drugged, half-sleeping state.

They took the path with the most trees, hoping the sidewalks that had been shaded during the day would not give off so much heat.

"Thanks for going along," said Jacob, looking at the walk in front of them. "I'm not sure why you did it, but it was a nice thing to do."

"This town is sort of a huge, dysfunctional family, isn't it?" she asked.

Jacob didn't say anything for several steps. "That's one way of looking at it, I guess."

"That's how it seemed to me last night, when I stepped outside the church and saw all of that. At first it was so unreal, this woman getting beaten up. But then, I don't know; it looked familiar."

They were in the little park, next to two or three oak trees bowed together, under which a small fountain gurgled in near darkness. The air around their legs felt cool, like the coolness of black earth and very green grass.

"What was familiar about it?"

"I had an aunt and uncle who used to fight a lot. They were well-off, had a place on the north lakeshore. I'd visit my cousin, Cynthia, during the summers. And I liked the private beach and eating out in nice restaurants. But there was always this ugly undercurrent. One minute everything would be beautiful and refined, the next Uncle Lewis would be slamming doors and breaking things."

"Were you afraid? Did your folks know what went on?"

Sarah paused, remembering the night, the lapping of the lake against the shore just outside Cynthia's bedroom window, and the feeling that all control was gone from life. "It was scary sometimes. But I had the feeling it wasn't something we could ever talk about. Aunt Jerene finally divorced him when Cynthia and I were nearly out of high school. People found out a lot then."

Jacob was leaning against one of the tree trunks. "So, all this at the church reminds you of him?"

"The fight made me feel the same way I used to feel."

"I'm sorry." She heard him sigh. "This town has turned out to be one booby trap after another, hasn't it?"

"But feeling like I used to at Cynthia's made me think more about what church people really are. Just a big, dysfunctional family. You know what I'm saying?"

His face was still in darkness, but she could feel his concentration.

"They make their own decisions, Jacob. They want what they want, and they're devoted to God or not. It isn't up to you."

"I'm their pastor, Sare. A shepherd. Shepherds take care of their sheep."

"There are limits, though. I mean, if God can't get them to behave, what makes you think you can?"

They left the trees.

When they came to Elm and Washington, she pulled him in the direction opposite their house. "I want to show you something."

In the dim, muggy evening, Mamie Rupert's house came into view like a ship out of the fog. Since it was the corner house, the streetlight reached its front porch and eaves.

It looked glorious.

"Wow!" Jacob let go of her hand and crossed the shallow, dry ditch in one stride. Sarah came close to his side, enjoying the wonder on his face.

"It sort of evolved," she murmured. "They'd accidentally used two colors of paint on the trim, and somebody decided to doctor it up. I suggested the pink." She smiled.

"Did you do the artwork?" He pointed to the flourishes under the eaves.

"No, Randy Kluver did that."

"Really! It's beautiful."

"You're the fifth person today to stop by and admire my house!" Mamie's voice drifted out to them. They heard the creak of a swing and saw her emerge from the porch's recess. She came down the steps, fanning herself with a newspaper. Her white hair was in tiny, round pin curls, close to the scalp and all over her head.

"I wouldn't have planned it that way myself, but I never had much imagination." She shrugged her tiny, old-lady shoulders and stood with them to gaze upon her home. "How do you like my little vines down the posts?"

"Outstanding," Jacob said.

"Want some iced tea?"

"No, thank you, Mamie," said Sarah. "We're on our way home. I need to put Miranda to bed."

"Well, before you go—I've been meaning to ask you about something, Pastor." Mamie put her hand to her mouth, as if she were afraid she'd say too much at once.

"What's that, Mamie?"

"Do you think that if God was angry with me about something, he'd let me know what it is?"

"Uh, I don't know that God stays angry like a person would. The Holy Spirit will let you know if there's anything specific that is causing grief to God's heart."

"Does he ever let us know through dreams?"

"I suppose he could. I wouldn't count on that always being the case."

"Well, I've had these horrible dreams all summer, and I thought they'd go away when I prayed the prayer with your seminary boy. But they're bad as ever, and I don't know what to do."

Sarah waited for her husband's response.

"And Rev. Miracle prayed for my arthritis, and nothing happened."

"I can't speak for why God answers some prayers and not others—"

"I'm wondering if he's just put out with me. I know I'm not very religious, not the way Louise Filcher thinks I should be."

Sarah could tell that a smile was lurking underneath Jacob's calm. Louise Filcher was well-known to every pastor in town. "Mamie, it's been my experience that God lets us know when we're in the wrong—in a way we understand," Jacob was saying. "I don't know much about dreams, but sometimes they tell us more about the way *we* think than about what God thinks." He raised his hand then and placed it gently on Mamie's cheek. Sarah was jolted by the tenderness of it; it wasn't something she'd seen him do before.

"I think these dreams will pass, Mamie," Jacob said. Sarah heard the love in her husband's voice. She felt the blessing of his hand on Mamie Rupert's cheek. She saw, suddenly, Abraham blessing Isaac, and

Isaac Jacob, and Jacob Joseph. Loving hand to needy head, from person to person, wise to the innocent. Strong hands invoked blessing and chased away curses and fear and darkness. Hand to head, into infinity, and her husband's hand took its place in this eternal sequence.

Sarah felt the heat of the evening and breathed in the heavy fragrance of Mamie's honeysuckle vines. And she felt a contented breath leave the breast of that other Sarah, mother of all who learn to believe, as she settled into Abraham's bosom and rested from her journey.

31

MAMIE RUPERT: RECONCILIATIONS

Saturday, August 9

Rain was in the air this morning. Mamie smelled the damp of it as she peeked through the pink curtains of the high bathroom window. The sun wasn't anyplace in particular, its presence diffused through a high cloud layer. She watched her mimosa bend slightly with a breeze from the south. Air coming in the window felt cool. It had been weeks since anything had been cool around here.

Mamie's movements were ten years older this morning. The dreams of the night before had been so chaotic she woke up exhausted and with a headache. Everyone in her lifetime had shown up at one point or another. People had been running, screaming, playing ticktacktoe, and lying in state. They kept changing locations and giving Mamie new sets of information. Mamie herself had turned into her high-school math teacher, Charles's Aunt Beth, and Iris Miracle's niece. There were carnival noises in the background. She kept tasting tomatoes, rusty, like blood. After waking up for the fifth or sixth time, she had sat in the kitchen with a cup of cocoa and turned on the country-and-western station. It wasn't a type of music she liked, but at least it was familiar. Something moved her to turn on the light and look through old coffee cake recipes.

As the sky outside had lightened, she turned to the part of her old Betty Crocker cookbook with the tried-and-true casseroles. The robin family was well into morning choruses by the time Mamie put the chicken-and-rice mixture into the oven. Her sigh was nearly as loud as one of Ruthie's best, and she slumped back into the kitchen chair. As tired as she was, there seemed to be an odd peace planted in the middle of her this morning. It sprouted out of the dreams and the decision she had made at dawn, about taking food over to Iris when she came home from the hospital. Town talk claimed it would be several days. She had sustained multiple injuries and was in shock when they reached the hospital. Mamie could envision the woman's large frame and snapping eyes and suspected that Iris would be out by this nightfall. At any rate, the casserole would freeze up just right and be ready to take the very day Iris returned to her yellow, unkempt house.

Liz called at nine and Alma at ten-twenty. They all thanked the good Lord that Ruthie had had to go to Elda's and had been spared the events of last night. They agreed to tell her in the middle of a pinochle play when she returned in a few days. That way it would seem more like old news; pinochle had a way of lending a gossip feel—and therefore a lack of urgency—to anything said during its play. They didn't exactly spell this out in their conversation, but Liz had said, "Let's not call her, just wait till she's back and bring it up during pinochle," and the good sense of that was obvious.

Alma, on the other hand, had aged a couple of years it seemed. To see her own granddaughter mixed up in the trouble at the church— well, in a way she wasn't too surprised, but the shock hit her anyway. She'd said one time that Lena had always been a different kind of child but that the real problems had started when Alma's son and his wife divorced. It hadn't been bad enough for them to divorce; they'd made a world war out of it, and a year or so into all the court fights, Alma had stopped talking about it. It was one of those things a person had to bear alone. Nobody could blame Alma; her other children had good marriages at least. But it was a sad thing now to see Lena going a bad direction. It was sad to see Alma with dark patches under her eyes from lying awake thinking about it. Liz and Mamie had said all they knew to say. Mamie had even ventured to say, "You'll just have to leave the part you can't fix to the Lord, Alma." For once Liz had not said anything sarcastic.

To look around the neighborhood, no one would know that such a horrendous act had been committed so recently just a few blocks from here. People wandered into their yards and fiddled around with garden hoses, looking tentatively up at the swollen sky. It was still unlawful to water anything fresh from a spigot. But it never hurt to have all the kinks pulled out and the soaker hoses in place.

Gideon had made his rounds early, the dust-covered Plymouth creaking to a stop at corners and driveways as residents approached and said their good mornings. It wasn't usual for him to stop or for anyone but closer acquaintances to come all the way to the car, but it seemed that, since the beating at the church, Gideon had taken on an air of sudden experience. No one could forget the force of his authority, dragging kids twice his size away from the poor woman on the ground. His voice had remained steady and clear. Afterwards when someone noticed wires dangling out of the van's stereo system, a bystander mentioned that it was the sheriff's doing. That was why, when the crowd gathered, the noise had suddenly stopped, the horrible sounds of Iris's pain punctuated by Gideon's commands in the sticky air.

Mamie didn't bother going outdoors. She was still incredibly tired, the exertion of casserole-making at dawn taking its toll on the morning. She saw Gideon through the bathroom curtain, and it crossed her mind to flag him down and check on what had been done about Bill Simpson's dog. But she hadn't seen the man or his pooch, and right now it seemed that Gideon had more important things to do.

The next day Mamie carried the casserole, wrapped in towels and balanced on one forearm, while she managed the cane with the other hand. She hated to use the cane in front of the woman who had prayed so fervently for her healing, but she didn't care to end up face first in her own casserole either. Humidity welled up under her housedress as she crossed her front yard and came to the road. Of all times, her nose itched. Then her right eyebrow. There was no place to set the hot dish down except in the grass, and Mamie doubted by this time that there was an unfouled patch of ground in all of her end of town. So she wrinkled her nose desperately and held the dish chest high. It hadn't seemed right to deliver a cold casserole. Twenty minutes in the oven had freshened it up, but then Mamie wondered if Iris would just stick it in *her* freezer and have to thaw it out a second time. Mamie couldn't guarantee how good it would taste under those conditions. But it was too late now. Maybe she could offer to dish up some when she was there.

Some high school boy roared by in a pickup truck loaded down with mowing equipment, and Mamie had to spin around to prevent dust from spattering her front. After a moment she hurried on her way, the heat of the casserole causing sweat to trickle from her hairline. She prayed that nobody else would pass who knew her, and see her in such a mess.

At the pale yellow house she turned up the walk, then left to get on the gravel driveway. The drive was empty; Mamie could see through a gap in the boards of the garage door that Iris's car was inside.

The girl, Leah, opened the door to Mamie's knock. The face looked out at her carefully, then disappeared. She came back again and opened the inner door a crack.

"My Aunt Iris can't come to the door. Can I give her a message?"

"No message. I just brought some food over."

"She brought some food over," the girl called to another part of the room.

"Ask her in," came a voice from inside. There was no resonant boom to it. Leah pushed open the screen, and Mamie came in.

Iris was on the sofa in a light housedress, a faded print of tiny flowers. Mamie walked over and stood in front of her, still holding the casserole.

The reverend's face was a study in bruises and degrees of swelling. There were raw purple spots on her bare legs. One wrist was in an elastic bandage.

"Hello, Mamie," Iris said, looking up. It was impossible to tell what expression she had on her face. Her eyes landed on the dish in Mamie's hands. "My heavens, what did you bring?"

"Just a little something." Mamie looked around her, spied the dining-room table partially covered with Bibles and papers, and set down the dish. She came back and stood in front of Iris, her hands folded before her.

"It's a chicken-and-rice casserole, made with cream of mushroom soup. Nothing spicy. It's not fancy, but you can get two or three meals out of it."

"That's so *sweet*," said the reverend, her voice gaining strength. "Thank you. I love chicken casseroles. You shouldn't have troubled yourself, Mamie."

On the word *Mamie* it seemed that Iris's eyes teared up. She'd said it as though it was the name of a good friend. Mamie didn't know what to say.

"Sit down," said Iris. She raised herself up to be in a more sociable position. Mamie sat in the chair.

"I just don't understand people," said Mamie, and her voice broke. She spoke rapidly to beat the tears. "There's so much meanness around, and people like you are always the ones to get it. I'm so sorry, and I hope that a judge throws 'em all in jail for at least twenty years. There's no place in the community for that kind of people." She took a breath and dabbed at her eyes.

"It's not people, Mamie; it's the evil one," said Iris. She was obviously in pain. Just sitting up seemed to take a lot out of her. "It's Satan, and we have to come against him. I should have prayed more. I knew it wasn't a simple matter, coming against children who'd been deceived by Satan. I should have prayed and fasted, like Jesus said. But I'll know better next time. The Lord protected me."

"How in the world did he do that?" Mamie sat up, her tears gone. "My lands, Iris, look at you. That isn't protection. It's those mean kids, hanging around in gangs and taking dope. That's what it is."

"But behind it there's another battle."

Mamie sighed, at a loss. "Can I get you anything? Go to the store for you?"

"No, thank you. Ax has been real good about that since this happened. Who knows? Maybe the Lord allowed this in order to bring him to his senses."

Mamie chose not to comment on that one, but said, "You look like you're in awful pain. Can I get you an aspirin?"

Iris gave up trying to sit and eased back down into the sofa. "Maybe I'll let you do that. They're on the ledge above the sink."

Mamie went into the kitchen and found the aspirin. Leah had followed her in and got a glass out of a corner cupboard. She filled it with water. Mamie took both in to Iris.

"Here. Aspirin's still the best thing I know for plain old pain."

Iris raised up again to take the pills. As she sank back down, Mamie backed a few steps toward the door. "You call me if you need anything. I'm going to let you rest now."

"God bless you, Mamie," Iris said in a small voice.

Mamie went out, Leah closing the door softly behind her.

Mamie felt a release as she walked home. It was foolish to hold anything against Iris—even if Ax had stolen that money back in June. Mamie had known Iris since Iris was a child in school. She never had fit, was always keeping to herself and talking a strange language, peppering her sentences with *sanctified* and *sin* and *ordained of God* and *sword of the Lord*. She couldn't help that her father had been a crazy old preacher given to fits of temper. Everyone had been afraid of the man. A person couldn't grow up like that and not be affected.

When Mamie sat in her chair with the floor fan angled toward her, she thought about the tears in Iris's eyes. She was just a person, after all. And for a minute there, Mamie had felt that she might be a good friend. Could be a friend.

Mamie rocked in her chair and reached for the *TV Guide* to see what was on this evening. She knew she could never be close to some-one like that. That kind of seriousness about life. And so familiar with things like Satan and the Holy Ghost. Mamie clicked on the TV and settled into her chair. She would call Alma and Liz later. Now she just wanted to cool off. She looked contentedly around her airy living room with the tan wall-paper and soon-to-be-replaced curtains. Not dark and cluttered like Iris's home. Maybe it was just the difference between marrying and not marrying. Mamie wondered what her house would look like now if she had never married, if Charles hadn't been in her life all those years to make decisions with. It was something to think about.

32

DAVE SEATON: WATER

Saturday, August 9

On Saturday morning, Dave thought he had woken up in hell. His head hurt, and his stomach was upset. He rolled over on the couch and remembered that he wasn't in his bed, and that made him remember why. After Lena had left yesterday evening, he couldn't bring himself to go into the bedroom. To that bed where he'd taken Lena, the bed Randy belonged in. Belonged in with him. He sat up on the couch and held his head in his hands, as much from regret as from the hangover. Now he understood what people said when they talked about something being like a bad dream.

He dragged himself to the bathroom and then to the kitchen sink. The thermometer read eighty-five degrees, and it wasn't even seven in the morning. He groaned and turned to the coffeemaker. A note leaned against it.

Dear Dave,
     We need to talk. I came over early, and you were sleep-
ing, and I've got some things to do for Mom today. I'll stop
by later, OK?
Love, Randy

Dave rubbed his face and read the note again. She didn't sound
mad. But a note never gave you the whole story. He placed the paper
on the counter and made himself coffee. No food sounded good to
him. Out of habit, he wandered to the back door to survey his place
while the coffee was brewing. The bare, ugly spot that had been his
garden yesterday glared at him, and he felt sicker than ever. What had
he been thinking?

He walked out to the place in his bare feet and stared at it up
close. Nothing he could do now. Something big had happened to him;
he didn't know what, and he didn't know if it was good or bad, but it
felt like the end of everything. He walked the length of the garden spot,
kicking aside leftover bits of tomato or squash that hadn't gotten tilled
under completely. As he made his way back to the house, he noticed
that his feet felt sticky. Probably juice from a tomato or something. He
looked at the bottom of his right foot; it was caked with mud.

He took two more steps toward the house and stopped and turned
around. He walked back over to the rectangle of mangled dirt. The
northeast corner of it looked . . . wet.

Had he turned on the hose when he was drunk? But the hose was
wrapped neatly around its caddy against the house. He walked over
the wet spot, and his feet sank. He was ankle-deep in mud.

"Oh, man, I screwed something up," Dave muttered to himself as
he saw Harry looking at him from across the yard. He waved.

"How you doing today?" called Harry.

"About like you'd expect."

Harry laughed. "You were lookin' bad off, kid."

"Well, I'm worse off now."

Harry came over and stood at the edge of the bare garden. "What
happened?"

"I don't know. I mowed all this down yesterday, got up this
morning, and look at it. Must have hit a pipe or something. Didn't
notice any difference in the water pressure, though." Dave looked
toward his house and murmured some choice words. "Fine time for
a water leak."

"Better call the city works."

"Anybody in the office on the weekend?"

"No, but you can call Bob Thomas at home."

Dave called Bob, then stood by the garden and swallowed some coffee. After a few minutes he put the coffee down and got a shovel out of the shed. He dug carefully where the ground seemed to be the most wet. He'd only gone a couple feet when water bubbled up. "Oh man, oh man."

He heard a car door and saw Bob Thomas walking toward him. "Hey, Bob."

"What've you got? Oh wow." Bob stared at the water that was quickly pooling around Dave's bare feet. "Looks like a burst pipe."

"I don't have pipes here that I know of."

Bob bent down to look closer and dip his hand in. He looked up at Dave, surprised. "This here's cool water."

It hadn't occurred to Dave yet that the wetness on his feet was cooler than any tap water had been in a while.

"Well," Bob said, grabbing the shovel, "let's see what we've got."

Bob dug, and the water kept coming. Not gushes of it, but it seemed to have a current all its own. Bob stopped a minute and wiped sweat off his forehead.

"Don't make sense, Dave. Your water lines are supposed to run over there." Bob pointed out a line between the kitchen and the street, a line perpendicular to the garden. "When we redid the sewer, we closed off those old mains that went to the alley. What the Sam hill did you do to your garden, anyway?" Dave waved him away. His headache was getting worse.

"You about to puke?"

Dave nodded and headed for the house.

Dave sat in his recliner. He'd gotten over being sick a while ago, and Bob had left to look at plumbing blueprints at city hall. Meanwhile, water bubbled out of Dave's garden and had already dug a tiny trail along the edge of it and on through the yard to the ditch by the street—the ditch that had been dry for over two months. The water was a worry, but Dave's mind kept jumping to other things.

He wanted Randy to be here. But he didn't want her, either, because Lena had made clear that what happened wouldn't stay a secret. She'd probably try to make out like he'd gotten drunk and raped her or something. There were all kinds of ugly possibilities. He closed his eyes and tried to think.

The knock on the door woke him up. It seemed like early afternoon. He heard machinery sounds coming from somewhere close by. Mamie Rupert was standing at his back door.

"It was so late when you finished the other night, I forgot to pay you. There's a little extra there, for the special job on my trim." Her eyes and mouth crinkled as she smiled.

"Now, Mamie, we already said that was on us."

Mamie dismissed him with a wave of her hand. He put the check in his shirt pocket.

"What's the excitement out here?" Mamie pointed to Dave's garden spot, where Bob and a high school kid were running a backhoe.

"Oh, uh, water leak or something. Got up this morning and the ground was wet." Dave stepped onto the porch, and he and Mamie stood on the edge of it, watching the commotion.

"The waterworks guys dig up your whole garden?"

"No. I did that last night." He met her questioning look. "Too much beer."

Mamie's eyes got wide, then a hand went to her mouth and she started to laugh. Her shoulders and belly shook.

"Yeah, it's real funny now," Dave said grimly. He laughed a little too, as Mamie shook harder and wiped at tears that were streaming out of her eyes. Finally, she brought a hanky out of her dress pocket and blew her nose.

"Let's get out of the heat," Dave said, opening the door wider. "You shouldn't be out in this."

"Neither should you."

"I'm in it every day out on the crew. Doesn't bother me that much."

"Where's that girl?"

"Randy?"

"Yes, the one who painted all the fancy stuff."

"At work," he said. "She works at the Cupboard."

"I waitressed for a while. Awful work."

"I hope she finds something better."

"She could paint."

Dave thought about that. "Yes, she could. So you used to be a waitress?" It hurt too much to talk about Randy.

"Just for a summer when I was sixteen. At Barber's Café, the old one they tore down some years ago."

"I didn't know there was another one."

"You probably weren't born yet."

"I guess there's a lot of stuff used to be here I know nothing about. My dad used to talk about the newspaper."

"*Bender Springs Daily News*. Boy, the town was bigger then. They were dragging coal out of the ground by the trainload."

Dave put two glasses of tea on the table. They sat and sipped. Then Dave noticed Mamie looking at him in a strange way.

"You OK?" he asked.

She lifted her glasses to rub her eyes. "I just thought of something. May be nothing at all."

They sipped some more.

"It might just be something." She turned to him. "I'd like you to drive me up to city hall."

"This is Saturday. I'm sure it's closed."

"I'll call Helen and have her open up. I clerked there for forty years; they can just let me in."

Helen, the present clerk, was opening the door when Dave and Mamie pulled up in front of the one-story, gray-brick building.

"You comin' back to work, Mamie?" Helen was fortyish, plain, and obviously up to dealing with all kinds of requests. Half the time the electric guy in Helmsly didn't make it to Bender Springs to read meters, and Helen closed the office for a day to do the job herself.

"I've got some looking to do," said Mamie. She turned to Dave. "Go on home. Helen can take me back."

Dave shrugged and went home. The roar of earth-moving equipment drew his attention to Harry Steeps's place. Dave walked up the little rise to the alley between their properties and looked into the hole that was growing beside the east wall of Harry's house. Harry was shirtless with a soda in hand, overseeing the two men who were digging up his yard.

Dave didn't try to make himself heard over the noise. He lifted a hand and his eyebrows in question. Harry made his way around the mess and stood close enough for Dave to hear.

"Building a new family room. Putting in a basement."

Dave nodded. "Looks good. Lot more space."

"Now that you've given up gardening, maybe you'll expand your little hut too?"

"Got to find out where the water leak is before I do anything. Besides, what would I build?"

"Huh?" Harry hadn't caught the last part, with the machinery shifting gears behind him. Dave waved and went back to his house. Bob Thomas and the kid were gone, the backhoe sitting there. Dave stood at the edge and stared down at the water hole, full as ever, and then at his house and felt as empty as he'd ever felt. It was afternoon, and Randy was still gone. No, she was just gone. By now she probably knew everything. What he'd done couldn't be undone. Maybe it didn't matter anyway. Since Randy had gone to the revival meeting, life had been shifting out of gear for them. Maybe this was the only way things could be.

Dave sat miserably on his back porch, watching Harry Steeps expand his house and his future. Dave had no beer left and decided not to buy any. He sat a pitcher of tea on the porch and sipped at leisure. An unfamiliar car pulled up around four, and Mamie got out. She had something in her hand and walked pretty darn fast for a woman with a cane. Dave gave her a hand up the three porch steps.

Mamie stopped to catch her breath. She fanned herself with a manila folder that looked to be as old as she was.

"That Louise Filcher," she said finally. "So sure of her story. When she sat down to write the town history, I offered to help—after all, I was clerk for forty years. But no, she wouldn't hear it. I should've knocked her off her high horse then."

Dave half listened. "What's she done to you, Mamie?"

"She didn't get her facts straight. See—," She pointed the folder at Dave's nose. It smelled like a basement. "When I first got the clerk job, the place was such a mess I cleaned it stem to stern. War was on, a lot of people gone, and not so much business to tend to. So I spent weeks sorting through the clutter."

"Put the town into shape, did you?" Dave smiled. "You want some tea or a Coke or something?"

"No. I thought I remembered a folder—of things dating before the town. This folder." She handed it to him.

Dave bent the tab to look at the label: *Dissension Springs.* "Huh."

"It's kind of hard to make out, but these are pages written down by your great-granddaddy, James Seaton."

Dave opened the folder to brown sheets of paper, faded ink in neat lines across them. Some of the letters looked odd, but it was readable.

"Helen and I got out the maps and pieced it together. We wouldn't have been able to, but the old boardinghouse at the end of Oak Street made it fit. And this water of yours—,"she pointed meaningfully—"that's the original spring of the original town, which was called Dissension Springs, which is *not* in Louise's little history."

Mamie stopped talking. Dave didn't mean to be cynical, but he knew that the look Mamie saw on his face was what had shut her up. "I never heard *this* before," he said.

"Well, you should have, seeings as how your dad's people founded this town. Go ahead, read it." She tapped the folder.

Dave looked at the last page and saw "James Seaton" written quite legibly. "I have his desk. But he was dead long before I came. Nobody ever talked about him."

"Well, his son—your granddad, Hank—was kind of a mean one. As I recall, they hardly spoke. There was a falling-out of some sort when Hank came back from running all over the country to claim this place, old James not even dead yet. Heavens, I don't remember myself a lot of what happened in my own family. The years shift the memories around."

An oath split the air suddenly. It wasn't an angry oath. It was full of surprise, and it came from Harry's backyard.

"Jeanne Anne, come look at this!"

"Oh my," Mamie said quietly.

"What?" Dave looked from her face to the excited crew in Harry's yard.

"That might be the bodies. If I've got it figured right, Harry's place is on top of the graveyard."

"The *what?*"

"Just read." Mamie patted his arm and reached for her cane. "I've got to get home. My bones are tired. You can keep these papers. We made copies."

Dave watched her and her cane march out of his yard. He saw her head turn toward Harry Steeps's place, but she kept a straight path toward home. Dave wanted to walk over to Harry's but decided to go inside. He took the folder with him.

The house was dark when Dave finished reading and rereading. He struggled to keep track of it all. Right after Mamie had come and gone, Randy had called.

"Did you hear about the beating at the church last night?" she asked.

"No." He'd listened, not quite comprehending, while Randy talked about Rev. Miracle. She didn't mention Lena at all.

"You coming home?" he asked.

"Not tonight."

"Your mom pretty sick?"

A pause at the other end told Dave what he'd been afraid to hear in words. Randy's voice sounded tired, or maybe it was tearful. "Yeah, she's sick. I'll come by in the next day or so, OK?"

"Your note said you wanted to talk."

"I do, but I'm not feeling too good right now."

"OK. Whenever you're ready. I want to see you."

Then Bob Thompson had appeared at the back door to inform Dave that there were no broken pipes.

"That's a natural spring, Dave."

"How is that possible—in a drought like this?"

Bob made a big shrug. "Half this town has old mine shafts underneath it. Could be something's shifted and redirected a current. I honestly can't say. We'll need to build a culvert so it can drain into the sewer. I'll have a guy out on Monday to take some water samples, see what you've got in there. Tastes fresh."

"OK, whatever."

"If I were you, I'd fix myself a little pool out there." Bob looked happy. Dave guessed it wasn't every day a brand-new water source just popped out of the ground.

"That's a good idea."

Bob laughed. "Maybe you can get some flat rocks from Harry over there. He's dug up enough today. D'you see the old coffins they found?"

"Uh, no, haven't been over there yet."

"Been quite a day in our little metropolis, huh? Get some sleep, Dave, you still look sick as a dog."

Dave sat in his recliner and tried to piece it all together, but his mind was on overload. He felt so sad about Randy he could hardly stand it. His backyard was mud, with no good explanation. And this folder on the lamp table beside him—this folder was telling him about people who were related to him, people he'd never even heard of.

Dave could feel cool air coming through the house. It smelled like rain.

33

MAMIE RUPERT: MEMORIES

Tuesday, August 12

Mamie knew it was Iris at the door; she could hear the front porch creak like it did when a heavy person walked across it. Alma was plump, but not enough to make the boards sound like that. Liz was slim, and Ruthie was almost nothing at all. And any of Mamie's next-door neighbors knew to come to the back door. The only person it could be was Iris.

The woman preacher was in a housedress, not her usual polyester church suit. Her hair looked flat, and Mamie noticed that it wasn't piled on top of her head, sprayed, curled, and shining as usual, but gathered in a bun in the back. Mamie wasn't sure, but it looked as though the woman may have used a little makeup, probably to cover the purple and yellow bruises around her cheek, chin, and right eye. The uneven-looking face smiled warmly through the door.

"Hello, Mamie. I brought your casserole dish back. That chicken and rice was just delicious."

"Why, thank you." Mamie opened the door and took the glass dish. "Come in for a minute."

"Just for a minute. I've got loads to catch up on. Spent too much of the last few days on my back."

"Well, you needed your rest."

"Your house looks real nice."

"Some of the kids painted it. Kind of wild for me, but I'm getting used to it."

The two women sat on the sofa. Iris noticed an oil painting on the far wall. She nodded toward it.

"That's a pretty painting. Did you do it?"

"No. That was Charles's. He painted some—oh, by the numbers, you know, but I always thought it looked like a professional had done it."

"I've always loved horses. My grandpa had one that looked something like that."

Mamie looked at her. "I don't remember you being on a farm—were you?"

The woman shook her head. "We always lived in town, next to the church. But we visited my mother's people, a few miles outside Coffeyville. They were farmers. A lot of our church members were farmers too. A couple of them rode their workhorses in to Sunday services—when I was a little girl." Iris's face looked soft and happy. "I spent most of my summers on that farm, working in the big vegetable garden, helping Grandma and Aunt Macy do the canning. And—,"she winked at Mamie—"I preached to the pigs. I wasn't even half Leah's age, putting out those sermons on the south side of the barn."

The house was very quiet around them.

"So I guess you always liked to preach?"

Iris straightened her back and smoothed the print dress over her lap. "It came to me more naturally than anything else I ever did."

"But didn't you ever want to do anything else?" Mamie thought immediately that she hadn't the right to ask such a thing, but the words hung in the air between them.

"You mean like get married and have a family?"

Mamie tried to back out but ended up shrugging a little and saying, "Well, that or move away and get some other job."

"No." Iris looked again at the picture. "Not for any length of time. I was gonna get married once, but then I received the call. When the Lord calls, nothing else is important."

"Oh," Mamie said, as if she understood.

"A person can never really be happy if they're not doing what God called them to do." Iris cocked her head. "Just like he called you to be Charles's wife for all those years. You wouldn't have been happier anywhere else, would you?"

Called to be Charles's wife? Mamie didn't remember anything special about how it had happened. She met him right after the war when she was city clerk, and he came in to put down his utilities deposit. He'd just moved to town and bought the little house she and Iris were sitting in now. He was young and handsome and excited about that beat-up old house, stood there in the April sunlight in front of Mamie's desk and told her about all he was going to do to it. Put on a new roof, build a better kitchen, plant trees. He just went on about it.

Then, instead of mailing his payments like everybody else did, he delivered them in person and would stand there and tell her what he'd finished and what was next on his list. For four months he visited like that before he ever got around to asking her out. And when they finally went on a date, they spent half the evening in a carpeting warehouse, because it was on the way to the restaurant and a big sign outside said that all goods were marked down 50 percent. So she helped him pick out the living-room carpet. She never imagined she was choosing her own pattern that would be in her own home within a year's space.

Mamie didn't recall getting a single hint from God in this whole matter. But what Iris said made some sense. Mamie couldn't look back over her life and imagine being so happy with anybody as she'd been with Charles.

"I've got to go, Mamie. Thank you again. That was so sweet of you to bring over the food. It was a big help." Iris said all this as she pulled herself up and walked over to the front door. She gave Mamie a pat on the arm as she left, then headed down the street, humming some tune Mamie didn't recognize.

The rest of the day Mamie daydreamed about the past. She took care to dust the frame of the horse oil painting. And she walked around the house and looked at the boards and the windows, the nooks and crannies, and thought about the work she and Charles had done together. There was hardly any of the original place left, they'd done so much rebuilding. It was truly their place. Her place now.

When afternoon came, she felt too sad to watch her game shows. She dug around in the bedroom closet and brought out a photo album, one of the early ones. In the first pages were a few childhood shots of her and Cassie. Cassie was the sloppy one, her dresses hanging crookedly and her hair half down in her eyes. Mamie had been Miss Priss, eternally worried that her hair bows were not straight.

The family teased them all the time about how different they were. Mamie was Priss and Cassie was Smudge. When the uncles came over, their voices barreling through the house, the first question was, "Where's that Priss and Smudge?" It was cute when they were small. Trouble was, they didn't change that much as they grew older. Cassie never became graceful or beautiful, and Mamie never let her clothes stay wrinkled.

When the war broke out, Papa went overseas, and their one brother, Sam, took over as best he could at the small bakery. Sam was only sixteen then. Business went down, and money ran out. Cassie and Mamie were forced to leave school their junior and senior years respectively. Within a month they were both working in a dog-food factory down the highway (long gone now), taking over line jobs that men had occupied. It was miserable, messy work, and their supervisor was a harsh, thin-lipped woman. She and Mamie hit it off wrong the first day, but Mamie stayed with the job until her health gave out. Doctor Brenner said it was the stress and her delicate constitution, and Mama decided they would just do without that salary, try to find Mamie another job somewhere. Lottie Woods, the city clerk, had to leave for Indianapolis about then to be with her sister, who had just lost her husband in Italy. Mamie became the new clerk.

But Cassie—sturdy, strong, and homely Smudge—stayed at the factory. She hated every hour of it, but she stayed until the war was over and Papa got home. He'd hardly put down his bags and hugged them all when Cassie put herself on the first train to Kansas City. A month later they heard from her; she was stocking and keeping records in a department store.

It struck Mamie's heart, as she looked over their history in pictures, that Cassie never really smiled back then—or ever. She'd never gotten over being Smudge. She'd never forgiven them for the wrinkled clothes and those long months in the factory. And she'd never forgiven Mamie for being happy, either, for finding a man like Charles and having a nice home.

Mamie put the albums away. The day had grown heavy. She thought again of Iris and wondered if what she'd said about God's calling people was true. What had Cassie's calling been? Had she missed it because of the war? Did things like war interrupt God's business? It was too much to think about. Besides, Cassie was long gone, her life spent the way she'd chosen to spend it. Mamie shook her head where she stood there in the hallway. It was time to stop thinking about Cassie. She was tired of feeling so sorry about things. She went to the kitchen and poured a glass of orange juice, then settled into her easy chair and picked up the phone to give Liz a ring.

34

DAVE SEATON:
SUMMER'S END

Tuesday, August 12

She came to him in early evening, between thundershowers. The whole town was under shadows and smelled of water. People came out to their porches and sidewalks, stood with hands on hips, gazing up into the boiling gray of the sky. The birds hushed, and cars slid by in silence.

And she walked across his grass barefoot, her face open and expectant as always. Dave watched her move and searched her face from a distance. He hadn't seen her since their argument the other night. And after that was the thing that had happened with Lena. Lena had as much as said that she would tell Randy. Now Dave couldn't see anger or hurt. Maybe Lena hadn't told after all.

Randy wore a sundress, a light blue with different colors of turtles on it. It hit her midthigh. Her thin legs were a bit tanner now.

She came right up to the porch and sat beside Dave on the step. "Hi."

"Hi. You sort of disappeared. How's your mom?"

"About the same. Mainly she's tired a lot. I like your pool." She nodded toward the new thing in his yard.

"Thanks. Pretty weird, huh?" He noticed a rolled-up book sticking out of the side pocket of Randy's dress. It said *Teacher's Guide.* "What's that?" He pointed to the book.

"Sunday school lessons."

"They've promoted you to teacher already?"

"No. I just help with the little kids."

"I figured you'd be in the big people's class." He grinned.

"This is more at my level. Adult classes are more like school. Little kids' class is Bible stories. I like stories." She grinned back. Dave felt his heart breaking. Something had changed between them. It had happened silently under the cover of all the craziness of arguments and revivals, but it had definitely happened.

"So, uh, I heard Lena had a run-in with the law down at the Baptist church the other night."

"Her dad flew her back to Denver yesterday."

"Really?"

Randy was staring at the ground just beyond her feet. "I don't understand what's made her this way. She's done things this summer she never would have done before."

Heavy clouds drifted and rumbled far above them.

"What kinds of things?"

"Beating up people. Doing things just to be hateful." She looked at the bare garden. "What she did with you."

Dave felt his scalp tingle. "I was drunk. And mad. I wanted to. . . . I don't know, show her, I guess."

"I thought you didn't even like her."

"I don't. Don't like her at all."

"Then how could you do that?" Her voice was surprisingly calm.

"I think I did it because I hate her. It was absolutely wrong. And I wish it'd never happened. But I don't want you thinking it had anything to do with you."

"She always was the sexy one."

"You've got her beat any day."

"Sexy girls get the prize."

"Oh, babe. It wasn't even sex. It wasn't what we have."

They watched a sudden wind bend the fruit trees just yards away. The light that filled the air around them was changing color from gray to yellow.

"I don't expect you to forgive me," he said. "It's too much to ask. Just don't let it make you think I've stopped being crazy about you."

"I can forgive you, Dave."

"I don't know how."

"I've felt what it is to be forgiven. Your mistake's the same as mine. Your hate and stupidity, same as mine. If there's no forgiveness, what's left for anybody? We've run out of good things by the time we're eight years old. How can anybody start over without it? How can we get out of bed in the morning?"

Dave felt sudden tears heat up in his eyes.

"It hurts, what you did, and maybe it'll hurt for a long time, but I've already decided to forgive you."

He very carefully took hold of her hand. "But then this Jesus thing happened."

"Jesus' love took up where yours left off. If you hadn't loved me first, there wouldn't have been enough left of me for Jesus to save."

"But now my love isn't enough for you anymore."

"No person's love is enough. Your love is better than anybody's, but it doesn't reach down and heal the worst hurts. That's not what human love was made for. There was always supposed to be a place in us special-made for God's love."

He wanted to understand what she was saying, but none of it lined up right in his head. "The thing with Lena was a fluke—"

"I can't talk about that now. Please." She put her hand on his, and her eyes looked more sad—and more alive—than Dave could remember seeing them. "Let's do this the right way, not screaming and getting hateful. I just need to pray about all this. A lot."

Dave groped around in his mind for something to say that would let them just kiss and make up. Instead he heard himself saying, "The feeling I'm getting from you now is that we're finished."

She leaned back against the porch post, facing him. "A while back my spirit woke up. And there's a whole new person in there. I need some time to get to know her." Her eyes shifted up to the yellow sky. "There's so much to learn about life, now that it's eternal."

"I want to be part of your life."

"Me too. But I don't know how it will all fit yet. For now, I can't stay with you. I've got this stuff to work through. Mom and Dad need me around more. Teri needs me too. She's only twelve, and she's feeling so lost and lonely these days." She nudged Dave's leg with her toe. "I have to get over being mad about Lena. But mainly this isn't about that."

Dave stared at her foot and nodded. "OK. Time for this other stuff. That's how I'll look at it."

"Yes. Please look at it that way."

Gideon's squad car went by slowly. He saw them and waved, and they waved back.

"Were you at the church when all that stuff happened the other night?" Dave asked.

"I meant to be, but Mom was having a hard time, and somebody needed to cook supper. Then I was just too tired. Glad I missed it. I heard Tony was there."

"I don't think he was in on the worst of it. Hope not, anyway."

"So, you can take that job in the city now."

"Maybe."

"This would be a good time, don't you think?"

"You'd rather we not live in the same town?"

"No! I thought you really wanted to work somewhere else for a while. That's all."

"I'm thinking I should stay now." He looked at her and cocked his head. "Turns out I've got roots here."

"That's what I heard! The café was buzzing yesterday about the old graves at Harry's place." Randy was looking toward Steeps's backyard, still dug up. "Somebody said they were your relatives."

"Some are, but it's hard to know who's who. They've moved them all to the cemetery. As it turns out, I'm the sixth generation of Seatons to live around here." He patted the step near his elbow. "Thaddeus Seaton lived on this very spot—in 1913. Before that he had a farm a couple miles south."

"Dave, that is *so* cool!"

"He was actually the mayor, but the town had a different name then."

"What was it?"

"Dissension Springs." He told her about Mamie finding the old file. He told her about crazy Lewanda Thompson and about Corrie Bender, who'd died so young.

"This is, like, the story of your life, but you didn't know it yet!" Her eyes were bright, and he knew that she didn't hate him. Already she was thinking about him, how good it was that he had this history all of a sudden.

"Mamie gave me a file with records my great-grandpa James wrote. I think you should read it sometime. Parts of it would be interesting to you, with all that's on your mind now."

"I'd like to read it."

"Anyway, since we think this is the original spring, I'm thinking of turning the yard here into a little park. Leave the fruit trees, put in a couple of maples, one or two benches. Maybe the town council can put up a plaque."

"That'd be real nice."

The rain began again. It started out easy, like a conversation between friends. As Dave and Randy scooted back under the porch roof, the sound changed to hearty applause. Dave heard another sound and turned to see Randy laughing. She looked at him and said above the noise, "Sounds happy, doesn't it?"

She jumped up then and ran a few steps into the yard. Dave watched her lift her arms to the drenching and turn slowly, her eyes closed. Her face was as calm and strong as any face Dave had ever seen. Her mouth opened, and she laughed some more. The sundress was soaked and clung to her. Water streamed down her hair and face. Their eyes met, and Dave saw her face change, still almost laughing, but in a way that looked painful. He realized she was crying.

"You're my very best friend, Dave!" Her voice wavered like water ripples across the cool, noisy air. "I love you." Her arms were still raised, but now looking more helpless than joyful.

"I love you too." Dave spoke it not loud enough to be heard over the rain and thunder. Randy was looking right at him, and he knew she read it on his lips.

He watched her walk away, the air shining around her, full of silver darts of water. He almost ran after her, to hold her one last, long time. He wanted to cradle her slight body and smooth face, wrap his love around her so well that she would never forget how it felt.

But they couldn't love anymore just because they needed to. They were going and coming as different people now, people thinking more deeply and making choices, opening doors to the past and the future all at once, doors that had just shown up in front of them and opened without warning.

Dave Seaton felt the summer close against the soft watery spat of Randy's steps as she walked away from him. She was soaking wet and swinging her arms just a little.

35

THE MIRACLES: REDEMPTIONS

Tuesday, August 12

Ax's little girl was still awake when he arrived home and made his rickety way to the sofa. He collapsed and lay there a few moments before he realized he had to relieve himself. He passed Leah in the hallway near the bathroom.

She was standing there solemnly when he reemerged, her hands folded in front of her, large gray eyes scanning Ax's face. He knew she had grown used to figuring out how drunk he was on a given night. It usually irritated him, but at the moment he was almost comforted to know that she knew him well enough to know if it was time to guide him to the toilet, get him something to eat, or just stay out of his way. Her understanding so much took some of the responsibility off him. He grunted as he passed her and sought his resting spot again.

He could feel her follow him into the room. She sat on the sofa near him, which meant he couldn't stretch out, so he hoisted himself out of the barely upholstered foam rubber and sat at the one clear end of the dining-room table. He propped himself up on his elbows and linked his fingers. Yesterday's newspaper was conveniently in front of him, so he decided it wouldn't be a bad idea to read it. Leah hovered closer and finally sat down in the chair to his right. She rested her arms on the table, too, over photocopies of songs used in vacation Bible school.

"Aunt Iris still hurts a lot and feels tired," Leah said.

"I know that."

"You think you could help me clean up the house for when she comes in?"

Ax didn't look up; he kept his eyes fastened on the newsprint. "Why should we clean up? When has this place ever been clean?"

"I just thought it would be a nice surprise." The voice was suddenly that of the ten-year-old she was, trying to do something worthy of adult appreciation. "I guess I can do it."

"I can do something in the morning. Not feeling any good tonight."

"You never feel good. You'll feel worse in the morning, 'cause you'll need a drink."

Ax shot a look at her but found no indictment in her face. She had made the statement as a matter of fact. Everyone knew that morning was his worst time of the day. He tried to think of something to say, but instead merely looked at her and she at him.

"Will you *ever* stop drinking?" she said abruptly.

As Ax gazed, a soft quality came over his daughter, and he recognized that she really was not an extra conscience born into the world to haunt him. Her child's eyes were steady and her hands so calm on the table that she seemed like an ever-present image, dark and vivid like the picture of Jesus walking through the storm, his hands outstretched. For just an instant, Ax felt that God had given him a vision of himself. He jumped a bit on the inside from the shock of it. The God in this vision was patient. Through Leah, God seemed to be saying in those steady gray eyes that he would always be around. Ax had assumed God was everywhere all the time, but this was the first time the thought had come as a comfort.

"No, honey," he said firmly. "I'll never stop. It's just got into me and won't come out."

Her lip trembled, and a tear slid down her cheek. Ax reached over to hold her chin in one of his hands. She stiffened and drew away, not in rejection but in order to maintain her steadfast composure. She rose from the table and pushed the chair back into its place. As she left the room, Ax said softly, "I'm sorry."

The next evening, it was well past dark, and Iris had not arrived home. Ax and Leah had cooked, in somewhat a joint effort, with Leah in her aunt's shapeless apron giving orders in a voice both mild and driven. She had set her father to peel and slice potatoes, which he did from the couch, the large bowl balanced on a flimsy TV tray, with *Wheel of Fortune* crowd noises bouncing around the gray room. Ax got absorbed in the game and peeled twelve large potatoes before his daughter checked up on him. She fussed over the scraps of peeling caught on the couch's nubby upholstery. "And we only need four or five of those."

"Stick the rest in the fridge," he answered.

"They'll get all brown." She wrinkled her face at him.

The man muttered and cursed, carrying the bowl of gritty white potatoes to the sink. He rinsed them, put eight in a smaller bowl, covered them with water, and shook salt over them.

"What're you doing?" Leah asked, toothpick arms jabbing the air. One shoulder of the apron had slipped down to her elbow.

"If you salt 'em, they don't get as brown."

She looked at him as though he had just spoken French.

"I know a few tricks myself, missy," he said, placing the bowl inside the refrigerator.

"Put the others on to boil, please." She turned her back to him and raked raw hamburger back and forth in a skillet black from numerous meals overdone.

"Just look at my little darlin', putting on dinner!" Iris's voice rang out behind them suddenly. She stood at the dining-room table looking triumphant.

"Where you been?" Ax was opening one cabinet after another, looking for plates and glasses.

"Been to the jail," his sister announced, plopping giant Bible and giant purse on the dining table. She had to scoot magazines and restack them to make room.

"They want you to fill out more papers?"

"No, it was a counseling visit."

"Who's up there that you know?"

Iris took the plates from him and began to set the kitchen table. "Why, those two boys."

Ax's eyes cleared, nearly sober, as he worked over what she'd just said. After a moment, realization came to his face, and he swore loudly. "Iris, don't go tryin' to save their worthless souls. You got no sense at all."

"Oh, I pressed charges. They need to learn they're responsible for their actions." The small table was set, and Iris eased into the old couch for a moment's rest. "But their souls are another matter. And I'll have you know that one of them is born again this night."

"Praise the Lord!" cried Leah, the box of Hamburger Helper half emptied into the skillet.

"That's right. I was hardly there half an hour when he just broke down and wept, and we prayed together. The Lord has touched that child."

Ax grunted and plopped into the overstuffed brown chair. "Easy as that, is it? Little twerp. How old is he?"

"Eighteen. He confessed to me that he'd worshiped the devil. He and those other children." Iris fairly levitated from the couch. "But he's delivered now."

"Thank you, Jesus," murmured Leah.

"We'll see how your new little saint is doin' when he's lived awhile." Ax continued his tirade on medium volume while Iris related to Leah the details of her visit. They prayed there at the sink for the delinquent's soul to stay in God's keeping.

"He *knew* he had sinned, that there was no way out." They were at the kitchen table eating, and Iris had revived bits and pieces of the narrative to chew on along with the stroganoff hamburger. Ax avoided listening to her by carrying on his own monologue—little explosions, for the most part unintelligible, erupting from his lips periodically.

When the meal was over, Iris moved to the dining-room table with a cup of tea while Leah washed dishes. The woman pulled out a large manila file and started to scribble on one of the pages. At intervals she hummed hymns and lifted her head to think, silently moving her lips and making little sounds in her throat.

"What are you working on?" asked Ax.

"I'm writing a book."

"Ha!" he said from the couch. "What about, pray tell?"

Iris turned to fix him with a look. "What are you doing home, anyway? Isn't this a Perky's time for you?"

"You want me to leave?"

"No. But I don't understand you hanging around here so much lately. I'm completely healed, you know. Don't sit there on my account."

"What's the book about?" Ax sounded more interested than disgruntled.

Iris leaned back in her chair and took a deep breath, seeming to search the ceiling for an answer bound to come at her wish. Then she closed her eyes and said, *"The Sanctifying Breath of God: Lessons Learned in the Dark, Proclaimed in the Light."* She opened her eyes and looked at Ax for comment.

"So what's it called?"

"I just told you the title."

"Sounded like three or four titles to me."

Iris turned in the chair and pursed her lips at him. "There's a title and the subtitle. That's how they do books. The title is more inspirational, and the subtitle tells what the book's about. If you read books, you'd know that."

"You still haven't told me squat what it's about."

"Lessons learned in the dark."

"What lessons?"

"Spiritual lessons. Things God teaches us in hard times."

Ax looked thoughtful himself. He sucked on a toothpick for a minute while his sister went back to her writing.

"You know, Iris, you'd better change that subtitle. People could take it wrong. Me, for instance. There's some lessons I've learned in the dark I *sure* wouldn't want to tell nobody." He cackled at his own joke.

"Don't be so foolish. Here! Maybe if you read it you'll be quiet and leave me alone." She handed him several pages. "That's chapter 1." She went back to her work. Leah was still at the sink, craning her neck to hear their conversation.

Ax belched and shuffled the papers, then quieted down and read for several paragraphs. Then he grunted and slapped the papers on his legs.

"Iris, nobody's gonna read this stuff."

"Nobody like *you.* People interested in spiritual matters will be blessed by it. I don't know which publisher to have do it, though. I'm thinking—"

"'For a beautiful and eternal instant, the glory of the almighty God shone in the dank jail cell,'" Ax broke in, reading from her first page. "'All was silent in that overpowering presence, and no one dared breathe lest they break the peace, the wonder, the holy tranquillity which surrounded them like the first clouds of Eden.'" Ax cleared his throat and riffled over another two pages, then resumed reading, his boozy voice grating against the small room's evening quiet.

"'And what sayeth the Lord God Almighty to you, O soul, O sinner yearning to break free of the enemy's bonds? What light does your spirit thirst for, as the woman at the well thirsted for living water? What is the answer to our every prayer? Is it Jesus Christ, who was the water in that well? Is it Jesus Christ, who was the light at the beginning of time and shines even now in our dark and tortured world? I say to you: It is to him we must turn in our darkness, him whom we must drink until we are full, him to whom we must give our confused minds and wounded hearts.'" Ax stopped as abruptly as he'd started. "This is a sermon, Iris. It's just a sermon written down."

His sister looked genuinely offended. "What's wrong with the word of the Lord? Our lives are a sermon too."

"But it ain't interesting on paper. Sermons need people to say them out loud. Nobody likes readin' this if there's no person to watch or listen to."

"Since when are you such an all-fired expert, Mr. Maxwell Miracle?"

"This is just like those stories you wrote back in high school. All up in the air with holy language nobody understands who ain't in church every other day."

"People will never understand the truth until they've heard it, just like the verse says: 'And how shall they believe in him of whom they have not heard? and how shall they hear—'"

"It's all up in the air!" Ax sat up on the couch and waved the pages at her. "You got too much heaven in your head, Iris, to be any earthly good. This may go in a pulpit, but you may as well save your time."

"You're upset because that boy got saved, that's all. Here he is young and his whole life ahead of him—" Iris choked with tears suddenly. "And he's made the right choice, and you know it. It just makes you entirely mad to see grace come to anybody else, doesn't it?" Her voice quaked, and she was standing now, towering above him, looking like someone who had been disappointed for the millionth time. "I just ask myself, *Why can't Ax do that? He's heard! He knows the truth. He could be as brand new as that boy!* But here you are! And you can't stand knowin' that you're in the wrong. You'd just like to bring the whole world down to your level, wouldn't you?" She had begun to cry, and she stalked her heavy form out of the room.

"Aunt Iris?" Leah stood in the doorway, the apron untied, looking toward Iris's bedroom.

"She's all right. Just gets tired of her ol' drunk brother. She'll be OK, honey." Ax tried to comfort her from the couch, but Leah didn't look at him.

"She'll write a wonderful book. You'll see," she said to her father.

"She's got too much heaven in her head. You may not like to hear it, but it's the truth. Most people in the world don't want to hear about heaven. One of these days you'll learn that."

Leah finally looked at him. He could see the beginnings of conflict somewhere in the little-girl face and knew she'd heard what he said. She was saying something, scolding him, but he tuned out the words and gazed at his daughter, tall and full of a growing grace. There was still time for her to escape both of them—him and Iris. He could still look at Leah and see what had appeared in her face yesterday, when she understood for the first time that he would always be a fallen drunk. He could still construe a smile of God on her serious lips, see God's patience in the hazel-gray of her too-old eyes.

When Leah turned to go to the refrigerator, Ax pulled a wilted Montgomery Ward catalog on top of Iris's "book," scattering some of the papers. If he got lucky, she would get a new inspiration and not bother to find this one again.

36

Sarah Morgan: Jacob's Walk

Wednesday, August 13

Sarah awoke to someone shaking her. She vaguely recognized Jacob's face above her, and she panicked. He never woke up before she did.

"Is something wrong? Where are Miranda and Peter?" The room was dark.

"Shh. Everybody's fine. Come on, get up." Jacob's face looked untroubled, and he held a finger to his lips. He took hold of her hand and helped her out of bed. "Get dressed and put on your walking shoes." As the picture came in clearly, Sarah could see the smile on his face.

"What time is it?" Sarah pulled on the first pair of shorts she found.

"Three."

"In the morning." She said this to herself, trying to grasp the moment.

"Here." It was then she saw that Jacob was fully dressed. He held her walking shoes out to her, and she took them. He waited patiently while she combed her hair and sloshed some mouthwash around. As he guided her toward the front door, she turned to him.

"We can't just leave the kids."

"Joe's here. He knows we're going out for a while."

"OK." Sarah shrugged. She'd been sleeping soundly. The air was almost chilly. Since the rain yesterday, the whole town had felt different. It smelled luscious.

"So," she said, speeding up some to get even with her husband, "what's this about?"

"You've been enjoying these walks so much I thought I'd join you."

"No, Jacob, you've got that wrong. You woke *me* up. I'm joining *you.*"

"Whatever." His voice was light. "This way."

"Why?"

"Why not?"

They were headed toward downtown, or what Bender Springs called one.

"You know, there's not much in this direction. Deserted buildings aren't real inspiring at three in the morning." Sarah was surprised at how grumpy she sounded. She knew that if she were fully awake, she would appreciate this gesture Jacob was making. He didn't offer to change direction, so she walked silently beside him.

"At this next block we'll turn south, OK?" He was looking toward the streetlight ahead at Adams Street. Sarah followed his stare and saw two people under the light. Two people in jackets, just standing there.

"Hey, Jacob, who do you think that is? Maybe we should turn off the street here."

"They're waiting for us. Hurry, Sare."

Madison and Rona looked like kids ready to board the bus for their year-end field trip. Rona waved a little at Sarah as she and Jacob approached. Madison whispered loudly, "Let's avoid Pine. The dogs are really loud." He scrunched his face to emphasize.

"What is this?" Sarah asked and laughed.

"It's a spiritual renewal walk. Only pastors and their wives are invited. Once we get the kinks out of it, we'll invite the Danceys."

Sarah stood back and looked at the three of them. They smiled back at her, proud of themselves. "This is nuts, you guys."

"We're a nutty bunch." Madison took her elbow, and they started down the street together. "You don't mind, do you?" he asked in a more serious voice.

"Of course not. This is so sweet."

"It was Jacob's idea."

Sarah looked over her shoulder at Jacob, who was arm in arm with Rona. She sent a kiss to him so slight that she doubted Rona had even seen it. He winked back.

"It's so pleasant out now, isn't it?" Rona said, the tone of her voice low enough to blend into the breezy sounds around them.

"That's why I like it so much," said Sarah. She turned back to Madison. "Where are we going?"

"Just around. No plans really. I hate plans."

They walked past the park, past the senior center. The small building seemed to watch them go by. A breeze made whispering sounds in the trees that lined the sidewalk. The shadows thrown by the streetlights danced crazily at their feet.

"Thank you, Madison, for coming along."

"We've got to keep tabs on each other. Jacob tells me the two of you will see Jaymee again next week. How's that going?"

"Only one session so far, mainly introduction. I don't know. This is all new to me."

"Well, we're rooting for you. What?" Madison's head turned suddenly. Rona was tapping on his shoulder.

"Change places with me. Let us visit." Rona slipped up beside Sarah. "Is this a nice surprise, or would you rather be sleeping?"

"It's a very nice surprise."

They turned down Oak Street, toward the older part of town. Madison and Jacob started talking shop behind them. Rona nodded back at them. "Amazing, isn't it, when two of them get together. They just push each other's little ON switches."

Sarah smiled. "I guess I'd be worried if they never wanted to talk about the ministry. Better that they're passionate about it."

"Or even if they're not. Passion comes and goes."

Sarah thought Rona might use that to lead into a discussion of passion in general, and about marriage, but she didn't. The four of them stopped and tried to look in the windows of the old grain elevator. It had stopped operating only two years ago. When they left there, they crossed railroad tracks and found themselves on more uneven pavement. Just old houses in this part of town, many of them run-down. A couple of dogs yowled from a stand of several mobile homes some ways from the road.

"You know, it's strange how the mind works," Sarah said, looking up at the dark fringe of treetops spaced along the road ahead of them like very old guards. "I've thought lately of things I hadn't thought about in years."

"That happens to me sometimes too," said Rona. "I don't know why."

"The last time I saw my mother, she was dressed in a navy blue suit with a small suitcase in her hand. Going on a visit. I don't know what she had in the suitcase. I remember helping her pack, but I don't remember any of the contents."

Their steps made soft echoes down the pale street. The men's voices had fallen farther behind them. Sarah sucked in a long breath. "I didn't see her again. Whoever she went with lost control of their car early in the morning—the morning they were coming back."

"How awful."

"I was so young, barely Miranda's age. I always thought it shouldn't have mattered that much, that I hadn't known her long enough to have a lot of memories or even to miss her as much as other people did."

"She was your mama, Sarah." Rona's voice lingered close to Sarah's ear.

"And now, all of sudden—" Sarah felt her throat close up painfully—"out of nowhere I've got to see her again. I miss her so much I think I'll go crazy if she's not here."

She felt Rona's arm come lightly around her shoulders.

"I need her advice," Sarah said, as tears ran down her face and neck to the collar of her shirt. "I have a little girl, and I don't know if I'm doing this right. I feel like I'm headed out into the world for the first time, and I'm scared to death."

"You're never completely disconnected from your own people," Rona said. "I miss loved ones at different times for different reasons. My grandmother's been dead for forty-odd years, but still, some mornings, when the sun shines on the pansies a certain way, I cry for her all over again. It's the bittersweet part of having people in your life."

"Thanks." Sarah sniffed back the last of her tears. "I guess I'm not going crazy."

"No. We couldn't let you do that."

The four of them had reached the old boardinghouse. There was a sign, its paint rubbed almost completely away, that merely said, "Saxton Boardinghouse." The place was empty, gray plywood over the windows. No one had bothered to mow the yard, and they walked carefully through the weeds to the back of the place. There, facing a soybean field, was a split-rail fence that had been kept up by the field's owners. They sat on it and looked over the expanse that moved like a huge organism as the night wind hovered over it.

Jacob took Sarah's hand and squeezed it. "You OK?" he asked softly.

"Yes. Really OK." She tried to read his features in the low light of the early-morning sky.

"This place almost feels like it's still in another century." Madison's voice was barely louder than the crickets in the weeds of the yard behind them.

"So peaceful. I love the way it smells," Rona said. She bent to examine some of the tall plants around them. "I've got to get some of these seeds—going to have a wildflower patch in the northeast corner of the yard, I think."

"I've only been here a couple of years, but sometimes it feels like a century," Jacob said, "or like I'm caught in a time warp."

"Kind of gives the place an everlasting feel, doesn't it?" Madison cleared his throat. "It can be discouraging, because you feel that nothing will ever change. But it's encouraging, too, because some things you really don't want to change. A field like this—kind of gives me hope."

Sarah could see the incredulous turn of Jacob's head. "Are Presbyterians just naturally optimists, or what?" he said. "It's a *soybean* field."

"Oh, you know us. Those Calvinist roots. Sort of makes us able to dig in for the long haul and accept what comes."

"Shh," said Jacob.

"What?" The three of them looked at him.

"Car coming." They leaned back to look at the road behind them. A car crunched over gravel and passed the boardinghouse slowly. A man hung one elbow out the driver's side.

"What's Gideon doing out here?" Rona asked.

"Making rounds. He does it once a night," Jacob answered.

"You're kidding."

"No. I've heard him before, from our bedroom."

"*I* haven't," said Sarah.

"You have to tune it in. After two years in this wilderness, I can hear a grasshopper eating his lunch."

When the car was well past, they walked back to the road and toward the Carrutherses'.

"Maybe listening is your spiritual gift right now, Jacob," said Madison.

Jacob was quiet. Sarah knew he doubted his spiritual existence at the moment, let alone any gifts.

"Madison and I talked far too much the first twenty years of pastoring," said Rona. "I feel certain of that now."

"One person I do need to talk to, though, is the Gardino boy," said Jacob. "I've got to call over there again tomorrow. I've tried a couple times but keep missing him."

"I think that will mean a lot to him," said Rona.

When they reached the Carrutherses' home, Sarah and Jacob said soft good-byes and waited until they saw the two figures go inside the door before walking on.

They held hands and didn't say much on the several blocks to home. They were getting close when Jacob said, "I don't have any expectations or any plans, Sarah, except that we have to stay together somehow."

"Yes."

"I'm not sure anymore what God has called me to, in the ministry, anyway. But I'm sure as ever that I'm called to love you the rest of my life."

Sarah felt a sensation—old and wonderful—pass through her. "Me too."

"If this place isn't good for one of us, then that's a signal we need to recognize."

"But we can't run away. We have to go because we know it's the best thing. I just don't know what the best thing is."

"Could you really stay? If you felt it was the right thing to do?"

They sat on the steps of the porch. There was enough light now for the grass to be turning from gray into dark green.

"I could stay if I found the resources to keep going. I can't stay the way I've been."

"Well, we'll have to find whatever it is we need, then."

They were quiet, but Sarah felt a jubilation of sorts—or at least a relief—between them.

"So you still believe there's some purpose in all of this, in us?" Sarah said. "I'm not even sure I believe enough to pray these days."

Jacob gazed into space. "I still believe, but I don't expect to understand it as much. I'm beginning to think that people never really understand a thing until they look back on it, if they understand at all. Maybe it's not so important to know why, or to draw conclusions."

Sarah leaned against Jacob slightly. "Thank you for the walk."

"You're welcome." She could tell by his pause that he would say more. "I'm sorry I've let you walk alone all summer."

"Sometimes we have to be alone first, Jacob."

"But it's not good to stay alone."

Sarah scooted close and kissed the softness of his cheek. She breathed in the smell of him, which was part of her, in her permanently, like her own blood. "I'm not alone. I feel you with me."

He kissed her on the lips. They stayed there for a long moment, and Sarah felt tenderness return between them. She allowed it to ease hurts that had raged inside her far too long. When she reached up to stroke his face, it seemed that other things—ugly things she couldn't even name—slipped from her fingers.

37

TONY GARDINO: SUMMER'S END

Saturday, August 16

Tony woke up with sun in his eyes. He'd slept until nearly nine, after lying awake until four-thirty. When he sat up in bed, he felt different somehow. He stared at the things in his room—the candles that had burned themselves out, the music he hadn't played, and junk he hadn't touched for most of the summer.

He stood up and looked out the window. The yard looked greener now that it had rained. The air was cooler, too, as it sifted through his window screen. He sat down again and tried to put together why today felt better than the other days up to now.

Mrs. Petersen's house was in front of him, and he didn't know how it got there. Before he knew it, she was at the back door, looking at him through the screen. Had he rung the bell?

"Why, Tony!" She seemed at a loss, for the first time, of what to say.

"Hi. Is Lena here?"

"*Why, no, Tony. She's back in Denver, with her aunt. I thought you knew.*"

"*No. I hadn't heard from her or anything.*"

"*You look like you're about to die from the heat. Come in where it's cool.*"

"*No, I can't—,*" Tony backed down a step.

"*Just for a few minutes, till the red goes out of your face.*" Mrs. Petersen held the door open wider and gave an authoritative nod toward a chair, and Tony relented.

He sat in Mrs. Petersen's kitchen and drank a root beer. From there he could see the Feel-Better Room. It looked quiet and green and like a place he had been to in a dream.

"*Your mother told me you aren't mixed up with those kids. I'm glad to hear it. That Lena just isn't careful enough about her friends. You're the only boy I've trusted her with.*" Mrs. Petersen's face looked tired.

"*She's with her aunt?*"

"*Yes—my daughter Irene—her dad's sister. Maybe she can help the two of them work things out. I always told Mark the divorce was a selfish thing to do, that the kids would suffer.*" She got up from the table and started washing dishes. "*But I'm just his mother—ha—what do I know?*"

"*Thanks for the root beer. Let me know if you hear from Lena. I want to know how she's doing.*"

He didn't expect to hear anything ever again about Lena. Even her grandma hadn't looked very hopeful. But without Lena—her skin, her smell, her voice—to fill him up, there was nothing left to make him look forward. He looked at the blood-red candle glasses, their former brilliance muted with dust. He'd hardly lit them since Lena came. Now they looked like discarded toys; he knew their light would never comfort him again. "A few good things," she had said during a philosophical moment one day, "that's all we're given. We make up the rest on our own. And if we can't make them, we just pretend."

I'm through pretending. The darkness hit him, like ground rushing up. He wanted the comfort of the ground again. He considered sneaking out to lie under his tree. But he knew it wouldn't be enough this time. When he went to the earth for comfort, he would go deep and bury himself in its blackness. He would go for good.

That's why he felt better now. He finally knew for sure the best thing to do. He'd played around all summer, finding this thing and that thing to help him through it, but he'd only prolonged the darker reality behind it all. None of it mattered in the long run. It felt good to understand that now.

He spent the rest of the morning pitching things in the trash. He took a whole garbage bag out to the trash can in the alley. No one was home. Mom and Dad had gone to town. Granddad was at the hardware store, and Annie had gone swimming in Helmsly. By some miracle, so small no one else would see it as such, he was alone in the house. This was a sign, too, that he'd made the right decision.

But no guns this time. They took too much time and thought. No, Lena had showed him a better way. It had been a joke to her, but he could use the knowledge in dead seriousness.

He didn't write a note; there was nothing to say that anyone would understand. He saw the candle glasses and decided it would be a good thing to return them to the church. He looked at the clock by his bed. Eleven-thirty. By the time he got to the church, Father Ricardo would be eating lunch.

He gathered up the glasses and a few candles he hadn't burned and put them in a Supreme Video sack. He put on some old jeans and the T-shirt he'd worn yesterday. On his way through the kitchen, he saw a big sign on the refrigerator with his name on it: *Tony, call Pastor Jacob this morning.* Tony laughed out loud. Fat chance. The sun was out bright. He put on an old ball cap and left the house.

He didn't plan it that way—maybe his feet went there automatically now—but he ended up walking by Dave Seaton's place.

He saw Dave out by the new well, puttering. It would be good to say a decent good-bye. He and Dave hadn't spoken since the paint job on Mamie's house. Tony walked over and stood quietly a few feet away until Dave noticed. When he did, he actually smiled.

"Hey, Tony, what's up?"

Tony shrugged.

"Uh, we squared away on your pay for the painting?"

"Yeah. You didn't need to pay me for that, since I screwed it up."

Dave waved him off. "You came out a hero on that one. I've got requests from all over town now, for three-color trim." He grinned, shaking his head at the irony of it. "You want some more work? 'Cause we've got it now."

"No. Thanks for hiring me, though. Sorry I wasn't with it more of the time."

Dave shrugged, looking toward Harry Steeps's place. "No harm done. You doin' OK?"

"Yeah. Bizarre about the water, huh?" Tony nodded toward the well.

"That's for sure."

"Nothing like your own personal miracle."

Dave's eyes widened a little, and he didn't respond right away. "That's one way of looking at it, I suppose."

"Why not?"

"I heard Lena's back in Denver."

Tony couldn't think of a response.

"Probably best," said Dave.

"Randy moved out?"

"Her mom's pretty sick now. And, you know, we have some stuff to work out."

"Hope things turn out OK."

"Thanks. Take care now."

Tony walked away feeling nothing. A part of him thought he should feel something, since, in a way, Dave had been a friend. But he couldn't concentrate on that now. His heart was already racing. He wasn't sure when the next train came through the field in back of the school, but he knew several of them came through every day. Two minutes to put the candles back, and then the short walk over there. Then he'd just sit in the tall grass and wait. Suddenly he felt ultimately patient with life. He felt that he could hang around all day if he wanted. The end was determined, so everything leading up to it was cool. He couldn't remember feeling so free, even contented. Not happy. Not full of peace, really. But OK with everything.

Tony entered the church by a side door, out of public view. The early afternoon came through the heavy stained-glass windows and felt dim and old inside the church. Father Ricardo wasn't there. No one at all was there.

The remaining candles knocked together inside the plastic bag. Tony decided to take them out of the bag and place them neatly on the shelf beside the candle rack.

Tony had almost reached the foyer when Father Ricardo entered suddenly by a side door on the opposite side of the room. He carried some papers. He saw Tony and stopped.

"I came to return these," Tony said quickly. He held up the bag. "I guess you know I took them. I just borrowed them for a while. And I bought new candles to replace the ones I burned. Sorry I didn't ask first." He held up one of the ruby glasses. His heart thudded, but he made himself imagine high grass and the train coming through. It would hit hard and instantly. If he stood just right, he would die with no memory of it.

"I appreciate your returning the glasses. But why don't you consider the candles a gift? Are you finished using them?" The old priest walked a few steps toward Tony. He didn't look angry. His eyes were dangerous though, because they asked Tony to look back.

"I'm finished," Tony said. He continued toward the candle rack, sensing the priest's steps, which were coming at a leisurely pace from the other side of the room. Tony's hands shook a little. He figured it would be fine just to leave the plastic bag there or to hand it to Father Ricardo. But he didn't want to wait until Father Ricardo was that close. He wanted to turn around and speak to the priest to give him just a minute. He would leave then. He would leave.

But they reached the foyer at about the same time. Tony practically rushed to the candle rack and stopped in surprise. There were twice as many candles there as he'd ever seen before. And every one of them was lit. The brightness took his breath for a second, but he said as casually as he could, "There are more than usual."

The priest didn't reply. They stared at the silent, dancing flames. Tony tried not to be taken in by them again. He pictured Lena, walking away from him, and Pastor Jacob, screaming at him. Candles didn't matter at all. Just one more fake thing. He closed his eyes and imagined the field, the freight train roaring through, a single, powerful blow.

"Are you all right?" Father Ricardo's voice pressed at him. Tony opened his eyes.

"Where are all the people who lit these?" he asked.

"Oh, I lit most of them myself."

Tony gave a small surprised laugh. "Trying to make it look like business is good?"

Father Ricardo chuckled. Tony had never seen so many crinkles around two eyes. He stood back to protect himself from another pretense of someone being nice to him. The priest was still talking.

"No. It's not a thing I usually do. I just started it lately."

Ricardo looked at Tony, his eyes suddenly full of wind and waves, storms breaking and streaks of sun peeping through. "I light them for you."

Tony felt the bottom fall out from somewhere. The laugh left the muscles of his face. As Father Ricardo locked eyes on him, there was a tremble deep in his gut, and he sensed something slipping abruptly from his grasp. He tried to think of the steel wheels of the train—and absolutely nothing afterwards. All he wanted was a feeling of not existing anymore. Of being blank.

I light them for you.

"I don't get it," Tony whispered.

"Tony, why is it so hard for you to believe that there are people who care about you?"

Tony jerked his head, disconnecting their gazes, and looked back at the flames. The trembling was moving up through his body, gaining on him.

"Your grandfather comes in and lights one every morning, and Mrs. McGeever who sits there in the fourth row, she lights one. She doesn't know anything about you, but she can see how troubled you are. She had to ask me your name."

Tony felt a sudden hotness spilling from his eyes. He clutched at the thundering feelings, but they scattered away from his reach.

"So I think that between all of us, we're covering you pretty constantly." The priest's voice was calm, almost congenial.

"I never asked anybody to do anything." In spite of the growl in Tony's voice, the tears continued, running down his face, cooling in the medieval air of the church, splattering on his shirt and on the floor.

"But you need someone to do something, don't you?" Father Ricardo had moved closer. Tony could feel energy between them. It seemed as though he were being pulled toward the priest, and so he wrapped his arms tightly around himself and dug with his feet through the soles of his shoes and to the floor below. The water just kept running out of his face, like he was some little kid, a stupid little kid who couldn't control himself.

They stood for a long time, inches apart, the flickering glasses in front of them, the day outside gleaming through the peaceful, sad faces of the Virgin Mary and some apostles. Father Ricardo handed Tony a tissue, and he blew his nose. He was tired suddenly, his body like lead. The feelings he had tried to chase down and hold in place were God-knows-where by now. He felt as though his insides were spilled all over the room.

When he thought he could speak again without sounding like an eight-year-old, he said wearily, "I'm afraid of the dark." This time a sob came out without any warning. Tony covered his face.

"I know," said the priest. He ventured a hand to rest lightly on Tony's shoulder. "Let's sit down for a while." He guided Tony toward a pew. "I don't like the dark either."

A timid blush of sun came through the west windows. It struck through the hand of the suffering Jesus, and Tony could feel warm colors on his face.

38

MAMIE RUPERT: DREAMS

Saturday, August 16

It was Bill Simpson, sure as the world, That Dog straining at its leash. Mamie happened to be on her front porch, celebrating the washed-off look of the neighborhood, when the man and his beast were there all of a sudden, at the edge of her yard. As the dog lifted a leg at the base of her oak tree, Mamie stepped straight off the porch and shouted at once.

"You! Bill Simpson! I want that mutt off my property!" She had already reached him, taking giant strides in her house slippers. Simpson looked up at her, the general vagueness of his face shot through with surprise.

"He messes all over my yard to where I can't even walk through it! He ruins my roses and dirties my mint patch! How could you be so *unneighborly!*" She didn't allow him an answer, although he looked too stunned to formulate one anyway.

"From now on you keep him *off* my property. I'll *sue* you, so help me!"

"Don't want no trouble," grunted the man. He tipped the grimy bill of his work cap and pulled That Dog to the other side of the road. The dog didn't seem to mind the change of direction, and Simpson didn't turn back. The dog's chain collar and leash clinked in the clear morning.

"I don't want an argument now," Mamie called after them. She walked to the middle of the street, arms in the air, not sure whether to fold them across her chest or put hands on her hips. Simpson and the dog were moseying along the rain-freshened grassy edge of the street.

"What's his name?" Mamie called at the old man's back. Simpson, deaf as ever, kept moseying. Mamie strode several more steps and shouted, "Bill Simpson!"

The man turned around, looking frightened.

"What's the dog's name? If he comes in my yard again by himself, how do I call him?"

"Doc." Simpson turned back around. The dog glanced back at him, hearing his name. The tail wagged.

"All right. Well. You heard what I said." Mamie went back to her house. She walked to the kitchen and wrote "Doc" on the calendar that hung down the side of the refrigerator.

In the living room the television sat blank and silent. The *Today Show* had started ten minutes ago, but Mamie sat in the easy chair and stared at the black screen, her heart pounding. After two months of trying to nail down the old man, her release was almost too much to bear. And other things were fresh on her mind.

*T*he porch swing sways in wide motions, the air filled with lilacs. Mamie loves the big swing Papa built for them. It is big enough for three people to sit comfortably. Papa is beside her now, smelling of raisin muffins, his apron still tied around him.

Smudge is wearing her Easter dress. Her hair hangs neatly in shiny curls, and she's grinning ear to ear. She looks so lovely and happy, happier than ever seemed possible for Smudge. She climbs the steps on skinny legs to sit between Mamie and Papa.

When she reaches the top, little-girl Smudge becomes grown-up Cassie, fortyish and plump. She moves more slowly, but the smile—the uncharacteristic smile of a happy Smudge—is unmistakable. She wears the pretty green dress she bought for Papa's funeral. Mamie knows that he is no longer beside her on the swing.

Now Cassie is bending toward her. She takes Mamie's hands in hers. Cassie's hands are warm and deliciously soft. She sits beside Mamie in the swing. They hold hands and sway in the lilac air.

It is so wonderful, holding Cassie's hand and feeling her smile to the bone. They hug and clasp hands like schoolgirls, and the swing moves as if weightless. Behind them in the house, Mama is listening to George and Gracie on the radio, cackling like a contented hen. Mamie feels warm and sweet and completely loved. Cassie's shoes are new and smart; her job in Kansas City has worked out after all. Cassie's happiness sends waves like angel voices through the morning. The sisters inch closer together, and Mamie can feel the cool softness of Cassie's arm.

Mamie pulled the handkerchief out of her dress pocket and wiped tears from her cheeks, thinking of Cassie and last night's dream. The small house hummed with the busy quiet of morning. Mamie reclined in the chair and kicked off her house slippers, still wet from her walk across the grass.

When she closed her eyes, she could hear neighbors in their yards. She recognized the particular voice of Gideon's Plymouth as it glided by on morning rounds. It was late summer, and the season had its own constant sound—the ruffling of grass in the heat, the metallic chirps of insects hidden there. But mixed into the sound and the sunshine was the scent of stirred-up earth, the smell the rains had left. In the last few days the town had greened and spread its leaves.

In a bit Mamie would call Alma, then relish the farm report over chicken noodle soup. But for now the memory of dreams was comfortingly close. She rested her head back and waited for yellow light to walk across the room.

The History:
Dissension Springs, 1895

In 1895, surveyors came through Dissension Springs. They found only deserted buildings and an overgrown road where the town's street had been, and they landed eventually at Thaddeus's gate down the road. A coal company was coming into the area, they said, and they needed to know boundary lines. The nearest land office had no information.

"What's the name of this place?" asked a young man brown from days in the sun.

"Bender Springs," said Lewanda before Thaddeus could respond. He looked at her, and she looked back. Her eyes told him nothing.

"Springs, is it? There a spring here?"

"Used to be. Dried up some years ago."

"And Bender? Somebody's name?"

"Somebody's."

The young man shrugged and made a notation in his little book. "Good a name as any. Anybody else here?"

"No. Folks didn't have very good luck."

"And who are you?" he asked Thaddeus.

"Thaddeus Seaton. I'm mayor."

The man laughed. "Mayor of what?"

Thaddeus indicated the land around them. "This farm, the graveyard by the old church. I was honestly elected mayor, back when there were enough people here to vote." They heard suddenly, clear as a bell, the call of a meadowlark close by. Wind moved over the grasses like an accompaniment.

"Well, Mayor Seaton, it's good to meet you."

By the time the young man had gone back out the gate, Lewanda had found some chore to do. Thaddeus didn't ask about her giving the man the wrong name for the town.

After supper, the two of them sat on the porch. Thaddeus smoked, and Lewanda drank some sassafras tea. The porch was but a year old and Lewanda's idea. Even though she'd settled into a home, she still missed the outdoors at night, she said. Now she gazed toward the western sky, streaked with gray and dusty rose.

"It wasn't good, the way the spring happened in the beginning," the old woman began.

"I don't know that it was a bad thing."

"But it went bad, real bad."

"You think the name Dissension Springs might curse it more?"

"No. The old name was all right. But it's better to be named for her now."

Thaddeus was quiet, the memory of young Corrie still sweet enough to give him pain. He'd often imagined what their life would have been like had she lived.

"The night you brought the girl to me," Lewanda said, "she said Jesus sent her. I laughed, but not too loud. Her eyes could hold a person, couldn't they?"

"They sure could," said Thaddeus, fingering the pipe.

"I said, 'Why would Jesus send you to me?' And she said, 'Because your soul is hurt, and you don't know how to mend it.'"

Thaddeus stared at Lewanda. He thought then how she didn't seem hurt or crazy at all anymore.

"She said I'd been given a gift but didn't know the One who gave it to me. Well, I was hungry to hear it said I had a gift—so many folks called it evil, but it was with me, that was all, this ability to feel the weather with my mind. We walked to town that night. It was a night like this—cool and quiet, but just a sliver of moon. She took my hand when we got to the church grounds. She led me to the spring. It was just a flat, bare piece with some old scrubby grass grown over it."

Thaddeus had become mesmerized by Lewanda's voice. The yard in front of him seemed to float in milky light. He could picture Corrie and Lewanda, sneaking around his wagon and going off to town, two figures looking like ghosts.

"She got down on her hands and knees, and then she stretched out across that old spot. Spread out like an angel over that dried-up spring.

She prayed over it. She prayed for the town, but more for the spring itself, that it would bubble up again. And then, most of all, she prayed for me—that I'd meet the God who'd put me in such close connection to natural things."

Lewanda's voice trembled, and she stopped abruptly. She spoke of these events as though they'd happened a week ago.

"She got up, dirt all over her dress, and she kissed my cheek. Then we walked back to where we'd left you. And all along that road she told me stories from the Bible. Stories about water. About God dividing the waters in the heavens from the waters on the earth. How he opened up the Red Sea for the people to cross in safety. And about the river Ezekiel saw that started in the temple and got deeper and wider the further it went, about the well Jesus sat by when he was thirsty. About the water coming out of the ground for the woman Hagar and her little boy. She talked about Moses bringing water out of the rock and about Jesus being the rock—and being living water so we wouldn't be thirsty no more. About him changing water into wine. And him being baptized in a river and coming up blessed. All the way along the road that little Corrie Bender told me about all the other times God had done mysterious things with water and with people.

"When we got back to the creek, she said, 'Lewanda, do you hate the One who brought water out of the rock?' And I said, 'No, I've never hated that One.' And she said, 'You must believe that that One has never hated you. The One who brings water out of the bare ground loves you with love that will outlast all the springs and all the rivers and all the seas.'"

Thaddeus listened while Lewanda wept. It was a soft sobbing, weary and relieved, filled with the memory of forgiveness unexpected.

"But Lewanda," he ventured to say softly when she had quieted, "the spring never came back."

"No." She straightened a little and sniffed. "Not yet. That's not important. Doesn't have to come back for you or for me. That was a special gift, the night we found it, and we were foolish little children who didn't know anything. It doesn't have to come for us, and it doesn't have to come now."

"I suppose you're right about that."

"It's enough for me that the water's there, always was, always will be, and it comes at the Almighty's bidding, one way or the other."

They went to bed shortly after. Thaddeus lay awake long after the sounds of Lewanda and the children settling up in the loft had ceased. He could look back now at the changes in Lewanda and see the sense it made. That Corrie would have healed her that night, and that neither one of them would have talked about it. It made sense how Lewanda seemed to perk up especially when the children read from Exodus or Ezekiel at their suppertime Bible readings. And Thaddeus understood now that the times he spied Lewanda standing alone, still as a deer, out away from the house, she was praying to the One who brought water from the ground.

Even though the spring remained dry, Bender Springs came to life again as the coal mining started in 1896. By the time Maryanna had married and moved to Ohio, an entire new settlement had sprung up about a mile north and east of where the original few buildings were. New folks tore down the remains of the grocery and smithy and church and put what lumber was good enough into new buildings. They left only the boardinghouse, because its lumber was newer and the building sturdy. About the time Samuel married and moved to work at the telegraph office in Cape Girardo, Missouri, Bender Springs elected what all the new folks believed was its first mayor (no one ever got around to telling them about Thaddeus, the old man who lived off to the south). That was 1897.

When Lewanda died, six years later, Thaddeus laid her next to Florence. He knew that Florence welcomed Lewanda's soul now. None of them were foolish children anymore.

The year Thaddeus turned sixty, he gave up the farm. He felt old and sick and couldn't keep up with things. Either he would have to repair his house or build another one. One sleepless night he decided to move to where the old church had been, so that he could better care for the graves, now that no one in the new town knew or cared anything for those long dead and unknown to them. Thaddeus found a young man to help him and built a small place next to the graveyard. One of the few times Samuel made his way back for a visit, he suggested putting proper stone markers over the graves of his mother and the others. But Thaddeus saw no need. He knew where they were, and Florence and Corrie and Lewanda would all favor, he thought, becoming part of the wildflowers and wide, rosy sunsets. Thaddeus knew their places by heart; once his heart was gone, it didn't seem important for others to decorate memories they didn't even own.

A few years later, Samuel's young son, James, came back to live with his grandfather, who was now blind and needed someone to help him around. In Thaddeus's last years, he and young James tended the graves together and kept a little vegetable garden.

On a night very similar to the hot evening Thaddeus and Lewanda had discovered the spring, he sat out on his small porch with James and told him the story. He talked of Florence and the people who'd died in the drought. He talked of the little girl who died before being born, and about the other girl, Corrie, who'd healed old Lewanda's soul.

"So Corrie was sort of a faith healer?" James asked. He was writing down every word his grandfather said, in a tablet, his eyes wide and hungry behind a studious boy's spectacles.

"Something like that."

"And the old spring never came back?"

"Not yet." Thaddeus, too blind to see his own hand, pointed precisely to the place where the spring had been. "When God decides, it'll come back."

"Grandpa, do you still pray over that old spot?"

"I still do." Thaddeus felt cool tears run down his cheeks. He could still feel that long-ago night on the parched land, the church house wailing, and Lewanda following God's finger. If it hadn't been for her, the town would have blown away with the dust devils that very year. Even now, it was hardly a town—would probably never amount to more than a pause in the road for folks on their way to someplace bigger. But he remembered moist earth gathered back in his arms and the overwhelming feeling that God had taken notice of them kneeling in the dust down on the vast world. If Thaddeus closed his eyes, the memory of loamy water tickled his nose. It was the one smell in all of life that made him think eternal thoughts.

"I'll stay after you're gone, Grandpa, and tend the graves."

"Son, there's nothing here for you but the mines. You've got intelligence and spiritual feelings that are better off in a place where you can learn."

"What about the graves? Papa and Aunt Maryanna live too far away."

"You can help me plant them in hollyhocks. That was one of your grandma's favorites. We'll fill the place with hollyhocks."

All of the people who'd been important to Thaddeus seemed close to one another now. He thought that possibly they waited for him on the other side, the group of them, happy and wise in heaven.

And, as his years squeezed tighter and tighter around him, his memories came more clearly than they ever had. And he understood things he hadn't understood before. He understood that Florence's faithful hymn-singing and his silent anger had been part of the same prayer, that summer long ago. That, and Lewanda's wandering all over the country. And Corrie Bender's strange ways. They'd all been one long prayer that stretched over them like the farmland's pale heaven. And from that heaven the Almighty had reached down and dealt with each of them as he saw fit.